WIRETAPS & WHISKERS

THE FAERIE FILES BOOK 1

EMIGH CANNADAY

Cover design by Fantasy Book Design.

In ancient times cats were worshipped as gods.
They have not forgotten this.

— Terry Pratchett

CONTENTS

ELENA

"Watch out. Harris is on the warpath," Allan warned me as I swiped my FBI badge and walked into the office of the Occult Crimes Division. "You might want to . . . " He hesitated long enough to give me a blatantly judgmental once-over. Was it my uncombed hot pink hair? I was on day three of dry shampoo. Was it the slept-in makeup look I was rocking today? My ripped up black jeans? Or was it my wrinkled Arctic Monkeys t-shirt that smelled like the dirty laundry bin I'd pulled it out of?

Probably all of the above.

Compared to the neutral ocean of boring gray and navy business suits that surrounded me, I stuck out like a sore thumb. On the other hand, I'd worked at the OCD long enough that nobody gave me a second look anymore. I think they'd given up on expecting me to conform. Allan pursed his lips as if coming to the same realization. "Just stay out of his way. He's in a mood."

"Thanks for the heads up," I said, sliding into my cubicle. I took a chug of my Mountain Dew and spun around in my chair, taking a look around my workspace. Even by my standards, it was a disaster. Pulling open the top drawer of my desk, I rifled through piles of papers and broken pens until I found a bag of Sour Patch Kids. As I crammed a few into my mouth and washed them down with another drink of soda, I was aware of Allan still hovering nearby, watching me with a curious expression.

He'd started as an intern at the end of last summer and had somehow never left the office. Nobody knew quite why he was still hanging around, or what he did exactly, aside from gossip. He was a prissy little neat freak and he had shit on everyone, which is why I never went out for drinks with him after work. I looked up to see his nose poking down over the cubicle wall.

"What are you looking at?" I frowned.

"All the candy on your desk," he said, clearly disapproving of my life choices. "It's like a piñata factory exploded. Where do you even put it all? You're skinny as a rail."

"I dunno," I shrugged. "Faerie genetics?"

"You know, if you didn't do that weird magic spark thing with your hands, I'd believe you weren't human like everybody else."

"That's kind of the point of being undercover."

I'd been living up on the surface since I was a little kid. Only one person alive knew what—and *who*—I really was; my boss, Chief Harris. To everyone else, I looked like a normal human. Well . . . as normal as a human with long hot pink hair can be.

Fine. So I ate an alarming amount of sugary junk food and I thought cake and gummy worms were two of the basic food groups. Sure, I had the ability to understand animals, to talk to the forest, to feel the pain of plants, and to hear what the music of an oak tree sounded like. And maybe my eyes were a peculiar shade of green no one had seen before, and *maybe* my skin was a bit more shimmery than it should be. But unless you knew me, I mean *really* knew me, I was just like everyone else.

Kinda . . .

"How do you get any protein?" he pestered. "Aren't you worried about your health?"

Shutting the desk drawer, I slowly spun around in my chair to face him, taking care to keep my face completely deadpan.

"Some people like coffee. I like sugar. Is there a reason why my food choices are affecting you?"

Allan's eyes narrowed. "No."

"Awesome. Now be a doll and fuck off, would you? I have work to do."

He disappeared back over the wall like a cat that had been sprayed with a squirt gun. Finally alone, I was free to log into my computer and start my day. Sometimes it felt as though the FBI was more interested in pen-pushing than actual fieldwork. And that sure as shit wasn't what I'd agreed to when I joined the bureau. For better or for worse, the very moment I loaded up my first spreadsheet, a voice boomed across the room.

"Agent Rivera!"

I craned my neck to look over the cubicles. I could see Chief Harris standing in the doorway to his office staring right at me. Not wanting to give him the satisfaction of seeing me race to him like a lapdog, I took my time standing up and slowly ambled my way over to him.

"Late night again?" he asked, looking me up and down.

Everyone in the building was scared of him. Everyone except me.

The guy might have towered over me at six-foot-three

with the personality and looks of a grizzly bear, but I'd seen things more terrifying than his worst nightmares. I'd seen the things that go bump in the night—and laughed in their face. Well . . . most of the time. Sometimes they hit back, although I was still standing. As far as some lowly human in a suit was concerned, I wasn't scared of shit. And I think he knew it.

"Yeah, I had a late night."

Harris lingered in his doorway for a moment as though he was waiting for me to apologize for my unkempt appearance, but I just stared at him impatiently and crossed my arms. I wasn't here for decoration. I was here to get shit done. And unlike most of my coworkers, the FBI had recruited *me* . . . not the other way around.

"I'm guessing you didn't just call me down here to talk about my night," I said, already bored.

"No. You better come inside."

Ushering me into his office, he closed the door behind me and to my surprise, closed the blinds.

Shit.

This must be serious. He hardly ever closed his blinds.

Harris was a man of ritual. He left the door open when he wanted a quick word, and he left the blinds open when he was having a regular meeting. But *closed* blinds? I'd only seen him do that when the bigwigs from the Pentagon showed up.

"Please, take a seat," he said, waving his hand over to the chair across from his desk.

I didn't like to sit in other people's spaces. It made me feel small, almost vulnerable. But the expression on Harris' face told me something was deeply wrong and he had no time for my games. I lowered myself into the seat and watched as he reached into his desk for a bottle of Scotch.

"Sir, isn't it a bit early for a drink?"

He glowered at me in response.

"Maybe not," I added with a fake smile.

"Are you joining me? After what I'm about to tell you I think you'll need it."

"Sure."

It felt surreal to watch him hand me a glass of Scotch. Not just because it was nine in the morning, but because it almost felt like we were friends. Were we bonding now? Did this mean I was in his good graces? Was he going to expect to be invited to dinner to discuss work?

"So what's the news?" I asked him. "I'm guessing you didn't call me in here just for your usual run-of-the-mill case."

"No," he said. "It most definitely isn't run-of-the-mill. And you're not one of my run-of-the-mill agents. Which is why you were the first person I thought of when I received a call in the middle of the night from a concerned sheriff in Tennessee."

He sat back in his seat and took a sip of his drink, swirling it around his mouth for a moment. He frowned into space as though he wasn't quite sure where to begin.

"What's the case, sir?" I prodded.

"Kids," he began. "They're going missing right and left."

His words hit me with a deep uneasiness that wormed its way up from my gut. Missing persons cases were par for the course, but *kids*? Only sick fuckers preyed on kids. My eyes flicked over to the photo on his desk, where his two chubby-cheeked kids were cuddling the family dog. No wonder this case had him all torn up.

"It started in the Smoky Mountains, but now the situation has reached a crisis point."

"Crisis point?"

"And beyond," he replied. "The Smokies are just the tip of the iceberg. The phenomenon is spreading, mostly in the Rocky Mountain states. We even have reports south of the border in the Sierra Madres. Children are vanishing under almost identical circumstances."

"Sir, with all due respect, kids go missing and fall victim to crimes every day. It's tragic, but it's not a single phenomenon. The way you're talking about this would suggest it's one crime taking place. All the children going missing because of the same cause." I crossed my legs and leaned back into my chair. "If it's happening in Mexico, it might be the cartels."

Harris sighed as if I should've known better than to suggest such a thing.

"Rivera, I'm not talking about your standard abduction cases!"

The anger in his voice stunned me. Not because he was practically shouting at me. He was always shouting at everybody. I could see beyond his anger, and he wasn't just angry for the sake of it. He was mad because he cared. It wasn't just testosterone-fueled anger gushing out of an alpha male. This was a paternal sort of passion that set his eyes ablaze with the need to find those kids.

"You need to understand something," he growled. "These disappearances don't fit any mold of the expected child abductions we're used to. You know, the ones taken by sexual predators, random wackjobs and human traffickers. Even the cartels don't want kids this young. This is something different."

Springing from his seat, he ventured over to his filing cabinet and pulled out a beige file. Slamming it down on his desk, he pointed at what looked like an ordinary spreadsheet. But as I leaned forward, I saw the statistics it held were far from ordinary.

"These are for the last twelve months alone," he said, stabbing his index finger into the page. "Last November, seventeen children vanished in the Appalachians alone. In December, twenty-three. Fast forward to September of this year and we see the disappearances spreading out to Colorado, Montana, and even California. As many as three hundred kids simply walked off the face of the Earth that month. They've never been seen again. Then there was last month . . . "

He paused as though he was trying to mentally prepare himself to tell me the number. Slowly, his eyes moved up from the page and met mine. His gaze appeared more haunted than ever before.

"Four hundred and seventy-three," he said.

For a second I thought I'd heard him wrong.

"In October?"

He nodded.

"Four hundred and seventy-three children. All in the woods. All with their parents. All healthy, well cared for, and thriving. All of them were standing beside their parents one second, then gone the next."

"That sounds . . . " I trailed off, rubbing my temple in confusion. "That's almost unbelievable."

But I knew it was possible. In my job, I'd seen things that nobody would believe. Things that brought me to the brink of sanity more than once. It didn't take long working in the OCD to figure out one very certain fact. Absolutely anything, no matter how crazy it sounded, was possible.

"Sir, that's . . . that's a fucking epidemic."

Harris nodded and took another drink of his Scotch.

"And just shy of three hundred of those took place

within the Smoky Mountains. By the looks of it, that seems to be the hub of activity. A base from which the phenomenon spreads out. Here—look at this."

He flipped the spreadsheet over to reveal a map of the US covered in red dots. There were so many around the Smokies it looked as though the entire area was completely covered. The red dots spread out further, leaving a slight rash in Colorado and Montana, with only a few specks in Wyoming and California.

"Should I assume that you're telling me this because you're not entirely convinced humans are the cause of this phenomenon?" I asked.

"That's exactly why I thought of you. But there's another reason. I think it's something that only you would understand. Follow me."

Without waiting, he jumped out of his seat and left the room as though he just expected me to be on his heels. I followed him out the door, but not before grabbing my drink. Then when I reached the door, I changed my mind, returned my glass of Scotch to his desk, and reached for the bottle instead. By the sounds of it, I was going to need it.

The cramped computer room had me and Harris squashed up shoulder to shoulder in front of the screen. It was the closest I'd ever been to him, and I didn't like it one bit. I could smell his sweat, the sour kind of human perspiration that I found slightly nauseating. His cologne on top of it was overkill.

Holding my breath, I took a swig from the bottle of Scotch and handed it over to him.

"Don't let the other agents catch you with this," he said, holding it to his mouth. "They'll get jealous."

"Do you really think I care what the other agents think of me?" I laughed. "I'm not here to make friends."

Which was almost true. It wasn't that I didn't like any of the other agents or that I loathed them to the point of being enemies. It was simply that there was a divide between us . . . a major one. They were human, I was fae. I put up with them but I couldn't trust them. Not entirely, anyway.

There were people I occasionally met like Harris or even Allan that I thought I could trust, but I could never quite extend this feeling to the rest of the human world. It just wasn't in my nature.

As we both stared at the screen, Jake from IT fiddled with his mouse until he brought up a video.

"Skip to fifteen minutes and nine seconds, Jake."

"Right on it, Chief," he squeaked back.

I could see he was starting to sweat too. The back of his shirt was growing damp. I got the impression he never spent much time with Chief Harris. When he looked up at him, there was a childish sense of wonderment in his eyes as though he was meeting a celebrity.

"Right there. Stop. Alright, Rivera. Look at this."

As Jake pressed play, a video began to play showing a small interview room where at the back, a small child no older than seven was hunched inside a giant coat. Beside her, a crying woman I assumed to be her mom nervously fiddling with her long, brown hair with one hand and pressing a tissue to her eyes with the other.

In front of them, a police officer with a thick country accent spoke softly to the child. He looked more like Santa Claus than an officer of the law, appearing almost as wide as he was tall, yet the girl didn't appear afraid of him. If anything, she was leaning towards him as though he was bringing her much needed comfort and safety.

"Haley, can you tell me what you saw?" he asked her, bending down to her height.

The little girl nodded, her head bobbing up and down inside the oversized neck of the coat.

"Can we begin when you were out on the trail with your mommy?"

Again, she nodded.

"Can you tell me what you told your mommy you saw?"

She began fiddling with the sleeve of her coat before raising her thumb to her mouth to nibble on her nail.

"We were walking," she began, her voice barely audible. I could hear it just fine, although Harris was straining to hear. As though sensing his difficulty, Jake turned up the volume.

"We were walking to go on a picnic," Haley said.

"And who was there?"

"Mommy, Daddy and Pop-Pop."

"That's her grandpa," added her mom.

"Ah," replied the officer. "So it was just the four of you?"

"Uh huh . . . " replied the little girl. She began fidgeting with one of the buttons on her coat.

"And you were walking. Can you remember the name of the trail?"

"Yeah! It's got a funny name; Pinkie Pie Trail," she replied. "We go there every Sunday."

"Well done for remembering," said the officer, scribbling in his notebook. "From the sounds of it, you know this Pinkie Pie trail well."

"Yep."

"And do you like the trail?"

"I like it a whole bunch," she smiled back, pulling down the coat from her face.

Now I could see just how young she was with chubby cheeks and brown pigtails.

"But I love all of the woods," she continued. "My favorite tree to climb is the oak because the branches are really strong."

"I used to love to climb trees too when I was your age," said the officer. "And did you climb trees on this day?"

"No."

"Why not?"

"Because I never got the chance. We were just walking on the trail and then I saw the little man so I couldn't climb the tree."

"The little man?"

"Yes. The little man," she confirmed with a vigorous nod.

I could feel a nervous energy build in the room. I glanced over at Harris and saw he was staring deep into the screen with that passion still on fire in his eyes. I followed his gaze back to the officer who was now leaning even further forward to the point that he was almost falling off his seat.

"Can you tell me what the little man looked like?" he asked, his pen poised over his notebook.

"Smaller than me," she said.

"Smaller than you?"

"Yes. This tall."

Sliding off her seat, she held up her hand to show his size compared to her. By her description, he was no higher than her shoulder. The uneasiness that had already been washing through me intensified. Something told me that I knew what she was going to say next.

"Haley, can you remember his face?" asked the officer.

"Ugly," she replied.

"How ugly?"

"Like reeeeally ugly! He had these big ears like this," she said, flapping her hands at the side of her face. "And this big long nose that was pointed at the end. And his eyes were completely green."

"Shit," I whispered to the room.

That was all I needed to hear to know exactly what we were dealing with.

"You know what she's talking about?" asked Harris.

Jake slammed his finger on the mouse to pause the tape.

"That sounds like a goblin to me," I said.

Jake frowned in confusion, but Harris gave a silent nod.

"Roll the tape," he ordered and Jake reached for the play button once again.

I watched as the girl's mom pulled her back onto her seat and held her tight.

"Sweetie, you have to tell the sheriff the truth."

"But, Mommy I *am* telling him the truth! That's what the little man looked like!"

"I'm sorry," said her mom to the officer. "She has a vivid imagination. She watches a lot of cartoons."

"No, it's okay," he replied. "I'd like to hear more about what she has to say."

He gave the girl a warm smile and continued to scribble in his notebook.

"So you saw the little man, and he was ugly," he continued. "Where did he come from?"

"He popped out of a tree!"

Her mom, looking a mixture of exasperated and embarrassed, lowered her head into her hands.

"He popped out of a tree . . . " repeated the officer.

Until now, he had been able to hide his skepticism, but now he couldn't stop it seeping out his voice. Miraculously, he wrote down what Haley said.

"Was he hiding behind it? Or in the bushes beside it? Or did he climb down from it? What exactly do you mean when you say he *popped* out of it?"

"He just popped," replied the girl. "There was a hole at the bottom of the tree. I thought it was just filled with leaves at first, but then I saw his face and he sort of popped up out of it."

"Okay . . . " The officer paused to make a few more notes. "And your parents were there?"

"Sort of," said the girl. "I was walking way in front of them."

"We were right behind her," the mom quickly added. "No more than ten feet away. I knew where she was."

"It's okay, Mrs. Brown," said the officer. "I'm not suggesting you were neglecting your daughter."

The mom, relaxing a little at hearing this, sat back in her seat and took a deep breath.

"So could your Mommy and Daddy see this little man too?"

"No, I don't think so. There were bushes in the way."

"Okay . . . " The officer, bless him, scratched his head before continuing his interrogation. "So the little man popped out of the tree. Can you remember what happened next?"

Haley's eyes grew wider.

"He told me we were going on an adventure!"

"Oh, he did, did he? What kind of an adventure?"

"He said I had to follow him into the tree."

The little girl's mom grew distressed again and began crying silently into her sleeve.

"You had to follow him into the tree," said the officer, flipping his notebook to jot down some more notes. "Are you sure about that?"

"Uh huh."

"Completely sure?"

"Yes!"

"And did you follow him into the tree?"

"I did," Haley said with an emphatic nod of her little head. "He held my hand and led me towards the hole in the tree and we took one big step and then we were inside!"

"You were inside the tree?"

"No, we were inside his *kingdom*."

It felt as though my stomach was about to bottom out. Suddenly I regretted my breakfast of Mountain Dew, Sour Patch Kids, and Scotch.

"Chief . . . " I said. "This is so much worse than I could have imagined."

"Keep watching," said Harris. "It gets weirder."

Resting a hand on Jake's shoulder, I gestured for him to move away so I could take his seat. Lowering myself into his place, I leaned forward until I could feel the light from the screen burn my retinas. I needed to take in every single detail.

"You were taken into the little man's kingdom," said the officer. "Can you tell me what it looked like?"

"It looked magical," replied the girl without missing a heartbeat. "Everything was green and shiny and so pretty! And it was filled with more little people. Maybe a hundred billion jillion of them! And they were all smiling at me."

It looked as though the officer was trying his best to remain calm but the look on his face said he was ready to burst out of his skin.

"What happened now you were in this kingdom?"

14

"The little man took me to this place. He said it was called a court. And there were all these tiny people in long dresses sitting on sparkly glass chairs. There were really big mushrooms everywhere . . . they were bigger than Daddy's golf umbrella!"

The girl was growing more and more excited. She didn't appear to be the traumatized victim of some terrifying abduction. She sounded as though she was talking about a trip she'd taken to Disneyland.

"Little people sitting on glass chairs beneath giant mushrooms," the officer repeated to himself as he scribbled in his notebook. "Okay. Got it. What happened next?"

"They said I was never going to see my Mommy and Daddy again. They said I was going to meet the Queen and then I had to say goodbye to everyone up above the ground forever."

The mom grew even more distressed at hearing this and began to sob heavily.

"They said you'd never see your parents again?" asked the officer. "If that's what they said, then how come you're here right now? How did you get back up above ground?"

"They asked what was in my backpack."

The officer, looking confused, cocked his head to the side.

"And what was in your backpack?"

"Treats," replied the girl with a smile. "It was my job to take the desserts for the picnic so I had the chocolate chip cookies in my bag. When the little men saw the cookies, they got really excited. They said I could return to the surface world if they could have all of my cookies."

"And what did you tell them, Haley?"

"Well," she kicked her legs, swinging them back and forth before turning to look at her mom. "I didn't want to live with them forever. I wanted to see Mommy and Daddy again. I gave them my cookies, and they brought me back up through the tree. But when I popped out it was nighttime."

"Was it?" asked the officer. "I thought this happened on Sunday morning?"

"That's when she disappeared," the mom chimed in. "She was missing for almost twelve hours. By this time I called you, I'd called everyone in the neighborhood. There had to be nearly fifty people out looking for her at this point. But she keeps saying she was only gone for a couple minutes."

"Time slip," I said under my breath.

A moment later, Harris leaned over my shoulder and shut off the tape.

"Time slip indeed," he said. "What do you make of this?"

"From the sounds of it, I'd say she encountered a goblin."

"And what is a goblin?"

"The bad guys of the Fae world," I explained. "They're tiny chaos causing bastards who'll ruin the life of anyone they cross. They wouldn't think twice about taking a child."

"Are they known for taking children in particular?"

"That and a lot more. But I gotta say, if all these disappearances are linked to goblins, then they're taking kids at an unprecedented rate. It's unheard of for them to operate at such a large scale."

Jake, who was now leaning against the wall with sweat pouring down his face looked as though he was trapped in a room with two crazy people. He was new to the OCD, and like most of the other agents in the division, he was on a need-to-know basis. He didn't need to know all the details about the faerie realm that shadowed his world. Only a privileged few were privy to such information.

"Do you really think all these cases are connected?" I asked Harris. "Is there enough similarity between each disappearance?"

"It's starting to look that way," he said with a shrug. "If it wasn't for Haley, we'd never have known where they went. That's if what she's saying is true."

"I'd bet my life she is. I've been to these courts. I know firsthand that goblins are exactly like how she described."

"But you *really* think they'd swap her for some chocolate chip cookies?"

"Um . . . have you *seen* my desk?" I replied. "Nothing can win faeries over more than sugar. An entire package of cookies down there would be like finding a suitcase of cash up here."

"I'll keep that in mind," Harris said, still looking skeptical. It didn't deter me from elaborating further.

"Throughout history there have been countless stories of people making deals with faeries by leaving out treats for them. It's usually honey, but faeries love anything sweet. Hell, some even like booze."

I winked and took a liberal gulp from the bottle in my hand. Jake's eyes grew wide like saucers as he backed himself into the corner.

"The cookies are what saved Haley's life," I said. "She'd have disappeared into the fae underworld forever if it wasn't for that bargaining chip."

"If you know that's how to stop the abductions, will you be able to stop any more from happening?" asked Jake.

"That's Rivera's assignment," Harris replied before turning to me. "You leave Monday."

"Sir, I'm happy to go," I said, rising from my chair, "but

with hundreds of kids missing, it's going to take me a while to figure out what's going on."

"I realize that," he said, sitting down and returning to his work.

And then, to my sheer and utter horror, he told me of his genius plan to help me solve the case.

"Seems about time you had a partner."

2

LOGAN

"Holy shit, Logan! Senior special agent." My dad swallowed hard, trying not to get too choked up. "I couldn't be more proud."

"Thanks, but it's not *that* impressive. When you were my age, you were already in FBI management."

"Pfft . . . When I was your age, the world was a different place," he assured me with a laugh. "Rising through the ranks is just plain harder these days."

He slapped my back so hard it knocked the wind out of me, but I smiled anyway. I may have been right about him ranking higher than me, but that didn't stop the pride swelling up inside my chest.

I'd worked my ass off the last few years to graduate from a humble field agent to where I was today. And there were so many times when I thought it would never happen. The cutthroat office politics, the long hours, the exhaustion, and the competition. Sometimes it felt like I'd have more luck pulling a sword from a stone. But here I was at long last, a senior special agent. And with it less than a week after my thirtieth birthday, it couldn't have come at a better time.

Having a plan and sticking to it got me to this point. Hell—I had friends from high school who were still trying to 'figure themselves out.'

Maybe when you're a freshman in college. But at *thirty*? No way.

Not me.

There was only ever one path for me in life—to follow in my father's footsteps. I'd always been the most driven student among the rest of my classmates, finishing high school with a perfect GPA of 4.0. I worked part time for the college police and managed to graduate at twenty-one with degrees in Political Science and Russian. Then I went to Quantico and finished at the top of my class.

So yeah. I knew how to put my nose to the grindstone. Special agent by twenty-four, senior special agent by thirty. Married at thirty-two, first kid by thirty-four, second by thirty-eight, and middle management at the bureau by forty.

I was already engaged. Now that I'd just been promoted, everything was falling perfectly into place.

"Your mom would be so happy if she could see you today," said Dad, walking over to the fridge to grab a beer.

I clenched my jaw but said nothing. Why did he have to mention her? For a second there, I was walking on air. Now I was barreling towards Earth.

"Don't look like that," he said, sliding a beer across the kitchen table towards me.

"Like what?"

"Like you're all miserable and shit, like one of those emo kids."

"I'm not miserable," I shrugged. "I'm just . . . like you said, Mom would've been really happy."

"Yeah, she would have. She knew how much you

wanted to join the FBI when you were a kid. If she could see you right now, she'd be so proud."

Now he was the one that looked miserable. For a second, he looked as though he was going to cry, but then he took a deep breath, blinked a few times, and swallowed a mouthful of beer.

I took his lead and chugged some down as well. I would've preferred something stronger, but all Dad ever kept in the house was beer.

"You know, you look just like her," he said, setting his bottle down with a *clunk*.

"I *do* know. You don't stop telling me."

"And you should be grateful for it," he said, grinning as if he were about to impart some sage wisdom. "My side of the family wasn't exactly blessed in the looks department."

That was definitely true. I had an uncle we called Tater because he had the face, charm and complexion of an actual potato. As I looked into Dad's face, I could see a hint of his brother's looks.

The large forehead, the long jaw, the bulbous nose. I always wondered what attracted Mom to him when she was younger. She could've had anyone—was a legit beauty queen. The year I was born, she was crowned Miss Ashland County.

I looked for similarities between my own face and Dad's but saw nothing except the same brown hair color. It made my blue eyes stand out. People—usually women—always felt the need to comment on my eyes. They'd say it made me look mysterious, but I always thought blue eyes were boring. I'd much rather have the deep chocolatey shade of brown like my mom had. When I was a kid she'd tuck me in bed and sing me to sleep. Those big eyes of hers would shine in the dim glow of my Teddy Ruxpin nightlight.

When I was getting bullied at school, I remember her telling me that she was a bear too. A momma bear. And nobody messed with a momma bear's cub.

The bullying stopped shortly after that confession.

Sadness welled up inside me again as I made that trip down memory lane, and I swallowed more beer to stifle it. I made a mental note to get a bottle of Scotch to keep at Dad's house for times like these, when beer just didn't cut it.

"Anyway," said Dad, reaching over to grab a bag of potato chips off the counter. "You got any big celebration planned for tonight?"

Looking around the kitchen, I noticed it was getting messier each time I visited. There used to be a time when there wasn't a speck of dust in the whole house. I used to come home from school to be greeted by the smell of fresh laundry and a scented candle. Now it just smelled like stale beer and tobacco. Mom would've hated what had become of her home.

"Nah. No celebration tonight," I said. "I was gonna go home and surprise Bridget with the news. Thought I'd take her out to dinner."

"You mean you haven't told her?"

"Haven't told anyone but you," I replied, and he shot me a warm smile.

As soon as I heard the news about my promotion, he was the first person I'd thought to tell. I raced right over here as soon as I left the office. And I was glad I had. It had been a few weeks since I'd made it over to his house, and it was looking worse than ever.

"Well, I think we should have our own little celebration," said Dad, wandering back to the fridge. "Another beer?"

"Actually, I better get going."

Looking over the pile of dirty dishes out the window, I saw the sky begin to darken as twilight approached. A little bit of rain was starting to fall across the abandoned flower garden, settling on the tall weeds and making them shine.

"Really?" asked Dad with a frown. "You can't stay for one more?"

The look on his face told me he didn't just want me to stay to celebrate; he needed me for more than that. I wondered when he had friends over last. Did he even still *have* friends? Every weekend when I was younger, the house was always filled with the sound of music and tipsy voices. I used to go to sleep to the sound of my parents and their friends laughing and playing cards as they fought over which radio station to listen to.

But that was when Mom was still alive. When she died, she took most of the life and joy from this house. Well, from Dad anyway. I never expected him to fully recover after she went. Grief like his could last a lifetime. But I never expected him to sink lower and lower every year. If she could see him now she'd give him a piece of her mind. She'd tell him to stop feeling sorry for himself, and to do something more productive.

"I guess I can stay for one more," I relented, taking another icy beer from his hand. "But I really do have to go soon. I thought I'd take Bridget out for dinner and tell her. And I wanted to stop and see Mom before it gets too dark."

Dad smiled weakly and slumped into his seat.

"I didn't know you still went to visit her."

"Whenever I can."

"You're a good son, Logan." He reached across the table and patted my arm. "Don't know what I'd do without you."

"I saw him today, Mom," I said, kneeling down with the daisies I brought whenever I visited her.

She didn't say a word, and I wasn't expecting one. As I knelt in front of her headstone, I felt a warm rustle through my hair. The months were growing hotter and it wouldn't be long until the heat of the swamp made every inch of my clothing stick to my skin.

"He's looking real bad, Mom . . . like he hasn't slept in months. And the house? You should see it. Well, actually, you shouldn't see it. It's such a mess. You would have hated it."

I didn't know why I was spilling my guts to her. It wasn't like she could hear me, and it wasn't normally something I did. But for some reason, as I knelt there in the dark and contemplated two huge milestones in my life, I felt full of nervous, excited energy.

"Anyway, you don't wanna hear me complain," I said to the wind. "I wanted to tell you that I got the job. How crazy is that? Never thought I'd get it this fast, but here I am. You're looking at the FBI's newest senior special agent."

I suddenly felt ridiculous, talking out loud to a grave like this. I stood up, brushing the dew from the wet grass off my knees.

The breeze picked up around me, moving through the trees like it was whispering secrets in their leaves. I looked around and saw nothing but lonely headstones surrounding me. Some were old and weatherbeaten, others were new. Some were neglected, some were well-maintained, but none were as pristine and well cared for as Mom's.

"Seems like I just saw you this morning," I said. "It's hard to remember that it's been fifteen years since you went. Fifteen years . . . That's half my life."

The realization weighed me down as it came to me.

She'd missed out on half my life. Hadn't seen me graduate high school or college. Hadn't watched me play football in high school. She hadn't even met Bridget, the girl I was going to spend the rest of my life with.

"Anyway," I said, turning away. "I better go. I haven't told Bridget about the job yet. She'll go nuts when she finds out."

I paused for a second, not wanting to leave just yet.

"You know, you'd like her so much. She's the sweetest girl I've ever met."

Taking another step away from the gravesite, I looked back towards my car. It was getting darker, and it wouldn't be long until I wouldn't be able to see the path back to the parking lot. But I still felt the need to stay a moment longer. I knew Mom had been lying here for years, and that it was just her bones down there, but I still couldn't bear the thought of leaving her out in this lonely, dark place.

"Maybe you'll see Bridget at our wedding," I said as I walked away. "I'm sure you'll be watching us from wherever you are."

By the time I arrived at Bridget's condo, I was completely soaked through. It wasn't until the elevator doors shut that I caught a glimpse of myself in the reflection. I looked like a half-drowned rat. Bridget was going to throw a fit if I tracked any mud on her white carpet.

My stomach growled, and I knew it was close to dinner time. Usually Bridget texted to see how my day had gone, but I hadn't heard anything from her all day. My small handful of texts had also gone unanswered.

Weird, I thought, looking at my phone. The background

wallpaper was a picture of her taken on the beach in Mexico last summer. She was sipping on a fruity drink with her blonde hair dancing in the sea breeze. I laughed to myself, thinking about how many dozens of pictures she'd told me to take until she got the perfect one for her Instagram feed. I couldn't care less if that snapshot had over a thousand likes. All that mattered was that she was engaged to me.

The first time I saw her was at a frat party back in college. She'd walked into the room with a group of sorority sisters, but all I saw was her. I'd never been shy with girls before, but with her, it felt like I'd never spoken to a woman in my whole life. She was a trust fund kid from a wealthy family. I was nobody. Like a chicken shit, I'd admired her from a distance until the end of the night. Just as I was about to leave, she tapped me on the shoulder and smiled.

"Aren't you going to talk to me?" she asked. "You've been staring at me all night."

And just like that, I was sucked into her orbit. A week later we went on our first date. A year after that we graduated from college and she gave me a key to her condo. A few years later, I got down on one knee at her favorite restaurant and proposed. She wanted a long engagement. I didn't care. I just wanted to be with her. Sometimes it didn't feel real. And at moments like this, when I looked at her picture, things felt too good to be true.

"Bridget?"

I entered the hallway, making sure to take my shoes off at the door. My jacket shed droplets of rain onto the carpet as I hung it up, and I shook the rain from my hair. I decided to keep my holster on.

"Bridget? Are you home?"

Her place was completely dark and eerily silent. That

was the weirdest thing of all. Bridget didn't have many faults, although she was one of the noisiest people I'd ever met. There was always a television blaring, or a blow dryer running, or music playing with the bass thumping until the walls shook.

Ascending the stairs softly, I listened out for any signs that she was in, but there were none. Intrusive thoughts ran through my mind.

Is she hurt?

Is she sick?

Did she fall in the shower and knock herself out?

I tried to stop the nonsense in my head, but I just couldn't shake the feeling the something wasn't right. When you're with someone long enough, you just *know* when something feels different. And right now, every cell in my body was screaming that something was wrong.

"Hey, Bridget!"

Reaching the landing, I looked down the hall towards our bedroom. The door was closed when it was normally left open. Then I noticed something else. A black shape lay in the shadows to the side of the hallway floor. Flicking on the light switch, I saw it was a strip of black lace. Bridget's panties. All the hairs on my body rose to attention. Now there was another feeling mingled with my anxiety.

Suspicion.

Marching towards the bedroom door, I pushed it open so hard it smacked off the wall with a bang, leaving a hole in the drywall. Bridget gave out a startled scream as I stormed in.

"What's going on?"

But then I saw her lying naked, stretched out on the bed. On the bedside cabinet, candles were lit. Their flickering flames dancing across her spray-tanned skin. Beside them, I noticed two wine glasses beside a freshly opened bottle of Chateauneuf du Pape.

"Hi honey . . . " she purred. "What's got you so worked up?"

"I was worried," I said. "I haven't heard from you all day."

She slipped her tongue out along her bottom lip and stretched out even further to accentuate the curve of her waist.

"That's because I was here, waiting for you," she said, parting her legs ever so slightly.

In an instant, the worry drained from my body as all my blood rushed below my belt. I crawled onto the bed and gazed down at her.

"Why didn't you answer my texts?" I asked. "It's not like you to not call all day."

"Maybe I was playing hard to get."

Raising her hand to my chest, she began popping open the buttons on my shirt one by one until her warm hand was sliding across my cold skin.

"You're freezing," she said, scratching her nails down the center of my pecs. "Come here, baby. I'll warm you up."

She pulled me close and I tried to relax into the feel of her body. But I couldn't help but notice a peculiar, strained quality to her voice. I looked into her eyes, but she glanced away nervously. Again, the feeling that something was wrong entered my mind and I began to tense up.

"What's wrong, baby?" she asked, rising to kiss me. "Just relax."

As her lips met mine, I noticed there was a different taste to her kiss. A different feel.

And it wasn't the wine.

Pulling away, I tried to figure out what was going on.

You're just paranoid, I told myself. *You're exhausted. You're imagining things.*

But at the same time, I knew this wasn't just some woo woo sense of intuition. I was trained to be observant, and although I couldn't quite put my finger on what was bothering me, I knew something was wrong.

"Come lie down, baby," Bridget breathed, grabbing my tie to lower me down beside her.

There was an urgency to her voice I didn't like. I looked at the two glasses of wine, searching for smudges from fingers or lips. And that's when I heard it. A sneeze came from under the bed. Springing to my feet, I dove onto the floor, hand on my gun and heart in my mouth.

"Logan!" screamed Bridget. "Wait!"

But my stomach was already against the floor.

"Who's under here?"

I didn't need to wait long to get my answer. Through the darkness came the whites of two eyes peering right at me. Drawing my gun, I pointed it at him, and that's when all hell broke loose.

Bridget jumped on my back with such force my chin smacked against the floor. And her momentary distraction let whoever was under the bed make their escape. I pushed Bridget off me just in time to see a naked figure fleeing with their clothes bundled in their arms.

"Freeze or I'll shoot!"

The figure froze in the doorway.

"Logan, don't do anything stupid!" cried Bridget.

Her voice was background noise. My eyes were pinned on the naked man cowering in front of me. I took in the salt and pepper hair, the stunned expression on his face, the wrinkles around his eyes. Then I saw his body; flabby and pale with a trail of hair that traveled from a barrel chest down to where his dick was hidden behind the balled-up pants in his hands.

Fuck. He was old. Like, in his seventies.

Raising his hands in a panic, he stumbled and dropped his clothes at his feet to reveal a still hard cock, albeit a small one, pointed right at me.

"Please don't shoot!" he begged. "I have a wife and kids!"

"Get the fuck out of here," I snarled. I put away my gun and waited until he'd left before I turned to Bridget.

"Who the fuck is he?"

She looked down into her lap which was now covered in her thin, satin robe.

"One of Daddy's business partners," she said. "You didn't have to be so mean to him. He has a bad heart. You could have killed him!"

"He has a bad heart?" I raged. "Then what the fuck was he doing taking *these*?"

I grabbed the pack of Viagra I'd found in the bathroom and hurled it at her. It landed on her lap and she just stared at it.

"And you've got some fucking nerve. I was being mean to *him*? *Mean*? If that's your definition of being mean, what the fuck were you doing to *me*?"

Her eyes remained shamefully planted on her thighs.

"Hey! Look at me!"

She sniffed and wiped the tears away from her eyes.

"I'm so sorry, baby!" she wailed.

"Don't bother apologizing. You think your apology means shit?"

She sniffed again and mumbled something into the palm of her hand as she wiped her face.

"I just don't fucking believe it, Bridget!"

Falling into the nearest chair, I buried my head in my hands.

"How could you do this? And with him? Why?"

She shrugged, tears tumbling down her cheeks onto her satin robe.

"I just don't understand. I thought you and I had it made."

"We do! I love you, Logan! We can work through this."

"Doesn't look that fucking way to me." Unable to hold back my rage-filled energy, I jumped out of the chair and began pacing up and down the living room. I didn't know what I wanted to do more, punch the wall or burst into tears. "Why him? What's he got that I haven't?"

Bridget swallowed hard and rubbed at her eyes. It annoyed me that even though I'd never been angrier with her, I still thought she looked beautiful. Even though her face was red and swollen from crying. Even though she'd clearly broken my heart.

"He's retired," she replied in barely more than a breath. "He wants to take care of me."

At first, I wasn't sure I'd heard her right. Was this about money? Could she be so shallow?

She began to sob, and pinched the bridge of her nose as though she'd been attacked by a migraine.

"You know how I've always wanted to open a lingerie boutique?"

I said nothing. I just stared right through her waiting for her to give me some sort of explanation where this would all make sense.

"Well, he said he'd bankroll me to open it and the more time we spent together . . . " She started to cry harder, picking up one of her half dozen pillows and pressed her face into it. "I love you so much, Logan. I fucked up. I really fucked up!"

Lifting the pillow slightly to reveal a wet face print on the fabric, she looked into my face pleadingly. But the more I looked around the room, the more I realized I'd been missing the signs for months, if not longer. All the expensive designer shoes, the Birkin bags, the long weekends in the Hamptons with 'the girls.' Add to that the fact that we still hadn't set a wedding date, and now I knew we never would. The more I thought about it, the more glaringly obvious it was that Bridget and her retired, wealthy sugar daddy had been carrying on a lot longer than I'd realized.

"Do you think you could ever forgive me? We can make this work—I know we can! Daddy knows all sorts of counselors we could talk to, because every couple has problems, and . . . "

"No."

Her mouth dropped open slightly in shock. I'm not sure that I'd ever said that word to her before. Maybe no one had.

"What do you mean, *no*?"

"I'm not sure how I could be more clear. We're done."

Using a couple Whole Foods grocery bags for luggage, I began collecting what little I kept in Bridget's apartment. Electric toothbrush, a few pairs of socks and underwear, a pair of wireless headphones, and a few shirts and pants.

It wasn't until I reached the inside of my car and closed the door that I let the emotional floodgates open.

"Fuck!" I screamed, hitting my hands on the steering wheel. I didn't think it was possible to feel such anger. To feel as though my blood was boiling in my veins. I was so angry I was dizzy, although it could've been low blood sugar. I was hungry when I'd arrived, even if I wasn't anymore. Beneath all the turmoil was another sensation starting to eclipse the rage. Sadness. As I drove away from the condo, it began to fill me up and consume me with its darkness.

Bridget and I were over. The perfect life that I thought would last forever had come to an end. As I turned left at the end of the road, I began to feel tears burn at the corners of my eyes.

"Don't fucking cry," I told myself. "Don't you dare fucking cry over that bitch."

But I couldn't help it. The last few years of my life had all been a lie.

3

LOGAN

I was still bleary-eyed and yawning continuously when I arrived at the office the next morning. I'd gone through the motions of showering and shaving, of ironing my clothes and straightening my tie, but I somehow still felt like complete shit.

"Argh, fuck," I grumbled as I entered the elevator and saw my reflection.

My eyes were so bloodshot I looked like I'd spent the last twenty-four hours sampling blunts with Snoop Dogg.

After leaving Bridget's place, I'd gone straight to Dad's where I spilled out everything. He wasn't the best person to go to in a crisis, but he tried his best. I ended up sleeping on his couch. Well . . . *trying* to sleep. I tossed and turned until I woke up with a neck that felt like it was trapped in a vice. The 4am drive back to my apartment was not how I'd expected to start this day.

What a perfect way to begin my new career as a senior special agent.

Stepping out the elevator, I entered the bullpen of offices and tried to find my desk. Snaking my way through the labyrinth of cubicles, I tried to avoid all the curious looks I was getting from the other agents as they caught sight of my tired face. But I doubted they would've looked any better if they'd just found their fiancee in bed with a crusty old millionaire.

At last, I found my cubicle which was, thankfully, situated in the back left-hand corner out of sight. I slumped into the creaky office chair and lay my forehead on the desk. This was officially the second worst day of my life. I was convinced I'd aged thirty years in the last twelve hours. I swore that my insides were rotting away from the misery chewing through my entire body.

I lay there for a long while, unable and unwilling to move. It wasn't until I heard the click of high heels approach my desk that I raised my head to see a young intern with a clipboard in her hands.

"Agent Hawthorne?"

"Yeah?"

"You've been summoned."

"That sounds ominous."

From her clipboard, she pulled out a note and handed it to me. Damn. It *was* ominous. I was supposed to report to the Occult Crimes Division.

"You're to meet Chief Harris in his office at nine o'clock. And on your first day, too." She stopped and smiled. "That's quite an achievement. Details are on the note."

"Nine o'clock," I said to myself, looking down at my watch. It was two minutes to nine.

"Shit!"

Leaping out my seat, I ran down to the elevator, the note held tight in my hand like the golden ticket that would get me into Willy Wonka's chocolate factory. In a way, it kind of was a golden ticket. Nobody got invited to Harris's office unless they were the creme de la creme, and for special agents to get invited on their first day? That was fucking unheard of. A thousand thoughts rampaged in my head.

Am I in trouble?

Am I going to be recruited into some special program?

Shit! Am I going to be sent to chase down a terrorist?

Then another thought crossed my mind.

How am I supposed to see him looking like this?

As the elevator doors opened, I ran out into the foyer of the top floor and slapped my hands on the receptionist's desk.

"Where's Harris' office!"

"Um . . . Good morning to you, too."

"Sorry, ma'am, can you please just tell me where to find Chief Harris?"

"Last room on the left," she said, pointing into the distance. "Have a good day."

I jogged down the hall, my shoes slipping on the tiled floor until I arrived at Harris' office. I practically tumbled through the door.

"Hello . . . " came a masculine voice. It was about as welcoming as the sound of broken glass being rubbed by sandpaper. The man it belonged to looked formidable. I didn't want to screw this up. Not on day one.

"You must be Special Agent Hawthorne," he said, barely looking at me from his stack of paperwork. "Please, take a seat."

Only now did I come to realize there was someone else in the room. I caught sight of a long, bright pink mane, and vivid green eyes that looked unnatural. The slender figure was clad not in the official uniform of the FBI, but a cropped leather jacket on top of a black t-shirt.

"Hey . . . " came a bored voice from the mysterious figure.

"Hi." I wasn't sure whether or not I should reach over to shake her hand. For all I knew, she was an informant. Or maybe she was Harris's daughter, home on break from college.

That had to be it.

I settled into the seat next to her, unable to take my eyes off of her for very long. Despite her disheveled appearance, she was stunningly beautiful in an almost otherworldly way. Like she didn't quite belong in the room with us mortals. Her skin shimmered like she'd been sprayed with the finest diamond dust. I found my hands begin to sweat with nerves.

Get it together, man! That's the chief's daughter!

My gaze was only pulled from her when I felt Harris lean in close to me. Then came the sound of him sliding a file across the table.

"Thank you for being here," he said. "And congratulations on your promotion."

"Thank you, sir. I'm honored to make it to senior special agent."

"Ooh, you're *extra* special?" said the young woman. "I'm just a lowly special agent."

She smiled to show she was joking and crossed one lithe leg over the other. Her jeans were so ripped up that it was a wonder they stayed on. Then I saw the sidearm resting against her hip. It was impossible to miss. It was a standard-issue Glock just like everyone else's, except unlike everyone else's, this one was gold-plated.

"Special Agent Logan Hawthorne," said Harris, clearing his throat. "This is Agent Elena Rivera."

A mess of hot pink hair turned my direction. So she definitely wasn't the chief's daughter. That made things less weird. I gave her a courteous smile, which Elena neglected to return.

"I'm so pleased to meet you."

The mocking tone of her voice was impossible to miss. She wasn't pleased to meet me in the slightest. And those eyes . . . those fucking eyes. It was like they were staring right into my soul.

Harris looked uncomfortable in her presence. If she could rattle a bear of a man like him, then what hope in hell did I have?

"Alright, let's get down to business," said Harris, pointing to the file in front of me. "I've heard good things about you, Hawthorne. Your dad was a fine agent too, and your performance over the last few years has been nothing short of exceptional. That's why I couldn't think of anyone better than you to join the OCD's latest task force."

"Task force?"

Shit, this is serious.

"Affirmative. I know it's your first day in your new position, but what better way to learn than to get thrown into the deep end?"

He paused for a second to gauge how I was reacting, but I was numb, blank, totally confused. It was always my dream to be brought in on a big case and be selected for a major task force. It's what all the agents aimed for. But my joy was being eclipsed by a growing sense of nervousness. All thoughts of Bridget were gone now that duty called. But something kept bringing my attention back to Rivera and her unwavering gaze. Something about her was bugging the shit out of me, but I couldn't quite put my finger on what.

"I couldn't agree more, sir," I replied. "I'd like to hear everything we know about the case."

"Of course," said Harris. "I suggest you keep an open

mind. This isn't your average terrorist or serial killer we're dealing with."

I nodded, but my brain had questions.

What the hell is an average serial killer? And what could be more serious and difficult to capture than a terrorist?

"Rivera," the chief began, "perhaps you would like to brief Hawthorne."

"With all due respect," I interjected, "a field agent isn't really in the position to be briefing me on—"

"Hey F.N.G.," spat Rivera. "Shut the hell up." The venom in her voice forced me to the back of my seat. Did this disrespectful little punk just call me the Fucking New Guy?

Yes. Yes she did.

"You've been on the case for what, five minutes?" she said, glaring at me. "I'm the expert in this room, so save your questions and comments for *after* the briefing."

She wheeled her chair closer to mine, carrying her scent along with her. She smelled sweet, but not the cloying kind of sweet. No, there was an earthy edge to it . . . like a picnic of sugar cookies in a flower garden on a summer day.

"There's one thing I want you to know first," she began. "I don't *know* you, so I don't *like* you."

"Okay . . . " I wasn't sure if this was an elaborate joke or not. "I'm glad we got that established."

Harris flashed me an apologetic look. This was definitely not a joke. How was she getting away with being such a bitch? Especially in front of the chief?

"And another thing," she continued. "I don't think you're qualified to be working on this case. I know Harris said you're a good agent, but that doesn't mean you belong in the OCD. This is *my* area of expertise. I'm the only one around here who knows how this works."

"Okay, Rivera," I said with a cocky grin. "Now it's *your* turn to shut the hell up. I don't know who you think you are, but the FBI is in my blood. Every man in my family for the last four generations has worked for the bureau, so if anybody knows how shit works around here, it's *me*. And to be perfectly honest, I don't think I like you either."

Her green eyes practically blazed in anger. In that moment, I wasn't sure if I hated her or was terrified of her. Either way, I didn't want her near me. I wheeled my chair out of reach in case she decided to throw a fist my way. She seemed more than capable of it.

Agent Rivera stared right through me. I was hoping my retort would have dampened her spirit somewhat, but it only appeared to make it stronger.

"I told you this wouldn't work out," she complained to Harris. "I want him off the case."

Now I was just pissed.

"I don't even know what the case *is!*"

Harris sighed and held a hand to his forehead.

"*Both* of you shut the fuck up. If I wanted to deal with this kind of shit, I'd be running a fucking daycare." He stood up, circled around us and walked over to the window. Staring out across the skyline of Washington DC, he held his hands behind his back and took a deep breath.

"Apologies for stepping out of line, sir," I said, earnestly trying not to get fired on my first day. To my surprise, Agent Rivera just rolled her eyes.

"I'm the chief here and what I say goes. You two are the most qualified agents for what this case requires. I couldn't give two shits if you get along or not. You *will* be working together. Am I making myself clear?"

He turned around and we both nodded.

"Perfectly clear," I said. "Now can one of you tell me what the case is?"

"Goblins," replied Rivera. "We're gonna go hunt goblins."

My brain was drawing a complete blank.

"Goblins? Is that code for something?"

Harris returned to the table, sat down and spread his hands down over the wood.

"Hawthorne . . . You ever been to the Smoky Mountains?"

"No, sir."

"Well, lucky you. It's where you're heading right now."

"But, sir . . . can you tell me what a goblin is?"

He turned to Rivera and they shared a solemn glance.

"Faeries," he said, looking me dead in the eye. "You're hunting faeries."

4

ELENA

What an absolute ass hat, I thought as I looked at Agent Hawthorne. He was tall, handsome, and a total dick.

Why exactly did Harris think this arrogant frat boy would make a good partner for me in this case? In fact, why did he think I needed a partner at all? Nobody in the whole of the FBI knew more about goblins than me. So why did he have to bring in this clown who looked like a page torn from the dress code section of a 1950's training manual?

I studied his clean-shaven face and neatly trimmed dark hair, mentally preparing myself to hear him call women dames or broads. The dark blue suit wasn't insanely expensive, although it had been tailored to look that way. It barely concealed his thick, beefy arms. The color made his blue eyes pop, unnerving me with their twinkly sapphire effect. I was a fiend for sugar, it was true . . . but I was *obsessed* with anything that sparkled.

"I'm sorry," Hawthorne said, looking in between Harris and me. "For a second there I thought you just said we were going to the Smoky Mountains to hunt faeries."

He was trying to force a laugh, but he also looked as though he was on the verge of cracking up.

"Yep," I replied seriously. "That's *exactly* what we're going to do."

He held my gaze for a second, then burst out laughing.

"Oh, I get it. Very funny. A nice, big practical joke for the special agent on his first day. I bet you're not even the chief, are you? And you, Rivera . . . I bet you're not even an agent at all, are you? Who are you? The girl that brings the sandwiches?"

I leapt to my feet.

"What the fuck did you just say?"

"Alright, alright!" interrupted Harris. "Both of you calm down."

"Calm down? This guy's a fucking meathead, chief!"

"Hey!" moaned Hawthorne. "Don't you dare call me a fucking meathead. You're the one rambling about goblins or some shit and—"

"*Enough!*" yelled Harris. "If you both don't shut the fuck up immediately, I will knock both your skulls together . . . *after* I write up each of you for insubordination!"

We both fell silent, shrinking into our seats.

"Look, Hawthorne, I understand this is difficult for you to comprehend," said Harris. "But this is all very true. The Occult Crimes Division works on cases involving devil worship and witchcraft, but that's just scratching the surface. Your case involves another . . . *dimension*, if you will. It's a world that remains largely hidden from the one you're familiar with."

That appeared to pique Logan's interest, and I watched as his ears perked up.

"You won't have heard of this world," said Harris. "In fact, only twenty-five people within the bureau have ever heard of it. And with you on board, that makes twenty-six."

I could see the realization fall across Hawthorne's face as he came to discover that maybe this wasn't a practical joke after all.

"Wh—what's it called?" he asked. He sounded like a child asking about the reality of Santa Claus. Harris gave him a slight smile and looked deep into his face.

"It depends who you ask. Some people call it Faerieland. We just call it the Hollows."

For a long, excruciating moment, there was nothing but awkward silence in the room as Hawthorne processed what he had just heard.

"The Hollows?"

He glanced over at me as though he hoped I could give him some much needed clarity. All I could do was nod in agreement.

"Everything originating from the Hollows falls within my area of expertise," I told him. "So if you don't believe in magic, you better start real soon. Or, you know, you could just go back to running sting operations on counterfeit checks, or whatever it is you're good at."

Hawthorne's mouth hung open as though he was trying to catch flies.

"No . . . " he said. "This can't be right. You're just messing with me on my first day in my new position. This is all some kind of elaborate joke, isn't it?"

But the look on my face told him it wasn't.

"Seriously?" he asked Harris, pleadingly. "You expect me to believe all of this is real?"

"Hawthorne, listen," said Harris. "I understand your reticence to believe in certain matters, but the OCD is a very real division that deals with real cases. There's no room for practical jokes or time wasting. Rivera? Tell your new partner why he's here."

I flipped open the file and showed Hawthorne the same spreadsheet I had only become acquainted with myself that morning.

"Missing children," I said. "Hundreds of them. The disappearances started in the Smokies but they're moving south and west and at a hell of a rate."

"Child abductions? That's what we're really investigating?"

"It is," I said. "And we need to get moving right away. I don't have time for you to keep questioning who I am, or whether the world we're investigating is even real or not."

"Understood," he replied, but I could tell there was a massive wall of skepticism behind his eyes. "I gotta ask . . . what makes *you* such an expert in these crimes?"

I brought the palm of my hand to my face. It was like the meathead didn't even hear what I'd just said.

"Rivera has insider knowledge," explained Harris. "And she's worked on numerous cases in the OCD. Everything from exorcisms and poltergeists to UFO phenomena."

"Get outta here," Hawthorne snickered.

"It's true," I said. "And I don't care if you believe me or not. Right now, all that matters is that we track down these missing kids and find the little faerie shitbag that's abducting them. Are you in or not?"

Hawthorne stared into space for a long moment, clearly wondering if he'd lost his mind. It wasn't every day I got to witness a human having their entire belief system shaken to the core, so this was a real treat for me. Right about the time when I thought he'd completely dissociated, he turned his eyes towards me before glancing down at the spreadsheet. I knew what he was thinking. Whether faeries were real or not, kids were going missing. Hundreds of them. It didn't matter if he believed us; the numbers didn't lie.

"I'm in," he said. "I can leave as soon as you need me to."

"Good," Harris beamed, standing up and clapping his hands together. "You'll both fly out first thing in the morning. I'll set up a rental car after you land in Tennessee." He paused and glanced at Hawthorne's long legs. The motherfucker was tall—taller than anyone else I saw around the office. "It's a couple hours drive from Knoxville to get to where you're going. I'll try to get you something with plenty of legroom."

"Nice. I'll drive," Logan volunteered before I had the chance.

"I always drive," I hissed through my teeth.

"There's a first time for everything," he said, not flinching. The two of us stared each other down for a few seconds. The last thing I wanted was him joining me on this trip, but what choice did I have?

"Play nice, Rivera," warned Harris. "Your job is to *find* kids, not act like them. Do you understand?"

"Loud and clear, sir," I said, and mustered up the decency to offer my hand so Hawthorne could shake it. "Let's get to work. For the kids."

"For the kids," he replied, leaning close to lean into my ear. "But I'm still driving."

"I'm glad to see all that hard-working taxpayers' money is being so well spent by this bullshit division," Hawthorne said coolly from behind the wheel. I whipped my head in his direction.

"Fucking *excuse* me? Bullshit division?"

"C'mon. A Lincoln Navigator? For ghost hunting?" he scoffed as we rounded a bend in the road. "You know this is all bullshit. When's the last time the OCD had an audit?"

"Maybe you should be asking Harris. You know, your new boss."

It was obvious that Hawthorne had gotten a good night's sleep. He was less dazed and had essentially taken charge of our entire operation so far, treating me like a first-year cadet instead of the expert I was. His confidence soared, which was a real pain in the ass for me since I'd been stuck with him all morning.

He'd been making snide comments and talking shit the entire time. Most of it was like water off a duck's back to me. But bullshit division? Threatening us with an audit? I wished more than anything that the Navigator had an ejector seat. Why in the name of all that was holy did Harris think it was okay to dump this tool into my lap? Not only was Hawthorne a cocky shit of an agent, but he was a skeptic through and through. Would it have been so hard to find someone who actually believed in what they were assigned to investigate?

But I knew things didn't work like that around here. Hawthorne's dad was retired FBI upper management, and so was his father before him. This was nothing but pure favoritism among the good ol' boys club.

I switched on the radio before he could say another word, and I didn't stop until I heard The Strokes playing over the speakers.

"Dear god, change the station, will you?" he groaned.

"Nah . . . I like this song."

"Fine," he said, and tapped a button on the steering wheel. The music stopped. "We won't listen to anything."

"You are literally the *worst*," I replied through my teeth.

"Aww, the feeling's mutual, partner," Hawthorne said, glancing at the navigation screen. "Like I wanna be stuck in the middle of bumfuck Tennessee with some emo punk alt-chick who believes in faeries. I joined the FBI to work on serious shit."

"And you think I didn't? I've worked on things that would turn your hair gray. Things that would scare the ever-living shit out of you."

"My ass, you have. I don't know how you convinced Harris that you've worked with exorcisms and little green men, but it's all horseshit. You're nothing but a scam artist."

I wanted to leap out of the seat and strangle him with his perfectly knotted necktie, but the SUV was cruising into a sharp descent of another mountain valley. Then the landscape gave way, revealing the small and *very* rural town of Yarbrough.

Looking out the window, I saw stunning green scenery. Thick virgin forest mixed with the damp gray of the misty air. Even from all the way up here, I could sense the mystery and energy of the place. All my irritation drifted away, leaving my body and my mind within seconds.

"The goblins are here," I breathed. "I can feel it."

"The *what*?"

"The goblins. They're here. This is the perfect place for them."

"You're nuts," Hawthorne muttered under his breath. "I hope I don't die out here. You're actually insane."

5

LOGAN

The town of Yarbrough barely qualified to be called a town. It was nothing but a county highway making up the main street. There was a police station at one end, a school at the other, and a gas station-grocery store combo in the middle. A few hundred houses peppered the landscape all the way up into the foothills.

"It's an honor to meet y'all," said Sheriff McKinney as he greeted us in the parking lot of the police station.

He was everything you'd expect from a small-town sheriff, masculine with a weathered face and raspy voice, but full of country charm. I got the impression he was a darling to everyone he met, but I could sense beneath his exterior that he was capable of being one tough motherfucker when he had to be. Nobody became a sheriff in this tough-as-nails region for nothing.

"Thank you, but the honor is all ours," I said to him, giving him a firm handshake. "I know it's difficult for a police department to hand over a case to the FBI. Many aren't so willing."

He held my hand for a fraction of a second too long, his thin, chapped lips turning up into a boyish grin.

"We're here to work with you any way we can," my partner butted in. "Our top priority is getting to the bottom of whatever's happening to these kids."

"I'll be honest, Agent . . . "

"Rivera. Elena Rivera."

"Well, Agent Rivera," he said, giving her a goofy smile. She smiled right back, lapping it up. "I don't mean no disrespect, but when I heard two agents were coming down from DC, I didn't expect one of them to be so lovely as you."

"She's far from lovely," I joked. The Sheriff glanced over at me and laughed.

"And you're not quite what I expected either Agent . . . "

"Hawthorne. Or Logan. Whatever you prefer."

"Hawthorne. Damn, son. You're a tall drink of water. What are you, six-six?"

"Six-seven," I replied. McKinney nodded.

"Did you play basketball?"

"Football. Wide receiver."

"I'll bet that came in handy against the cornerbacks," he chuckled.

"Yes, sir. It sure did."

He took a step back and gave me a casual once-over, shaking his head.

"I know FBI agents are known for being clean cut and slicker than snot on a doorknob, but fuck me. You look like you're gonna audition for the next James Bond movie."

"That'd be one hell of a commute," I laughed. McKinney grinned in such a way that I knew he'd already warmed up to me. Perfect.

"Anyway," he continued. "I guess I have a lot to learn

52

about y'all. And you sure both have a lot to learn about what's been happening in our town. Where would you like to go first?"

"Could you swing by the hotel so we can drop off our bags?" I asked. After sitting on a plane and in a car all morning, my shirt was as wrinkled as a crumpled up paper bag. I wanted to change into a freshly ironed one.

"Hotel?" chuckled the sheriff. "Aw, bless your heart. There ain't a hotel around here for over forty miles. I didn't think you'd much care for that commute, either."

Me and Rivera shared a curious glance.

"So . . . where are we staying?" I asked, growing worried.

"The missus and me have a little Airbnb setup," replied McKinney, puffing out his chest with pride. "It's our side hustle. Martha takes care of all the bookings. Her nephew just wired it up for electricity last week. Turns out people love being out in nature, but they gotta keep them phones charged."

I shot Rivera a thinly disguised look of concern. To my surprise, she didn't seem the slightest bit worried about the situation. I waited until we were back in our car, following the sheriff down a long dirt road to our questionable lodgings.

"Is it even up to code?" I wondered out loud. Rivera just pursed her lips and tossed her pink head of hair. I was half expecting the big bun on top to go flying across the room.

"What's the matter, Hawthorne? Were you expecting a Nespresso every morning?"

"No, but it would've been nice," I admitted. There hadn't been any sign of a coffee shop, and I was already wondering how I was supposed to get my caffeine fix. I had a feeling I was going to be in for a rude awakening.

I wasn't disappointed.

"It ain't the Hilton, but it'll do nicely," said Sheriff McKinney as he stomped his way towards his two-story log cabin . . . and subsequently walked right past it. Each of his hands held our heavy suitcases as though they were nothing but lunchboxes. At first I thought he was heading for a side entrance to the house, but he was making a beeline for the back yard. The only thing I saw was a freshly mowed lawn and a backdrop of tall trees battling an ever-encroaching wall of kudzu.

"Are we camping in his back yard?" I whispered to Rivera. "Is that normal for you?"

"Um . . . No. I usually get a room at the Hilton."

I narrowed my eyes at her, but kept my mouth shut.

"Okay, here we are!" announced McKinney as he motioned above his head.

We'd arrived at our dwelling, a structure cobbled together with reclaimed wood planks and secondhand windows, all resting on a perch of thick oak branches.

"We're staying in a *treehouse*?" Rivera gasped.

"*Luxury* treehouse," he corrected her. "It was my eldest's favorite hangout spot until he flew the coop. It's real cozy up there now that we fixed it up."

He began climbing the ladder while juggling our suitcases, if you could call them that. I'd brought a nice carryon with an adjustable handle and wheels that spun 360 degrees. Rivera had crammed all her shit into a worn-out army surplus duffel bag that looked older than her. Down on the ground, the two of us stared up at McKinney. It was impressive that this treehouse could support a man of his size and stature, but three adults seemed a stretch.

"Come on up, kids," McKinney laughed from the top. His bright, bushy beard stared down at us expectantly.

"Ladies first," I said, and shoved Rivera in front of me.

Her slender limbs climbed the ladder with graceful ease. She'd reached the top in a matter of seconds.

"Coming?" she asked me. "I'll give you a hand if you want."

"I'm fine."

But I wasn't fine.

I could hear boards creaking and limbs groaning above me. I was convinced one more person up there would send the whole thing crashing down. It was also a lot higher up than I'd initially realized. It was one thing to risk life and limb while chasing down a suspect or in a life-or-death situation, but this? Please. The last thing I wanted to do was end up in a body cast from falling out of a treehouse.

"Why aren't you up here yet? Are you scared?" Rivera asked. The gleeful look in her eyes ignited a flame of anger in my gut. If I refused to do this, I wouldn't hear the end of it from her. And I sure as shit wasn't letting some emo punk faerie-loving hellion get one over on me.

I placed one foot above the other as my palms grew sweaty around the sides of the ladder.

"You okay?" McKinney hollered down to me. "You look a little wobbly."

"I'm fine."

Don't look down. Don't look down. You're tough. You work out. You're a senior special agent. Even if you fall, you'll be fine. You can climb a fucking ladder.

"Are you sure you're okay?" McKinney called out. "You're sweating like a whore's tush."

"I said I'm fine!" I snapped a little too loudly. I could hear Rivera giggle and my anger grew.

Get up there to prove her wrong. Imagine the look on her face if she saw you quit.

Motivated by rage, I pushed my fears to the side and forced myself up the ladder until at last, I could see the tops of McKinney's shoes.

"Hope you'll be comfortable here."

I was so busy focusing on the overall stability of the structure that I hadn't put much thought into the accommodations. I took a quick glance around, noting that I'd seen walk-in closets bigger than this. It was still bigger than expected. The large windows facing the trees made it open and airy. There was even a tiled area sectioned off with a curtain, pulled back to reveal a sink, a shower head, and what looked to be a composting toilet.

One thing caught my eye in particular. It wasn't the kid-sized chest of drawers, the lone wicker chair, or the single nightstand. It was that there was only one bed.

"So . . . we're *both* staying up here?" I asked.

"Well, sure!" grinned McKinney. "If you don't want to go top to tail, there's plenty of room for a sleeping bag. Bedding's in that built-in storage bench."

"I call dibs on the bed," Rivera announced, dropping her duffel bag on the mattress. "Hawthorne can sleep on the floor."

"I'm not sure what I think about this arrangement," I said.

"Alright then, I'll let y'all figure it out," McKinney said, and started down the ladder. "Let me know when you're ready to go back to the station. I'm sure you're eager to have a look at our files."

Through the large screened window, I watched the

sheriff amble across the lawn and into his house. When I turned to look at my partner, she'd already started to empty her carryon. Clothes, makeup, and hair products were strewn across the blanket, intermingled with bags of gummy worms, Snickers bars, Ding Dongs, and pink Snoballs. A six-pack of Mountain Dew sat on the floor next to a beat up pair of Chuck Taylors.

"This can *not* be the only option," I said, wrinkling my nose in disgust. "There has to be a hotel or a bed and breakfast nearby."

Rivera grabbed a handful of her personal items and took the four steps required to reach our bathroom . . . if it could even be called that.

"Sounds great to me," she said, placing her various hair products on the tiny shelf until it was completely full. "You can call Harris and ask him for another rental car while you're at it. I'm sure he won't mind you burning up more of his bullshit department's budget, not to mention all the time you're going to waste driving back and forth to wherever the hell you're going. I'm sure your new boss will be thrilled. You should ask him for a Nespresso while you're at it."

I held my tongue and took a deep breath. Rivera had dug in her heels. She wasn't about to leave. She was barely willing to give me a spot on the floor. I briefly considered phoning headquarters to see about getting a different room somewhere else, but Rivera had a point. Another room in another location would require another vehicle, more gas, and would waste more time. I thought about the video with Haley, and the tired, distressed expression on her mom's face. She was one of the lucky ones. How many parents were lying awake at night, worried sick about their missing children?

I set my carryon next to the built-in storage bench,

claiming my spot on the floor. And for the first time in perhaps my entire career with the FBI, I wished I could turn back time and never get this promotion.

"I've seen the spreadsheet," I said to McKinney as he handed me a cup of much needed steaming black coffee. It wasn't good, but it was good enough. "Are these numbers right?"

"Are these numbers right?" the sheriff grumbled. "What do you think—that us country bumpkins can't count?"

"I don't think that at a—"

"Because the numbers are right! I know because I investigated each and every case around Yarbrough myself. *I'm* the one who's met the families . . . .comforted crying moms and devastated dads. I interviewed everyone who's ever set foot in them woods. I *know* these numbers are right."

He sat down at his desk and took a defiant gulp of his coffee. Beside him, Rivera was standing at a nearby bookshelf perusing the various volumes that were stacked up in dusty piles.

"I think . . . " she began, running her spindly fingers down the spine of a beat-up hardback, "that my colleague here is just surprised. The numbers aren't ordinary. Nobody has seen a phenomenon so . . . "

"Shocking," I cut in. "It's just a real shock to discover so many children have gone missing. And from this area alone. In such a short period of time. It's highly unusual."

"Yeah, that's why you're here," said McKinney, pointing his coffee up at each of us. "You're supposed to be the experts with all this paranormal and occult stuff."

"Actually, when it comes to all the woo-woo stuff, *she's* the expert," I said, smirking at Rivera.

"Yep," she said, turning around with a book in her hand. "I'm the expert."

I squinted to take a closer look at the title, revealing it to be an anthology of Native American folklore. The other titles on the shelf seemed to focus on UFOs, astrology, ghosts, divination, alchemy, and witchcraft. Not exactly the sort of reading I saw floating around the libraries at the FBI.

"This one's a skeptic," she added, nodding at me. "He doesn't believe in any of it."

McKinney screwed up his face like he hadn't heard her correctly. Then he turned his gaze on me.

"Not even ghosts?"

"No."

"What about demons?"

"No."

"Faeries?"

"Uh uh."

"Witches?"

I shook my head.

"You really don't believe in *any* of it?" asked McKinney, horrified. "What are you? Stupid?"

"No," I frowned, wondering if I should be worried about this guy's mental capacity for carrying a firearm. "I just haven't seen any evidence befo—"

"Evidence shmevidence." He waved a hand in dismissal, as if having evidence for crimes was just an afterthought. "You gotta believe in the paranormal. Ain't no other explanation for why there's so many dead black cats in the woods after Halloween. It's gotta be the occult."

Despite how serious Sheriff McKinney was, part of me still clung to the belief that I was the butt of an elaborate practical joke. There was no way in hell a salt of the earth guy like him—a county sheriff, no less—could believe in ghosts and demons and witches who sacrificed black cats on Halloween. It was an urban legend at best.

"I don't think it's anything occult or paranormal," I said, firmly. "And neither should you. You're a man of the law. Don't you think child abductions require a bit more critical thinking, instead of assuming it's the work of faeries or witches?"

McKinney crossed his arms and looked at me dead in the face. So much for making nice with the guy.

"Sure . . . " he said, unable to hide the bitterness in his voice. "Some things require critical thinking. But *some* things, as you're about to discover, fall beyond the realm of logic." He turned to Rivera. "How did a goon like him end up in the Occult Crimes Division, anyway?"

"It wasn't my choice," Rivera said without looking up.

"Don't you have to believe in the things you investigate?"

"That's what I used to think," huffed Rivera, turning the page of her book. "But he only started yesterday morning. He's got a lot to learn."

"Yesterday morning?" laughed McKinney. "I don't fucking believe it. I thought the FBI was sending the cream of the crop."

I clenched my jaw, keeping my frustration in check. I *was* the cream of the crop. That's why Harris had chosen me for this assignment. I realized I wasn't going to make any friends with my current outlook, but at the same time, there was no way in hell I was going to drink whatever Kool-Aid McKinney and Rivera were chugging. Without proof, I didn't believe anything. Maybe it was time to change my approach. Just a little. Try and at least pretend I was interested in learning about all things occult and paranormal.

"Sheriff McKinney," I began, pulling out my notebook so I at least appeared interested. "You'll have to forgive me. I'm a city boy. Given what kids are wearing these days," my eyes darted over to Rivera's hot pink hair and ripped jeans, "I probably wouldn't recognize a faerie if it was standing right in front of me. I hope you'll cut me some slack and help teach me whatever you know about the paranormal."

"Well, I can't tell you everything." His tone was begrudging, but he'd taken the bait. Good. "We'd be here for a lifetime. I can, however, tell you what I know about what's happening here in Yarbrough. I can tell you a whole lot because it's been happening long before Yarbrough was even called Yarbrough."

"That would be great," I said, nodding my head as I scribbled in my notebook. "So you're a bit of a historian?"

"You could say that," he nodded. "But a lot of us here are. The history of this area is rich in legend. We all grew up hearing the stories from our grandparents that they heard from their own grandparents."

He relaxed a bit as he spoke and stood up to walk over to the coffeemaker, topping off his mug. Then he moved into the top drawer of his desk. I expected him to pull out a bottle of whiskey or even a mason jar of moonshine, but instead, he presented us with a package of soft molasses cookies. Rivera's eyes widened like a cat's when she saw them.

"Don't tell Martha," he said, offering me a cookie before taking one for himself. "She'll have kittens if she finds out I'm back on the carbs."

Clearly unconcerned about her own carb intake, Rivera

practically lunged at the package, coming away with three in one hand, and another in her mouth.

"Wow, hungry?" laughed McKinney.

"For molasses cookies? Always."

I tried to ignore her talking with her mouth full, but she didn't seem to mind making a spectacle of herself. She took her time licking the crumbs off her fingers, swirling her pink tongue around each tip. Good god. Did she have any idea how sexually suggestive that came across? Maybe. Did she even care?

Hmmm . . .

Shaking some inappropriate thoughts from my mind, I doubled down on trying to focus on my notes.

"Right. The history of Yarbrough," I blurted out, eager to get back on topic. "You said you know a lot about it. Is there any of it's that relevant to the missing children?"

A solemn expression fell across McKinney's face as he lowered himself down into his seat with a groan.

"Where should I start?"

"Wherever you want. I prefer the beginning."

He placed a cookie into his mouth and began chewing thoughtfully.

"Well then . . . The very beginning was thousands of years ago for Yarbrough. That's what the legend says anyway."

"There's a legend?"

"Uh huh. A Native American one. Cherokee, to be precise." Without turning around, he motioned out the window to the nearest peak. "Up there on that mountain there's a cave full of paintings. Weird paintings of little people coming out of the ground. Every generation's got stories of kids being taken by these little people."

"Is there any evi—any record of these earlier occurrences that we can review?"

"Sorta," McKinney shrugged. "The thing is . . . all the Native American's history is oral. That's how they passed it along from one generation to the next, was tellin' stories. It wasn't until settlers started showing up that people started writing things down. There's an old newspaper clipping somewhere that talks about pioneer children disappearing. One minute they'd be playing near their covered wagon . . . and the next they'd be gone. They blamed it on the Cherokee, but later on, after they'd all been run off their land and put on reservations, the kids kept vanishing."

Rivera had finished her cookies and miraculously waited until she'd swallowed her food before she began to speak.

"I don't understand," she said, confused. "If children kept disappearing from this area, why was nothing done sooner? Wasn't this investigated?"

"Now you're getting somewhere . . . " McKinney's bushy eyebrows lifted as if to impart some deep wisdom. "Some big shots from Washington came out back in the nineties, but nothing happened. Seems Uncle Sam doesn't care what happens to a bunch of broke-ass, backwoods rednecks. Course . . . if it happened in Beverly Hills, you bet there'd be some answers by now."

There was no arguing with that.

"Besides . . . " He leaned back in his chair, propping his feet up on the edge of his desk. "The disappearances weren't constant. And they weren't predictable, either. In one year it could be one child, then there would be no disappearances for a decade. Then suddenly there would be three in a weekend, then none for twenty years. We knew nothing of how to deal with these disappearances. Only that they were happening when we least expected it."

"Alright," I paused to write more notes. "How long have you been in the Yarbrough Police Department?"

"It'll be thirty-three years next summer. But I know what you're going to ask me." I caught his gaze, waiting for him to speak. "You're going to ask how many missing children's cases I've dealt with in my career." I gave him a faint smile and nodded my head. "The answer is that until this recent spate I only dealt with two. Two in three decades, then suddenly there were hundreds. I'm at the end of my tether, Agent Hawthorne. There's not much more we can do here without the resources. That's why we need you guys."

The man truly believed what he was saying, but I was struggling to feel his enthusiasm for the old local stories. Cave paintings? Little people? It all sounded like folklore to me. Not real life.

"Agent Hawthorne. You're looking at me like I'm talking nonsense."

"No, sir. Not at all."

"I can see there's a part of you who thinks none of this could really be happening. That us country folk are just imagining it all. I guess to a certain extent that's healthy. But if you want to become a believer, I suggest you go visit some of the parents yourself."

"Actually," interjected Rivera. "I was thinking our first visit should be to the Brown family. I've watched Haley's interview. It's pretty compelling stuff."

"Indeed," McKinney agreed. "But I better warn you. The Brown family ain't the friendliest to outsiders."

6

ELENA

Sheriff McKinney wasn't kidding when he said the Browns were suspicious of outsiders. We'd barely made it halfway down the driveway when Mrs. Brown stepped out onto her porch with a shotgun in her hands.

"Who are you?" she bellowed through the misty air. Hawthorne stepped on the brakes and I leaned out the window, flashing her a disarming smile.

"FBI," I called back cheerfully, raising my badge at her.

Slowly, she lowered her gun and motioned for us to continue driving up to the house.

"You don't look like FBI," she said when we got out of the car. She took a moment to look me up and down. I'd taken my hair out of the messy bun it had been in all morning and now it was shaped into big fat waves. I thought it looked fabulous, but it did have a tendency to make people not take me seriously. As if to prove the point, Mrs. Brown glanced at my tall, handsome, asshole partner before giving me a questioning look. "I mean, *he* looks like he's from the FBI, but you don't."

"She's not your average agent," Hawthorne said, sounding smug and condescending. He stepped forward to shake the woman's hand, but she just stared up at him, his hand hanging in the air for a few awkward seconds before he lowered it. Man . . . what a tool.

"So does that mean you're average?" she asked. "The FBI sent someone average to find out what happened to my daughter?" Mrs. Brown's gun was still lowered but her grip on it was firm. I might've laughed at her snarky jab if it weren't for her hand on the shotgun. Then again, she was only protecting her little girl. She had every right to be defensive.

"Agent Hawthorne is one of our very best," I assured her. My partner's eyes flicked my way, probably wondering why I'd decided to be so nice to him when he'd been a complete dick since day one. Whether or not he was one of the bureau's best remained to be seen, although Mrs. Brown didn't need to know that. "We're here about your daughter, Haley. I've seen her interview with Sheriff McKinney."

"You have?"

"Yeah. And I believe everything she said."

She softened at hearing this and lowered the gun even further, relaxing her grip as well.

"So then . . . you're here about them little people?"

"We are," Hawthorne said in all seriousness, although the look behind his eyes told me he still thought we were all crazy. That was fine. I couldn't wait to see firsthand the moment when he realized he was completely wrong.

"I suppose you better come on in then," said Mrs. Brown. "Y'all want something to drink? We got water, milk, and coke."

"Thanks. What kind of coke?" I asked, following her up

the steps to the front door. "You don't happen to have anything fruity like Fanta, do you?"

Mrs. Brown's stony face melted into a smile.

"That's funny. Orange Fanta is Haley's favorite. I have to drive all the way to the Piggly Wiggly in Scruggsville to get it."

As we entered the house, I became aware of how rundown and tired the whole place was. It looked like a half-trailer, half-wooden cabin with bits and pieces built onto the crude building over years and years. On the wall above the sofa hung three coyote pelts, draped across the thin wood paneling like they were part of some macabre ritual.

"My husband," said Mrs. Brown, noticing my gaze. "He loves to hunt. Of course, most of our family loves to hunt. It's how our ancestors survived out here for so long."

She walked away into what I assumed to be the kitchen. I caught sight of a battered old stove next to a stick-thin kitchen table piled full of magazines. Children's artwork had been stuck to the wall with Scotch tape instead of fancy frames. Taking a seat on a nearby rickety chair, I started to relax. Although it was slowly falling apart, the house felt safe and full of love. It was evident from all the clutter that it was the home of a lively family.

"So," said Mrs. Brown, fetching some glasses from the cupboard and filling them with ice. "You really came all the way from Washington DC to find out what happened to Haley?"

"Yes, ma'am," replied Hawthorne. He stood stiffly beside me, obviously not sharing my sense of ease with the place. His expression was a mixture of disgusted and nervous. With a gentle hand, I nudged him in the direction of the sofa. Sitting down on it gingerly, he opened his note-book and crossed his legs like he was trying to place a barrier between himself and the rest of the house.

"I'm amazed they really sent y'all down here," said Mrs. Brown, rummaging through the fridge. "I mean, we're just a small town. We ain't ever had the FBI here before."

"There's a first time for everything," I smiled. "And if it was up to me, I would have been down here a long time ago."

She smiled back and for the first time since we arrived, I felt as though I had gained a little of her trust.

"I've seen the numbers," I continued. "So many chil-dren are missing. You must've known some of them. This is a small town, after all."

She looked down into the ice-filled glasses. Her face seemed to droop with sadness as she thought about them.

"I knew *all* of them," she said, filling one of the glasses with water and one with a can of orange soda. "I've worked at Yarbrough Elementary for the last fifteen years as a teaching assistant. Met every single one of those kids at one time or another. I just . . . I just . . . "

She cleared her throat, holding back tears. Before any could fall, a clock chimed and she jumped at the sound.

"Sorry, I've just been so on edge recently. Can't stop thinking about it at all. I mean . . . all those kids . . . "

"It must be really hard for you," I said, trying to soothe her. "For everyone in this town."

"It is. It's . . . it's just not right. And . . . "

A single tear ran down her bronzed, wrinkled cheek and she wiped it away with the heel of her hand.

"It's just always on my mind, you know. This town is real close, so when a kid goes missing, it's like everyone's kid goes missing."

"But thankfully Haley came back," said Hawthorne.

It was the most he'd said since we entered the house, and his voice pierced the atmosphere. I wasn't sure if Mrs. Brown was apprehensive of him because he wore a suit, because he was a man, or because he was so obviously uncomfortable. Regardless, there was tension between them, and as she set a stainless steel glass of water in front of him, she did so with an aggressive clunk.

"Yeah, Haley came back," she said. "I thought she wouldn't. She was gone for twelve hours, but it felt like twelve damn years."

"I'm sorry to ask, but do you have a different cup I could use?" I asked with an apologetic look. "I've got a metal allergy."

"Sure, but the only thing I got that's clean is a mason jar."

"That's perfect," I said, hoping she realized how grateful I was. "Thanks so much."

She swapped out my Fanta into the glass jar, then joined us around the coffee table. It was more than a little amusing when she took the chair next to me instead of sitting on the sofa with Hawthorne.

"Do either of you have kids?" she asked.

"Not yet," replied Hawthorne. "But I plan on it someday."

"And what about you?" she asked me while I gulped orange soda. It tasted like nectar of the gods.

"Kids? I suppose someday."

She nodded with a knowing smile. "You're probably focused on your job right now, aren't you?"

"I guess you could say that, Mrs. Brown."

"Please, call me Shelly. I'm sorry, I didn't catch the name on your badge."

"Agent Rivera," I said, mentally facepalming myself. For fuck's sake. How come human interaction was always so hard for me? Well, I knew the answer to that, and I wasn't about to tell Shelly my secret. I had to do something quick to earn back some of my credibility. "But you don't have to use my last name. Just call me Elena."

"Elena," she said, staring at my long pink hair. I was glad I'd actually washed it this morning. I'd forgotten how shiny it was when it wasn't loaded down with four days' worth of dry shampoo. "That's a pretty name. I'd say it suits you."

Our small talk was interrupted by the sound of little feet running down the stairs.

"Mommy!"

We all turned to see Haley run into the room at full speed before she saw us and froze in her tracks. Clearly, she wasn't used to seeing strangers inside her house.

"Sweetie," said Shelly. "These nice people are here to learn about what happened to you."

The little girl stood in the doorway with her wide eyes jumping between the three of us. In her hands, held against her chest was a sheet of paper with messy green ink stains around the edges.

"What you got there?" asked Shelly.

"A drawing," replied Haley.

"A drawing? Would you like to show us?"

The girl nodded and edged closer towards her mom, but her eyes were on me. I was used to getting those kinds of curious looks. Hot pink hair and bright green eyes tend to have that effect.

"Here," she said, handing the sheet of paper over to her mom. Shelly took the drawing and squinted as she held it up to the light.

"What do we have here? Are these . . . "

"They're the little men," said Haley. "The little men I saw under the tree."

Shelly's face blanched and she lowered the paper.

"Can I see?" I asked Haley. "I love drawing too and I'd sure like to see what you did. Looks like you're quite the little artist."

She smiled and took the drawing from her mom's hand before sliding it over to me.

The first things I saw were large green ears and wide eyes. If I didn't already believe the kid about who or what she'd seen underground, I sure as shit did now. It was the most accurate drawing of a goblin I'd ever seen in my life.

"This was the little man you met?" I asked her, pointing to his ugly face.

"Yeah."

She didn't seem remotely afraid of him or traumatized by her experience. If anything, she looked like she was remembering a pleasant dream or a recent pretend tea party.

"Was he scary?" I asked.

"No, he was nice. He was ugly, but he was really nice. He talked like Uncle Larry." She started to gurgle and make a series of wet coughing sounds.

I was intrigued. I turned to Shelly.

"Uncle Larry?"

She shook her head. "Uncle Larry was in an ATV accident a few years ago. Got clipped by a low-hanging tree branch. Went right through his windpipe. He's lucky he didn't get himself decapitated, but now he sounds like he's got a permanent frog in his throat."

"Ah . . . " I nodded as Haley stepped closer between me and Shelly.

"The little man had these big, green eyes and—"

She stopped and looked at her mom for a second before returning her attention to me.

"He had green eyes that were the same color as *yours!*"

I bristled in my seat and hoped the other two would take her words as nothing more than a throwaway comment. But Hawthorne was now staring intently at my face.

"Oh, yeah. Green eyes are more common than a lot of people realize," I said, laughing it off like it was nothing. "Anyway, can you remember anything else?" I asked, hoping to deflect her attention from my eyes. "Something you didn't mention to the sheriff? Maybe it's a teeny weenie little detail that didn't seem important at the time?"

The little girl swayed side to side for a second as she thought. Then she shook her head and frowned.

"Nuh uh. I told him everything."

"You did a great job today, hon," said Shelly. "Thanks for—"

"Oh, wait!" burst Haley. "There was one thing I forgot to tell the policeman. I won't get into trouble, Mommy, will I?"

"Of course not," said Shelly, while rumpling her daughter's hair. "It's okay to forget things. What do you remember?"

"Honey," Haley said with an amused little laugh. "There were jars and jars of honey and sugar down beneath the tree. Like, a hundred billion jillion jars of it! The little man, the one who was holding my hand, he said it was their most favorite thing in the world. He said candy and cookies and sweets were like silver and gold to people like us."

Hawthorne frowned, obviously thinking the girl was just having fun elaborating on her story, but I knew exactly what it meant. And of course, that's when

Hawthorne's gaze met mine. I knew he was thinking about the comment on my green eyes, and recalling the piles of junk food spread all over my bed back in the treehouse.

"Sweets are good as gold . . . " he mused out loud, tapping his pen against the side of the table. "That's an interesting concept. That means it's not just something they like. It's something they value like currency. You could barter with it, in theory."

"Absolutely," I agreed. "And Haley, didn't you say you managed to get back to our world, up here on the surface because you had cookies in your backpack?"

She nodded.

"Yeah! I had a whole box of chocolate chip cookies! They thought I was rich!"

"As long as it worked," smiled Shelly. "I've never been so glad for chocolate chip cookies in all my life."

"I think that's the key somehow," said Hawthorne.

I narrowed my eyes at him. Was he starting to believe now? Or was he merely throwing ideas around?

Haley, now leaning into her mom, was starting to grow tired of the excitement. She wrapped her chubby arms around Shelly's neck.

"Mommy? Can I have a snack?"

"Of course, sweetie."

Looking up at the clock on the wall, I realized a full twenty-four hours had passed since I'd been assigned a new partner.

"We'd better get going," I said, standing up. "I'm glad we got the chance to swing by and introduce ourselves. We'll be around."

"You staying in town for long?"

"As long as it takes," said Hawthorne, not missing a beat.

Although Shelly hadn't completely warmed up to him, she appeared slightly comforted by his confidence.

"Here, take my number," I said to her, fishing in my pocket for my business card. "If you think of anything—and I mean *anything*—you can call or text me anytime."

"Thanks," she said, taking the card. "I'll let you know if me or Haley remember any other details."

Haley was still hanging off her mom, but smiled and waved as we departed. I waited until Hawthorne started the Navigator before I spoke.

"So? What do you think?" I asked him.

"I haven't got a fucking clue."

"Maybe we should visit that Pinkie Pie Trail so you can get a fucking clue?"

Hawthorne looked like he was fighting with a hell of a comeback. Instead, he just nodded his head and pulled out of the driveway. He didn't seem to need the navigation anymore—but just when I thought he'd already figured his way around the town, he turned left when he should've turned right.

"The trail's that way," I said, pointing my thumb towards the east.

"I know," he said, continuing to drive us west, and into the main strip of Yarbrough. "I need something to eat if we're going to go on a hike."

"I have Snickers bars in my bag," I said, giving my duffel bag a soft kick. "Want one?"

He made a disgusted face.

"No. I need *real* food, as in protein and vegetables. We passed a diner on the way over to the Brown's. Hopefully it's halfway decent."

As much as I was not looking forward to sitting down to lunch with Hawthorne, my stomach began to growl at the thought of anything covered in syrup and whipped cream.

Twenty minutes later, I had my pancakes sitting in front of me, along with a strawberry milkshake. Hawthorne had just taken a huge bite of a double bacon cheeseburger across from me.

"So? Do you believe her?" I asked.

"The girl or the mom?"

"Both."

"Oh, I definitely believe them."

I started to get my hopes up. Then, of course, he went on to crush them.

"I mean, it can't be faeries, but I believe that they believe they saw something. The two of them are as honest as they come. I don't think they're lying. They might be nuts, but they're not lying. That house is in pretty bad shape. Maybe we should have it tested for carbon monoxide poisoning."

Making zero effort to conceal how I felt about that reply, I rolled my eyes, shook my head, and went back to my gooey pancakes.

"I'm guessing from your melodramatic body language that you believe them."

"Obviously. It's my job to, and besides . . . "

He popped a French fry into his mouth and waited for me to finish my thought.

"Well? What else were you going to say?"

"Nothing. Forget it."

"Anyway," he continued, "whatever the fuck it all means, I think the honey or cookies or whatever is important. It's what set Haley free. By the sounds of it, the sweets have some kind of value to our suspect."

"No shit?" I was busy with my spoon, digging around

my milkshake for the elusive maraschino cherry. "You already figured that out? Damn. We're going to have this whole case solved by the end of the week."

Instead of arguing with me, Hawthorne pulled out his phone and ignored me for the rest of the meal.

7

LOGAN

One outlet.

One.

That's all we had in this damn treehouse.

I was charging my phone and laptop when Rivera had the genius idea to plug in her turbo-charged hairdryer. Of course it blew a fuse. But what really pissed me off was that her hair wasn't even wet; she was heating up some stupid goop that she put on her hair at night. And of course, it was *me* who had to climb down that rickety ladder, through a cloud of mosquitoes, and go ask Sheriff McKinney to help me fix it.

"Just so you know, I am *not* doing that again." I took off my shoes and set them at the foot of my sleeping bag, then lay down and pulled the cotton sheet over me. "Everything about this arrangement sucks."

"Oh, you think I'm thrilled to be here?" said Rivera through the darkness. "Because it's totally my dream come true to be stuck in a treehouse with a douche like you."

"Hey! At least you get the bed. I'm stuck on the fucking floor. And douche? Really? How old are you? Twelve?"

I lay against the floorboards, listening to the hordes of mosquitoes whining at the window screens, begging to get in and make me even more miserable than I already felt. This was like the worst sleepover I'd ever had. No horror movies to watch, no popcorn. There was no television or radio. All we had were the four walls of the treehouse and the sound of the bugs whining outside. That's when the coyotes started howling. I looked over to where the branches from the trees outside were dancing against the screen and squirmed even more. It wouldn't take much for a broken branch to fall and poke a hole in the screen, letting in all the bloodsucking, disease-ridden mosquitoes.

I hated this place.

The whole town was weird, too. Not weird enough to have little faerie people living beneath the trees, but weird.

"Hey, you still awake?" came Rivera's voice after a few minutes.

"What do you think?"

"I thought maybe you already fell asleep."

"Oh, you thought it was so comfortable down here on the floor that I somehow fell into a deep sleep the minute my head touched the pillow?"

"Damn, you're touchy," she snapped.

"Me? *Touchy*? You've been a prima-fucking-donna from the minute I stepped into Harris' office. Who the hell uses a blow-dryer when their hair's not even *wet*?"

"I needed the heat to activate my split end prevention mask," she said, like I gave a shit.

"If your hair's that messed up, maybe it's time to think about cutting it."

"Ugh, just shut up."

"Why would you bother to wake me up if you were going to tell me to shut up?"

"I thought you said you were awake!"

I sat up in the dark, wondering what the hell I was doing here. For a brief moment, I thought about zipping myself up in the sleeping bag and knocking all the screens from the windows to let the mosquitos have their way with her. They'd probably love it, what with the amount of sugar in her bloodstream. But I quickly abandoned the idea and took a deep breath instead. Someone had to be the adult here.

"I'm sleeping downstairs," I muttered, and began rolling up the sleeping bag. "I'm sure McKinney won't mind if I crash on his couch."

I pulled my laptop cord from the single outlet and started to pack it up, along with my phone. Grabbing my thin blanket and pillow, I stepped across the dark, creaky floor towards the treehouse opening and reached for the handle.

"Wait!" Rivera hissed. "If you go out there, you're going to let in all the mosquitoes!"

"That's a price I'm willing to pay," I said, grinning at the thought of them swarming her. I imagined them forming into an arrow and aiming straight for her ass. "At least McKinney doesn't screech like a velociraptor every time he opens his mouth. He might even let me get some sleep."

I reached again for the handle, when the little LED lamp above the bed switched on.

"Hawthorne . . . don't," Rivera protested. Her voice had lost the sarcastic edge and become soft, like when she'd interviewed the Browns earlier that day. There was even a hint of tenderness to it. "You don't have to go bother McKinney. He and Martha are probably sleeping by now. At least wait until morning if you'd rather sleep on his couch."

I sat back and considered the offer. She had a point. I was going to be here for weeks, if not months working this case. The last thing I wanted to do was piss off the sheriff who'd been nothing but cooperative and given us a free place to stay. Just then, the coyotes started another round of yips and howls. They sounded closer. I looked at my partner, who didn't appear overly concerned, but she definitely wasn't thrilled about the idea of sleeping out here with a pack of coyotes nearby.

"You can even have the bed if you want," she offered, and pulled back the covers. "I'll sleep on the floor."

She started to climb out of the bed, and I forgot all about what the hell I was supposed to say next. It might've had something to do with the unwitting peek she'd given me of her black lace-trimmed boy shorts, or the round, supple ass that was filling them out. They looked expensive, handmade even. But I could tell she wasn't wearing them for me. She was the type of girl who never did anything to please a man. No, those sexy panties were for her enjoyment alone. The oversized FBI t-shirt she wore only called more attention to her bare thighs. Was it normal for her skin—including her legs—to have that shimmery glow to it?

"You should keep the bed."

"Honestly, I don't mind. I've slept on worse."

I wouldn't hear of that. First, she was a chick, and making her sleep on the floor wouldn't be very chivalrous. Second, I refused to give this chick the pleasure of me accepting such a peace offering. I knew I'd never hear the end of it if I called her bluff.

"Don't worry about it." I plugged my laptop and phone back into the single outlet, then unrolled the sleeping bag and lay the sheet and pillow on top. "Besides, whatever glitter lotion you're wearing is probably all over the sheets. I'd rather not change our sleeping arrangements."

I kicked off my shoes and lay back down, but I was wide awake. I scrolled through my phone, studying a satellite image of the Pinkie Pie trail in hopes of discovering an old mine or a river or a cliff. But we'd hiked out there until it had grown dark and come up with nothing. We even found the tree that Shelly had described. There was nothing particularly special about it. It was just a tree.

"Do you want me to turn out the light?" Rivera asked. And, of course, that's when I looked over and saw her climbing back into the bed, giving me another shot of that lacey apple bottom. I snapped my head back to its previous position and went back to studying the green landscape on my phone.

"Nah. I don't think I'll be falling asleep anytime soon."

"Me, neither," she said, situating herself until she was perched on the edge of the mattress. "May as well go over the case notes until I pass out."

"That's what I'm thinking," I said. I leaned over and showed her the picture on my phone of Pinkie Pie Trail. She gave me a faint smile and I returned it.

"I also have snacks," she said reaching into her suitcase at the bottom of the bed. "If that helps."

Remembering those packages of unnaturally pink Snoballs, I was about to turn down the second peace offering, but then she surprised me with a grease-stained white paper bag.

"Homemade blueberry muffins," she said, pleased with herself. "From the diner."

My eyes widened.

"When did you get those?"

She snickered.

"When you were in the can."

She smiled again, this time more brightly. Were we finally starting to get along?

"Okay, well hurry up and take your shit, Brad. We've got work to do."

The harshness was back in her voice as she tossed the paper bag at me and ripped open a bag of Skittles.

"My name's Logan."

"I know, but you look like a Brad."

"What the hell does that mean?"

Rivera crammed a handful of rainbow candies into her mouth and chuckled in response.

"Aw, shut up. You know exactly what it means. I'm talking about spoiled momma's boys who play football and date cheerleaders and drink energy drinks. You know, Brads."

"I think you're insulting everyone in the world who's called Brad. Anyway, what the hell's wrong with playing football and all that other stuff?"

"Nothing," she smiled.

But her eyes told me she was repulsed by all of that.

"Oh, I get it," I said, throwing myself down on the opposite end of the bed from her. "You think you're too cool to be around someone who actually knows how to dress like a professional *adult*. I bet you were one of the chicks in high school who hung out behind the art building smoking clove cigarettes and reading Sylvia Plath. I bet you thought you were a real badass. You probably had a Facebook profile where you called yourself fucking Azrael Lovecraft or Raven Reznor or some other gothic punk shit."

"I did not!" she exploded, throwing a pillow at me.

"I think I hit a nerve," I taunted. "You just don't like me because I was one of the popular kids. One of the cool kids.

And if that makes me a Brad, then fine. I'm a Brad. But you should probably call me Logan or Hawthorne if you want me to give you the time of day."

Her cheeks flushed an angry shade of deep pink as she crunched her candy menacingly at me.

"Am I wrong?" I asked. For the first time, she said nothing and just glowered at me.

Good.

Hawthorne one, Rivera ZERO, I thought triumphantly. I'd finally figured out how to put this nippy little brat in check.

"Whatever, Logan," she said, trying to sound bored, but I knew better. "Let's get to work. We've got some kids here who might never grow up to smoke cloves *or* read Sylvia Plath if we don't find them first."

After that sobering comment, she grabbed her notes and began scanning through her pages. I joined her, flipping through my own notebook as I skimmed over my frantic handwriting. I started to wonder if I'd been too much of a dick.

"Just so you know," I said cautiously, "I hate energy drinks and I've never dated a cheerleader. I did play football, though. And I was a total momma's boy. How did you know that?"

She was quiet for a minute, then looked up. I could feel her gaze burning into the side of my face.

"You part your hair on the left side," she replied. "Since most people are right-handed, your mom would've parted your hair like that when you were facing her. Then it just becomes a habit as you get older."

I raised my eyebrows in surprise.

"I'm impressed. Good observation skills, Rivera. Did I get anything right about you?"

She pursed her full lips and nodded her head.

"Yeah. I smoked behind the art building," she confessed. "You were right about that. But if you played football, didn't that make you popular, too? I thought guys like you were supposed to be kings in high school."

I rubbed the bridge of my nose in quiet exasperation.

"There you go again with the sweeping generalizations. What the hell does *guy like me* mean?"

"You know exactly what it means."

"No, I really don't," I insisted. "So why don't you tell me?"

"It means you've been handed everything," she said, getting flustered. "I bet you've never really worked that hard for anything, have you? I know you're only in the FBI because your dad and grandpa and a bunch of uncles were in it."

Was Rivera for real? It was like she was doing everything she could to make me abandon our assignment. I took a deep breath, not willing to let her reclaim that point she'd lost earlier.

"If anything, that family legacy meant I had to work *harder* to prove myself. And why do you give a shit what sport I played in high school? I was too busy studying to bother with dumb shit like being the most popular kid in my grade. I'm guessing this tough girl act of yours stems from you not getting enough attention from your parents."

She tensed up, her face turning pale again.

"Oh, am I on the right track *again*? I bet you were a mean girl in high school. Bet you threw little temper tantrums when you got cut off from your credit card. I bet you were mommy and daddy's special little snowflake and you always got what you wanted."

I could see the anger rise within her like a boiling kettle.

I imagined steam coming out her ears as she finally blew her lid. I wondered what insult she'd hurl at me next. Quietly, she seethed with rage as though she was going to erupt at any second.

Aww shit . . . I've driven her crazy, I laughed internally.

But just when I thought she was finally going to go apeshit crazy bananas, a single fat tear ran down her cheek. It caught me so completely off guard that I was instantly filled with regret. I didn't even think it was possible for her to cry.

On the other hand, she might be completely manipulating me. She seemed the type. I decided even if she was, I could still be the better person.

"Look, I clearly crossed a line," I said, raising my hands. "I didn't mean to upset you. I was just—"

"My parents are dead."

Thick, heavy silence filled the space between us. Even the frogs and crickets chirping outside seemed to quiet down. I could just imagine them judging me.

Ohhhhh fuck . . .

"Rivera, I'm so sorry . . . " I said. "Honestly, I really am. I never would've said those things if I'd known."

"It's okay," she replied. "It's not like you had a clue."

The silence returned for a long moment as the tension built between us. She'd even stopped chomping on those Skittles. I could see her morph before my eyes as she reminisced about her parents. Her entire demeanor shifted before my eyes. Somehow, someway, she managed to appear smaller and younger as she withdrew into herself.

Eventually, she raised her face to look at me. Her eyes had dried up, but I could still see the raw emotion in them.

"They were murdered when I was a kid."

For a second, I looked into her eyes for any sign that she was joking, but of course there wasn't one.

"That's so fucked up," I whispered. "Oh, man, Rivera . . . that's awful!"

I meant everything I'd just said, but my words sounded far from comforting. They sounded hollow. What do you say to someone who's lost someone so violently? In my job, you meet tons of people who've lost a loved one, and there was never anything wise or profound to say that made them feel better. Even in our sensitivity training class at Quantico, you just had to let people feel their feelings and empathize with them.

"I'm really sorry that happened to you," I said to her. "I mean it."

"Thanks . . . " she said, looking down at her lap. "I'm sorry for being such a bitch. I'm not really that good with . . . people."

I shrugged and took the opportunity to dig into that paper bag for a blueberry muffin.

"I kinda figured that when you kept calling me Brad."

She lifted her head, then realized I was joking.

Shuffling further up the bed, I approached her the way I would a feral cat. Laying a hand on her shoulder, I prepared myself for her to pull away, but to my surprise, she didn't.

"I lost my mom too," I told her before taking a big bite. Man, it was good.

Rivera looked at me with wide, inquisitive eyes.

"You did?"

"Yeah. Cancer. I was fourteen."

"Oh, that's so sad," she replied. "That must have been awful for you."

"It was, but . . . " I swallowed the bite and took a swig of bottled water to wash it down. "I like to think she's still with me somewhere, somehow."

"I'm sure she is," she said and gave me a soft smile.

"You said that like you know."

"I do know."

"How?"

She didn't reply. Just looked back down at her lap.

"What about your parents?" I asked. "Do you think they're watching over you?"

"In their own way." She smiled bigger, her eyes shining like they were filled with the sun.

Holy crap, I thought as I looked over at her. *She's not like anyone I've ever met before. It's like she's not even from this planet.*

"So," she said, snapping herself back to her usual tone with a shake of her head. "Our case notes."

"Yeah, right . . . our case notes." I finished the muffin and tidied up my papers, eager to return to professional adult mode.

"We've got a lot to go through. Where do you wanna start?"

"I think we should go back to Haley's testimony," she said. "She's given us the most insight into possible locations of the children."

I scrunched my face in confusion at her.

"What do you mean, possible locations? As in underworld faerie kingdom with crystal thrones and giant mushrooms?"

"You sound so skeptical."

"I *am* so skeptical."

"You shouldn't be."

I set down my pencil and put on my most practical, sensible face.

"Show me the proof. Show me the facts. The whole faerie world doesn't make sense. It's nuts, right? It's more likely that something else happened to Haley and she's simply interpreting the event like any creative child would. Then you factor in the whole folklore of the area seems to be centered around faeries, moonshine, and bingo, of course the locals are going to say their kids are being abducted by little green men. It's probably some child trafficking ring that lures kids by dressing like Disney princesses or something. What if they're being kept in a basement? That would explain the mushrooms."

A smirk twitched at the corners of Rivera's mouth. With her head cocked to the side, she regarded me in the same way I'd seen old ladies look down at their yappy chihuahuas. She was simply waiting for me to stop flapping my jaws.

"What?" I asked. "What is it now?"

"Nothing. You just have so much to learn," she said and ate another few pieces of candy. "So fucking much."

8

ELENA

I woke up expecting to see the roof of my bedroom, not expecting to see the low beams of the slanted treehouse roof above my head. As I rolled over, intense orange sunlight stung my eyes.

What the hell? Was it dawn? Was I really up at dawn?

Ugh.

With a grumble, I sat up and felt something cold and damp stuck to my cheek with drool. Slapping a hand to my face, I realized I'd fallen asleep on top of my notes sprawled out across the top of the covers.

Peeling the page from my face—and a Skittles wrapper from under my boob—I looked around for Logan but there was no sign of him. His bag was still on the built-in bench, although his sleeping bag and sheet had been rolled up and folded in a neat little pile. Huh. Even when he was sleeping on the floor, he still made the bed.

Weirdo.

"Good morning!" came McKinney's friendly voice from the ground below me. With a yawn, I sauntered over to the window and looked down. Mist had gathered in the night and was now pooled just a few feet above the ground. The sheriff stood there in a plaid bathrobe with his hair stuck up on end. He was holding two steaming mugs, with a thermos in the pocket of his robe.

Clever. I'd have to try that trick sometime. First I'd need a robe.

"I remember you don't like coffee, so Martha made you some hot chocolate," he said. "Hope you ain't one of them lactose-intolerants."

"Aw, Sheriff, you're a lifesaver!"

Reaching for my over-sized sweatshirt and joggers, I quickly slipped into them before shimmying down the ladder.

"Have you seen Agent Hawthorne?" I asked McKinney, taking the cup from his hand.

"Nope. Must've given us both the slip."

I held the cup of cocoa beneath my face and hoped the steam would wake me up.

"I, um, heard you and him arguing last night," he said, taking a sip from his thermos. "y'all are like a cat and dog."

"Sorry," I replied, embarrassed. "We're just really, *really* different. And like I said yesterday, he's the new guy."

McKinney snorted. "Oh yeah. Breaking in the ol' F.N.G. Been there before. *Lots* of times. Well, I sure hope you work things out."

"Yeah . . . me too. Logan's heart is in the right place. He wants to find those kids as much as anyone."

The sound of footsteps approaching quickly stopped me from going on any more about my partner. After opening up to each other about losing our parents, I felt like the least I could do was not talk shit about him to the local law enforcement.

McKinney and I both turned around to see Logan

jogging across the yard and out towards us. Soft white mist swirled behind his wake, parting gently as he slowed down to a steady walk. His shirt was tucked into the back of his running shorts, making them hang low on his hips. It also called attention to the heavy equipment he was packing inside his shorts. I could tell it was grade A beef. The only thing he wore from the waist up was a watch and a thin sheen of sweat. I wanted to look away, but I couldn't.

Those arms. And those abs.

God damn!

I could grate cheese on those abs.

"Is there a yellow lab that lives nearby?" he asked, pointing his thumb back towards the driveway. "One ran with me for about two miles before she saw a squirrel and took off. Weirdest thing."

"Yeah, that's Tempie," laughed McKinney. "She's a sweet pup. Great bird dog, too. Hope she behaved herself."

"Oh yeah," Logan said, having just about caught his breath. "I love dogs. Can't really have one in this line of work, though. It wouldn't be fair to the dog."

Was he pulling out the shirt from his shorts to wipe himself off with it? Oh fuck . . . he sure was. A whiff of his clean sweat floated through the air, mingled with just a touch of woodsy body wash or soap. I closed my eyes and took a deep breath of that fresh fragrance.

"What about a cat?" McKinney suggested. No sooner had the words come out of his mouth than Logan was groaning like he'd just realized the milk in his cereal was chunky.

"No way. I hate cats. I'll never be a cat person. My fiancée—I mean, my ex, she was always begging for us to get a couple of five-thousand-dollar Persians. I'm not spending ten grand on cats when shelters can't even *give* them away."

McKinney handed him the mug of coffee, and I just stood there like a fly on the wall as the two of them blabbed about fools and their money. I wasn't listening to a single word they said. I was too busy unpacking the two huge nuggets of info that Logan had unwittingly volunteered. One, he hated cats. Interesting.

But the offhand comment about his fiancée—I mean, his ex, was *way* more interesting. It must've been a fairly recent break up if he was still accidentally calling her his fiancée. Maybe that explained his "I'm not taking any shit from a woman" attitude? I didn't agree with it, but at least he had an understandable excuse for treating his new partner like shit. I didn't have a good excuse for why I treated him the way I did.

Sometimes I was just a bitch.

As I finished off my hot chocolate, I took another long look at Logan's body. It was unnerving how casual and relaxed he was, standing there half-naked as he swapped stories with McKinney about the dumbest shit people wasted their money on. He just grinned and drank his coffee, probably enjoying the feel of the soft morning air on his bare body. Who would've guessed that beneath the boring suit he was hiding all of *this*?

And I found myself hating him for it. Even in this day and age, I'd never have that experience . . . to stand outside topless and chat with someone over drinks like it was no big deal. I even hated myself a little bit for being so weak and practically drooling over this human. They looked a lot like Logan, but humans sure as hell didn't smell as good as he did. Now here I was, bug-eyed with my brain in my panties over the sight of Logan's hunky, ripped, shirtless glistening body.

"I should get dressed!" I suddenly blurted out,

desperate for a reason to leave the conversation. Before they could respond, I was already racing back up the ladder. Once at the top, I realized just how fast my heart was beating.

What the hell was all that about? I scolded myself. *Why did I just act like it was the first time I'd seen a shirtless dude? Maybe cuz it's the first time I've ever seen someone that fine?*

You're just sleep-deprived, I reasoned as I walked over to my duffel bag and searched for my makeup bag. *You just need to wake up and get your head on straight. That's all.*

🐈

"What do you think?" asked McKinney.

But I couldn't think of a single word to say. I was speechless . . . which didn't happen too often. But now I was completely overwhelmed at what had been set out in front of me.

The incident room at the station had been set up long before we'd arrived in town, complete with the missing children's photographs placed along each wall. Their faces stared back at me with chubby cheeks and innocent faces. Seeing numbers on a spreadsheet was one thing, but this . . . this was heartbreaking.

"There's just so *many,*" I said scanning the photos on the walls. "Too many."

"It's almost too much to process," said Logan from behind me. "It doesn't seem real."

"No. It doesn't," I agreed. "How can so many kids go missing from this area alone?"

"And how can only one come back?"

The three of us stood in the center of the room taking it

all in. Hundreds of eyes stared out at us, begging for us to find them. I felt crippled by the weight of all their hopeful gazes. Paralyzed by the realization of how many children we needed to find.

"This is a fucking epidemic," I said to the room. "Something like this hasn't happened on this scale before."

"Actually it has," said McKinney.

"It has?" I asked him. "*Here?*"

"No. In Europe." He scratched his chin and perched on the edge of the nearest desk. "Ever heard of the Pied Piper of Hamelin?"

"Obviously," replied Logan. "Some guy with a flute got a bunch of kids to follow him out of town. But that's just a faerie tale."

"I don't think you realize the irony of what you just said," snorted McKinney. "You're right. It *was* a faerie tale. A real one."

Logan blinked at him in response.

"Right then . . . listen up," continued McKinney, pulling out a chair and making himself comfortable. "It was the medieval times and there are rats everywhere, right? So they get this exterminator called the Pied Piper to play the flute and lure the rats out of town. And he did, but the townsfolk refused to pay the bill, so he came back and took all the town's kids with him as payment. Fucking hundreds of them."

"But . . . that didn't really happen," Logan said with a frown. "It's just a story like Sleeping Beauty or Hansel and Gretl."

"Will you cut your shit and open your mind a little?" I told him. "Don't you know that all these so-called faerie tales came from someplace real?"

Logan's frown deepened as McKinney gave me a nod of alliance.

"Exactly," he said to my partner. "These stories didn't just spring up out of nowhere. And believe me, I've read everything there is to know about faerie tales and folklore."

"I know. I saw the book collection in your office."

"Then you'll know that I'm not an idiot in this field. I consider myself quite the amateur historian actually." He drew himself up as though he were getting ready to launch into a litany of examples.

"Anyway, the Pied Piper," I interjected, wanting him to get back on topic.

"Yeah . . . the Pied Piper. He lured the kids out of town, but do you know where he took them all?"

Logan shook his head.

"Into a hole in a hill."

The frown across Logan's head deepened ever further until it looked as though his head was about to implode.

"A hole in a hill? Would we maybe call that a cave?"

"Or compare it to a hole in a tree?" I mused.

"Exactly," said McKinney.

Logan, looking as though he was being afflicted by a tremendous migraine, raised a hand to his head and stared into space.

"Let me get this straight. Are you suggesting all these kids in this area were lured away by . . . the Pied Piper?"

"Something like that," said McKinney. "He's got the same MO. Just look at the similarities. Hundreds of missing kids from one area. An entrance into the ground like a hole in a hill or a tree. An otherworldly little fella luring them away. Seems uncanny, don't it? What do you think, Rivera?"

Before I could answer, a timid knock came from the door.

"Who is it?" bellowed McKinney.

"It's Billy, sir."

"Alright come in, son."

In walked a skinny slip of an officer with a shock of blond hair, ruddy cheeks, and a uniform that looked like it was wearing him than the other way around. He anxiously glanced over at Logan then me and lowered his head, obviously intimidated by us.

"Don't worry about these two," said McKinney. "They're from the FBI. They came all the way from Washington DC to help us. Now, what's up, son?"

Billy looked over at me and said, "There's someone here to see you, ma'am."

"Someone's here for *me?*" I asked. "Who?"

"It ain't a fucking reporter, is it?" raged McKinney. "Because if it's a reporter, I'll fling their ass to the curb!"

"No sir. It's not a reporter," said Billy. "It's Sylvia."

"Oh, for cryin' out loud," McKinney said with a groan. "That's just as bad. Should've known the minute word got out that the FBI was here investigating these kids, she'd come snoopin' around."

"Who's Sylvia?" I asked.

Billy and McKinney both sighed in unison. Their exasperation was real.

"Sylvia's a sweet old dear who's lived here in Yarbrough since the beginning of time," the sheriff droned. "Legend has it she used to babysit Moses when he was a boy."

Logan stifled a laugh, sending it huffing out his nostrils instead.

"And she's here to see *me?*" I asked. My curiosity was growing more palpable by the minute.

"That's what she says," said Billy. "Just you. Not your partner."

I glanced over to Logan and he shrugged at me.

"Fine with me," he said. "Doesn't sound like I'm missing out on much."

I looked back to McKinney. He was still muttering and grumbling under his breath.

"Damn woman. Always in here with her lunatic nonsense."

"I take it you don't like her very much," I laughed.

"Lemme put it this way—she's a real pain in my ass. Been that way my whole life. Even when I was a kid, she used to yell and scream at me and my friends if we ran over her lawn. Even stabbed a knife through my football once when it went in her yard."

"Yeah, she's a bit wackadoo," said Billy. "She comes in here at least once a week to report stuff."

Oooh, once a week? No wonder she rubbed these guys the wrong way. Then again, what else was the sheriff of a sleepy little mountain town going to do with his free time? There was only one way to know.

"What kind of things does she report?" I asked. "Barking dogs? Rowdy teenagers?"

"If only!" Billy snorted with a grin. "She once called 911 because she thought a squirrel had cursed her and was trying to poison her with a noxious gas. Turned out to be a rotten sack of potatoes underneath her sink."

Logan blinked for a moment, making sure he'd heard the officers correctly.

"Maybe this is the wrong question to ask, but why did she think a squirrel was to blame?"

"Easy," McKinney said with a dismissive wave of his

hand. "She ran over its mate the week before. Obviously, the little critter wanted revenge."

"Obviously," said Logan sarcastically, and returned his attention to the images taped on the wall at the back of the room.

"Alright, so, she's a little eccentric," I shrugged.

"She's more than that," replied McKinney. "She's a mean old wench. Always likes to cause trouble and come in here blaming just about everybody for everything. I don't think there's a single person in this town she hasn't reported for something or another. Whether it be stealing the dirt from her plant pots or looking sideways at her cats."

"And she has a lot of cats," added Billy. "Like . . . a *lot*."

Even from the back of the room, I could see Logan's face scrunch up at the mere mention of cats. All the more reason for him to not be the one to speak to Sylvia.

"The cats ain't even the worst of it," continued McKinney. "The old girl claims to be a psychic. Said a ghost came into her garden one night and gave her the powers to read people's dreams."

A loud burst of laughter exploded out of Logan. When his blue eyes met mine, I saw they were filled with tears. He was laughing so hard he struggled to breathe.

"A ghost with magic powers?" he wheezed. "For the love of God. Next thing you know, she'll be related to Bigfoot."

As tired as I was of his skepticism, I couldn't help grinning along with him. If this batshit little old lady was half as interesting as I was being led to believe, I was in for quite a treat. I had half a mind to drag Logan's ass along with me.

"I can't wait to meet her," I said, heading for the door to where the reception area was located. "She sounds like a blast."

Sylvia sat across from me in the small interview room we were given, cradling a cup of tea she'd brought from home. She was swimming inside a huge pink cardigan straight from the '80s, with large coke bottle glasses covering half her face. Her thinning, gray hair was pulled into a bun so tight I could make out the shape of her skull.

"You asked to see me," I said. "Why me?"

She gave me a shrewd, knowing look. "Because I heard you were here."

"From who?"

"Pfft. From everyone. This is a small town, Agent Rivera. People talk."

Her voice was surprisingly forceful for someone her age and behind her glasses, her eyes were alert and directed right at me.

"I hear you went to see little Haley yesterday," she said. "Did you learn a lot?"

I nodded.

"It was informative, but I can't discuss details."

"I understand . . . "

She took a long sip of her tea and let out a satisfied exhale.

"I reckon that McKinney bastard told you a whole lot about me," she said, appearing downright proud of her status in the Yarbrough police department. "Reckon he said I was crazy, too."

"He may have mentioned that you're one of the most . . . *colorful* characters here in town."

Sylvia beamed, revealing a full set of sparkling dentures.

"That sheriff is a goddamn hypocrite," she said into her

travel mug. "He's always claiming to be a man of the people. Always saying he listens to us. Folks even say he's into all sorts of esoteric stuff. Folklore and whatnot."

"He is," I replied. "I've talked to him about it and he seems pretty knowledgeable on those subjects. Most guys in his position wouldn't be so eager to admit they believe in things they can't see. It's been my experience that people shy away from that stuff."

"That sheriff shies away from me, I can tell you that," spat Sylvia. "And he doesn't give a hoot when I have something to tell him."

"And what do you have to tell him?"

"All the things that are happening in this town."

I raised a curious brow at her.

"Things like the curse put on you by a squirrel?"

"Ah . . . So he got to you, eh?" she seethed, wagging a finger at me. "I should have known the gossip would have started flying already."

"So . . . are you saying it's not true?"

Sylvia settled into her chair, shaking her head.

"It was a misunderstanding. That's all."

I was trying to be patient, but this particular human was starting to test my limits.

"Look," I said. "I was told you came here specifically to speak to me. Can you tell me whatever it is you have to say?"

Sliding her cup to the edge of the table, she leaned forward and grabbed my hands between her liver-spotted, gnarled arthritic fingers. Her skin was paper-thin, and it was anyone's guess how old she truly was.

"There are things that happen in this town that are beyond our realm of understanding. Strange things. Terrifying things." Looking deep into her eyes, I tried to figure out just what was going on in her head. She was right, there were strange things happening in this town, but the things she spoke of? They couldn't be true. Squirrels didn't curse anyone. Well, actually they *did*, but usually other squirrels, not humans.

"I've seen lights in the sky and creatures in my yard. I've seen things look back at me from the mirror that wasn't just my own face. I've seen the faerie rings at the bottom of the garden, when all that anyone else can see is a circle of mushrooms. I know you've seen all these things too. Maybe not here, but you've seen them."

Her grip on my hands was so tight her nails were on the verge of breaking through my skin. I tried to peel myself away from her, but she only held me tighter.

I tried to hear a ring of truth to what she was saying, but sadly, as I looked into her face, all I saw was a lonely, old, grief-stricken woman who'd driven herself mad with too much solitude. Whatever she had to say wasn't connected with what we were investigating.

"I can tell you think I'm just some old, crazy, grief-struck woman," she said, on the verge of a smile. "I bet you think I've gone nuts living alone with no one to talk to but my cats."

"Uh . . . well . . . " I stammered. Sylvia nodded and eased up on her grip. Not by much, but enough.

"I know I might be a little nuts. I accept that. The thing is . . . I'm not stupid. I know what you're thinking."

"Do you?" I had to know where this was leading. The suspense was starting to make me jittery. Or maybe it was the liter of Mountain Dew I'd had for breakfast.

"I'm extremely perceptive and I can see the skepticism in your eyes," she went on. "I can also see something else. Something not . . . human."

Shivers ran down my legs. She'd touched on something secret. How could she have any idea? Could she actually read my fucking mind?

"Sylvia, what exactly are you saying?"

"I'm saying I could feel your presence the moment you drove into this town. You're not one of us, are you? You're one of *them*. One of them folk from below. You're one of the fae. I can see it from the color in your eyes. I can smell it on your breath. You got that cotton candy smell like all the good ones have."

I yanked myself out of her grasp and reeled back in my seat. Never, in my entire life up here on the surface had a human guessed what I was. People may have thought I was a little weird at times . . . a little different, but they *never* guessed I was fae.

"See? I'm not just some crackpot," she said with a contented grin. Sylvia had swagger for miles. "I can see things and I can see the fae in you."

Nodding my head, I got my shit together as quickly as I could. Fine. So she knew what I was. She knew my secret. I had to make sure she kept it that way.

"Sylvia, this is really important," I began, trying to keep my voice quiet and steady. "You have to—"

"Keep my yap shut. Don't worry, hon. I won't tell a soul." She made a motion of locking her lips and throwing away an imaginary key. "I'm on *your* side."

When she leaned forward and took my hands again, this time her grasp was soft and gentle.

"You might not believe all the stories that damned Sheriff McKinney tells about me," she said. "But if you don't believe anything you hear while you're investigating this case, you gotta believe this one thing. This town, it's at the center of everything. People have known about what lays beneath the land for thousands of years."

"What lays beneath the land?"

"The realm of the dark fae," she replied matter-of-factly. "Yarbrough sits on one of them ley lines, and since a ley line is all full of energy, it takes a lot of energy to open it. I'm thinking they need something powerful, like a couple hundred youngin's life force."

"The children?" I whispered. "Are you saying you think they're being sacrificed?"

She nodded.

"But you can bring them back. You're halfway to the other side already. I reckon that's why you were fated to come to our little town—to solve this mystery. Only *you* can bring the children back, Elena."

9

LOGAN

Rivera stood beneath an oak tree with the leaves lightly grazing her hair. Her gaze was fixed on some faraway spot in the distance, her eyes noticeably glossed over. She'd been a little off ever since she'd come out of the interview room with Sylvia.

I know, I know. Off was an understatement. The girl was a few crayons short of a full box. She was patient and understanding with kids like Haley and then turned around and acted like Godzilla whenever I was around. Her idea of a hearty breakfast was a bottle of soda and a package of gas station donuts. No wonder her moods were all over the place, given what she was doing to her blood sugar levels.

I bet her pancreas hated her.

But I knew something was off with Rivera because she'd gone to meet Sylvia with curious enthusiasm. The pink-haired punk-ass who'd come out of that room now had a serious expression on her face that hadn't budged all day.

"Hey, Brad, what are you staring at?" she yelled across the rocky space between us. Brad? Really? Well, it looked like she was back to her usual self. As much as she might try to chum the waters, I wasn't going to take the bait.

"I was just wondering when you were gonna snap out of it, Azrael Lovecraft. You've been staring into space for a full five minutes."

Her eyes narrowed, and her mouth pinched into something between a snarl and a pout. Aww . . . she was kinda cute when she was angry.

"I was *thinking,* you meathead. You should try it sometime."

The cops beside me shot me an amused look.

"Is Elena always like this?" asked the younger one.

"Nah. Sometimes she's in a *bad* mood."

"She worth it, though?"

"What?"

"Is that hot Mexican ass worth it?"

I ignored him and walked away towards the rest of the team. After departing the incident room at the police station, it was decided we'd comb the woodlands on the outskirts of Yarbrough along with a few officers to fill us in on any local knowledge.

We'd been walking for over an hour through fields of emerald grass towards the more rugged terrain. It was only a ten-minute detour to the treehouse for us to change into our hiking gear. It would've been a beautiful day if I wasn't putting up with sleazy banter from the young officers and crabby comments from a sulky Rivera who insisted on brooding beneath the trees.

This meant that over the last hour we'd found precisely jack shit. Not that any of us really had a solid idea of what we were looking for. Little green men? A hole in a hill? A pedophile with a pan flute and an affinity for rats?

We were searching the area that McKinney had designated as the hot spot, the general spot where most the children had disappeared. There was some hope between us that even the smallest clue would present itself. A few fibers of clothing, some kid-sized footprints, anything that could tie us to what was happening. But there was nothing.

You'd be forgiven for thinking not a single person had traveled through this neck of the woods. The foliage was thick, the trees as tall as skyscrapers and the mud deep and treacherous. The only relief on our feet was the smooth asphalt tourist path that traveled down the center of the virgin forest. A route you had to be crazy to venture off if you didn't know the area.

"This is pointless," Rivera complained, finally coming out from under the tree. "We can't just search the site like you would any other. The kids haven't been abducted in a regular way, so you're not gonna find clues in a regular way, either."

"I'm inclined to agree," I said, surprised at myself for agreeing with her. "We'd need to have hundreds of law enforcement combing the area to find anything."

We both looked around us. All there was as far as the eye could see was thick, green forest and rocky outcroppings. The view was stunning, but that wasn't why we were here. And as much as I'd love a team of one or two hundred to help with the search, I didn't think Chief Harris would appreciate the OCD getting that much publicity.

"I think we should be focused on this Hollow kingdom Haley spoke about," I said. "Maybe there's an abandoned mine shaft or something around here? I could try and get in touch with the Army Corps of Engineers."

Rivera looked up at me and rolled her eyes.

"You still don't get it, do you? This isn't a normal case!"

"Don't worry. I'm pretty fucking well aware of how abnormal all of this is."

"But you're really not. Get your head out your ass, Hawthorne. We can't just enter the kingdom like we're walking into a post office. Well, *you* can't, anyway."

"What do you mean, I can't, but you can?"

Rivera rolled her eyes.

"It's not a regular physical place. Not like the diner, not like the police station, not like the houses or the gas station. The Hollows isn't like what you know. It's . . . it's . . . "

Putting her hands on her hips, she thought for a second, glaring at the two officers who were watching her and trying not to crack up.

"It's another dimension," she finally said. "It's on another plane of existence."

The youngest officer chuckled to himself, thrust his hands into his pockets and leaned back on his heels.

"Man that crackpot Sylvia must have got to you," he laughed. "Next you'll be preaching about Bigfoot."

"Shut up, officer—what the fuck's your name?"

"Davis."

"Officer Davis, shut your goddamn mouth until you're spoken to."

"Wooooo . . . Aren't you a spicy little thing?"

Rivera's green eyes glowered.

"I would listen to her, if I were you," I warned him. "She's tougher than she looks."

"Whatever, man. You're just pussy-whipped," he said to me with a shake of his head. "Letting some crazy-ass Mexican bitch like her boss you around. You're nuts."

"What the fuck did you just call me?" Rivera growled through her teeth.

I could swear for a split second that her eyes caught fire

with anger. Her legs were practically pawing at the ground like a bull who'd seen a red flag. I decided to stay out of it and enjoy the show. While I had no desire to get caught in the crossfire, the truth was that I was dying to know how this would all play out.

I put my money on Elena.

"Yeah, if you're talking about chasing perps in alternate dimensions, I'd say that makes you a bonafide crazy-ass bitch," he sang at her, rocking his head from side to side.

"No, that's not what you said." She took one step closer. Then another. That moron didn't shut up. He just kept right on taunting her.

"I bet the FBI only hired you to fill a quota, and now my tax dollars are goin' to some mouthy little bitch in big girl boots with an even bigger chip on her shoulder. You think you can just come into our hometown, waving your fancy badge at us and boss us around and—"

That miserable fucker didn't get the chance to finish his sentence. Rivera made a wild swing at his jaw, then faked him out and landed a solid knee deep into his crotch.

Now, there's getting hit in the nuts, and then there's getting hit. In. The. Nuts. This was the kind of hit that didn't just make me cringe—it was the kind of hit that made my balls try to crawl back up into my body until it was safe to come back out. We all watched as officer Davis sank to the ground and fell over in the fetal position. I'm not saying he deserved it, but . . . he shouldn't have poked the bear.

"What do you think about my big girl boots *now*?" Rivera coolly asked, standing over him like the badass she was. Davis was emitting a high-pitched whine as he tried not to cry. "C'mon, Davis. How do you like them?"

Davis made a choking sound and then puked all over the grass.

"Alright then," she said, tossing her long pink hair over her shoulder like it was no big deal. "If you want to be involved in this case, great. If not, great."

"Hey! What the hell are y'all doin' over there?" came an urgent voice from behind us. Well shit. If McKinney told Harris that my partner had just assaulted an officer while I stood by and watched, we were most definitely off the case. Rivera and I both turned to see the sheriff climb over a fallen tree, waving with his hands like an air traffic controller.

"Get the fuck over here!" he yelled.

We ran towards him, leaving Davis and his buddy behind. There was a fear in McKinney's eyes and his cheeks were red and flushed from running. Before we reached him, the officers' radios sprung to life with a muffled voice masked in crackling static.

"Code Adam!" said a woman's voice. "Code Adam, Code Adam!"

"What's happened?" asked Rivera as she reached McKinney.

"What do you think's happened?" he said, breathlessly. "There's another kidnapping! Seven-year-old girl went missing from two miles east."

"Fuck!" I gasped. "How can that happen?"

"We need a BOLO out immediately," said McKinney.

"How long has she been gone?" I asked.

"Forty-five minutes?"

"And you're sure she hasn't just gotten lost in the woods?"

McKinney was too upset to give me the stink-eye for suggesting a rational explanation.

"Positive! Her parents said she stepped two feet off the trail and they were watching her the whole time. She ran around a big tree and never reappeared from the other side of it."

"Shit, that sounds just like all the others," said Rivera.

"Pretty damn near close," I agreed. "How can someone walk behind a tree and never be seen again?"

"Because we're not dealing with a normal kidnapper," said McKinney. "This isn't even from our world."

Officer Davis was looking increasingly uncomfortable. I didn't think that was possible. Turning to look at his officer, McKinney narrowed his eyes and motioned for him to get into the squad car.

"Believe me, kid. This isn't a time for logic. This is a time for Rivera and her willingness to chase down perps in alternate dimensions."

Davis's eyes widened in a mild panic.

"Yeah, I heard you," McKinney told him in a low roar. "Talk to her like that again and I'll chop your fucking tongue off, boy."

ELENA

The first thing I saw when I stepped out of the Navigator were two hysterical parents pacing back and forth in front of their parked sedan. Since the call came in about their daughter, the parking lot and trail they'd been walking was cordoned off. McKinney was in his squad car, giving an update on the situation over the radio. Climbing beneath the tape, I showed the distraught parents my badge and they both ran at me.

"Oh, thank god you're here!" the mom cried.

She looked the same age as me, but her eyes were red and there were deep lines down the sides of her mouth from the stress of the last hour.

"The police in this town don't do shit," she said, clutching her blonde hair. "The kidnappings have been going on for months now but they don't do nothing about it!"

Hawthorne caught up with me and placed a light hand on her shoulder.

"We're here to find her now."

"But *are* you?" she asked as thick tears fell from her

eyes. "Why do you think you'll be able to find Rylee? None of those other kids have been found apart from Haley."

"None of them," added her husband, a stout man with a bushy, red beard poking out from a UT Knoxville t-shirt. He looked like a raging, helpless bull stuffed into human clothing, his meaty hands clenching together in fists.

"What was Rylee wearing when you last saw her?" Hawthorne asked as he took out his little notebook.

"Um, a pink unicorn t-shirt, purple leggings, and red tennis shoes.

"Show me where Rylee went missing," I said, trying to keep my voice as calm as I could. The last thing anyone needed here was more emotions, although laying into Davis had left me refreshingly calm.

"She was up there," said the mom, already walking away towards the path. "Right here. We hadn't been out of the car for more than two minutes when she walked over towards the tree."

"What kind of tree was it?" I asked.

She looked at me and furrowed her brow.

"I don't know. A big one."

"Alright. Can you show it to me?"

After a few more seconds, we arrived at a gradual bend in the path just as a light summer rain began to fall. Each drop hit the hard, dry ground with a soft pitter-pat. The more drops that fell from the sky and sank into the ground, the more it gave off the smell of the grass, moss, and dirt. That smell was like Xanax to me. I immediately began to relax.

"This is the tree," said the mom.

"Ahh . . . an ash tree," I sighed. "Of course."

"What difference does that make?" asked the mom. If I

told her the real reason, she wouldn't handle it well. So I didn't exactly lie when I said,

"It's pretty. It makes sense why Rylee wanted a closer look."

"Yeah, I guess," the dad said with a helpless shrug. "When Rylee ran towards it we didn't think nothing of it. Why would we?"

"And where did she go?" asked Hawthorne. Which direction did she walk? Can you try to retrace her steps for us?"

The dad walked towards the tree and pointed around it.

"She walked up to it like this," he said, stepping around the trunk.

We could see that as he walked behind it, his large body was still visible, but seven-year-old Rylee's wouldn't have been. A small child could've easily disappeared behind the medium-sized trunk. But they were supposed to appear again.

"So she just walked around here like this," he said. "We had our eyes on her the whole time so we thought nothing bad could happen. We had no idea she could just . . . she could just . . . walk behind it and disappear."

His voice broke and he buried his face in his hands.

"Oh, God she's gone forever, isn't she? We've lost her. I told you we shouldn't have come here, Maggie. I fucking told you!"

"How were we supposed to know this would happen?" the mom cried back. "We were watching her the whole fucking time! What else could we have done besides hand-cuffing her to our sides?"

"We knew about the kids disappearing! It's all anybody's been talking about for months! How could we have been so stupid as to think it couldn't happen to Rylee? It's happened to fuck knows how many kids in this town."

The dad cried harder, balling his hands up into fists and hitting the side of his head in a mixture of pain and frustration.

"Please," I said, holding onto his hand in an attempt to calm him. "Try to take a deep breath. We're going to do all we can to find her."

"There's still a chance she's not far from here," said Logan, sounding hopeful. "For all we know, she's playing a joke on you and hiding in the brush somewhere. Kids don't always understand what's okay to joke about and what's not. It's only been less than an hour."

But as I looked into his eyes, I could see he was just bullshitting them to keep them optimistic. He knew as well as I did that little Rylee was gone. Taken. Captured and taken to another dimension.

Well . . . maybe not that last bit, but for Rylee's sake, I hoped the evidence was starting to add up with him.

I could feel my whole body become gripped with fear and tension. How long would it be until another child vanished?

Think fast, I told myself. *You need to think of a way to go back to the Hollows and find those kids.*

But I knew it wasn't as simple as that. It may have been a world I was once part of, but I wasn't welcome there anymore. I hadn't been welcome there in years and years.

"I do have to ask you something, and please don't take this personally. I'm just trying to cover all my bases, alright?" Logan said to the couple. The mom wiped her face and nodded. "If you knew about the disappearances, why did you come here?"

They both looked at him sorrowfully. He held up a hand and gave a sympathetic smile.

"I'm not judging here, okay? I get it—school's out for the summer, kids need to burn off some energy, it's a gorgeous day. I'm only asking because it might help lead to Rylee's whereabouts. I would've thought parents wouldn't want to bring their kids into the woods when there's so many abductions around here."

They both looked to each other, then back at Logan. I knew that look. They were about to tell him something. Something good.

"Tell them," urged the mom as she nudged her husband. "Tell them about the dreams."

The husband clapped a hand to his forehead and let out a long, exhausted exhale.

"Rylee kept having these really vivid dreams," he began.

"Anything specific?" Logan asked while he jotted down notes in that trusty pad of paper. The dad gave an anxious nod.

"She kept dreaming about a woman dressed in silver who lived in the trees. She wouldn't stop talking about her."

The tension in my stomach intensified until it felt as though my intestines were wrapped around someone's fist.

"A silver dress . . . " I said. "What else did she look like?"

"Rylee said her hair was black and flowed like a waterfall," said the mom.

"And her eyes were the same color," added the husband. "She said she had huge black eyes."

While Logan continued to scribble in his notebook, I started to feel a sweeping dizziness enter my head, and nausea rise up in my stomach. I knew those eyes. I'd stared into them myself when I was a child.

"Rylee dreamed of her?" I asked. "Have other children dreamed about her?"

The dad shrugged.

"I don't know. All I know is that Rylee kept talking about the pretty lady in silver from her dreams. She told us she lived in the woods."

"She wouldn't stop talking about her," said the mom. "It actually became quite a problem because she wouldn't talk about anything else. She dreamed about her last night, didn't she? Freddy?"

"Yeah, she did, which is why we came here today. We live on the other side of that hill." Freddy turned and pointed in the opposite direction of where the ash tree stood. "Our property butts up against this forest. Anyway, Rylee kept insisting that she had to come down here. She said the pretty lady in silver had a present for her."

"So you came here together, to make sure nothing out of the ordinary happened?" asked Hawthorne.

"She wouldn't stop asking," said the dad. "I'd never seen her want anything as much as this before. She didn't even behave like this when she wanted an iPad for Christmas. You'd have thought the world was about to end the way she was freakin' out."

"And she's a good kid," his wife pointed out. "But you'd never believe it if you'd seen the way she was behaving. She was throwing tantrums like she did when she was two and three. But seven? There's no excuse. She told us she had to come down to the woods and that was that. We had to keep the doors and windows locked. That's how bad it got."

"So we thought there was no harm in bringing her down for a little while," said the dad, regretfully. "Just to shut her up so she realized the woman she was always talking about didn't exist."

The four of us stared at the ash tree as though Rylee would reappear from the other side.

"Did she mention a name?" asked Hawthorne.

"Huh?"

"The lady in silver. Did Rylee ever give her a name?"

"She never called her by a name," said her mom. "But she drew a picture of her once and wrote a name underneath. I've got a picture of it somewhere on my phone."

"Can you text it to me?" I asked, handing her my card. I could feel the breath become sucked out of me as I anticipated what I'd see or hear next. I already knew exactly what that name would be.

"What did she write?" Logan asked, blissfully ignorant of who and what we were dealing with.

"I think it said Solana," said the mom, peering at her phone. Then her face softened as she found the photo. "Yeah. Queen Solana."

She held up the screen and I almost puked right there. My knees felt as though they'd turned to jelly and suddenly my legs stopped working. I felt myself fall against Logan as the dizziness overwhelmed me. The last thing I remembered before everything went black was the intense smell of grass and mud as my face hit the ground.

11

LOGAN

Rivera was so pretty when she was unconscious. Mainly because it was the only time she ever shut the hell up. Unfortunately, that serene moment was blown to bits when her green eyes fluttered open.

"Where the fuck am I? And why the hell are you staring at me like that?"

"Hey, slacker. You feeling okay?"

She dragged herself up to a seated position and rubbed her eyes.

"Where *are* we?"

"The urgent care clinic in Scruggsville," I explained. Oooh, that stink-eye was out in full force. Rivera scowled as she took in her surroundings.

"Clinic? It looks like a fucking bomb shelter," she griped, recoiling at the chipped gray paint on the walls and the low ceilings. A fluorescent light flickered to an erratic beat.

"Yeah. It's Scruggsville, not DC," I reminded her. "Don't worry. I've met your nurse and she's great."

Rivera rubbed her eyes again, trying to sort out her thoughts on how she'd arrived at this place.

"How were you able to meet my nurse? You're not family."

"Easy. I told her I was your husband."

Rivera's long dark lashes blinked in confusion, so I added to my story.

"I also told her I needed you back in working order as soon as possible because we've got four boys at home who need help with school. Since I'm working two jobs to make ends meet, I don't have time to help them. They just kind of run wild. They don't even help with chores like cooking and cleaning. I told the nurse what I'd *really* like is for you to help me open a miniature golf course. It's been my lifelong dream."

By the grace of god I managed to keep a straight face. I waited on pins and needles for Rivera's reaction.

Three.

Two.

One.

"What the actual fuck, Hawthorne!" she howled. Then she started to wrench her face into that familiar, pinched, angry expression that I knew. "Did you really say all that shit to my nurse?"

"Hell no." That was about all I could manage to get out before I started laughing at her. "That's the plot of Overboard." The pink-hair punk ass in the hospital bed just glared at me. "You know, with Goldie Hawn? Kurt Russell?" Rivera wasn't amused.

"It's something my dad used to do to my mom when she was still alive," I explained, still laughing. "Since he was privy to a lot of sensitive information, he couldn't exactly tell her how his day went when he came home from work.

So he'd tell her the plot of a movie they'd seen and see how long it took for her to figure out."

Rivera glanced around the almost empty ward, purposely avoiding eye contact with me. I wasn't sure if she was being standoffish on purpose or whether she was just embarrassed.

"Can you please tell me what really happened?" she asked. Wow. That might've been the first time she'd said please and sincerely meant it. Her voice was slightly hoarse and her eyes were red from rubbing them. Although she didn't sound it, she looked vulnerable to me. At least, she did in that moment. I chalked it up to old memories of my mom lying in a hospital bed.

"You passed out," I told her, suddenly feeling sheepish. "I tried to catch you, but . . . it all happened so out of the blue. You really hit the ground hard."

"Aw, shit. I can't believe it. I've never done anything like that before. How long was I out?"

"A while. Long enough to stuff you in the car and drive you here. You're lucky Scruggsville is a small town. The only other person in urgent care just needed a couple stitches. Got bit by squirrel. I suppose it's better than being cursed by one."

Rivera reached for a bottle of water sitting on the bedside table. Then something snapped in her mind and she suddenly bolted upright like she'd been zapped with a defibrillator.

"Rylee!" she gasped. "We need to find Rylee!"

"The officers are on it," I said, holding her hand. "Just take a breath for a minute. We'll get back out there as soon as you're ready."

"I'm ready now."

"Hey . . . Rivera . . . give it a minute, okay?"

She wasn't listening. She was starting to get out of bed.

"Elena!"

That got her attention.

"Look—you're obviously exhausted. You didn't sleep for shit last night. You haven't eaten anything but garbage since we left DC, and we're both under crazy pressure. It's no wonder you passed out."

Her eyes shifted away from me as she slid off the bed and reached beneath a nearby chair for her boots.

"I'm not hanging around in here a minute longer," she said, zipping them up. "Come on. Let's go."

"The nurse said she wanted to keep an eye on you."

Rivera rolled her eyes.

"She doesn't need to. I can keep an eye on myself."

Unbelievable. It was like dealing with a teenager. Time to act like the professional adult . . . again.

"Elena. Stop!" I said in what I call my 'dad' voice. It was the 'I'm done with your bullshit' voice. Surprisingly, it worked. Rivera sat still and gave me her undivided attention.

"Just chill for a minute and hear me out. You're no use to the team if you're unconscious. And you won't find any of these kids if you're only running on fumes. You need to look after yourself. You don't have to set yourself on fire to keep other people warm. Know what I'm saying?"

She paused for a second, gazing at her feet, then gave a reluctant nod.

"I guess I could take a break for a little while. My head's still fuzzy anyway."

"Exactly. The officers are finger combing the woods right now. They've got half the town searching for her . . . even Tempie the lab is out there sniffing for clues. I know how bad you wanna be out there looking for her—I feel the same way. But we don't know the lay of the land compared to the locals who've lived here their whole lives."

"Okay, okay . . . " She put her hands up in surrender and I relaxed. This was good. We were making progress.

"Wanna get something to eat? You need to get your energy up."

"Sure," she said. "Food sounds good."

Standing up, she slung her jacket over her shoulders and ran a hand through her hair, pulling out a few blades of grass.

"Thanks for being here, I guess," she said.

"Of course, Rivera. We're partners."

She gave me a weak smile and jammed her hands into her pockets.

"You don't have to keep calling me Rivera."

"So what do I call you? Azrael? Raven?" Her eyes flashed, and I took a step backwards in case she decided to pull an officer Davis with my junk. Wearing a cup might not be the worst idea with her for a partner.

But then her expression softened, and she actually grinned.

"Good one, *Brad*," she teased back. "But I prefer Elena, if you wanna call me that instead."

"Does that mean we're friends now . . . Elena?"

"It means you're on trial . . . Logan," she smiled, grabbing her phone and the bottled water off the bedside table before we headed out the door. "I mean . . . I suppose if we have to be stuck out here together we should at least be on first-name terms."

🐈

Finding ourselves back at the diner on the edge of Yarbrough, in the same booth with the same waitress, we both looked out at the gray clouds as rain lashed the cars in the parking lot. I genuinely felt bad about Rylee and all the folks out in that crappy weather looking for her. But I knew I had to take care of my partner.

It had been a challenge to find something I thought was acceptable for her to eat. I was thinking something along the lines of a protein, a complex carb, and some fruit or vegetables. She was thinking something along the lines of a strawberry shake and a full basket of French fries.

"Could you at least get a side salad?" I asked when our waitress took our order. Elena looked at me like I was an idiot. I mean, she *usually* looked at me like I was an idiot, but this was different. Maybe she thought I was a full-fledged moron.

"Potatoes are a vegetable."

All I could do was sigh in defeat.

"We use fresh strawberries in our shakes," the waitress added with a wink. "That's what makes them taste so good."

I gave her an appreciative nod and returned my attention to the gloomy gray sky outside.

"I hope the next case we're on is somewhere sunny, like Arizona," I said. Elena's nose wrinkled in disgust.

"Ugh. I hate the sun."

"Of course you do," I laughed under my breath. "You hate most things."

"That's not true. I like the rain. And I like trees."

"I noticed. What was all that earlier about the ash tree? You made it sound like there was something significant about the specific kind of tree."

"It was nothing," she said, trying to throw me off the trail I was on. "I just like trees."

"Then why did you ask Rylee's parents what kind of tree it was?"

Our waitress returned with our order, and I waited until she left before trying to get Elena to open up more.

"C'mon . . . why'd you ask them about the ash tree? I think there's more to it that you're not saying."

Ignoring me, Elena dug into her purse and pulled out the personal silverware kit I'd seen her use before. I guess she wasn't kidding about that metal allergy. There was even a plastic straw tucked in with the plastic fork, spoon, and knife. Then, to my horror, she reached for the jar of honey she'd requested earlier, and began squeezing a steady stream of it into the puddle of ketchup on her plate.

"Um . . . What the hell are you doing?"

"I'm eating. So what if I like to dip my fries in ketchup and honey?"

"That is . . . That is disgusting."

She laughed and dunked a couple of thick fries into the puddle, creating a red, sticky sauce. Then she crammed them into her mouth before dunking another fry, reaching across the table, and gleefully shoving it in my face.

"Try it," she said.

"No! Get it the hell away from me."

"Aw, stop being a little bitch and just eat it."

"What's up with all the peer pressure? I said I don't want it."

I tried to swat her away like a fly, but she was fast and nimble with her hands. I was so distracted by the French fry in my face that I didn't even think about the burger on my plate. By the time I realized my mistake, she'd taken off the top bun, dipped it in the sauce, and slapped it back on the burger.

"There," she said with a defiant grin as she set it down next to my side salad. "I fixed it."

"Gross! You asshole!"

I took off the top bun and reached for a napkin, wiping off as much of the sauce as I could from the burger. Then, either to spite Elena or to find out if I was really missing out on some culinary gem, I took a bite and chewed in silence. She seemed absolutely delighted.

"Well? Isn't it better?"

I wiped my mouth with a new napkin and frowned.

"No. It tastes like a preschooler's interpretation of barbecue sauce. Why would you do that to my food, you evil demon spawn?"

"I was just trying to open your eyes to other possibilities," she said loftily. "Obviously you don't have the same sophisticated palate as me."

"Says the chick whose veins are full of Mountain Dew."

"Oh, you think coffee is so much better?"

"Yeah. You know why?" I challenged. "Because it's only made of two things; coffee beans and water. Do you even *read* the ingredient labels on your food?"

Elena rolled her eyes. "You're such a snob."

"I'm not a snob," I retorted. "I just have *standards*."

She continued to eat her fries in her sacrilegious manner and I did my best to ignore her. But I was glad to see the color back in her cheeks.

"You're doing it again," she said with a crunch.

"Doing what?"

"Staring at me."

"No, I'm not."

She shot me a deadpan gaze like she could see into my head.

"Fine," I said. "It's your eyes. I've never seen anyone with such bright green eyes before."

"Yours are a crazy shade of bright blue, but I don't stare at you."

I couldn't help smirking.

"That's because you have standards."

Popping the last fry into her mouth, she patted her full stomach and leaned back in her seat.

"Thanks for bringing me here. I needed that," she said, licking salt off her fingers. "I was hungrier than I realized."

"It's good to see you with an appetite. You had me worried back there."

"You were worried?"

"Yeah, you went all pale and wobbly and you had this thousand-yard stare. Then you just hit the deck." I took a long drink of my water in hopes of getting the taste of honey out of my mouth. "I don't know your medical history or whatever health issues you might have. A partner ought to know some of those things if they're relevant."

"It was nothing. I just fainted."

"Hmm . . . That's not right. You probably should have stayed at the hospital to get checked out. What if you have diabetes? With the way you eat, I'd be surprised if you don't."

She brushed it off with a confident grin, but I was only half-joking.

"Like you said, I was probably just sleep-deprived and hungry. I'm fine now."

I couldn't help but be skeptical. The look she gave me right before she fainted wasn't going to be forgotten anytime soon. There was a look of real terror on her face. One that seemed at odds with her usual strength and feistiness.

"You wanna talk about it?" I asked her.

"Talk about what?"

"What happened."

"There's nothing to talk about," she laughed, but I could tell she was lying.

"Cut the crap, Rivera. I mean, Elena. The look on your face back there was scared as hell. I want to know what you saw."

She pursed her lips and picked a napkin off the table, which she started to fiddle with, tearing it to shreds. With a tell like that, she better never try playing poker. It was obvious that I was onto something.

"If we're going to work together, we have to be honest with each other," I said.

"I *am* honest with you."

"Then tell me what happened back at the trail. What did you see right before you passed out?"

"It was nothing. It was just . . . "

She lurched forward in her seat ever so slightly, as though she'd been nudged in the back. Then she did it again, this time more violently as she clamped a hand to her mouth.

"Whoa, you okay?"

Her nodding head said yes, but the rest of her body was saying no. She jumped out her seat and hauled ass towards the bathroom. A second later I heard the clatter of a toilet stall door being slammed open and the sound of her retching into the toilet. The only other person in the place, our waitress, made a beeline for me, looking worried.

"It wasn't the food, was it?"

"I doubt it. Mind if I go into the ladies' and see if she's alright?"

She shrugged.

"There's no one else here to give a damn," she mumbled before tidying up the sugar packets at the next booth over.

There were some things you just didn't do. You didn't date your cousins, you didn't take a rawhide away from a dog, and you didn't look in the top drawer beside your parent's bed. You also never dunked French fries in honey. But you also never, and I mean never, *ever*, went into a girls' bathroom. For a guy, the inner sanctum of the ladies' restroom was a sacred space that we entered at our peril. It was a mystical place where girls entered in pairs and came out transformed . . . laughing at private jokes and wearing a fresh layer of makeup.

I had never entered the women's bathroom before, and as I pushed the door open, I had no idea what to expect. I was almost disappointed then when I realized it looked exactly like the men's room minus the urinals.

From the first stall, I heard Elena still puking her guts out. Approaching her from behind, I saw her lustrous mass of hot pink hair spread out across the toilet bowl. Bending down to scoop it up, I pulled it into a makeshift ponytail.

"How ya doing, champ?"

She replied with a couple of dry heaves. Luckily, I'd missed the worst of it. As she pulled her head up from the toilet and flushed the last of her dinner, I saw her face was a mess. Tears had smeared her mascara from the corners of her eyes to the outsides of her cheeks.

"Thanks for holding my hair," she whispered as I let it fall through my fingers. It was softer than I was expecting. "No one's had to do that for me since college."

"I don't think I've done that since college, either. What happened?"

Elena gave the saddest, most pathetic shrug.

"I'm not sure. It's like my stomach spontaneously decided to turn itself inside out."

"It sure sounded like it. Come on. Let's get you back to urgent care. You're obviously not okay." I motioned for her to come out of the stall and join me at the sink. Her hair might've been soft and pretty, but it had just been draped over a toilet full of puke. I lathered up and washed my hands. I looked down at her when she stepped beside me and reached for the soap. It almost felt like a little dance in that small bathroom, us trying to share a sink.

"Really . . . I'm fine. Just give me a minute."

She hurried to wash her hands, then returned to the stall for some toilet paper to wipe the mascara off her face.

"You know it was the ketchup and honey, right?" I joked.

"Shut up."

"Then what was it?"

"Nothing! I'm fine!"

"For fuck's sake, Elena—why can't you admit that you're not okay? It's not a sign of weakness to ask for help."

She turned away from me and huffed. I wanted to lean over and pat her on the shoulder, but honestly, I was afraid she might try to claw my eyes out. Instead, I kept an eye on her, all the while wondering what might be the problem. I only had one other idea.

"Shit, you're not pregnant, are you?"

She looked at me as though I'd just taken a shit on the floor in front of her.

"*Pregnant?*" she screeched. "Not fucking likely!"

"Alright, alright! I was only asking. Geez."

I remained quiet for a minute and tried to think what else it could be.

"Are you *sure* you're not pregnant?" I asked her.

"Yes!"

"But . . . "

"I'm not fucking *pregnant*!"

She threw her hands over her face and grumbled.

"But you know what's up, don't you?" I said more than asked. She said nothing, just continued to hide her face behind her handful of balled up toilet tissue.

"Elena . . . I can tell you're hiding something. I know you think I'm just some idiot football jock, but I'm smarter than I look. Not sure if Chief Harris told you, but I'm actually a highly trained FBI agent. And I know when people are lying."

Still, she refused to reveal her face. Leaning over, I gently held her wrist and removed her hand from her face. It was dripping in fresh tears. Her green eyes weren't fiery with anger. Now they held an emotion I'd never seen in her before.

She was scared.

"Please, Elena, will you tell me what's going on? I can't help you if you don't tell me."

"Fine," she said, tossing the tissue into the trash can. "I'll tell you. But not here."

12

ELENA

"Solana," I whispered, pulling my arms tight around my body. Although it was summer, and as much as I liked the rain, I was cold. The kind of cold that chilled you from the inside out. "Solana was the one who . . . "

Holy fuck. This was harder than I thought it was going to be. I gave up trying to explain and looked out the window instead. After cleaning myself up in the bathroom, Logan had paid the bill and cranked up the heat in the Navigator so it would be warm when I got in. That was sweet of him. He didn't have to do that.

Now he was sitting there patiently in the driver's seat, waiting as long as it was gonna take me to finish what I had to say.

"Solana," he repeated. Hearing that name made me want to puke again, but there wasn't anything left. "That was the woman who Rylee's parents mentioned."

"Yep."

"I'm going to go out on a limb here and suggest this Solana person has something to do with whatever you're about to tell me."

"I know her." I nodded ever so slightly and squeezed my eyes shut. "She's the one who . . . who . . . "

Why the hell couldn't I say what was racing through my head? It might've had something to do with the fact that I hadn't spoken them out loud in years. But when I turned to look at my partner, I didn't see some stupid meathead football player. I saw someone who wasn't the type to walk away from a problem just because it was going to be difficult. If Logan was that type of person, he'd already have ditched my ass and begged Harris for another assignment. No . . . I needed to tell him the truth. There was no way I could stay on this case without cluing him in about my past.

"She was the one who killed my parents," I blurted out.

Logan was quiet for a moment. Eventually, his investigative skills began firing off.

"I don't understand. Solana was the woman in Rylee's dreams," he said. "How can she be real? Or is Solana less of a person and more of an idea? Is that the name of a cult? Is it some kind of social movement?"

"Will you shut up and just listen to me?" I could feel the fire as it returned to my voice. "I don't know how many more times I need to tell you this, but so many things you don't believe in are real. It's all fucking real. Solana is real. *Faeries* are real."

"I realize you believe that," he said. "And I know this whole fucking town believes in all sorts of that stuff too, but there has to be some logical explanation for these kids going missing."

"Will you stop with your fucking logic already? The fae aren't logical!"

Logan threw his hands up in exasperation.

"Fine. If those are the parameters we're dealing with for this case, then humor me for a minute. Right now our prime suspect is a woman with big black eyes and long black hair who appeared in a seven-year-old's dream. How are we supposed to bring Solana in for questioning?"

I felt my nails digging deep into the upholstery of the seat, and I gritted my teeth as wave after wave of anxiety washed over me.

"Faeries. Are. Real."

Logan let out a heavy sigh.

"But how the hell do you know that for sure?"

"Because I *am* one!" I yelled. The words came out my mouth with such force that strong, steady, stable Logan Hawthorne actually flinched.

"You want proof?" I asked as I turned to him. "Watch this."

By the time we climbed out of the car, the rain had turned to a light drizzle. Normally I would've reveled in it, but tonight I couldn't care less.

"Where are we going?" Logan asked.

"Follow me."

I headed straight to the edge of the parking lot to where the asphalt gave way to grass, finding exactly what I was looking for.

"What do you see?" I asked him.

He squinted through the soft rain and shrugged.

"Just a bunch of mud."

"And what else?"

"And . . . I dunno. Can't we do this back in the car?" he asked.

"No. Tell me what you see."

Again, he looked down at the ground.

"Um . . . Some torn up grass, some crumpled weeds . . . a smashed dandelion. Looks like a car backed over it."

"Exactly."

Puzzled by how glad I was that he'd noticed this, he frowned and shook his head. I looked back down at the dandelion, so sad lying there, all smashed down into the mud. In that moment, I mourned for the small plant.

"Why do you look like you're about to start crying?" he asked me. "It's just a weed."

"Just a weed? This plant had a life, and it gave others life, too!"

He took a step back and wiped the rain from his face.

"Whoa, sorry. Didn't realize you were such an eco-warrior."

"Just watch me, okay?"

Kneeling down in the mud beside the flower, I placed my hands on either side of it and created a little shield with my fingers.

"What you gonna do?" Logan teased. "Say a prayer? Give it a eulogy?"

Ignoring him, I gazed at the shriveled leaves and what was left of the annihilated bloom. It looked like a lost cause, but not to me. I could save it.

I filled my lungs with damp air, closed my eyes, and then, as gently as possible, sent a current of energy out of my hands and over the dandelion. Logan towered over me, probably thinking I was a legit crackpot. But *I'd* be the one who had the last laugh.

I rose to my knees and waited. A few seconds went by.

Nothing happened.

"Elena . . . "

"Just watch."

"I'm watching. Nothing's happening."

"Give it a fucking minute, would you?"

To an untrained eye, and especially a human one, I'm

sure it *did* look like nothing was happening. But I could see the signs of life as clear as day. The withered stem started to plump up. The faded leaves began to fill out and grow more vivid in color. I could hear the sound of life being drawn back into the plant. I could even smell the chlorophyll return to its cells.

"Keep watching," I whispered, feeling a little buzz from the excitement. "This is my favorite part."

With curiosity overwhelming him, Logan knelt down beside me. Another whiff of his clean, woodsy scent wafted over me in the drizzle. I pushed the observation aside and focused on the dandelion.

"See?" I couldn't help pointing it out to him as I studied his expression. "Can you see what's happening?"

At first, he just stared with his perpetually skeptical expression. Then he started to notice the changes. The damage from the tire that had run it over vanished as the stem filled out, green and plump. It pulled itself out of the mud to stand upright. The mangled flower turned to the sky as its petals grew back and fanned out in a vibrant shade of yellow.

"What . . . the fuck?" he whispered. "How are you doing this?"

With a smile, I leaned forward and cradled the dandelion in my hand, giving one last surge of energy to nudge it back to its full splendor. It fanned out its leaves as though it was stretching after a long nap.

"Did that just happen?" Logan kept looking at the dandelion, then back at me before staring at the dandelion again. "Is this some sort of magic trick?"

"It's not a trick. It's magic."

"I just . . . I just . . . " Aww . . . The poor guy was at a loss for words. His face went alarmingly pale as he couldn't take his eyes off the plant. "I just don't understand."

I laughed under my breath.

"Dude, we've barely scratched the surface. I don't expect you to understand everything, but it would be great if you'd accept that I'm a fae."

He was deep in thought, frowning as he scrambled for some sort of logical explanation. He must've remembered me telling him that the fae weren't logical, because he opened his mouth, closed it, then hesitated before speaking.

"So . . . you're not human. You're fae."

"Yep."

"Do you have powers? I mean, *clearly,* you have powers." He gave me a curious look, although he wasn't anywhere near losing his shit. "What else can you do?"

"Lots of things. It's all on my resume."

He pinned his eyes onto mine.

"Really?"

"No, dumbass!" I laughed. "But asking me what I can do is like me asking what you can do. We'd be here forever."

Logan took another long, deep breath, oblivious of the world around him. Meanwhile, I noticed that it was getting dark and the rain had stopped.

"I still don't . . . I still don't understand what just happened."

"I took something that was almost dead and brought it back to life—*that's* what just happened." I gave myself a mental pat on the back. "Call it a blessing my tribe has."

"So . . . can you bring people back from the dead?"

"No," I said with a disgruntled shake of the head. "It only works if there's still enough life left in the body. If someone's like, a hundred percent dead, that's it. Game over. I've seen actual dead things brought back to life, and . . . well, let's just say it's not good."

Logan shook his head, still bewildered, but he was right there on the edge of coming around.

"Are we talking zombies here?"

"Pretty much," I nodded. "It's not like the movies where there's a virus that spreads. You'd need some pretty serious dark magic to reanimate a dead body. The more magic is used, the more it takes. That's why I used a dandelion as an example. I'd rather not have a magic hangover in the morning."

He nodded slightly as he processed what I was saying.

"Right . . . so, there's a kind of balance. A give and take. That makes sense. I mean, none of this makes sense, but I guess that part does."

Gradually, he turned to face me before putting his hands on his hips to keep them from trembling.

"Ever since we first met, I knew there was something different about you," he confessed. "I'm guessing this explains your obsession with sugar."

Not bothering to hide my grin, I nodded. As I looked into his eyes, I could actually see the paradigm shift taking place inside his brain. I could see how the world as he knew it was starting to peel away and reveal that there was so much more to it, if only he was willing to see.

Looking down at the dandelion, I saw it was closing for the night. I knelt down and gazed at it, thinking about all the bees and butterflies it would feed the next day.

"Sleep tight, little guy," I said, gently tickling the yellow petals as though it was a tiny little hummingbird. "I'll come back and visit."

Logan's deep-thinking frowny face was kind of cute, although his eyes were still full of disbelief.

"Now *you're* the one who looks like he's gonna pass out," I said. "You okay, partner?"

"I'm not sure."

Standing up, he kept his eyes focused on the dandelion, now the brightest plant for miles. Its new vibrant yellow petals outshone all the nearby flowers so it sat like a beacon of vitality amid the mud and dirt.

"I've got so many questions," he said, turning towards our rental car.

"I figured as much, but can we get something to drink? I'm dying for a soda."

He shot me another quizzical look.

"Soda? I was thinking of something stronger."

I had a fondness for dive bars and had quite a few favorites back in Virginia and Maryland, but nothing compared to The Drunk Chicken. It was the only watering hole in Yarbrough and brought with it a whole new level of dive-bar realness.

Even the smell was authentic.

It was hard to pin down; it wasn't good, but after sitting in it a while you got used to it. Tobacco smoke permeated everything. There were notes of mold from countless spilled drinks that had been wiped up in a hurry . . . or not at all, and the stank of sweaty roughnecks was so thick you could almost taste it.

Situated in what looked like a dilapidated barn, it was filled to the rafter with loggers, miners, farmers, truckers, bikers, and other salt-of-the-earth folks who made up the backbone of this community. Their hands were thick and calloused, with dirt and grease under their nails and tattoos on their hairy arms.

The best thing about this crowd was that they took one look at my hot pink hair, glanced at the gold-plated Glock holstered at my hip, and went back to their drinks like it was no big deal. I'm sure we weren't the only ones packing heat.

I climbed onto one of the available bar stools and ordered a Jack and Coke and an order of nachos.

"Half size or full portion?" the burly bartender asked.

"Full. Thanks." I set down a twenty-dollar bill and had a drink in my hand within thirty seconds. It was exactly what I needed right now . . . the perfect mix between adult beverage and sweet, caffeinated goodness. The burn at the back of my throat comforted me and I relaxed back in my seat, hoping that the duct tape patch on the cushion wouldn't stick to my ass.

Tuning out the noise of the other patrons, I focused on Hawthorne as he hung up his jacket on the coat rack near the door. Although his trembling hands had grown steady, he still looked a little pale when he asked the bartender for a beer and a shot of Jameson.

"Are you seriously that shook over seeing a dandelion come back to life?"

"Shook? I don't know about that. A little unsettled, maybe," he admitted. "That shit was weird." I watched as he took the shot and ordered another.

"Well, if you want a career in the OCD, you'll have a lot weirder stuff to contend with. Believe me, zombie dandelions are the least weird thing you'll see."

He took a long sip of his beer and ran his hand through his hair absentmindedly, leaving it sticking up in some places like a toilet brush. As the color and warmth returned to his cheeks, he looked about ten years younger. I had to hand it to him—he was taking this information pretty well. I suppose he never would've graduated from the academy if he was the type to get flustered at the drop of a hat.

"So . . . Are you gonna tell me how you did that with the flower?"

"I told you. I'm fae. That's why I have my own special cutlery and a shiny gold Glock. I can't touch iron. It burns me."

"It burns you?" he asked. That shrewd skepticism was back in full force. "Prove it."

I rolled my eyes, half-tempted to kick him in the shin. The whole cute jock from next door look he had going on was losing its charm fast.

"Fine," I said, reaching for the roll of silverware the bartender had left for when my nachos arrived. I peeled off the paper holding the napkin in place, letting the spoon, fork, and knife slide onto the counter. "Pick one up and rest it against your arm. See what happens."

Hawthorne reached for the spoon and pressed it into his forearm.

"How long do I do thi—"

"That's long enough. Now do it to me." I held out my left arm and pushed up the sleeve of my jacket. He'd only set the back of the spoon against my skin for a few seconds when it started to sting and burn. I grimaced, but I waited as long as I could before jerking my arm away. Hawthorne's jaw fell. Not a lot.

But enough.

The perfect oval of burned skin was dark pink and was starting to puff up and blister. All from a run-of-the-mill stainless steel spoon.

"So *that's* why you carry around your own silverware?" The half-haunted, totally bewildered look came back into his eyes. "That's why you asked Mrs. Brown for a different glass, isn't it?"

I nodded my head.

"Shit, Rivera—we should put some ice on that."

"It'll be gone in half an hour," I said, and carefully pulled down the sleeve. Just then, the bartender set down a massive platter of nachos underneath my nose. I was so hungry I started to drool. I took another sip of my drink before plowing into my second attempt at a meal that day.

"But why would stainless steel burn you?" Logan asked. "That's not iron."

"Sure it is," I replied. "It's 98% iron. Hard pass."

"What about soda cans? I've seen you carrying those around just fine."

"Aluminum cans are made of aluminum," I explained. "They're fair game. So is tin, copper, silver and gold. I just can't deal with iron."

I loaded up a corn chip with fixings, then shoved it into my mouth.

"So you're really a fae . . . " he said into his glass of beer. "It's like finding out you're an alien or Sasquatch or something. Although . . . " He trailed off, watching me scarf tortilla chips covered in shredded chicken, cheese, sour cream, jalapeños, black beans, and corn salsa. "Are you sure you're not a ghost? Watching you eat is giving me flashbacks of Slimer from Ghostbusters."

"Whatever," I mumbled with my mouth full of food. "I'm way cuter than Slimer."

"Your eyes are almost that same shade of green," he pointed out with his glass before swallowing another gulp of beer. "It's not natural. It shouldn't exist."

"But it does, and so do I."

He set down his drink and fiddled with a coaster, but his eyes remained on mine.

"How many of you are there?"

I was grateful that the Drunk Chicken was quiet enough to hear each other talk and loud enough that eavesdropping would be tough. The music was steady, yet soft. An old jukebox was playing oldies on it, and every now and then we'd hear a scratch or a pop, which only added to the atmosphere.

"Not a lot. I mean, not up here on the surface. I shouldn't really be up here either. I should be down in the Hollows . . . back in my home realm."

"So why aren't you?"

My stomach dropped as I prepared myself to tell him my story. In all my years up on the surface, I had only confided in Chief Harris about where I came from, but even he didn't know all the fine details.

Should I tell him? I asked myself. *Would Logan understand? Would he believe me?*

As I sat across from his watchful gaze, I felt a vulnerability that I'd never experienced before. I was going to lay myself bare to this man who, until today, didn't believe in a single thing he couldn't see or touch.

Could I really trust him?

13

ELENA

No, don't tell him! the protective part of my brain yelled at me. *You can't trust humans with your true identity. As soon as they find out, they'll find a way to exploit you!*

But as I looked into Logan's eyes, a sense of calm came over me. I could feel his energy. I could feel that he wasn't like most humans. He was . . . dare I say it, trustworthy and kind?

One more look deep into those dark blue eyes, and I knew my instincts were leading me in the right direction. I swallowed my nacho, slammed the rest of my drink, and wiped my mouth on the back of my hand.

"The reason I left the Hollows . . . " I began, feeling my heart beat a little faster, "is because of *her*—Solana."

A deep rage drifted up from far, far down inside me the second I said her name out loud. To me, it wasn't just a name. It was an evocation of evil. A sound so dark it wasn't a name at all but an utterance of pain and heartache. It was a name that didn't deserve to be heard from my lips.

"She's the current Queen of Elphame," I told Hawthorne. I could already see the wheels spinning as questions popped up right and left in his brain. Luckily, he kept his mouth shut and just listened to me. It was refreshing.

"The thing is, she shouldn't have ever been queen. Elphame belonged to *me*—I mean . . . my family. They'd ruled over it for thousands of years."

Logan regarded me suspiciously as I spoke, as though he wasn't quite sure whether I was playing a joke on him or not. Regardless, I pressed on. He'd asked to know my story, so he was going to hear it.

"So yeah. Thousands of years," I continued. "Can you comprehend how long that is? My ancestors were hard, wizened old fae who ruled the Kingdom of Elphame with an iron fist. They were irrational tyrants. It was normal for them to be at war with different kingdoms for centuries at a time. Nobody wanted to get on their bad side."

Grabbing my new Jack and Coke, I took a mouthful and hoped it would burn out the lump in my throat. It didn't go away completely, but it helped.

"My parents were totally different. They weren't like the rest of my family. Especially my mom. All she wanted to do was help people, and all my dad wanted was to love and support her vision for what Elphame could become."

Tears stung my eyes, and I debated how hard I should try to keep them from falling. If I didn't let go now, the pain would find me in the middle of the night during my worst nightmares. The ones where Solana came and stole my parents from me. The ones where their deaths were played back to me in vivid, awful slow-motion over and over, where I'd watch their blood dripping down . . . down . . .

"Elena, you don't have to talk if you don't want to," Logan said, laying his hand softly on mine. There was no trace of suspicion in his eyes. He could see my pain. I almost thought he could feel it. Nobody was that empathetic. At least, nobody had been this way with me. Not until now.

"I have to tell somebody," I insisted. "No one else knows and now . . . Solana's back. Her kind of evil will never stop unless everyone knows what she's capable of."

I swallowed another gulp of my drink and slowly pulled my hand out of Logan's. It was starting to feel weird. Like, too warm. The last thing I wanted was to leave my sweaty, salty nacho hands all over him.

"Most people in the kingdom adored my mom," I said. "They loved the fact that she wasn't like the warmongers before her. She actually cared about her people. Genuinely concerned for each and every one of them. She ended all those long wars and tried to make things better for everyone in Elphame. But not everyone appreciated her kindness. There were some like Solana who thought being a queen meant being feared. They said my mom's compassion made her weak."

As the tears began to fall, Logan grabbed a few paper napkins from a nearby dispenser and pressed them into my hands. It was so strange to open up to this human, and a man at that. Instead of it feeling wrong, or like I was betraying myself and my tribe in telling him about our people, I felt . . . appreciative . . . and relieved. He felt like a true friend.

It surprised me as much as it frightened me.

"Your mom wasn't weak for caring about other people," he said. "There's no shame in showing mercy."

"I don't think there is either, but Solana . . . " Ugh. That name. Maybe it was the Jack and Cokes, but it was getting easier to say her name out loud. And I really didn't want to start throwing up those nachos here in the Drunk Chicken. I took a deep breath and let it out slowly.

"Solana said my mom was naïve and stupid. And I suppose she was, in a way. If she'd been more careful . . . if she didn't always insist on seeing the best in people . . . and kept her guard up, then maybe . . . "

My throat started to close up once again and brought my drink to my lips, swallowing a strong, sweet mouthful before I could speak again.

"Sorry for being such a hot mess right now. I just miss my mom so much. I miss both my parents."

And instead of bailing or being distracted with his watch or his phone, Logan simply sat there and nodded his head in understanding. He'd lost his mom too, after all. He had an idea of what I was going through.

"Elena, you don't have to apologize for anything. I get it," he said, continuing to give me his full attention.

"Oh yeah?" I sniffed. "You know all about fae grudges?"

Logan shrugged. "I'm guessing they're like human ones, times a hundred."

"Something like that," I agreed. "Solana was a princess from a neighboring kingdom. My tribe never went there because only a few had gone and lived to talk about it. They came back all shriveled and twisted—mentally and physically. It was like something had sucked all the life out of them."

It felt surreal to walk down memory lane from the warm, dim confines of the Drunk Chicken. Men drank and threw darts, talked shit on each other, and laughed, oblivious to the shadow worlds that lay beyond.

"That's one of the things I'm worried about with all these missing kids, is that Solana's using them like human batteries to fuel whatever she's got planned," I explained. "She can lure people to their deaths with a smile or a song. How does Rylee have a chance when my mom was killed as an adult?"

My fingernails dug themselves into the wood at the edge of the bar as I thought of her. There were so many emotions running through my head; anger, guilt, sadness, longing. All of them made me sick. If it wasn't for Logan's calm, steady presence, or that extra shot of whiskey, I might've puked again.

"What did Solana do?" asked Hawthorne. There was an edge of caution in his voice, but the rational, stable person it belonged to gave me strength.

"She set a trap," I told him, feeling more at ease. "She knew that every morning my mom would visit the local townsfolk, healing the sick at the village square. I was always with her. I loved to watch her work her magic. I wanted to be a healer just like her when I got older. I never gave much thought to becoming queen. I figured I'd be just like my mom."

I grabbed my glass and realized the last drops had been drunk.

"Here," said Hawthorne, handing me his second shot of Jameson.

I took it gratefully and swallowed it down to feel its calming effects. But nothing could stop the tension building inside me or the intense sadness that seeped through every fiber of my body like an invading virus.

There wasn't a day that passed when I didn't remember the death of my parents, but with each time I recalled the day, the pain only intensified. I'd heard people talk of grief. They often said it got easier, but my grief never healed. It just burned deeper inside me until it sometimes felt it was burning out my entire heart, leaving me damaged and hollow.

But as much as it hurt, I knew I had to tell my story. So although it felt like my heart was splitting in two, I pushed onward.

"Solana waited until Mom had finished up for the day. She ambushed us on our way home to the palace," I said. I took another gulp of my fresh drink and remembered each detail of that morning.

"We heard a woman crying and found her lying in the middle of the road. She said she'd been attacked by thieves and that they hurt her. Of course, my mom ran to help her, and that's when she cut her throat."

I could feel the shock ripple through Hawthorne's body as he held me.

"Jesus!" Logan blurted out. "Right in front of you?"

I nodded my head.

"That's . . . that's fucking demented!"

"I know," I agreed, and swallowed another mouthful of Jack and Coke. "And since I was heir to the throne, Solana came after me with that fucking knife, chasing me through the woods. I've never run so fast in my life. All I wanted was to get home and be with my dad. I had no idea I'd never see him again. I didn't know it at the time, but he was already dead."

Hawthorne gasped ever so slightly.

"She'd charmed her way past the guards to his tower," I explained. "It wasn't difficult for her, not with her looks. It was like she cast a spell whenever she appeared. People just did what she told them, as though their heads had been emptied. So all she had to do was wait until my mom and I left for the day so she could sneak into their room. They say my dad was asleep when it happened. She stabbed him right in the heart."

Hawthorne's response to this was nothing but silence. He was too shocked to say anything. Nearby drinkers had noticed my earlier tears and my current empty facade. From a distance, we probably just looked like a couple having a lovers' tiff. Maybe they thought I was breaking up with Logan. Who knows? They never could've guessed in a million years the crazy story I'd kept private for so long.

"Anyway, Solana took over Elphame as her own. The people of our kingdom didn't see a murderer when they looked at her. They saw a beautiful warrior queen who'd taken what she believed was hers," I told him. "The faerie kingdom is savage. There's no place for genuinely kind people like my parents."

Logan ran his hand through his hair and ordered himself another beer.

"Your parents sound like wonderful people. They'd be so proud of you, doing what you do. You chase down bad guys. You try and protect people too, just in a different way. And I—I suppose the way you brought back that dandelion is an example of how your mom's healing powers live on through you."

"I suppose you're right."

"Exactly. So that means your mom l—"

"Don't say my mom lives on through me. That's bullshit."

"No, it's not," he said in a voice that was kind yet firm. "I'm saying this in the most logical, rational way possible. You're their daughter. Their DNA lives in *you* now. So in a way, they're with you in everything you do. That's how I think about my mom."

I didn't have an immediate comeback for that. He'd

actually just made a really good point. I didn't want to listen to him, although deep down, I knew I needed to hear what he was saying.

"Well, I might be alive, but my family's kingdom is gone. My family's legacy is gone. After thousands of years, I'm the last one left. I didn't even try to fight it, either. I just took off like a coward."

"Elena, you were just a kid when it happened. And from the sound of it, people weren't exactly rallying for justice after the woman who killed your parents stole their entire kingdom. Why would you think it's cowardly to lie low?"

"Because I didn't just lie low." I wrung my hands, avoiding Logan's piercing blue eyes as I took another look around the bar. In a past life, I would've been surrounded by all things bright and beautiful, sparkling and fragrant, rich and vibrant. Now I was surrounded by lumbering, slobbering, stinking humans. "I left the Hollows and I came *here* . . . to the human realm. Talk about desperate."

I paused long enough to take a sip of my drink. "I was homeless for a long time. I lived in the woods like a hermit. I didn't speak English. I didn't think I needed to. I just talked to the animals. Eventually, a hunter found me and I ended up in foster care. Somewhere along the way they assumed my parents were drug addicts because all I could do was tell the social workers that my parents were dead. After I learned English, I still couldn't tell them the truth. I didn't want to end up in a mental institution."

I looked towards the bar hoping to see a gap in the crowd. More than anything I needed another shot of whiskey, but the bar only seemed to look busier.

"Let's get outta here," suggested Logan. "You look like you need some air."

Putting an arm around my shoulder, he guided me out into the cool evening air. There was that woodsy, outdoorsy scent of his, of clean sweat and warm skin. It was so strange that I liked it so much. He didn't smell like any of the men in the bar. The rain clouds had drifted away and a soft breeze was rustling through the trees. Above, there wasn't a single cloud, so the stars shone brightly around a crescent moon. I lifted my head and cocked an eyebrow at him.

"I bet you don't believe a word I just said, do you?"

"Actually, I do believe you," said Logan, dropping his arm from my shoulder and jamming his hand into his pocket in search of the keys. "Like I said . . . I'm trained in this stuff. I know when someone's full of it, and when they're telling the truth. It also makes sense because you don't have anything to gain whether or not your story is true. So yeah. I believe you."

He'd found the keys, but instead of climbing into the Navigator, he just stood there beside the car, deep in thought as he looked up at the stars. It was still early in the night. I wondered what he was thinking about. Was he wondering if he shouldn't have put his arm on me? It was innocent enough, wasn't it? Or maybe he was thinking about his mom.

"Do you really think Solana's the one behind these disappearances?" he asked, still gazing at the sky. Surprised by his question, and even more surprised that he wasn't calling bullshit on everything I'd been telling him about fae and the paranormal, I perked up.

"Definitely. If Rylee said she dreamed of her then it must be. And we know she's a killer. She's capable of anything."

The reflection of the stars danced in his eyes as the wind ruffled his hair. I wondered if he was looking to the heavens to try and make sense of everything. The world as he knew it didn't exist. It was so much darker and vicious than he could've ever known. And it was kind of adorable to see his curiosity winning over any rigid beliefs that he held. It felt like I was witness to his mind opening and his beliefs bending just enough to accept who and what I was.

"What are you thinking?" I asked him.

"That I feel so small down here. That I can get straight As, graduate at the top of my class, be the best in my division, get promoted regularly, and still not know shit. At least, not in the grand scheme of things."

I gave a little half-shrug.

"The universe is huge. There are a lot of things out there we still have to learn about."

"A lot of things *I* need to learn about," he corrected. "Ever since I sat down in Chief Harris' office, I feel like I'm dreaming. How can this all be happening? You, the missing kids, Solana . . . "

"You'll get used to it," I told him as I walked around the car and opened my door. "Pretty soon you'll realize that all the things beneath the Earth and behind the veil are just as real as those stars up there. Either that or . . . "

I waited for him to climb into the car with me.

"Or?"

"Or you'll go insane. But I think you can handle it."

He started the car and backed up slowly, twisting in his seat to make sure he avoided the numerous potholes in the parking lot. In the lights outside the bar, I could make out a shadow of scruff on his jawline. And again, that scent. When he caught me staring at him, he gave the sexiest half-smile. All I could do was blink as I waited to see what he might say or do next.

"That might be the nicest thing you've said to me since we started working together, partner."

My brain started to race as I wondered how the hell to respond. Luckily, I didn't have to say anything. The two-way police radio in the cup holder was crackling with chatter as Sheriff McKinney barked orders at multiple deputies. It sounded like there was a new development in the case.

"Come on, Brad. Let's get back to the station."

Logan snorted a laugh as he took a right and stepped on the gas.

"You got it, Azrael."

14

LOGAN

I could tell something was wrong before we pulled into the parking lot at the police station. The entire building was in chaos and it looked as though McKinney had called every officer in the county to come out and find Rylee. Not that it looked as though they were making much progress. Most of them appeared to be running around like headless chickens with no plan of what to do. But I couldn't blame them. How exactly did you track down a missing girl when your only lead is that she'd vanished into a tree? And how did you trace a suspect that had only been seen in the little girl's dreams?

"Thank fuck you're both here," McKinney growled, stepping out of his office. The front of his shirt was covered in stains from whatever he'd eaten for dinner. My money was on sloppy Joe's. "Where have y'all been?"

"We were just—"

"Doesn't matter. You're here now. Please tell me you've got something good to tell me."

Both Elena and I stared at him, unable to be the bright-eyed, optimistic agents he wanted us to be. I so badly wanted to know the right thing to say, or at least think of a plan of action, but I felt as clueless as everyone else.

McKinney was still looking to us for answers. Before either of us could speak, a loud wail came from one of the nearby interview rooms.

"That'll be Rylee's mom," sighed McKinney. "She's been like that since she got here."

"Can you blame her?" asked Elena.

"Of course not. I'd be the same if I was in her position. She just keeps asking us why we haven't found her little girl yet. I don't know what to tell her."

Our conversation was interrupted by the squeak of boots on the tile floor. We all turned round to see a young officer running towards us.

"Sheriff! You gotta come see this. Shit has really hit the fan."

"What is it?"

"Reporters!" he yelled. "A news team from Nashville just showed up."

"Aw, shit!"

The four of us ran down towards the reception and looked out through the plate glass windows to see two large vans parked beside our rental car. The sound of slamming car doors and excited voices filled the air.

"This is an ongoing investigation!" Elena hissed. "We can't have the media here! Get rid of them!"

"How am I supposed to do that?" asked McKinney. "The general public has a right to know about the disappearances."

"Do you think they give a shit about the missing children?" Elena snapped back. "Or do you just think they're here to boost their ratings and make Yarbrough PD look totally incompetent?"

McKinney didn't reply. He pressed his thin lips together and blew an irritated huff out of his flaring nostrils. He looked out the window as a reporter smoothed down her hair before striding towards the main door with a cameraman in tow.

"Well, one of us needs to talk to them," I said.

McKinney's eyes lit up. "How 'bout you, Boy Scout?"

It took me a second to realize he was talking to me. My palms immediately began to sweat.

"You want *me* to speak to them?"

"Well, who else am I looking at right now? Yes, you! You've got the looks, the rank, the suit. People will trust you."

I raised a brow at my partner, who was clearly not interested in the job. Even if I refused, she was the last person who should be in front of a camera. Aside from her less than professional wardrobe, her long, tangled bright pink hair, the smeared makeup from crying, and the whiskey on her breath, she'd probably tell the reporter to fuck off on live television.

Not exactly a great look for the bureau.

"Go on then, Hawthorne," she huffed, crossing her arms. "Charm the cameras. I'm sure you've been briefed on how to deal with the press."

I never was good in front of a camera. Even on picture day in high school, I somehow managed to get sweaty palms before I sat down in front of the photographer. And despite the rise of YouTube stars and social media influences, there was just something I found so unnatural about appearing on camera. It felt like every inch of your appearance and behavior was being scrutinized and immortalized. I understood why the Amish weren't fans of having their picture taken. One of my worst fears was to become a meme.

And as for giving a statement or being interviewed, I felt grossly unqualified. I'd only spoken on camera once in my entire life when I was interviewed by one of the media students in college. My tongue had turned into a brick in my mouth and I suddenly forgot how to speak a word of English. My classmates called me Cottonmouth for a while, but luckily the nickname didn't stick.

But here I was, heart racing, palms sweating. More than anything, I wanted to channel Elena's fiery attitude and tell the news crew to fuck off. But I also knew I didn't have an option. Plus, it wasn't fair to the community. The media had every right to ask about the sudden uptick in kidnappings. And parents needed to know to avoid bringing their kids to remote trails until we had a better idea of what was going on. So, even though it felt like my stomach was about to fall out, I gritted my teeth and said, "Fine. I'll do it."

"Get your ass out there, Hawthorne," said Elena, slapping me on the back. "And don't tell them shit. The last thing we want is widespread panic in the whole state."

"Don't tell them shit? What am I supposed to say exactly?"

But McKinney was already pushing me towards the door.

I stumbled out onto the police station steps, I was immediately honed in on by a platinum blonde news anchor whose face looked like it had been coated with a thick layer of Cheeto dust.

"Hi there, I'm Melanie Brittle with WBR-Three News," she announced, shoving a microphone in my face. "And who am I speaking with this evening?"

"Uh . . . Senior Special Agent Logan Hawthorne, ma'am," I said, unsure of whether to look at her or the camera. The lights were blinding me, so I tried to focus on her instead.

"Can you confirm another child has gone missing in Yarbrough this evening?"

"Yes. I can confirm that."

"Can you also confirm that she is one of hundreds that has vanished in the region over the last few months?"

"Well, it's an ongoing investigation, so I can't speculate if this incident is related to the others."

Her eyes were like ice chips inside her orange face. As she looked up at me, her manicured hand clutching the microphone, she spread her red lips into a smile that didn't quite reach those chilled eyes. She may have been asking about missing kids, but the look on her face told me she could've been talking about anything from horse racing to pumpkin pie recipes.

Elena was right. She didn't give a shit about the kids. She was only here for her career.

"You said you're a special agent. Are you a detective working on the case?" she asked.

"FBI," I told her and her eyes lit up.

"So the FBI is on this now?" she smiled before turning to her cameraman. "Johnny, are you getting this?"

I'd had enough already and stepped back towards the door, but she was clearly not going to let me leave so easily. Pushing the microphone closer towards me, she stepped in so close that I could smell her sweet, sickly perfume.

"Why is the FBI handling the disappearances?" she asked. "Is it because the Yarbrough police department isn't capable of handling the case."

"Not at all. It's that—"

"So they're not capable of handling the case."

"I didn't say that."

"So what *are* you saying, Agent . . . Harmon?"

"Hawthorne."

"Agent Hawthorne, can you tell us your involvement in the cases? Is the FBI involved because of the esoteric nature of the disappearances?"

Shit, what does she mean by esoteric? She can't possibly know about Rylee's drawing or dark faeries, can she?

"I'm not sure what you mean by esoteric," I said, looking over my shoulder into the station.

I could just about see the faces of Elena and McKinney through the glare of the glass and longed for them to come out and rescue me.

"Esoteric," she repeated louder, as though being loud and repetitive would suddenly make her question make sense. "I'm talking about the rumors around the disappearances that have been circulating for years."

I was filled with a sinking feeling. Now I knew why she had really turned up. It wasn't just the missing children she was here for, it was the accompanying X-Files-esque storyline that she was really on the lookout for.

"The FBI is routinely called in to help with missing persons cases," I said. "And we don't comment on active investigations, but I do want to clarify that rumors aren't evidence. Now if you don't mind, I have to get back inside. There's a family who needs to find their daughter."

"One of hundreds of families," she continued, stepping in front of the door.

Fuck, she's really not letting go of this.

"Yes, a number of families," I agreed.

"Do you have an exact number of families? How about an exact number of missing children?"

"As I said, this is an ongoing investigation. I can't give precise details," I told her firmly. "But there will be a press conference at some time in the near future where you can ask more questions. Now please, I have a job to—"

"The rumors," Melanie Brittle interrupted, circling back to the subject. "What can you tell us about them?"

"Nothing."

"Agent Hawthorne, come on now." Ugh, again with that fake smile. "The public deserves to know what's happening to their children."

"I agree."

"So you must also agree that the rumors are shocking."

"I don't concern myself with rumors. I deal with facts."

Maneuvering my way even closer towards the door, I grappled for the handle, but she was still intent on discussing these rumors that were so damn entertaining.

"You can ask about them at the press conference," I told her.

"And when will that be held?"

"Soon."

"And Secret Agent Hawthorne . . . "

"I'm not a secret agent."

"You'll discuss the rumors then? For example, the Bigfoot theory, the alien abductions, or the Satanic child sacrifices?"

That last one made me do a double-take.

"Satanic child sacrifices?"

The genuine look of shock on my face must have made an impression on her because she lowered the microphone slightly and softened her determined expression.

"Satanic sacrifices," she repeated, this time softer than before. "It's what the locals have are talking about the most."

"I haven't been made aware of any theories involving Satan, let alone human sacrifices."

"But there have been sightings of men in the woods

wearing robes. What about rumors of chanting being heard in the surrounding forest? Or reports of a cult that operates on the outskirts of Yarbrough. Do you think there's something demonic taking place in this town?"

"No, I don't."

"And what about the rumors of a cover-up?"

"I think we're done here."

I pushed past her, yet she was relentless.

"How do you explain the fact that so many children have gone missing with so little media attention? Why hasn't the National Guard been brought in to search for the children?"

"No comment. Now, please, let me get back to work."

At last, I made my escape and shoehorned myself through the door, locking it in the camera's crew's faces.

"Fuck me . . . " I sighed as I stepped back into the station reception. It wasn't until I returned that I realized how much I'd been sweating.

"That sounded like it went well," said Elena sarcastically. She still had her arms folded and an exhausted look in her eyes.

"Please tell me you heard some of that," I said to McKinney.

"Satanic sacrifice," he said, closing his eyes for a second. "That's a new one."

"One we can't let the public fixate on," said Elena. "If anyone from the press gets an actual lead on that, there'll be a statewide panic. It's a miracle there hasn't been one already, given how many kids are missing."

"That's true," agreed McKinney. "Nobody cares when it happens in a backwater town like ours. I'm surprised Melanie Brittle came all the way from Nashville."

"There'll be more," I said, looking out the window

towards Melanie, who was now speaking into her camera. "They're like flies. As soon as one turns up, twenty come to join it."

McKinney's face turned a sickly shade of gray as he pondered on this.

"I can't handle all of this as it is, let alone with the media showing up to complicate things," he muttered. "The last thing we need is some stuck-up bitch with a microphone traipsing around the neighborhood asking for local folks' opinions."

"Opinions that include Satan, aliens, and Bigfoot," I said. "Fuck, this is a nightmare."

Once again, our conversation was interrupted by the sound of loud sobbing coming from down the hall.

"Why haven't you found her yet?" Rylee's mom cried, her voice bouncing off the walls. "Why are you not doing anything?"

"We're doing all we can," came the soft but nervous voice of the detective interviewing her.

"It doesn't fucking look like it!"

I turned to Elena and McKinney, the three of us staring at each other, feeling useless.

"We have to do something," McKinney said. "You guys are the experts. What should be our next step?"

What could I tell him? My best witness was a seven-year-old kid who'd only seen the suspect in a dream. My current police sketch was literally drawn in crayons. Right then, I felt like the furthest thing from an expert.

Elena, on the other hand, looked deep in thought, tapping her foot against the floor as the cogs in her mind cranked into action.

"Sacrifice . . . " she thought out loud. "I think I have an idea, but I'm gonna need Sylvia's address."

"Sylvia's?" asked McKinney, incredulously. "Why on Earth would you want to speak to her?"

"I'll tell you later," she said. "Just tell me where she lives."

"The last house on the road out east," said McKinney, pointing into the distance. "You can't miss it. It's the most ramshackle piece of shit house in the whole town. Looks like it'll fall down if you lean on it."

"I take it I'm driving?" I asked, fishing the car keys out of my pocket.

"Need me to come with you guys?" asked McKinney.

"No," Elena replied a little too firmly. "I mean, thanks Sheriff, but we'll be fine."

He eyed her closely as she hurried to the front door.

"Are you sure you wanna talk to Sylvia? She's a real nut job."

"I'm sure." Elena nodded at me to get a move on. "Come on, Hawthorne. If we slip out the back door, I don't think that reporter will notice us."

"Don't say I didn't warn you," the sheriff called behind us. "Make sure you watch her driveway for cats. She has about a thousand of them."

15

ELENA

McKinney wasn't joking about Sylvia being a crazy cat lady. When we turned the corner into her driveway, dozens of cats appeared from the shadows, snaking their way in and out of the overgrown grass. Their reflective eyes shone through the darkness at us, reflecting tiny glints of green, yellow, and gold.

"What . . . the . . . hell? There's like, an *army* of them," Hawthorne said through his clenched teeth. He was squinting through the darkness as he wound the car down the narrow path. "And how long is this fucking driveway? Feels like we've been driving for miles."

"McKinney did say it was on the edge of town."

"Edge of the world, more like. Good god—I almost hit *another* cat! I swear these little assholes are trying to throw themselves under the wheels on purpose."

"Obviously. How else are they going to file an insurance claim?"

He laughed, and it was good to see him smile despite the night we were having. Looking out into the darkness, I started to wonder if we'd taken a wrong turn.

Then I saw the house.

"Holy shitballs," I gasped. "What *century* is this thing from?"

"It looks like an old plantation," Logan said, slowing down as we approached the front door. "How is it still *standing*?"

Logan hit the brakes and we both gawped up at the building that looked like an illustration from The Fall of the House of Usher. Slanted at a precarious angle, the wooden siding looked ready to buckle and pop off at any second. All around it, thick brambles grew, creeping up the decaying walls so the branches looked as though they were tapping on the windows that weren't already cracked or broken. It was probably the thick vines keeping the house from collapsing on itself.

"I swear I saw this place on Scooby-Doo," said Logan, unbuckling his seat belt. "Or in my nightmares."

"Aww, it's not that bad. It's just . . . full of character."

He shot me an icy stare.

"Or hantavirus."

I grinned wide.

"Fine. It's sketchy as hell. Maybe it's better inside."

"Doubt it. Besides, you still haven't told me what we're doing here."

I wriggled in my seat and freed myself from the safety belt, eager to speak with the owner of the house.

"And you haven't told me what happened in that interview room with Sylvia. You went in there with a smile on your face and came out all dazed."

"She was a lot more interesting than McKinney wants us to believe," I tried to explain as I headed for the porch. "Now are you gonna help me find the doorbell?"

"Can't you just call her?" Logan said as he stepped out of the Navigator.

"I don't think she has a phone," I replied, and climbed up the narrow porch steps. I scanned through the darkness for signs of life. All I saw were the blinking eyes of the cats surrounding me. Maybe it was past Sylvia's bedtime? Old people usually went to bed early, although I hoped Sylvia was different. This looked like prime party time for her cats. I could barely hear the crickets and bullfrogs over their constant gentle meowing as they watched us poke around the wrap-around porch. I'd never seen anything like it.

"How many of those furballs do you think there are?" I asked.

"I dunno. Fifty? A hundred? It's too many damn cats, I can tell you that." He wrinkled his nose, shaking his head in disapproval. "McKinney should get animal control out here. There's no way Sylvia's looking after them all properly."

"I think they're the ones looking after her," I said, holding back a smile. "Look at them guarding the house."

Sure enough, they were acting as little sentries patrolling the doors and windows. Cats of all sizes and colors stalked back and forth, back and forth, shooting us wary glances as their tails twitched. An orange Tom with one eye and a broken tail looked especially menacing, while a cluster of calico kittens had climbed onto the porch swing to see what all the fuss was about. And then there were the tabby cats in every imaginable combination of spots, swirls, and stripes. If the orange cat was their one-eyed general, this was his army.

"Elena, is this normal?"

More cats were jumping onto the porch from the over-grown shrubs around the property, while other cats crept out of an open window. They slowly formed a circle around

Logan, surrounding him as they continued to meow. I was beginning to wonder just how averse he was to felines.

"I don't like this. What if they're planning to maul us when we step outside?" he asked, glancing around at them. "I've heard stories about cats eating people."

"Pfft. Whatever. They only eat people *after* they're dead."

"Oh, I suppose that makes it okay then," he scoffed.

Opening the screen door, I expected the cats to run at my ankles, but they didn't appear bothered by me. Keeping their distance, they watched me with wide eyes, twitching their whiskers as I knocked on the heavy main door.

"They're actually kinda cute," I pointed at a chubby white cat with a black mustache. "Look at this guy. Don't you think he looks a bit like Salvador Dali?"

"How can a cat look like Salvador Da—Oh." Logan actually stopped complaining long enough to look at the cat. "Yeah, he does look like Salvador Dali. Imagine that."

The cat meowed in response and flicked its tail from side to side. Bending down to pat its head, I felt the rumble of its purrs drift up through its body.

"Aw, he's a lover," I said. "What a cute little guy."

Logan, deciding he wasn't too freaked out by the cat after all, leaned down and put his hand up to its face for it to sniff. The result was that the cat screeched and hissed, batting his font paws at his hand before darting away into the long grass.

"Dammit!" screamed Hawthorne. "The little fucker scratched me!" A thin stream of blood was running down his hand. "What the hell? I did the same thing you did."

"I guess you're no good with animals," I said and knocked on the door again. As Logan took a few steps down the wraparound porch, I noticed the flock of cats split in two; half stayed still, keeping an eye on me. The other half closed in around my partner, following him every step of the way.

Suddenly, out of the darkness, a tiny gray tabby flew out the grass like it was spring-loaded.

"Fuck!" Logan screamed, jumping a full three inches into the air. "Where did that one come from? Aw, crap—there's another one rubbing against my leg."

"Will you relax?"

"How am I supposed to do that when I can't see shit around here?" he moaned, wiping the blood from his hand onto his pants leg.

"Aww, poor human. Can't you see in the dark?"

"Uh, no."

Flicking on his phone, he illuminated the spot in front of him with its electric glow. But the light brought him no comfort.

"Un—fucking—believable. Now I can see even *more* cats!"

"Oh my god, Logan! Would you stop bitching for two seconds?"

"What's all that ruckus out there?"

The heavy door swung open and revealed the faint glow of a single candle. Above it, Sylvia's face shone orange, the light from the flame seeping into the deep lines of her face.

"Agent Rivera? Is that you?"

"Yeah, it's me, Elena, and my partner, Agent Hawthorne," I said, approaching her slowly. "I'm so sorry if we woke you."

She shook her head.

"You didn't. I was just watching Matlock. Took me a minute to hear you knocking. Don't mind the pj's," she said, motioning to her full-length cotton nightgown. It was accessorized with a ratty bathrobe and Crocs. "I like to put them on after dinner. Never know where I'm going to fall asleep."

The dozens upon dozens of cats around us started to flock towards her, meowing and rubbing their heads up against her legs. It looked as though she was standing inside a cloud of fur. A very insistent, demanding cloud.

"Please, come in," she said, eyeing my partner's tall frame. "Watch your head. This house wasn't built for men like you."

Logan shot me an anxious glance.

"Agent Hawthorne," I said to him slowly. "This is the part where you say 'thank you'."

He hung back for a second before following me.

"Thank you, ma'am."

Following the light from her lone candle, we stepped cautiously through the cats until we entered her front door. The smell of herbs and cat piss immediately hit me, followed by notes of rot and mildew. There were probably bats living inside the walls, although I wasn't about to tell Logan. He was already muttering under his breath about the house needing to be condemned.

"You okay back there?" Sylvia asked. "I'll just take you through to the parlor."

"The parlor," Logan snickered behind me. I whipped around just long enough to tell him to shut up.

"Just in here," she said, pointing to a nearby door.

"Ow!" moaned Logan as a clatter came from beneath his feet.

"What's the matter?"

"Just tripped over a loose floorboard. Hey Sylvia, is there any chance you could turn on a light?"

"Wouldn't do much good," she said.

"What do you mean?"

"There's no electricity in here. Only have it in the kitchen."

Although I could hear my partner groaning and grumbling, I didn't share his negativity towards the dark, musty house. Aside from the moldy cat-piss smell, I enjoyed its primitive ambiance. It felt like we'd stepped into an alternate version of the eighteen-hundreds, exploring a parallel universe where humans had been replaced with cats. The flock of felines was still surrounding us as we entered, purring like tiny lawnmowers around Sylvia's feet.

"Please," she said as we entered the living room. "Make yourselves comfortable."

Now, in addition to all the cats, we were surrounded by dozens of photographs on the wall. They were all of the same handsome young man. Lighting more candles around the room, Sylvia handed one to a grateful Logan who used it to light his path to a nearby sofa. He took a seat, looking over his shoulder repeatedly as though he was afraid ghostly hands or angry claws were going to reach out of the darkness. Meanwhile, I lingered at the fireplace and studied the pictures on the wall.

"My husband," explained Sylvia with sadness filling her voice. "He was such a handsome man."

"He certainly was."

"I only had him for a few short years, but he filled my heart enough to last forever."

As she spoke, I noticed the golden glint of her wedding ring still on her finger.

"You must have loved him so much."

"I loved him more than anything. Still do."

She gave a little shrug, then walked away from the fireplace to sit beside Logan. If he was uptight before, he now looked as though he had a pole right up his ass. I didn't think it was possible for someone to look so uncomfortable in their own skin. He flinched as she cozied up beside him and lay a hand on his arm.

"I don't imagine you agents dropped in at this time of night to talk about my husband," she said. "You're here because of the little girl. The one who just went missing."

With the candle held beneath his chin, Logan looked up at me questioningly.

"I'll be honest," he leaned forward to set his candle down on the coffee table in front of him. "I'm not exactly sure why we're here. It was Elena—I mean, Agent Rivera, who wanted to see you."

Sylvia's gaze met mine and she smiled in understanding. Across the shadowy room a bond grew between us. Woman-to-woman. Spirit-to-spirit. It didn't need to be put into words. Somehow we just knew that neither of us belonged in this world.

"I did want to see you," I explained to her. "I know people laugh at you, but . . . you know things, don't you?"

Sylvia nodded her head and sat back in her seat.

"I know more than people believe."

"And you knew what I was. You figured me out."

"Indeed I did."

Taking a seat beside her, I watched the flicker of the candlelight in her sensitive eyes.

"No one's ever done that before," I told her. "People usually think I'm a little strange, but they never guessed I'm—"

"A faerie," said Sylvia. "I could see it in you the moment I looked into your eyes. I've met your people before."

Logan's eyes widened but he said nothing. Instead, he remained rooted to his cushion as a group of four cats jumped on the couch to sit beside their mistress. Soon, more of their friends came to join them and before he knew it, there was a clump of them surrounding him.

One solid black cat sat off to the side, swishing its tail as it eyed Logan suspiciously. Sylvia reached out her hand to invite him closer.

"Come here, Lafayette. Come get some snuggles."

Instead of joining the other cats, Lafayette narrowed his nearly fluorescent green eyes and turned away from her, pretending to be offended.

"He's still mad at me for giving him a buzz cut," she explained. "But my god, he was nothing but mats and burrs. It'll grow back, sweet boy. That's why you're getting fish oil at dinner."

Unwavering in his judgment, Lafayette swished his tail.

"You're not like everyone else, are you?" I asked her. "You have a gift that people here don't seem to understand or appreciate."

"Was born with it," she boasted with a smile. "Just like my mom and her mom and so on. All the women in my family were born with the second sight."

The purring around us grew louder and when I looked back at Logan he was swamped beneath a heavy pile of purring, kneading cats with a look of pure terror in his eyes. I'm pretty sure he was praying that they didn't sink their claws into his balls.

"I suppose you could call me a witch," said Sylvia. "That's what they called my ancestors before they burned them." She sighed heavily as though the witch trials were a recent memory. Judging by the age of the house, it might not have been so far-fetched of an idea. "Of course, they couldn't burn us all," she winked. "Could they, my little muffins?"

The cats purred and meowed in response.

"So, about your gift," I said. "It can make you see things on the other side, can't it? That's why you've seen all the weird things in this town that no one else has."

"That's right. They all think I'm crazy, but I can't help if their eyes weren't made to see what mine can."

"Wh—what can they see?" asked Logan, his voice muffled by a cat butt. He gingerly brushed it aside. I thought about telling him cats were more drawn to people who don't like them, but this was just too entertaining to watch.

"I can see different entities," she said. "Creatures, spirits, you know. Things that live in other dimensions."

"Like faeries?" asked Logan.

"Oh sure, among other things." Sylvia gave a knowing nod as she continued to cuddle her cats. "I've always had the ability to see things the normal people can't. Not unless they're trained or born sensitive like I was."

Logan, trying to softly push a tortoiseshell cat out of his face, sucked in a lungful of fur-free air. "So you're saying that all the things McKinney's been telling us are real?"

The old woman laughed to herself.

"What he knows is just the tip of the iceberg. Most people wouldn't believe the things I've seen . . . The lights in the sky, the entities, all of it. It can't neatly be packaged up into a traditional horror story. The things that happened to me, well, they're not your average ghost stories. It all goes deeper than that."

She paused for a second and stared off into the shadows with a serene look on her face.

"My people have always lived on this land, long before the town of Yarbrough was here," she said. "Us women always knew the land was sacred. I remember my great-grandma telling me it held a portal that could be opened by those initiated into the mystical realm."

"Like Skinwalker Ranch," I said, thinking out loud.

"Skinwalker Ranch?" Logan didn't bother to hide his contemptuous laugh. "I've heard of that place. Didn't some billionaire send a bunch of researchers out there to try and prove the existence of aliens or something?"

"It's a lot more complicated than that," I said, rolling my eyes. "The land there was sacred to the indigenous people for hundreds of years before the ranch was built. And things have been seen on that land that don't make sense. Things that defy explanation. Humanoid creatures, lights in the sky, monsters, orbs, black helicopters . . . everything. It's like the ranch won at paranormal bingo."

"Sounds a lot like Yarbrough," said Sylvia. "Just like here, the land at Skinwalker Ranch was thought to be a portal to another dimension. One that all the creatures from beyond could escape from."

"But Yarbrough is different," said Logan, trying desperately to appear rational even as he was surrounded by cats. "In this place, people get trapped *inside* of it instead of escaping from it. As far as I know, no one went missing at Skinwalker Ranch."

We all thought for a second, sitting in silence. Even the cats stopped purring as though they too were deep in contemplation.

"There's something different happening here," said Sylvia. "This isn't just a matter of things that go bump in the night. There's something methodical behind these missing kids. They're not stumbling into another dimension. They're being *taken* there."

"That's exactly why we need you," I said. "I think you

can reach the other side. If you truly have second sight, then you can see where they are."

For the first time, Sylvia appeared panicked and sat bolt upright. The cat in her lap plopped onto the floor.

"I can't do that."

"Of course you can," I urged. "Sylvia, you have the ability to see into the faerie realm like no one else can."

"Except *you*," she said. "You're fae. No one will know the kingdom like you do." I could feel Logan's eyes focused on me, but I was still looking at Sylvia.

"If I go, there's a good chance I won't come back," I told her. "It's a long story, but if anyone recognizes me I'll be killed on sight. I'm considered a risk to Queen Solana's throne. Do you really think she'll let me enter her kingdom and live?"

"No," she said, Even Logan appeared wary and concerned as the realization hit him.

"What good am I to those kids if I'm dead?" I was sitting on the edge of my seat, hoping that my point was being made. "We need someone who's skilled enough to go into the Hollows, into the fae realm, and not be recognized. I can't think of anyone more perfect for the job than you."

For a long moment, Sylvia looked down into her lap. Another cat had taken the place of the one that fell out. Finally, she raised her head and looked me in the eye.

"Alright. I'll do it. No one else can."

16

LOGAN

"It's called remote viewing," explained Sylvia as she cleared a space on the floor.

I knelt down beside her, moving my candle from one hand to the other, trying to avoid setting Sylvia or one of her four-legged minions on fire. Around us, the cats settled in a circle, their eyes reflecting green and yellow in the candlelight.

"What's remote viewing?" I asked, sitting cross-legged. Elena joined us on the floor, the three of us sitting in a triangle.

"It makes me a conduit," explained Sylvia. "Makes time and space irrelevant. Means that I can see right through the matrix of existence."

I looked blankly at her. Of all the responses I was expecting, that wasn't anywhere on my radar.

"So . . . you're saying that you can defy the nature of physics?"

"Pretty much," said Sylvia, reaching onto the lower shelf of her coffee table. "Let me just get my things and we'll get started."

Dear god. She was acting like we were about to dive into a ten-thousand piece jigsaw puzzle, but no. We were going to bend space and time to our will. I decided to keep my mouth shut and pay attention for the report I was inevitably going to have to write later.

Pulling a sleeping mask and a notepad and pen off the shelf, she set them down in front of her, running her hands over each item in a quiet ritual.

"You can see anything when you do this?" I asked. "Does that mean spirits too?"

"Sometimes. And aliens."

"Aliens?" Oh wow. I was in for a real show.

"Yes, I can see them too, although I'd rather not. They give me the heebie-jeebies."

"Let me get this straight. You're basically telling me your brain is a giant telescope that can see through all the different dimensions of the universe. Is that right?"

"No. I can see through all the dimensions of *multiple* universes," she said with a smile as she lifted the sleeping mask to her face.

"In layman's terms, she's a psychic," Elena said. "But remote viewing is a little different than just sensing the other side."

"That's right," agreed Sylvia. "I'd like to think this is safer."

"Have you always been able to do this?"

"Seeing to the other side is something I'd always been able to do," said Sylvia. "But controlled remote view like this? That took time and practice."

"I thought there *was* no time," I laughed. "Or whatever it was you said."

"You're learning quickly," chuckled Sylvia. "Now let's begin."

With the mask over her eyes, she took her notepad and hovered her pen over it for a second. Then, as though her body had been shot with a jolt of electricity, her arm started jerking wildly across the page so a variety of squiggles fell on the paper.

"Is that it?" I asked, craning my neck to get a better view of the paper. "Is that what you see?"

"I haven't even started yet," said Sylvia. "That was me just getting the excess electricity out of my brain."

I glanced over at Elena, feeling a little confused and a little concerned. I didn't know what was weirder. The sight of Sylvia on the floor blindfolded and humming to herself as she scribbled wildly, or the feeling of having countless cats stare into the back of my head. I could feel their eyes on me, giving me the impression that if I so much as spoke out of turn to their owner, they'd gouge my eyes out.

Turning to the one on my right, the black one she called Lafayette, I secretly thought, *Please don't kill me with your murder mittens.* He blinked slowly in response, as though he could hear my thoughts. Then he lifted a paw and proceeded to clean his toes, all while watching me with those bright green eyes.

With a shiver, I turned back to Sylvia. She was humming louder now, the pen in her hand making great big circular motions over the page as though she had no control over it. Elena was watching with mild interest, the same way you'd casually watch television. I wondered if anything unsettled her. Because so far, almost everything I'd encountered over the last couple of days had unsettled the shit out of me.

"Relax," Sylvia suddenly blurted out. "I'm talking to you, Agent Hawthorne."

"I'm perfectly relaxed," I said, my voice squeaking to betray me. Sylvia laughed softly and carried on scribbling.

"I can tell you're very tense," she said in between hums. "I can almost smell the tension coming off you. And I suppose the cats can smell it too. Just relax. This won't work unless everyone in the room is on the right vibration."

I looked to Elena for some guidance, but she just smiled.

"Don't overthink it," she instructed. "Just chill."

But chill was the last thing I could possibly do. Regardless, for the sake of professionalism, I took a deep breath to encourage Sylvia to do her thing.

Whatever that thing was.

"I'm calm," I told her. "I'm fine."

"Are you sure?"

I took another deep breath.

"Just empty your mind," she said. "Just think of nothing."

I closed my eyes for a second, but the more nothing I tried to think of, the more stuff entered my mind. Images popped up, dozens of them. Snippets of the last couple of days and worries I had for the future. Not just worries about these local families, but the family I'd hoped to start building with Bridget. I thought about finding her wrinkled up sugar daddy hiding under her bed. What was I even thinking? She would've been a terrible parent, and my mom would've hated her. Dad was only nice to her because she was pretty. I could imagine her forgetting to pick the kids up from school because she was busy getting her nails done. I could also imagine her calling them an Uber instead of picking them up. It was easy to imagine because it had happened to me once after coming home from a business trip.

The more I tried to empty my mind, the more it filled up with meaningless crap.

"Your brain is all over the place, Agent Hawthorne," said Sylvia. "Stop trying so hard. Don't think about anything. Don't do anything. Just be."

"Just be . . . " I repeated, feeling hopelessly lost. "Okay . . ."

"Just . . . be . . . "

That's when Lafayette chose to crawl into my lap and wedge his body against my thighs as I sat on the floor. The tip of his tail curled slowly to one side, and then the other. Was this a test? Had Sylvia sent him over here to keep my brain focused on one thing? Because right now, I only had one thought in my head.

Don't piss off the cat.

I rested my hands on my knees and sat as still as I could. I wasn't going to move. I wasn't going to push him away. I wasn't going to pet him.

Don't do anything . . . I thought. *Just be . . .*

And with that, my mind floated away on a cloud of nothingness, and all that existed were the sensations of my body and the breath that ebbed and flowed from my lungs. There were no more thoughts or worries, no time. Just blankness, and with it came a sense of serenity.

"Very good," said Sylvia. "You're a fast learner."

Elena smiled again at me, and for some reason, her smile didn't just reach my eyes. It reached into my soul, my heart, right into that sense of being Sylvia talked about.

Despite the darkness and the musty smell of the cats, that smile filled me with a fresh sunbeam of white light. And right then, with the three of us sitting together, I felt as though we were connected. I even felt connected to the damned cat in my lap, along with all the others around us. It felt like being linked by an invisible string that ran through Sylvia.

"We're ready," she said, and finally stopped scribbling. "Let's begin."

For a second, she sat in silence with perfect stillness. I could barely see the rise and fall of her chest as she breathed. The only flicker of movement on her face seemed to be coming from the candlelight. She reminded me of the wax figures at Madame Tussaud's. For a brief moment, I thought maybe she'd died, and I thought about leaning over to check for a pulse. But before I could move, she shifted abruptly and blurted out, "I'm going now."

"Going where?"

"Into the other side. I'm leaving this dimension."

I looked to Elena and saw her lean back against a chair, gently stroking a fluffy orange cat as it purred. There was no trace of worry on her face. It was the same look my mom had in her eyes when she used to watch Oprah.

"What do you see?" Elena asked Sylvia. "Can you see Elphame? Can you see any of the fae kingdoms?"

"Not yet. It's very dark. There's a lot of . . . noise. Not noise that comes from sound but . . . interference. Like static, as though someone's blocking the channel."

The way she spoke made me think of basic, rudimentary technical mishaps, not entering magical kingdoms in other dimensions.

"Yes, static," she confirmed. "There's a lot of it. I've experienced it before and it's very difficult to overcome. It's . . . a defense."

"What kind of defense?" I asked.

"Someone has put all this interference here so people can't see; so they can't get in."

"It's a psychic defense," explained Elena.

"Yes, that's exactly it," nodded Sylvia. "Whoever put it up knew there would be people seeking answers about the kingdom. This is meant to stop them."

She flinched as though she'd been hit, then held a hand to her chest as though she'd been afflicted with a terrible pain.

"It hurts," she cried, leaning forward. "All this noise, it's hurting me terribly."

I didn't understand what she was going through, but I could see the pain on her face. Whatever she was experiencing was very real. So real that it made her pale cheeks turn dark pink and made her eyes water. She wrinkled up her face as she dug her nails into the front of her nightgown and fell forward so her face was almost touching her knees.

"Sylvia, do I need to call an ambulance?"

"This is more than a defense," she said, ignoring me. "It's an attack. They're trying to push people out of the kingdom. Trying to force out those who can see their darkness for what it really is."

"Just stop this, okay?" I begged, laying my hand on her back. I could feel how hot and agitated she'd become as sweat poured through the thin fabric of her nightgown. "Sylvia, I'm worried about you."

But she just shook me off and said, "I don't ever stop. I never turn back! I've done this before and I've experienced worse."

Lafayette was still sitting in my lap, unfazed by what was going on. Even Elena appeared relatively fine with what she was witnessing. Seeing the worry on my face, she reached over and pushed my hand off Sylvia.

"It's okay," she assured me. "Someone as experienced as her knows what they're doing. She's prepared for this."

"Well, I'm not prepared for this. What if something happens to her? She looks like she's having a heart attack."

"She'll be fine," she insisted. "Sylvia's stronger than you think."

I was doubtful but felt like an amateur among experts. With no idea what to do, I sat back and gave Sylvia room.

Part of me still hoped none of this was real, that Sylvia was just a lonely, eccentric old woman playing the part of a psychic. Trying to be the skeptic I was raised and trained to be, I attempted to mentally detach myself from whatever Sylvia was experiencing. Instead, I tried to view it all as though I was simply examining a piece of evidence.

She was still clutching her chest and gritting her teeth from the pain as sweat poured down from her face. But the weirdest thing of all was the cats' behavior. The ones that were previously purring were now violently thrashing their tails from side to side. Their pupils dilated as if they were honing in on prey, and the hair along their backs was sticking up. I didn't know what they could see, but whatever it was angered them to the point of bringing out their claws which they scratched against the wooden floor.

"Where are you?" Elena asked Sylvia. "Are you still in the static?"

"I'm almost out of it. Good lord, it's thick! Like walking through electrified molasses. It still hurts to high heaven. Feels like these grains of electricity are attacking every cell in my body. But I can get through it."

She gritted her teeth one last time and held her breath as the beads of sweat on her brow trickled down her temples.

"Sweet baby Jesus," she grunted. "I haven't felt a defense as strong as this since . . . since . . . Since I entered . . . "

She paused for a second and I leaned forward to hear her better.

"Since you entered where, Sylvia?"

Her jaw was clenched so tight it looked like the muscles of her cheekbones were ready to pop. Drops of sweat continued to roll down her face. Even though she was wearing a mask, I could tell that her eyes were squeezed shut. The veins in her forehead pushed themselves to the surface of her paper-thin skin.

"Since I entered . . . ." she gasped. "Since I entered Hell."

Hell . . . Did she really just say that?

I looked for a sign that I'd heard her wrong, but the terror in her voice and the pain that ran rampant through her body was obvious.

"Hell?" Elena repeated. "You've been there?"

I nearly fell over.

Here was my partner, asking this poor old woman about visiting Hell like she'd taken a rare trip to Antarctica.

She clutched her chest tight one last time as though the very word itself had sent her into a tailspin of agony. Then she let go of her nightgown, sucked in a deep gasp, and fell limp across the carpet.

"Sylvia!"

Elena and I rushed to her pale, sweat-covered body. She looked up through her thin, silvery wisps of hair, and rubbed her eyes after pulling the sleep mask from her face.

"Don't worry about me," she croaked, her voice sounding haggard yet relieved. "I'm safe now. I've reached the other side."

17

ELENA

"We need to end this *now*," Logan said as he coaxed Sylvia up to a seated position. "Enough is enough. Someone's going to get hurt."

But as I noted the fear on his own face, I guessed it wasn't just for Sylvia's sake that he wanted to bring the session to an end. Whether he'd ever admit it or not, he was genuinely freaked out.

"I can keep going," Sylvia argued, gently pushing Logan away from her. "I can handle this. We have to keep going."

"But Sylvia, I'm worried about your safety," he said.

"We have to go on," she insisted. "It doesn't hurt anymore now that I'm on the other side of the static. Might as well take a look around now that we're here. Think of all those poor babies missin' their mamas. I gotta at least *try*."

And with that, she patted her hands down the sides of her arms as though she was dusting herself off, crossed her legs, and once again reached for her blindfold.

"Can we get on with it, then?"

"Are you sure you're okay with this?" asked Logan.

"She said she was," I reminded him. "Sylvia wouldn't do it otherwise."

"What if she has a heart attack for fuck's sake?"

Sylvia pulled down a corner of her blindfold and stared at him.

"I can hear you, Agent Hawthorne. Stop acting like I don't know my own mind. I said I can do this and I'm doing it. Now let's take our positions, shall we?"

Resuming our previous triangle formation, with the cats still forming a circle around us, we prepared ourselves to continue.

"I'm really not sure about this," whispered Hawthorne.

"Shhh!" Sylvia hissed at him. "Elena? Hand me my pen, will you, honey?"

I picked it up and slid it into her arthritic hands. I half expected her to jab Logan with it, but she held it above a fresh sheet of paper instead.

"What are you seeing?"

"I see lots of grey. Like a mist."

"What else?"

Her forehead wrinkled up over the top of her blindfold as she frowned.

"Figures," she said. "Small figures. Like people crossed with ants. Maybe they're sprites."

Hawthorne turned and shot me a quizzical look.

"Sprites are like goblins," I explained.

"But these aren't like the regular ones I've seen," elaborated Sylvia with a flick of her pen across the page. "They're darker with bigger eyes. They're more like a shadow. Oh! Their arms! Christ, their arms and legs are bent all over tarnation like they're made of wood."

Her arms began moving rapidly as though she couldn't stop it, drawing so fast the ink from her leaky pen smudged across the paper. She scribbled at lightning speed as though her arm had been possessed by a laser jet printer.

Finding himself enthralled, Hawthorne leaned in closer to see the result of her manic drawing. At first, neither of us could make out what we were seeing. It looked like nothing more than chicken scratch, a mess of tangled inky scribbles and cobwebs trailing across the paper. But then the figures started to take shape. They were tiny at first, and then there were dozens of them. They resembled spiders more than people. That was until she started drawing the eyes. In nothing but a few strokes of her pen she'd illustrated a gaze so full of malice that it sent a jolt of evil into the pit of my stomach.

"They're looking at me like this," she said, her voice breaking as though she was close to tears. "They can see me plain as day. Dear lord."

Logan's mouth was one flat line of nervous trepidation. If this was his reaction when he was seeing just a drawing of sprites, I couldn't imagine what he would feel if he saw them in real life.

"What are they doing?" I asked Sylvia.

"Just watching."

"Are they moving towards you?"

"No, I'm moving towards them. They're letting me walk through the grayness, but they're watching every move I make. Oh . . . this is so much worse than aliens!"

"Do they know why you're there?"

"They don't know anything," she said, gaining comfort from this observation. "They're simple creatures with hardly the sense that god gave a mule."

"Why are they there?" Logan asked.

Sylvia frowned again as though she was in pain, then

shook her head ever so slightly like she was trying to shake out a disturbing thought.

"They're telling me they're here to watch. That's all they do. They watch everything."

"Everything down there?"

"Well . . . sounds like they watch everything up on the surface world too? They're like . . . I don't know . . . CCTV. They can force themselves between the cracks in the dimensions. They watch from the shadows of the world so their leader can learn as much as possible."

"Who's their leader?"

Sylvia shook her head again, struggling to understand what she was hearing on the other side.

"I don't . . . I don't . . . I can't quite make it out. The Silver . . . " She frowned and tilted one ear down towards the floor. "The Silver Lady? The Silver Queen? The one with the big black eyes."

Logan's eyes darted over to mine, and if it weren't for the warmth of the candlelight, I'd have guessed he turned a few shades paler.

"Is she down there now?" I was desperate to know.

But Sylvia couldn't answer because once again her arm was possessed and she was scribbling wildly. Endless lines of ink traveling across the page until a form emerged through the spaghetti strings of her drawing.

The first thing I saw was the long hair, then the enormous eyes followed, staring out at me from the page. Even though it was a sketch on a notebook, I felt like they could see me just like they had when I was a little girl, fleeing from her in the forest. It was the first time I'd seen Solana since that awful day. She felt as real on that paper as she'd felt in real life.

"Sylvia? Tell me, is she there?"

She said nothing, just gritted her teeth together and continued to scrawl. The outline of Solana's long, flowing dress began to take shape.

"Sylvia? Sylvia! If she's there, you have to run!"

When she didn't answer again, I grew desperate. I grabbed her by the shoulders, pulling her towards me.

"Sylvia! Get out of there!"

She struggled against my grasp, thrashing in my arms.

"Elena, let her go!" Logan yelled.

But I couldn't. I had to know how close she was. I had to know if Solana was in reach.

"Listen to me Sylvia, you have to tell me if she's there."

With one hand still grabbing her left shoulder, I raised my other to her blindfold and gently peeled back the edge to look into her eyes.

Fucking hell. I really wish I hadn't.

The only thing I could see were the whites of her eyeballs as her eyes turned themselves back inside her head. She began to shake violently, her already stiff fingers twisting into unnatural shapes.

"Let her go!" Logan shouted, trying to pull her away from me, but I ignored him.

"Sylvia! Can you hear me?" I yelled.

"Agent Rivera! She's having a goddamn seizure!" Logan screamed at me. "Get her on her side, *now*!"

"She's not having a seizure! She's seeing things. She's seeing Solana!"

The two of us struggled against each other. Logan desperate to lay her down. Me dying to know more of her vision.

"Hawthorne, don't you fucking touch her!"

"Put her in the fucking recovery position *now*, Rivera! She needs medical attention!"

"No, she doesn't!"

"Goddammit Elena, listen to me right—"

His words were interrupted by a noise so loud it sent us both reeling back into the corners of the room with the cats sprinting in opposite directions. Even though my hands were pressed against my ears, it sounded like a train rattling through the house. The very walls were threatening to cave in. The air surrounding us roared like an airplane landing before promptly crashing into a fireball. It sounded like the descent into hell.

And that awful sound was coming from Sylvia's mouth.

Her face was now nothing but a black hole from which the caustic sound emanated, filling the room at such force and volume I was sure my eardrums were about to burst. It was so loud and ferocious that it blew red hot wind around the sides of my face. Windows shattered as loose papers and cat toys flew around the room.

I felt a strong hand curl around my wrist. I opened my eyes to see Logan's terrified face in front of mine.

"Elena! Run!"

The cats brave enough to stick around or too blind and deaf to care were now hissing and screaming with their claws out, ready to attack whatever force had possessed their owner. Logan's grip on my arm tightened as he pulled me away from the center of the circle.

"Run!" he shouted.

"No! We can't just leave her!"

I went flying through the air just long enough to realize he'd thrown me over his shoulder. I squirmed, but his strong arms held my thighs in place. He rushed through the dark house, his shoes crunching on broken glass while the candlelight in the living room dwindled to nothing but a speck at the end of the hall.

"Hawthorne, you idiot! Put me down! We can't leave her right in the middle of this!"

He stumbled down the steps, into the cool night air, leaving the chaos behind us as he finally set me down. We could still hear her screaming, along with the hissing of the cats. The windows rattled and walls of the house trembled from the force that continued to rush out from Sylvia's body.

"I'm not going back in there until I know what the fuck we're dealing with," Logan said and took out his Glock.

"Put your gun away before you hurt someone!" I yelled, walking towards him at a steady clip. "What's your target, huh? You can't shoot at something that doesn't have a body!"

He kept the gun aimed at the ground, but he wasn't ready to put it away. I suppose I couldn't blame him, given the chaos going on inside the house.

"That sound . . . " he yelled over the noise. "Fuck me, that sound! It isn't *human*!"

I shrugged, stepping a little closer so I didn't have to shout in his face.

"I've heard worse. Put your gun away. We need to go back inside and find out what she's seeing."

Fear dried the words up in his mouth leaving him breathless and pale.

"You've got to be fucking kidding me! I don't want a single part of whatever the hell she's doing. I don't even . . . I don't even know what that could be! It sounded like a battle cry. No. It was more than that. It was—"

His desperate attempts to explain the noise appeared to soothe him, and he started breathing deeper as the color returned to his cheeks. But I could still make out the sheen of nervous sweat as the moonlight fell on his face.

"Try not to pressure yourself into explaining it," I told him, moving. "You'll drive yourself insane if you try to understand everything."

The look of terror returned to his eyes.

"Whatever we started is evil!"

The moment the words fell from his mouth, the screaming from inside the house abruptly stopped. An overwhelming stillness lay over the house and the surrounding forest. No bullfrogs, no crickets. Nothing. Even the cats stopped screeching. The only thing I heard was my ringing ears.

We both turned and looked at the darkened front porch as though Sylvia would appear. I took a step forward, ready to head back in, but as I raised my foot onto the first step, I felt Logan's hand on my shoulder.

"Don't."

"What do you mean . . . don't?" I snapped while shaking him off my shoulder. "You were the one who said she needed medical attention. What if she's hurt?"

"There's evil in that house," he told me. "That woman . . . "

"That woman is our best chance at helping us find those missing kids!"

He thought for a second with his mouth dropped slightly open. I could see the fear and confusion on his face. He was out of his depth. Holstering his gun, he obviously had no idea what to do next.

Poor guy.

I guess my parlor trick with the dandelion hadn't quite prepared him for the levels of paranormal activity that we saw regularly in the Occult Crimes Division. He was still a total virgin.

Well . . . maybe not anymore. Not after what had just happened.

As I looked into his scared, nervous face, I was overcome with the most unexpected feeling; I had the strongest compulsion to nurture him. To care for him and keep him safe. Like a baby bird that had been knocked out of its nest after a storm.

It was a ludicrous feeling of course. He was a big guy. Strong. Fast. Highly trained. He didn't need some fae to look out for him, but the more I thought about it, the more I realized this was exactly what Chief Harris had in mind when he'd thrown us together. Logan needed me as much as I needed him.

"C'mon, Brad," I said, trying to lighten the mood. "Let's get back in there and finish what we started."

He shook his head and clenched his eyes shut as he struggled to process what he had just witnessed.

"How do I know what we're working with if I can't understand it? If I can't explain it?"

"You don't need to fully understand it. Not right now." He nodded in acknowledgment and straightened himself back up. "There will be plenty of time for you to come to terms with everything you're seeing. Until then, just observe it. Sit with it."

"How?" he said, stopping in his tracks. "How do you do it?"

"Do what?"

"Just go around without being scared of a single thing in the world?"

"I've been scared of stuff," I told him.

"I don't believe that. I know you've been angry. You've been overwhelmed or sad. But afraid? Does your faerie brain even allow for fear?"

I put my hand on my hip.

"Does your human brain ever—oh, nevermind." Realizing how much he needed me for guidance right now, I patted the side of his bicep. It was like comforting a brick wall. "Look, Logan . . . I know that seemed a little fucked up in there, but Sylvia's our best shot at rescuing these missing kids. And Chief Harris knew what he was doing when he assigned us as partners. I'm gonna go back inside. You can stay out here if you want, but I think you should come with me."

Logan nodded at me, then looked up at the house. From where we stood, it was barely visible behind the thick foliage, kudzu, and wildflowers. You could even be forgiven for thinking it wasn't there at all. From beyond the treeline, an owl hooted.

I stepped up onto the porch just as a white cat with a gray spot on its chest walked out and meowed softly to welcome us back inside. We walked in silence through the disheveled rooms, where the cats were now lounging in the moonlight, basking in its silver rays. Lafayette sat nearby, twitching his tail either in impatience or general disapproval. I could've sworn he shook his head at us.

"I'll never get used to all these cats," said Hawthorne as we reached the front door.

"Really? I think some of them like you."

"You think so?"

"Nah. I'm fucking with you."

We both stood for a second at the doorway and looked down another long, dark hall. From the back of the house, we could hear a gentle clanking noise as though someone was moving pots and pans.

"Hello?" I called out. "Sylvia, are you okay?"

"Yeah, I'm fine!" she called back.

I shared a surprised look with Logan, but I could see the worry visibly drain from his face.

We both eagerly stepped into the house and down the hall, following the faint glow of a dozen flickering candles from the last room.

"In here!" Sylvia called out. "I'm in the kitchen."

As we walked down the hall, we could smell the comforting, warm scent of coffee and pastries baking in the oven.

"Sylvia?" I asked, stepping through the doorway. After leaving her on the floor screaming demonically with her face contorted into an unnatural shape, I wasn't sure what condition she'd be in when we found her. Would she still have that god-awful black hole where her face had been?

But what I saw instead was a chipper Sylvia moving around her dimly lit kitchen arranging coffee cups and cutlery.

"Hey, y'all," she said with a smile. "I'm sorry I scared you."

"It's . . . okay," Logan managed to say, still shocked at the sudden transformation in her.

"I've put some biscuits in the oven," she said. "And I've made some coffee. Good lord, I need a pick me up right now. I'm sure you both do too."

"That's an understatement," exhaled Logan. "You wouldn't have anything stronger than coffee, would you?"

"Sure do. I made it myself," said Sylvia, reaching into the pantry and handing over a glass jar with a mysterious clear amber colored liquid inside it. The writing on the label was too faded to read.

"What is it?" asked Logan as he gratefully took it from her hand. "Moonshine?"

"Apple pie moonshine," Sylvia said while pulling on an oven mitt. "It's my secret recipe."

Logan raised an eyebrow, although I noticed he wasn't nearly as skeptical as he would've looked a day ago.

"Is apple pie moonshine even a thing?"

"Yep. I made this batch on the last full moon. And it's been blessed."

"By who?" I asked, watching Logan struggle with the lid.

"By me."

If Sylvia could see into other dimensions, I didn't doubt that she could also make her own moonshine and bless it too. She took a tray of biscuits out of the oven and set them on a plate to cool before plunking down a jar of honey next to them. My eyes widened like a cat that had caught sight of a moth.

While I slathered honey on a biscuit and shoved it into my mouth, I watched as Logan wrestled with the mason jar.

"You need a little muscle?" I asked him with my mouth full.

"Nah, I got it."

He tried to twist the cap off again, this time with so much effort he blew his cheeks out like a trumpet player.

"For fuck's sake, dude. Just gimme it."

Relieving him of the jar, I twisted the lid and gave it back to him, not bothering to hide my victorious grin.

With the booze now flowing, he took his dainty china coffee cup and poured in a liberal splash. We were all immediately assaulted by the smell of it. I couldn't detect any hint of apples or spices among the alcoholic vapors. It was alcoholic alright, definitely over 100 proof, but there was something else lurking in there . . . something deep and earthy.

"Are you sure this isn't gasoline?" winced Logan, screwing up both his mouth and eyes as the vapors stung his face.

"You be careful with that now," warned Sylvia. "Same old stuff went and blinded my grand-pappy."

"*Now* you tell me!"

But it didn't stop my partner from raising the cup to his lips and taking a long drink. He gagged as soon as it reached his tongue, then shook himself off like a wet dog before going in for round two.

"You okay?" I asked as he choked the stuff down. He nodded, and I turned to my cup of coffee. It was going to take a lot of sugar and cream to get it to a point where I could drink it. I started adding sweetener by the spoonful.

"Would you like a drop of something extra?" Sylvia asked me, nodding towards the mason jar.

Usually, I'd be the first to say yes, but right then, I didn't think it was the best idea. Especially not when my partner was still recovering from having his mind blown.

"No thanks. The coffee and biscuits are fine for now." I reached out for another warm pastry and slathered it in more honey.

"Suit yourself," said Sylvia, reaching for the jar. "Agent Hawthorne, can I offer you some more?"

Logan already looked like he'd had plenty. I could see his eyes had become bleary even though he'd only had two sips.

"No fank yoooou, Miss Sylvia."

"Are you drunk already?" I laughed. My partner gave me the goofiest smile. It was kinda cute. Actually, it was super cute.

"I might be." Logan held my gaze for a second, then threw his head back and burst out laughing.

"Are you sure it's just apples and spices you put in there?" I asked Sylvia. "And not some kind of psychedelic?"

Her twinkling eyes snapped wide open, and the grin fell off her face as she hurried back to the pantry. Her groan of frustration was not comforting.

"Dammit! I think I gave him the wrong stuff," she said, returning with another mason jar of amber liquid. I unscrewed the lid and was met with another whiff of alcohol, but this time it smelled like apple pie. I cocked my head as I closed the container and stared at our host.

"If this is the apple pie moonshine, then what did Agent Hawthorne just drink?"

Sylvia wrung her hands nervously as she gazed at the nearly identical jars.

"Pretty sure that's the ol' mushroom tincture I use for my vision quests."

I did a two-handed facepalm and took a deep breath. Then I slid my hands down my face and looked at Logan. Even in the dim light, his pupils were twice as wide as they should've been.

Fuck.

"Hey, Elena?" he asked, leaning across the table towards me. "Why does it look there are purple beams coming out of your ears?"

I blinked in disbelief.

"*What?*"

"Beams. Purple ones. They're like . . . all around your ears."

I looked back at Sylvia and briefly had an urge to strangle her. Who the hell kept hallucinogenic mushroom tincture in their liquor cabinet? I sighed, knowing exactly who'd do something like that.

Sylvia.

"We've just drugged a federal agent," I said, getting up from my chair. "How am I supposed to take him back to the station like this?"

"Oh, hush. He's fine. If anything, it'll open up his mind."

I supposed that was true, but it didn't change the fact that I was now the only competent adult out here. I stepped up to my partner and wrapped an arm around his shoulder.

"Hey, buddy. I'm going to have to confiscate your gun, okay? Just for a little while, until you feel better." Good grief—I sounded like I was talking to a puppy or a toddler. "Can you take off your belt for me and hand it over?"

Still grinning all cute and goofy-like, Logan nodded his head and unfastened his belt. I double-checked that the safety was on, then secured it around my waist. For good measure, I reached into the pocket where he kept the car keys and stole those as well. Taking what was left of his drink and dumping it into the sink, I set the cup in front of him and filled it back up with coffee.

"He's been wearing them shackles too long, anyway," Sylvia declared as Lafayette hopped on the table to join us. I half expected him to ask for a dish of half & half, but instead, he just sat near Logan, watching him carefully.

"Been carrying around all these rigid beliefs," Sylvia added. "The kind that makes a person stop believing in the magic of the universe."

"Yeah . . . I suppose you're right about that," I agreed. That didn't make my situation any better.

"This will set him straight. Just you wait and see. I bet he'll have his own vision quest. He'll wake up tomorrow morning with a slight headache, but he'll see things differently from now on. He'll be a believer."

"This is all still really new to him. That noise you made in the living room scared the hell out of him. I didn't know what to tell him. I've never heard anything like it before."

Sylvia glanced down at the table as though she was embarrassed.

"What did you see?" I asked her. "You mentioned a queen. Tell me what you saw her doing."

"You don't want to know."

"Of course I do. I'm the one who asked you to go to the other side. Please, you have to tell me what you saw."

Her eyes glossed over and she shrank back as if she was trying to disappear inside herself.

"I can't. Not right now. I'll tell you some other time. Just not now." Her hands began to shake as she stared into the distance.

"You talked about goblins," I pressed. "What else did you see?"

Her hands shook even more as her arms and legs joined in. Soon, her whole body was shaking so much the wooden chair she was sitting in began to wobble.

"I don't wanna . . . I can't tell you because . . . oh I just can't tell you!"

"Yes you can!" I said, holding one of her hands to steady her. "You have to!"

Standing up, she violently pulled herself away from me and ran for the door.

"Sylvia!"

I heard her stumble out in the darkness of the hall as a couple dozen cats scattered through the house.

"Sylvia!" I called out, hurrying after her.

The only light came from the candles behind me and

the kitchen beyond. Ahead of me, there was nothing but darkness and the sound of soft footsteps on the creaky floors upstairs.

"Elena?" came Logan's bashful, boyish voice from behind me. "You have such a beautiful energy around you right now."

I turned round to see him staring at me in awe.

"It's all around you," he said, raising his hands and pushing them towards me. "It's beautiful."

Fuck my life, I thought. *I need to get this idiot home.*

But there was no way I could take him back to Sheriff McKinney's place. Not in this state. It probably wasn't safe to stick him up in the treehouse, either. I could just imagine him wanting to commune with nature and fly with the bats and owls, only to fall out the window and bust out his teeth.

"Agent Hawthorne, I have an important assignment for you," I said, leading him back to the kitchen. I topped off his coffee and took a quick survey of the room for anything dangerous. I didn't see any knives, but who was I kidding? It should've been condemned years ago. "You sit here and drink your coffee, okay? I'm going to find Sylvia but I need you to stay here."

Logan nodded as he looked down into the cup. He smiled as if he was seeing magical visions of pure splendor. Maybe he was.

"Wow," he breathed in wonder. "It's just so beautiful. Every drop is just . . . whoa."

"Yeah, every drop is whoa. Just make sure you drink it. If you finish it all you can have some water from the sink."

Taking the candle, I left him there gazing wondrously into his glass. Out in the hall, I tiptoed over piles of broken glass and heaps of cats until I reached the stairs. They looked far too weak and rickety to hold the weight of a person. As soon as I put my foot on the bottom step, it creaked and groaned, threatening to collapse.

"Sylvia? Are you okay?"

I could hear her sobbing in the distance.

"Sylvia? Look, you don't have to tell me what you saw. Not right now anyway. But can you at least tell me you're okay?"

Her sobbing grew louder in response.

"Fuck," I said to myself as I realized I was going to have to go up and find her.

Hoping that every step I climbed wouldn't bring me closer to death, I ascended the stairs with bated breath and prayed I would at least reach the top alive. When I got halfway there, I looked down and sighed.

There was no turning back.

18

LOGAN

"Hey! Where are you going?" I called out to the shrinking figure of Elena as she disappeared down the hall.

Now alone in the kitchen, I was faced with nothing but a handful of cats and a single moonbeam shining through the window. It reflected into my cup, leaving a mesmerizing trail of colors in my coffee.

"Wow . . . "

It looked like a rainbow pearl held between my hands, and I lost myself in the image.

I could dive right into that pearl. I could live in those colors.

Out in the hall, I could hear Elena's footsteps with each creak of the floorboards.

"Elena? Come back here. You gotta see this moonbeam! It's like a pearl fell through a rainbow and landed in my coffee!"

The only response was the sound of her creaking her way up the stairs and calling out for Sylvia.

Ah, Sylvia, I thought as I looked around her kitchen. *She'd understand the beauty in this cup.*

I took another sip of my coffee and melted back into my seat. Staring at the walls, I was suddenly overwhelmed with the beauty of the wallpaper—pink with peony flowers. Why wasn't this in the Smithsonian? It was the most glorious thing I'd ever seen. But so were the kitchen cabinets in their off-shade of beige with rusted brass handles. And then there was the sink. Every chip in the white enameled cast iron told a story. It was such a beautiful sink.

As I watched the moonlight glint off the faucet, I had the most overwhelming urge to jump up take a closer look.

"Whoa! So shiny."

I leaned in closer and watched silver trails of moonlight leap out from the bottom of the basin.

Why has no one told me how beautiful sinks are before? Have I always taken them for granted?

As I stared, I realized a slight drip was coming from the faucet. Just a single drop falling every ten seconds. Or was it every ten minutes? There was no way of knowing, and it didn't matter, anyway. Time was useless. All that mattered was the shine of the moonlight and the hypnotic sound of each drop as it fell into the sink. It felt as though its energy was reverberating across the entire kitchen counter.

Splat . . .

Splat . . .

Splat . . .

A gentle meow sounded from my left. Looking over my shoulder, I saw Lafayette sitting next to the sink, watching me with a smirk on his face. Had he been there the whole time?

"Ah, hey dude. You see this?"

He cocked his head to the side inquisitively and meowed back.

"The sink," I elaborated. "Have you ever seen anything so pretty? It's so smooth . . . so shiny."

Lafayette brushed himself up against my arm before turning around and brushing the other side of his body against me. I reached out to pet him, wondering why his fur was cut so unevenly.

"Were you groomed by a weed wacker, little guy?" I asked. He rolled his bright green eyes and looked away, apparently insulted.

"Ohhh, that's right. Sylvia said your fur was full of mats and burrs, didn't she? So she probably had to cut them all out. I feel your pain, Lafayette. When I was in high school, one of the guys put gum in my football helmet. I had a bald spot for months!" Lafayette lifted a dark paw and cleaned his face. When his eyes met mine, he began to purr.

"Are we . . . having a moment?" I asked him.

I had never felt more connected to another being in all my life, and for what felt like a hundred years, we both stared into each other's eyes as the sound of his purring serenaded us. It somehow sounded like both an earthquake and a soothing lullaby as it rumbled through the entire room.

Closing my eyes, I listened to nothing but the sound of his purrs and relaxed even more.

"That's such a cool noise," I told him. "Real deep. You ever thought of playing bass? I think you'd be really good at it."

"I don't have thumbs, dumbass."

I opened my eyes and stared at him. Did he just talk? Did he just call me a dumbass? I looked for a sign, but he was busy gazing out the window, ignoring me.

"You know, I played bass for a while. For one summer, anyway. I was, like, fourteen and joined a band with these two kids that lived at the end of the street. We called ourselves—"

"Stop. Talking."

Suddenly, I was aware of deafening silence. Lafayette had stopped purring, and when I looked at him, he was jumping up against the window and pressing his paws against the glass.

"What's up?" I asked him. "You wanna go outside?"

He didn't so much as meow but scream in reply.

"You wanna go outside? I'll take you outside."

I'd always been slightly afraid of cats, but for some reason, I felt perfectly comfortable picking up the little guy and squeezing him beneath my arm like he was a set of bagpipes.

"Let's get you outside," I said to him as he burrowed his face into my armpit. "I could use some fresh air."

Holding him tight, I walked out of the kitchen into the darkened hall and stared down towards the front door.

"Shit," I said to myself. "How am I supposed to get down there?"

I had never been so acutely aware of the dark before. It wasn't so much an absence of light, but an inky abyss that I was sure I'd get sucked into. Lifting up my right foot, I hovered it over the threshold of the kitchen doorway and imagined placing it onto the floor. But as I lowered it inch by inch, I saw it sinking into the floor as if I was lowering it into wet tar.

"I can't walk on this," I said to Lafayette. "What do I do?"

He gave no answer, just dug his claws into my side and made a strange noise that resembled a tiny lawnmower.

"I know what we'll do," I thought out loud. "We'll climb out through the kitchen window. Sound like a plan?"

Carrying him back across the kitchen towards the sink, I leaned across the counter and twisted the latch on the window.

"Well, shit. This thing's pretty much rusted shut."

Refusing to give up, I twisted harder. A snapping sound came as I broke the rusted window frame. A moment later I was hit in the face by the smell of fresh woodland air. I sucked in a deep breath and sighed as I let it out.

"Aaaahhh, you smell that, Lafayette? Isn't that incredible?"

I watched as he jumped gracefully out the window, landing on the grass with a soft "meh!"

I couldn't say the same for myself. As I climbed onto the counter, my shoes slipped in the wet sink and I fell headfirst out the window.

"Aww, fuck!"

At least Elena wasn't there to see it happen. Rolling onto my hands and knees, I pulled myself upright, brushing the grass off my jacket as I looked around for my new friend. I caught sight of Lafayette making his way towards the nearby woods. I could tell he was on a mission by the way his tail kept flicking from side to side.

"Wait!" I called after him. "Don't go without me!"

I walked after him, following his lead into the treeline. Moonlight couldn't reach us in here. But for some reason, the darkness of the woods didn't scare me like the hallway had. If anything, it excited me.

With every step, I became more aware of how beautiful the moonlight was as it fell in silver strands across the leaves and tree roots. The sound of my feet crunching on dried leaves was like a tiny song in each footstep.

"Amazing . . . " I said to myself.

There was a tiny clearing where I watched a single

speck of moonlight dance on the edge of a broad, low leaf before jumping over to the next one. It was just about the most beautiful thing I'd ever seen. I wondered if Elena could see the silver beams of light wherever she was. I wondered if she'd appreciate it the same way that I did right now. I hoped so. I think she'd look at the moon the same way she'd looked at that sad little dandelion in the parking lot. She looked so cute, hunched down on the ground and playing in the mud. Not that I could ever tell her that. I knew she thought I was a dumb jock. At least I knew the reason why she was always such a jerk to me.

It wasn't about me at all.

It was about her past.

A few yards away, I could hear a gentle scratching sound and looked down to see Lafayette raking his nails down a nearby tree.

"Ooh, are you sharpening your murder mittens?"

He scratched faster, and it was then that I realized he wasn't just filing his nails. He was drawing his weapons.

"What's got you spooked, Lafayette?" I asked, bending down to gently pat him on the head.

"There's something out there," he said, his voice so low I could barely hear it. Then his eyes widened as he looked over my shoulder, his pupils dilating like I'd just dangled a sardine in front of him. Out of nowhere, he screeched an unholy noise and bolted into the shadows. I could see the leaves of a nearby bush rattling and shaking as he dove into them for cover.

"Hey! Lafayette! What's the matter? You're freaking me out."

Silence.

Even the crickets were afraid to chirp too loud. I became aware of a darkness creeping over me. Not dark as in nighttime, but dark like that terrible hole in Sylvia's face when that awful noise had poured out of it. Behind me, I could sense a presence . . . an energy. It was the opposite of the purple beams I'd seen swirling around Elena. This was a dark energy that crept closer and closer until my heartbeat was thundering in my chest. My hand instinctively reached for my gun, but it was missing.

I stood there, afraid to turn around, knowing that whatever stood there wasn't human. I could hear it breathing. I could feel its eyes burning into the back of my head.

Just look, I told myself. *Whatever it is, you have to face it.*

But I couldn't. Not yet. I stood shaking as the thing moved closer, its feet shuffling through the underbrush.

"Hello?" I called out, but there was no reply. "Who's there?"

My breath failed to come as I stood there, trembling.

"Elena? It's you, isn't it?" I hoped out loud.

Yeah, that's it. It's just Elena. She's playing some stupid prank on the Fucking New Guy. Of course she is.

But no matter how much I tried to convince myself, deep down I knew it wasn't true. Something was in the woods with me. Something that shouldn't exist.

Just turn and look. You need to know. You have to learn about what exists in the shadows.

I knew I'd have to look at some point. No matter how afraid I was, I had to see what lurked behind me. I'd gone through plenty of hand-to-hand combat training. So what if I didn't have my gun? I still had two hands.

Slowly, with my heart beating in my throat, I turned around inch by inch.

At first, all I saw were little black blobs creeping down low among the trees.

What are those? Cats? Coyotes?

But as I turned myself all the way around, I realized they were faces. The hairs on the back of my neck stood straight up. There were dozens of faces . . . all attached to small, spindly bodies about three feet tall. Their big black eyes reminded me of giant flies, and they all stared at me, their spidery fingers pointing out towards my face.

"These can't be real," I told myself. "They can't be real. I'm imagining it. It's just the moonshine."

But as I stared into their creepy, distorted faces, my eyes scanned their dark green, scaly skin, I knew exactly what they were. They were the same things that had scared the shit out of Sylvia.

Sprites.

19

ELENA

"Sylvia? What room are you in?"

Her sobs echoed down the hall towards me. I could see shapes of rotting furniture jutting out from the walls. There was a chest of drawers with clothes spilling out onto the floor, a chair missing a leg, a sofa with cat-claw-shredded cushions leaning away from the wall.

As a kid, I'd always loved to poke around abandoned houses, but I'd never seen anybody actually *living* in one before. This place reminded me of houses I'd seen on Hoarders . . . not with the amount of utter crap lying around, but the perilousness of it. It was a miracle nobody had died in here yet. The poor old woman needed so much help. It was hard to know where to begin. First, I had to find her.

"Sylvia? Where are you?"

I stood still and listened to gauge the direction of the crying. Just my luck—it was coming from the room at the end of the obstacle course that made up the hall.

Stepping over fallen books and the fleeting shadows of darting cats, I made my way down. As I reached Sylvia's bedroom, I caught the scent of rosewater and mothballs, a peculiar combination that should've been unpleasant but for some reason calmed me. Her door was open, but as I looked inside, all I could see was the corner of her bed covered in a pink, frilly blanket.

With a gentle knock, I peeked around the door and saw her sitting with her head in her hands. I tip-toed in, well aware that I was entering her inner sanctum. A woman's bedroom was her private sanctuary at the best of times, but for Sylvia, her privacy was more precious and guarded than most people's.

"Are you okay?" I asked, stepping closer. I set my candle on a nearby shelf and waited for her to respond. She nodded, her face still buried by her hands.

"You don't look okay."

Gradually, she lowered her hands from her face and glanced up towards me. Her cheeks were wet and red from crying. Her eyes were bloodshot and swollen.

"You didn't have to come up and check on me," she said with a sniff.

"Of course I did. I'm worried about you."

"You shouldn't be."

"I don't like seeing people upset," I said and knelt down next to her. She lifted her arm to her face and wiped away her tears on her bathrobe.

"You must think I'm a basket case," she said. "Running away and crying like a baby."

"I don't think that at all."

She rubbed her eyes again, making them even redder.

"Mind if I sit with you?" I asked.

She shook her head and swallowed down the last of her tears.

"Go ahead, hon."

Looking around at the walls, I noticed dozens of photographs, all of her in her younger days with her husband by her side. I imagined her lying in bed and falling asleep to the sight of those bygone memories. It was heart-breaking to think of her living in the past . . . but I suppose that was all she had. None of the pictures showed any relatives who might still be around.

As I sank down onto the bed next to her, a bundle of sleeping cats stirred, but didn't move.

"You've got quite the collection of familiars in here," I joked, trying to lighten the mood. "Ever worry you'll get allergies?"

She smiled ever so slightly and pet the nearest cat, a fat gray female with an obviously pregnant belly.

"I think I have enough herbs in my garden to treat allergies," she said. "Anyway, the cats are the least of my worries."

Strands of wet hair clung to the sides of her face. She brushed them away with her stiff fingers and faced the window so the moonlight glittered across her cheekbones. For a fraction of a second, the moonlight revealed the last of the youth in her eyes, and I caught a glimpse of who she used to be . . . who her husband must have known her as. But as soon as it came, it disappeared, and I was once again looking at the haggard, old, eccentric woman I'd become familiar with.

"I'm sorry about Agent Hawthorne," she said, sniffling. "Am I going to be arrested?"

I laughed softly.

"Nah. It was an honest mistake. We just have to wait for him to sleep it off. Luckily, he can't get into much trouble since I have his keys and his gun. He's probably downstairs talking to the cats."

Sylvia laughed softly and said, "I think Lafayette likes him. Which is funny, given that he doesn't like anybody. He told me so."

"Is that so?" I smiled and gave her a soft pat on the shoulder. "Well, let's make sure that he doesn't tell anybody that we accidentally drugged a federal agent. Especially not Sheriff McKinney."

"I won't say a word, and neither will Lafayette," she said with a wink.

Rising from the bed, she walked over to the window and tilted her head curiously to one side.

"Looks like Agent Hawthorn's going on an adventure."

I joined her and looked out at the darkened backyard. Amidst the tall grasses and wildflowers, I saw him following a black cat into the woods. Sylvia must've sensed my slight uneasiness because she turned and placed her hand on my arm.

"He'll be okay," she assured me. "If there's anything out there, it'll be more afraid of him than he is of them."

"I'll take your word for it, but if he comes in here screaming about seeing aliens . . . "

We both burst out laughing, the two of us cackling together like a pair of old witches.

"Bless his heart," she said, returning to her seat on the edge of her bed. "He's completely clueless about the paranormal. How does someone like him come to work with someone like you?"

"I've been asking the same question. My boss thought it was a good idea. Apparently, he's the FBI's golden boy."

"I don't have any doubts that Hawthorne's a good agent, but . . . he's not quite cut out for investigating the underworld, is he?"

I gave a doubtful shrug.

"We'll see. I suppose everyone has to start somewhere, but he didn't believe in any of it until today."

Sylvia stared at me as though she thought I was joking. When she realized I wasn't, she shook her head in disbelief.

"Well, he's a believer now I take it."

"I think so. I hope so. He's not a jumpy kind of guy. Like, nothing rattles him. But what he saw tonight really scared the shit out of him."

"It scared the hell out of me, too."

"I can see that."

The humor in her eyes vanished, and she was once again disappearing inside herself. I kept quiet for a bit to give her some space, worried that she might start sobbing again.

"I've only ever seen something like that once before," she said. "Years ago. A long time before I learned to control my ability. I never thought I'd see anything like that again. Never wanted to."

"What did you see?" I asked, leaning in closer to her. "I don't want to upset you or pressure you, but the whole point of me being here is to investigate. I really need your help, Sylvia. I know it's scary, but I need you to tell me what you saw downstairs. For the sake of finding those children."

She closed her eyes and winced as though she was in pain. Her fingers dug into her robe so tight that her knuckles were turning white.

"I saw the children," she said. "I saw them—"

Her words were cut off by the sound of a ferocious scream coming from outside. We both looked out the window just in time to see Logan running at full speed back towards the house like his ass was on fire.

"Elena!" he yelled. "Elena, where the fuck are you?"

20

LOGAN

In a panic, I climbed back into the nearest entrance of the house, the kitchen window, once again slipping in the sink as I scattered my limbs over the counter.

"Hawthorne!" came Elena's concerned voice as she bolted down the stairs. "What's wrong? Are you okay?"

I heard her footsteps rush towards the front door as her voice grew shrill.

"I'm in here!" I called out.

She emerged in the kitchen doorway just in time to see me fall onto the kitchen floor.

"What the—why did you climb through the fucking window? The door's right there!"

I looked up and saw her standing above me, pointing about three feet to the left of where I was lying. My cheeks flushed deep red with embarrassment. I went running every morning. I was supposed to be an athletic agent, a guy who could chase down the bad guys, but here I was, oblivious to the concept of doors and being conquered by a kitchen sink.

"Oh my god—did you break the window?"

"I'm sorry," I told her. "My brain's just melting."

Elena blew a strand of hair out of her face, then offered me a hand.

"I suppose another busted window isn't going to make much difference in this place," she said, helping me onto my feet. "That's what I get for not handcuffing you to the chair."

"Sprites!"

"What?"

"Goblins! There's dozens of them out there! I saw them with my own eyes! Lafayette saw them too!"

Elena looked deep into my eyes for a second, then screwed up her nose.

"Are you fucking with me?"

"No! I'm serious. Really fucking serious."

"Dude, you're tripping balls right now," she said, still eyeing me suspiciously. "I'm sure you're seeing all kinds of shit."

"Elena! I saw them! Ask Lafayette! He was there."

Her green eyes darted over to my new feline friend, who'd leapt up onto the counter and was rubbing his head into the side of my arm.

"C'mon, Lafayette. Tell her what we saw." I scratched his chin, trying to coax him into speaking. He continued pressing his head against me, keeping his tail low as it swished from side to side. "It's okay to talk in front of Elena," I said, trying to assure him that it was alright. "She's fae. If anyone's going to be fine with a talking cat, it's her."

Elena wasn't amused in the slightest. She was back to wearing that annoyed, pissed-off expression that had been on her face since the moment we'd met.

"He's just scared," I explained and gathered the black cat into my arms. "Believe me, Elena. Those freaky little spider goblins are all over the place."

I could see she wanted to believe me, but at the same time, something was holding her back.

"Tell me exactly what they looked like."

"Well, they weren't animals, and they weren't people. They moved slow and jerky at the same time. Little blackish-green fuckers with giant bug eyes. They were bigger than cats, but they weren't . . . I have no idea what they were."

"They were what Sylvia saw when she entered the other side," said Elena, speed walking around the side of the house. "The hall monitors to whatever hellish underworld she saw."

"And they're here now?" I said, following close behind. "How can that be?"

Elena closed her eyes and rubbed the bridge of her nose.

"I don't know, Logan. Just promise me you're not joking."

"I swear I'm telling the truth!" I practically yelled, holding Lafayette closer against my chest. "I saw them. They're as real as you standing right in front of me."

She glanced out the kitchen window towards the trees and narrowed her eyes.

"Show me."

"No way. I'm not going back out there."

"Yes, you are. Show me where you saw them."

"Why would I go back out there when there's demons or goblins out there?"

"Because it could lead us to wherever the kids are. We're here to find them, remember? If you're that worried about the sprites, I've got two guns and a taser. Let's go!"

I set Lafayette down and started to climb back out the window, but as I brought my knee onto the counter, I felt Elena's hand grab hold of my ankle.

"Through the *door*, Hawthorne!"

"Right."

I heard a shuffling behind me and turned around to see Sylvia standing in the doorway. Since the kitchen was the only room with electricity, it was also the brightest. I could tell that she'd been crying.

"You saw them too, huh?" she asked me. Shivers ran up my spine and down my legs as I nodded my head.

"There were so *many* of them."

"Too many," she replied, and stepped back into the darkness.

"Hawthorne!" shouted Elena from the back porch. "Where are you?"

"I'm coming!"

With my gun confiscated, I looked around frantically, searching for anything I could use as a weapon. All I saw were a bunch of hand tools that Sylvia used for the garden on her back patio. I grabbed a trowel and a hand rake and sprinted over to where Elena stood. She was staring impatiently out towards the trees.

"Over there," I told her, pointing in the direction I'd gone earlier. She didn't reply, just stormed off away from me faster than her legs should have been able to carry her. As she reached the edge of the yard where I'd come running out of, she hesitated, peering into the shadows.

"In this area?"

"Yeah. Just a few yards in."

She ran a hand through her pink hair and squinted into the darkness. Despite the panic and whatever influence I suspected I was under, having her close helped me calm down. The purple beams had stopped shooting out of her ears. The moonlight was covering her bare arms, illuminating the side of her face. I didn't think she was a makeup junkie, but it looked like she'd taken a bath in highlighter fluid. Her skin shimmered with a golden pearly glow, and combined with her bright green eyes and brilliant rose-colored hair, I couldn't take my eyes off of her. There wasn't anything ordinary about her beauty. It was otherworldly, a little devastating, and left her completely unapproachable. Sensing the way I was watching her, she twisted around and glared at me.

"What the hell are you looking at? We're supposed to be hunting goblins. Now show me exactly where you saw them."

I pointed again. She didn't hesitate for a second, just put one foot in front of the other and charged into the blackened forest that, for all she knew, was full of monsters sent from the bowels of hell.

"Are you coming?" she hissed, frustration pulling at her voice.

"Yeah, I'll be right there."

But I didn't want to be. I wanted to be running right back into the safety of the house. The last thing I wanted to see were those freaky little fuckers again. They'd sprouted a fear inside me that was so intense it was surreal. I didn't know it was even possible to feel a fear so strong. It didn't help that my only weapons were garden tools. I think what bothered me the most was the fact that these things weren't human. At least when I'd come across drug cartel members or serial killers, I had an idea what to expect.

But these things?

My past experience was nothing compared to the feeling of terror I felt when I'd seen those little green sprites in front of me. I couldn't move a single inch. It was like my feet were being tangled up in the grass.

"Logan, I know this is freaking you out, but I really need

your help right now," Elena said with a firmness that was impossible to argue with. "We need to find Rylee and all the other missing kids."

She was right. This wasn't the time to think about my own fear. I was here to find the kids, and if that meant coming face to face with the stuff of nightmares, so be it.

"I'm coming," I said, making a conscious effort to take a step forward. "Give me a second." My heart beat faster as I walked alongside of her and led the way through the darkness. "There's the tree Lafayette was scratching at and . . . I walked over here and then . . . They were suddenly behind me. Just . . . right there where you are now."

I pointed to the space that surrounded her. A bitter sense of uneasiness washed over me.

"Right here?"

"Yeah."

She glanced about as though hoping to see them, but to my relief, they were gone. Then she started sniffing the air.

"Why are you doing that?"

"Sprites smell nasty. Like the inside of a dumpster on a hot summer day. Didn't you notice?"

"Honestly, I was too busy trying not to shit myself to notice what they smelled like."

She knelt down into the grass, shining the light on her phone, looking for clues.

"There's gotta be something about this place," she thought out loud, brushing clumps of grass to one side. "Something significant. Maybe it's the rocks under the soil."

"Don't tell me you're into crystals and all that woo-woo shit."

"What are you, stupid? Of *course* I'm into crystals! Different types of rocks give off different frequencies. Some attract phenomena."

"Like sprites?"

"Like a lot of things. They can open portals, too, in the right circumstances."

She got down on all fours, propped up the light on her phone, and began feeling her fingers through the soil.

"Why here?" she asked. "Why would the sprites be *here*?"

"Uhh . . . because Sylvia's face turned into a black hole and everything unholy came flying out of it?"

"No, I mean right here. Why would the sprites have shown up at this particular spot?" She went on digging her fingers into the dirt.

"I'm confused," I said, handing her the trowel. She turned and looked up at me in sheer wonder before putting it to use. I think it meant I'd finally done something right. "If these things are inter-dimensional, they're not going to be found by digging, are they?"

"Shhh . . . "

She began digging wildly through the dirt like a dog searching for a bone. Instead of standing there like a dumbass, I knelt down and started clawing at the ground with my little hand rake.

"What exactly are you looking for?"

"I'll know it when I see it. It could be a sign or a symbol. Even a feeling, an energy, a splash of light that shows there's something strange going on here."

"Oh, there's definitely something strange going on here."

"I just don't get it," she said, ignoring my jab. "The trees around here aren't magic. Neither is the ground. So why were they here?"

"Fuck if I know. You're the expert in all this stuff."

The more we dug, the more desperate and irritable she

became. When one patch of soft soil brought up no results, she moved on quickly to the next, then the next, ordering me around until there were little piles of soil surrounding us. As I overturned patch after patch of soil, I became aware of how the light had changed. Hints of indigo and cobalt were staining the sky, and some of the stars had disappeared. The darkness was lifting its hold on the Smoky Mountains, and also my mind.

I was finally sobering up. Thank god for that.

I stopped digging and looked up. A blanket of purple lay on the horizon, waiting for the sun to rise.

"We've been here all night," I said.

"And what a fucking night it's been," Elena huffed, tossing aside another trowel-full of dirt. "Keep digging."

Plodding on, I poked and prodded at the ground with still no idea as to quite what I was looking for. The ground was soft and damp from the recent rain. Occasionally I found worms or beetle larvae, but nothing out of the ordinary. That was until I jabbed my garden fork into the ground and hit something so hard it almost shattered.

"I hit a really big rock or something. But it feels strange."

Elena shuffled over to me and knelt by my side.

"Where?" she asked.

"Here. It's probably nothing," I said, getting out of her way. "Just a rock."

"There's no such thing as just a rock."

Pressing her finger into the hole, she poked her tongue out in concentration.

"Hmm . . ."

"What is it?"

"It feels weird. I don't think it's from around here. Feels like it's carved or something."

Pushing her hand into the ground and scooping out the soil, she lifted the corner of the rock with a little grunt.

"Ugh. Got it. Just . . . One more second. Just . . . Ugh! Got it!"

It took all her strength and another grunt, but eventually, she popped the rock out the mud with a thud. It landed in front of us, the first of the morning sunlight falling across the stone.

I was expecting it to glitter or shine, or even just be an interesting color, but all I saw was a small boulder covered in dirt. An orange centipede was crawling across the top, desperate to escape.

"Um, wow," I said with a sarcastic sigh. "That's what the key to a portal looks like, huh?"

Not sharing my lack of enthusiasm, she pulled her sleeve down over her hand and began brushing the soil away.

"Look at it," she said. "It's been polished. It looks like . . . Shit, is that onyx?"

The more she cleaned it, the more obvious it was that the boulder didn't get that way naturally. You could see where it had been polished around the edges and cut with expert precision.

"Okay. This is weird," I admitted. "Someone clearly buried this thing out here on purpose."

"I think so too."

With a final sweep of her hand, the last of the dirt fell away to reveal the reason why. It was some kind of engraving.

Elena was ominously silent, staring at it with anxiety creeping into her eyes.

"Elena? You okay? What is it?"

Fear crept even deeper into her already worried face.

"Elena?"

Touching her delicate fingertips to the stone, she brushed her hand over the engraving and shivered.

"It's a sigil," she said. "It's a kind of magic symbol."

I took in its peculiar shape and crisscrossed lines, absorbing the look and texture of the mark. It was like nothing I had ever seen before.

"Do you think Sylvia stuck it out here?"

"No, but there's only one way to find out." She grabbed her phone and took a few pictures before slipping it into the pocket of her ripped up black jeans. "Let's get back to the house and see if she's awake."

"What in the hell happened to y'all?" asked Sylvia as we came into the kitchen. She was still in her nightgown and bathrobe and was in the middle of feeding her cats breakfast. The pungent scent of kitty kibble filled the air, covering up the undertones of cat piss and mold. Outside was fresh and clean and almost sweet. Now it was . . . a little soul-crushing.

"Why, look at you, all covered in dirt." She looked up from the bag of food she was pouring into a large mixing bowl and shook her head in disapproval. "You're making a mess all over my kitchen floor!"

Given the condition of the house, my jaw almost fell in surprise. I only kept it shut to keep out the cat hair that was floating through the air as dozens of kitties were scrambling for their food.

"Listen, Sylvia," said Elena, placing one hand on her hip as she took out her phone. "Dirt don't hurt. We need to know what this is."

Sylvia, bewildered, walked closer and peered at the image on the screen.

"Do you know anything about a big onyx boulder out in the woods on your property? It's gotta be two feet across."

Sylvia scrunched up her face in confusion.

"What's that doing on my land?"

"We were hoping you could tell us," I said.

"Well, I've never seen it before," said Sylvia with a shake of her head.

"Are you sure?"

"I'm positive."

"Has anybody else been staying here? Have you had any visitors or people on your property? Like hunters, maybe?"

Sylvia shook her head.

"Only people that's been on my property is the sheriff's department searching for those kids."

Elena studied her eyes for a sign of a lie, but even I could see the old lady was just as baffled as we were.

"What about this symbol?" she asked, swiping over to the next photo. "Does this look familiar to you at all?"

Sylvia froze and took a step back in horror.

"Someone's been doing black magic on my property?"

I wasn't sure what she was shocked about the most, that someone was practicing black magic, or that it was done on her property without her permission.

"Are you familiar with black magic?" I asked her.

"Some of it. But it's not my area of expertise. I'm a medium, sure, but black magic? If this is truly some sort of symbol or—"

"Sigil," interjected Elena.

"A sigil," repeated Sylvia. "If a sigil was carved onto a

rock and put on my property, it sure as hell wasn't by *my* hand."

"Are you sure you've never seen this symbol before?" I asked. "It's pretty distinct looking."

"I've never seen it in my life. I promise you." I could see the truth in Sylvia's eyes. "And I don't want to see it again," she said, her voice becoming strained. "I don't know what it means, but I know the damned thing is evil. I can feel the darkness coming out of it."

"Can you do a reading on it?" asked Elena. "Like you did when you were remote viewing?"

"No! I won't. It has an aura coming from it that's pure blackness. The blackest of black. I've got a mind to call in someone to come blow up that rock to pieces."

"Not yet," said Elena. "It's evidence. The best way for you to help us is just leave it alone."

"And if you see anyone out in the woods where we found it, let us know," I added, and handed her my card. Sylvia didn't look pleased, but she didn't object.

Good.

The last thing we needed was a townie with dynamite blowing up what little evidence we had.

21

ELENA

"Thanks for saving so much hot water for me," Logan said as he stepped out of the teeny tiny treehouse shower.

"I can't tell if you're being sarcastic or not." I stopped combing my wet hair long enough to look up and get a great view of him in nothing but a bath towel. Maybe it was because he was so tall and so muscular, but the towel looked downright tiny on him. Water dripped down his chest, soaking into the cotton fabric wrapped around those narrow hips.

"I'm serious. My ex used to stay in the shower 'til it ran out. But you were in and out in seven minutes."

"I guess I figured we'd sleep better if we weren't freezing our asses off," I said, and went back to combing my hair. It was only five-thirty in the morning, and I was just glad to have snuck back into the treehouse before Sheriff McKinney woke up. The last thing I wanted to do was explain why we were covered in dirt or why I'd confiscated my partner's gun. Luckily, he seemed back to his old self . . . for the most part.

I turned around and put my hair in a bun while he got dressed.

"It's safe. You can turn around now," he said after a few moments. When I looked again, he was only wearing boxers. If there were ab gods and tricep gods, they were all smiling upon me. I watched as he unrolled the sleeping bag and set the pillow up at the top. "I swear, if we'd stayed in Sylvia's house any longer, I was gonna have an asthma attack. And I don't even have asthma."

"Yeah," I mumbled from the comfort of my bed. "I didn't realize how bad it was in there until the sun came up. It looked like she hasn't vacuumed in a decade."

"She might not *own* a vacuum," Logan said. "Even if she does, there's no electricity, unless she runs extension cords from the kitchen. I can't imagine living like that. I feel bad for her. Do you think we should call social services or something?"

"We could ask someone at the county level to check in on her," I replied. "But I imagine McKinney's already done that."

With a big yawn, he rubbed at his tired eyes and closed the blackout curtains over the windows. It was barely light enough to see each other across the tiny space, but I could see that he was just lying there, staring at the ceiling as he tried to get comfortable. It didn't seem to be working. I set down my comb and sighed.

"I know you're being a gentleman or professional or whatever, but you need some decent rest. The bed's big enough for both of us, you know."

"Thanks, but I'm fine here."

"Really? You look exhausted."

"Aren't you tired?"

"Yeah, but I'll be fine. *You*, on the other hand, I'm not so sure about. What's wrong? Are you worried that you'll wet the bed?"

Logan's head whipped in my direction.

"What? No! I just . . . The last person I shared a bed with was Bridget, and . . . I don't know. It just seems weird."

"It's not weird. Back in the olden days, entire families used to sleep in the same bed."

I heard Logan snort a laugh.

"Back in the olden days, entire families bathed in the same water. Doesn't mean we should keep every tradition."

"That's not the point I'm trying to make," I huffed, but he'd made me smile. "One of my foster homes made me share a bed with two other kids. But we got along great and I loved it."

"You did?" he asked with a skeptical glance.

"Totally. I think I liked it because it made me feel safer than sleeping alone. Look at all this room in here." I scooted over to the far side of the mattress until I was pressed up against the wall. "See? There's a shit-ton of room. We're gonna have our hands full once we meet up with McKinney. I'd rather you weren't cranky from being up all night tripping on mushrooms."

Logan shook his head, then sat up.

"If I come over there, will you be quiet and actually let me sleep?"

I rolled my eyes.

"Dude, I'm only looking out for your best interest. That's why I took your gun and the car keys. I know how to adult when it matters."

"Fine," he said, grabbing his pillow. "I guess it's just for a couple hours." He climbed in beside me, lying stiff as a board as he tried to keep a decent amount of space between us.

As I closed my eyes I was aware of the bright sunlight streaming around the edges of the curtains, along with the sound of birds singing. Normally I would've loved their songs, but this morning I found it more of a challenge.

"I can't sleep," I complained.

"It's been like, ten seconds."

"I know, but I can't sleep." I rolled over and saw Logan staring at the ceiling. "What are you thinking about?"

He was quiet for a long time before he spoke.

"Every time I close my eyes, I either see Sylvia's face turning into a black hole or I see those creepy fucking goblin things surrounding me out in the woods."

"Yeah, I've never seen you that scared before."

"My brain feels like it's been turned inside out," he went on. "Like every horror movie I watched and laughed at as a kid is actually real. It's like everything I ever believed is a lie. Turns out the boogeyman is real after all."

He turned his head and looked at me. The bureau's big, bold golden boy had been replaced with a clueless football star who was way out of his league. To his credit, he was still here.

"Even faeries are real. And if I hadn't been high, a few hours ago I would've told you that talking cats are real, too."

"I know it's a lot to take in all at once," I said, trying to imagine what it must be like to be in his shoes. "But you'll be okay. In a few months, you'll look back on this night and laugh your ass off. You won't even recognize who that clueless FNG Agent Hawthorne was."

"We'll see."

"Trust me." I propped myself up on my elbow, shooting him a grin. "Before you know it, tonight's just gonna be another weird case you worked on. There's gonna be lots more."

Logan returned his gaze to the ceiling as the reality of his job struck him full force. This was just the first case of many. He'd spend the rest of his professional life investigating the unknown, being forced to face literal monsters head-on. It would mean more monsters, more dimensions, more scary things that I'm sure he couldn't even imagine.

He bunched up his pillow and maneuvered onto his stomach, looking at me curiously.

"How do you do it? How do you do this stuff day in and day out without losing your mind?"

"I don't know. I just do my job."

"But you're so fearless. They say fools rush in where angels fear to tread, but you actually know what you're doing."

"That's because I'm more experienced than you," I said, gloating with pride. "Look, you'll get there. Aside from me, nobody started in the OCD having much experience with this stuff. Pretty much the only way to learn the job is to get thrown into the deep end."

"Has anyone ever quit?"

"Pssshhh . . . *lots* of people," I told him. "Which sucks because I don't have anyone to talk to about work. I suppose that's what Jameson is for."

A soft snicker rose from Logan's chest.

"Now *that* I understand. My dad couldn't tell my mom about work, and I couldn't tell Bridget about work. Still, doesn't the whole magical paranormal spin on things make it harder? Aren't you worried you'll go nuts?"

"No. Not really."

He smiled softly at me. "I suppose you're already a little nuts."

"Hey, watch it," I laughed and gave him a playful

thump on the arm. He raised a brow at me, pretending to be shocked.

"Rivera!" he scolded, still smiling. "Did you just punch a federal agent?"

"No," I said, and did it again. "I *thumped* you. There's a difference."

He yawned again, this time so deeply that his whole body rocked up and down. When I looked up at his face, his eyelids were flickering shut.

"Finally getting tired?"

"Mmm-hmm . . . Must be having you to talk to that's calmed me down. You're better than Blanton's."

After hearing that, I couldn't stop smiling. I'd have to get him a bottle next time I came across one. I felt a rush of heavy, delicious, sleepy endorphins like no other. Fuck those goblins and the psychic visions and the black magic rocks. As I yawned and closed my eyes, I thought how lying here and feeling safe was what I'd remember most about this night.

There were a few things I'd never done in my entire career. I'd never taken my pants off in front of a colleague, and I'd never slept in a bed with one, either. Now I'd managed to do both in one shot.

My brain woke up long before I opened my eyes, although it was one of those times where consciousness didn't come easily. It was taking a lot more effort than usual, so I let myself glide through the process of fully waking up.

The birds had calmed the fuck down and mostly I just heard Logan breathing above me. His warmth had somehow come to surround me, shielding me from the terrors he'd witnessed the night before. I became aware of our tangled limbs right about the same time I remembered he was still wearing nothing but his boxers. My baggy t-shirt was now twisted around my body, and I was pretty sure one of my boobs was pressed against his ribcage. My face was stuck to Logan's muscular chest, and one of his long, powerful arms was draped over me with the weight of a dead log. I was trapped.

It felt incredible.

I couldn't remember the last time I'd been in bed with a guy. It had been months, if not a year or two since I'd gotten laid. And if I remembered correctly, I didn't let them stick around afterwards for Olympic-level snuggling. I got what I wanted and kicked them out before they could fill my place with their nasty human smell. What was it about Logan that made it so easy to let my guard down? For some reason, I wanted to get even closer to him than I already was. I wanted to be closer in a way I hadn't been with any other human being.

An identity crisis was imminent. I didn't even *like* humans all that much. I put up with them because I had to. Why the hell wasn't I repelled by this one? His smile, his laugh, and his scent had all managed to sidestep my radar. Instead of being annoyed, I only wanted more. I could see in his eyes that he could be trusted. And he was a virgin when it came to magic. There was no doubt that he'd been traumatized by what he'd experienced these last couple of days. I guess that made it easy to develop a soft spot for him.

Was I tapping into some latent, secret part of my brain that longed for companionship and connection? Or was it something more carnal? Maybe I was just horny as hell and wanted those hard, thick, long beefcake muscles holding me . . . wrestling me . . . manhandling me . . .

Fucking me.

A warm shiver flickered through my body at the thought. It would be so easy for me to slide on top of him and work that man meat into my pussy through the opening of his boxers. I imagined how it would feel to grind against him until I came, then begging him to fuck the living daylights out of me until he did too.

It would give a whole new meaning to the phrase 'rise and shine.'

It wasn't any secret that I gave conventionality the middle finger and liked to do things my way at the bureau. So what if I turned Agent Hawthorne into my personal boy toy? Even if Harris found out, I bet he wouldn't fire me.

Logan yawned, and I could hear the air being expelled from beyond the muscles of his broad chest as his heartbeat picked up. The strong arm holding me close moved away, careful to avoid touching my ass.

Dammit. He should've touched it. Should've grabbed a big handful of it.

"We probably shouldn't be doing this," he said softly, his voice tickling the top of my head. I was about to tell him that yes, yes we should, and that's when I realized my cheek was stuck to his chest by a massive, gooey puddle of my own fucking drool.

I bolted upright and wiped off his chest with the edge of my shirt, then used it to clean off my cheek. I didn't realize I was flashing my tits at him until I caught him staring at them.

"Oh fuck oh fuck fuck *fuck!*"

I couldn't scramble out of the bed and into the tiny bathroom fast enough. I couldn't even lock a door—all I had was a pathetic little curtain hook. And while I was having a mini-meltdown, Logan was laughing his ass off.

"Holy shit, Rivera!" he howled, still laughing. "I'm gonna need a towel to mop up all this slobber! What are you —part Saint Bernard?" Mortified, I stared into the mirror and tried to get my shit together. It wasn't like I'd wet the bed. I just drooled on him. A lot. On his chest. Right by his fucking nipple. And then I'd flashed him both of mine.

"Elena? I'm just fucking with you," he called. "It's no big deal." I could hear him moving around the room, rustling through his suitcase.

"Whatever! I'm fine!" I snapped. I wasn't fine, but what else could I say? That I leaked out of my mouth on people all the time?

"Can you hand me my toothbrush? I think it's in the cabinet."

I quickly found it and stuck my arm out of the curtain. I wasn't ready to look him in the eye. Not yet.

"Thanks." I heard zippers opening and closing, caught the scent of mint, and then heard the sound of him opening the treehouse windows while I brushed my teeth.

"Hey, I'm not feeling like a run this morning. You wanna grab some breakfast before we get back to work?"

I contemplated telling him to just meet me at the police station, but right about then my stomach started growling. All the puking from the day before had left me ravenous. Even Sylvia's biscuits and honey were no match for my metabolism.

"Sure. Give me a minute, okay?"

"Take your time. I'll meet you by the car."

I cleaned myself up and got dressed as fast as I could, then hustled down the ladder and high-tailed it across McKinney's lawn.

Logan was leaning against the Navigator, talking on his phone. He was dressed impeccably in a suit and tie, sporting a pair of aviator sunglasses. How had he managed to make himself so goddamn presentable in five minutes? Twelve hours ago he was telling me I had purple beams of light shooting out of my fucking head. Now he looked like James Bond's cuter younger brother.

We didn't say much on the way to the diner, although our waitress took great pride in seating us at what was becoming our booth. I ordered their "famous" giant cinnamon roll and a Mountain Dew while my partner got a black coffee and an omelet with a side of seasonal fruit. The two of us stared at our phones until our food arrived.

My eyes lit up when the giant cinnamon roll was set down in front of me. I understood why it was famous. It was the size of a bowling ball, taking up a full dinner plate, covered in icing, an extra dusting of cinnamon, and a hearty sprinkle of candied pecans. Shaking with excitement, I ripped off a hunk and shoved it into my face hole before Logan had even unwrapped his paper napkin. I caught him laughing to himself as he watched me inhale the bit of heaven on my plate.

"So . . . are we going to talk about the elephant in the room?" he finally asked.

"Mmmphhh?" Part of me wanted nothing to do with the elephant in the room. The other part of me—the hungry part—just wanted satisfaction at all costs.

"I'm not timing you on how fast you eat, Elena," he said, cutting his omelet into sensibly-sized bites. "Why don't you slow down long enough to breathe?"

"Oph cmmm brfff," I argued. He nodded and ate a few bites of food before speaking again.

"Look. I get it. We're partners. I know we're spending a lot of time together, and I'm glad we're starting to get along, but we can't lose focus on our work."

I managed to shove enough chewed-up cinnamon roll into the side of my mouth so I could talk.

"Sorry about flashing my tits in your face. That was an accident. So was the drool."

His blue eyes brightened as he held back a smile.

"I'm not complaining. Probably shouldn't make a habit of it, though."

"Duly noted," I grumbled, and tore off more of the cinnamon roll. I'd barely made a dent in the thing. "Although we didn't really do anything wrong." I stuffed more pastry into my mouth before I could say anything dumb.

"I suppose not, but . . . " He lifted his cup to his mouth, looking out the window as he sipped. "I just don't want you to . . . "

He might as well have waved a red flag in front of me. What exactly did he *not* want me to do? Did he not want me to get too attached, get the wrong idea, or be disappointed at being rejected? Did he not want me to take it personally that he didn't sleep with his coworkers? Whatever he didn't want me to do, it was way too early in the morning for this male-ego-centered bullshit. I washed down my cinnamon roll with some frosty Mountain Dew and reapplied my go-to look: resting bitch face.

"You don't want me to *what*?"

His expression was caught somewhere between confused and concerned. I noticed whenever he had that look, he got a little furrow in his brow and his bottom lip puckered just the tiniest bit. God, it was cute.

"I don't want you to be some kind of rebound," he clarified. "I'm glad we're getting more comfortable with each other, but . . . I was with my fiancé for years. We literally broke up the day before Chief Harris called me into his office."

Ohhhhhhh. *Wow.* I stood corrected. That wasn't *anything* like what I was expecting him to say.

"Damn, Logan. I didn't realize it was that recent. What happened?" The moment I blurted out that dumbass question, my hand flew up to cover my face. And because I was eating with my hands like a baboon, I got a big glob of frosting on my forehead. "Sorry. That's none of my business."

Ever the gentleman, Logan reached over and handed me his napkin.

"Yeah, well, you told me a bunch of private stuff about your life, so I guess I can tell you more about mine. We broke up after I caught her sleeping with her dad's business partner. Motherfucker's like, over seventy years old."

My jaw dropped enough that my half-chewed up cinnamon roll almost fell out of my mouth . . . while I was cleaning frosting off my face.

I don't get out much.

"You're joking."

"Nope." Logan shook his head. "Found him hiding under the bed, buck naked. I pulled my gun on him."

"Shit! Are you serious?"

"Yeah. So anyway . . . *that* happened." He lifted his fork and went back to eating.

Meanwhile, I had so many questions. Mostly wondering why the hell someone would choose an old, crusty geezer over the hot, smart, sexy hunk sitting across from me. I also wondered how it made Logan feel to be cast aside for someone closer to Sylvia's age than our own. No matter what her side of the story was, it was Bridget's loss. And even if Logan didn't want me to be some kind of rebound, he'd made a point of saying that he wasn't upset about seeing my boobs or snuggling in the same bed. He probably needed time to process his breakup, and he didn't want any distractions from this case while he did that. It made sense. The families of Yarbrough deserved our full attention.

"Let's make a deal," I said after gnawing through three-quarters of the cinnamon roll. "I won't tell Chief Harris about the mushrooms if you don't tell him about the drool."

With a boyish grin, Logan raised his cup of coffee and dipped his chin.

"Deal."

LOGAN

"Where in the hell have y'all been?" McKinney hollered as we walked through the doors of the station. "I haven't heard anything since you went to visit Old Mrs. Bonkers Mc Catface."

The sheriff was planted in his chair with his feet on his desk eating a Danish, oblivious to the crumbs in his beard.

"Have neither of you heard of a damn phone? I've been worried about you."

"I left a message with Davis," Elena said, sitting on the corner of his desk. "I can't help it if that moron forgot to tell you."

"Why, that son of a bitch!" McKinney growled. "He's been nothing but a pain in the ass ever since he joined the department. Causes more problems than he solves."

"It's been a long night," I said approaching the desk. "Looks like it's been one here, too."

Peering into the reception area, I saw a rag-tag team of officers in various stages of sleep deprivation. Two were leaning wearily against the counter as the coffee maker brewed a fresh pot. A few others were walking up and down the hall like caffeinated zombies.

"Any changes?" asked Elena.

"If by *changes* you mean have any other kids gone missing? Then no. Thankfully the numbers are staying the same."

He bit into his Danish and a dollop of jam spurted out onto his hand.

"Not that it makes things easier," he said, licking the jam off the palm of his hand. "We still got no leads. And to make matters worse, another news truck showed up this morning."

"Shit," said Elena. "Did you talk to them?"

"Yep," McKinney said, puffing out his chest. "I told the nice young reporter that he could go right ahead and suck a dick."

I tried to disguise my laugh with a cough and failed miserably.

"Yeah . . . 'Fraid I'm not as camera-friendly as Hawthorne here," he said, eyeing me. "Anyway, what have y'all got for me? Tell me you at least got something useful from the old bat last night."

Elena and I shared a nervous glance.

"Um . . . "

"Sort of . . . "

"I mean . . . "

"Sylvia was great, just . . . "

"It was difficult to get anything useful, you know."

We both fell silent. What exactly could we have told him? That we made a telepathic phone call to the underworld? That we watched her face melt into a black hole and shoot out a whirlwind of terror? That I mistook psilocybin mushroom tincture for apple pie moonshine and saw monsters and a cat that called me a dumbass?

I did *not* want to be the one to write that report.

"So basically," said McKinney, cramming the last of his Danish into his mouth. "You've found nothing and Sylvia was a great big waste of time."

"Not exactly," said Elena. "We've got a picture I want you to look at."

Fishing for her phone, she swiped to open the picture of our newly discovered rock and its corresponding symbol.

"What the hell is that?" asked McKinney.

"It's a boulder. But it's onyx. It's not from around here."

The sheriff frowned as Elena zoomed in on the photo.

"What's that graffiti on it? A gang sign?"

"We think it might have something to do with what's going on here."

He raised his eyebrows at her skeptically.

"Hear me out," she said, pinching the screen to zoom out a little. "It was buried in the woods in a place where there have been sightings of . . . " She hesitated for a second and looked up to me.

"Sightings of what?" McKinney asked. "And don't you dare say Bigfoot."

"Sightings of humanoid creatures," I said.

"Humanoid creatures," McKinney repeated. "Like that faerie lady that little Haley Brown described?"

"No, but I think they're connected," Elena said. "It's hard to explain, but I really think this rock has something to do with what's happening. And I think we'll find out more if we discover what this symbol means."

I didn't know if McKinney was entirely convinced, but I could see in his eyes that he trusted Elena.

"You found this at Sylvia's?" he asked.

"That's right."

"And you really think it means something?"

"I do."

"Okay well, Agent Rivera, you're the expert here in all things weird. If you think it matters then we can assign an officer to check out this weird thingmabob squiggle here."

"We don't need an officer," said Elena. "We need a library. One with an occult section."

McKinney scoffed at the idea.

"In this town? You ain't gonna find anything like that in little old Yarbrough. These are god-fearing people here, and they don't—"

"Wait!" I cut in. "You've got a bunch of those types of books in your office, don't you?"

"Sure, but nothing occult," he said, scratching his head. "Just books on folklore and whatnot."

"Perfect!" Elena jumped to her feet. "Let's start there."

Across the station, officers from around the county bustled back and forth between juggling the media crews, processing evidence, and interviewing relatives of the missing children. Meanwhile, Elena and I sat cross-legged on the floor in front of McKinney who was perusing his bookshelf. I felt like a kid waiting to hear a Christmas story from their grandpa.

"Hmmm . . . Let me think," he said, running his hands over the books lining the middle shelf. His fingers stopped at one and dug it out. "There we go. 'Folklore of the Great Smoky Mountains.' This would probably be the best place to start looking. Anyway, here you go. Knock yourself out. If you need me I'll be wrangling the rookies. Pretty sure they're about to go postal any minute."

Right on cue, an explosion of yelling came from out in the hall.

"For fuck's sake! What do I have to do around here just to get two fucking minutes to myself?"

We looked out the glass partition just as one of the detectives flung his file at a young rookie officer, pages raining down on him before hitting the floor.

"You got that under control?" I asked, raising a concerned brow.

"It's fine," said McKinney as he departed. "Sanchez is always a bit of a hothead."

As McKinney pushed the door shut and left us alone in his office, Elena looked down at the book.

I looked down at Elena.

"Did you see that huge red flag about Officer Davis?" I murmured under my breath. "McKinney said he's been a pain in the ass ever since he joined the department. He said the guy causes more problems than he solves. And given that McKinney's been here for decades, and Davis is relatively new, the timing of the abductions lines up."

Elena crossed her arms over her chest.

"The guy's a prick, but I didn't get serial-child-abductor vibes off of him."

I tilted my head to the side, putting my hands on my hips.

"Me either, but remember what Sylvia told us when we found that boulder? She said nobody's been on her property except local law enforcement."

"What do you wanna do? Interrogate Davis?"

"No," I admitted. "I don't think we have enough probable cause for that. But I can probably get a judge to grant us a warrant for wiretapping the station."

Elena's eyes narrowed in suspicion.

"*They're* the ones who called *us!*" she hissed. I gave a nonchalant shrug.

"*McKinney's* the one who called us. Not Davis. Anyway, isn't it better to be able to rule him out?"

"I suppose," she grumbled. "Do you wanna call Harris about that wiretap?"

I took in the sight of her skin-tight black jeans, her messy pink bun, and her surly, pouting mouth. Her arms were still crossed, squeezing her shimmering tan breasts together just enough that it took me an extra second to look away. I still hadn't gotten over the fact that they'd been pressed up against me less than two hours ago. Elena's body had smelled like warm, soft vanilla cupcakes.

I wouldn't be surprised if she tasted that way, too.

Down boy.

I cleared my throat and swallowed hard.

"Actually, I think it'll be better if you call it in. All the guys here are either terrified of you or wrapped around your finger."

"Fine. I'll take care of it," she said, standing up and stretching her legs. "Be right back. You make a start on that book."

I settled into one of the extra chairs in McKinney's office and turned to the table of contents. There were stories of Spearfinger, the Wampus Cat, and the Road to Nowhere. Skimming the paragraphs of text, it became obvious that none of these tales were going to be of any use. I pinched the bridge of my nose and groaned. What would I have done if this was a research paper for college?

I got out my phone and went straight to Google.

The first thing that came to mind was *rock*, but that seemed too simple of a starting point, so I changed my mind to *onyx*. I ended up with a ton of results, but they were all centered on the metaphysical and magical properties. Even the dry, analytical geography sites didn't have any useful information.

Next, I looked up goblins. That brought shit tons of results, but most of them were about monsters from role-playing games. Rolling dice wasn't going to solve my missing persons case.

I searched for elves, faeries, and magic. What I learned was interesting, but completely non-applicable.

"Magical creatures, not always benevolent, frequently found near ash trees, have healing capabilities, not all of them have wings . . . blah blah blah. What about this damn symbol?"

There was more ruckus out in the hallway. I glanced up, making sure I was still alone in the office. It wouldn't help if the yahoos from Yarbrough caught me talking to myself.

Running out of ideas on what to search for, I sat back in the chair and stared blankly at the acoustic tile ceiling. There had to be something I was missing. Something that was staring me right in the face that I wasn't taking notice of. My brain filtered through all the events of the previous evening.

I thought about Sylvia and her remote viewing and her deafening scream. I thought of all her cats and her filthy house and the moonshine she'd given me that made me think Lafayette could actually talk.

"Come on . . . What am I missing here? The boulder was buried on Sylvia's property. It has to be linked with her."

My mind traveled back to the image of her sitting on the

255

living room floor, pen in hand as she scribbled frantically across the page. She knew something we didn't. She'd seen something that scared the shit out of her. There had to be something she saw in that other dimension. Something that was the key to all of this.

And that god-awful scream . . . She wasn't putting on a show. She'd seen something evil. Something she said she hadn't seen since she last saw hell.

What the hell. Let's give that a shot.

At first, the only articles that popped up were all about fallen angels and fire and brimstone. There were endless pages about sinning and torture and living purely so as not to suffer an agonizing afterlife. Some interesting articles about Dante's Inferno. But my patience was dwindling, and so was my hope that I would find anything.

Just then, the door opened and Elena sauntered in holding an armful of chocolate-covered snacks from the vending machine and a can of Mountain Dew. Pinned to her chest with her chin was a bag of Skittles.

"What's all that for?" I asked, eyeing the Skittles on her chest. "You giving out treats to the deputies?"

"Hell no. I was hungry," she said with a little shrug and dropped the armful of little packages onto McKinney's desk. There were cookies, candy bars, peanut butter cups, and a little bag of powdered donuts. "Thought I'd grab a snack."

I didn't even bother to hide my incredulous expression.

"That's a snack?"

"I like having options."

"How can you still be hungry? Seriously! That cinnamon roll was the size of a watermelon! Have you ever been checked for tapeworm?"

Her eyes flashed as she drew in a sharp breath.

"You know, I was going to share this with you, but you can forget it!"

"Thanks, but I had a balanced breakfast an hour ago. I don't *need* a snack." I could see Elena's body trembling, either with frustration or sugar withdrawal. As much as I wanted to keep pushing her buttons—if only to see that adorable outraged look she constantly had—I decided against it. Tempers were already flaring in the station and I didn't want to see her go full-napalm.

I mean, actually, I kinda *did* want to see it . . . just not in front of an audience.

"Did you get ahold of Harris about the you-know-what?"

"Yep," she said through tightly drawn lips as she tore open the bag of Skittles. "Said he'll give me a call once a judge approves it."

"Great. Thanks."

"Have you made any progress with that book?" She stomped over to me and glared at the phone nestled inside the book McKinney had given me. More of that vanilla cupcake scent filled the space between us. "Ah. Fucking around on your phone, I see. Were you just waiting for me to leave so you could see what's new on Pornhub today?"

"No . . . " I picked up my phone and began scrolling through the latest article I'd come across, trying to ignore the sound of her chomping candy. "I'm researching Hell. So far all I'm finding is stuff about angels and fire and brimstone. Lots about sinning. Satan apparently has horns and a pointy tail, blah, blah, blah, and . . . wait a minute. Child sacrifice?"

I stopped dead, my heart beating a little quicker as the subject grabbed my attention. My focus went straight to my phone, where I saw words jump out of the screen at me.

"Countless children have been sacrificed to create a doorway to hell. This is a practice dating back thousands of years by primitive people who believed a portal to the underworld could be opened if the pure souls of young children were given to a demon as a form of . . . "

Elena shoved another handful of candy into her mouth, but her chewing had slowed down considerably.

"Hey, I think I'm onto something! It's about fucking time." I read even faster, growing desperate to absorb the words as I read out loud to my partner. "One dweller of the underworld, a king of the demons named Moloch, is said to be the one who they made the sacrifices to. His presence could be invoked in certain rituals using his sigil that . . . "

My heart began beating so fast I was scared it might burst. The hand holding my phone began to sweat and tremble. Right in front of me, the sigil of Moloch was displayed on the screen. It was the exact same symbol engraved on the boulder we'd dug up in Sylvia's yard.

"Hey, Elena? Have you heard about this demon Moloch?"

When she didn't respond, I looked up at her. She'd completely stopped chewing. For a minute it looked like she'd completely stopped breathing. Even her characteristically shimmering skin had gone dull. The fear on her face put me on edge. Elena wasn't the type of person to be afraid of anything, but here she was looking like she'd just been faced with Satan himself.

"There's a lot of different demons out there," she croaked. "Are you sure we're dealing with Moloch?"

I pointed to the picture on my phone, holding it up for her.

"A hundred percent sure. The sigil on the onyx boulder

is definitely his. From what I can tell, it's meant to summon him."

The blood drained from her face, and she took a step back. Then she took another one. It looked like she was ready to bolt out the door.

"Elena? Are you okay?"

"No . . . "

I could see her getting wobblier by the second. I rose to my feet and took her gently by her arms, guiding her towards the chair next to the one I'd just been sitting in.

"Hell," she said as she collapsed into it. "Isn't that what Sylvia saw when she was remote viewing? She told us that she hadn't seen anything like it except for hell itself."

Elena stared into space as though she was putting all the pieces of the puzzle together.

"Elena? Who is this Moloch?"

"A demon," she said, and leaned forward, burying her head in her hands. "A really powerful demon. One of the most powerful ones there ever was. If he has something to do with what we're dealing with . . . "

Slowly, she sat back upright and turned her face to mine.

"Logan, if this is what we're dealing with, we're fucked. This is bad. Like, worse than bad. We're in serious danger."

I reached over and rubbed her shoulder, trying to calm her down, but underneath my fingers, she started to tremble ever so slightly.

"It'll be okay," I told her, although I didn't have a fucking clue of how to go about that. I was out of my depth and had no idea about the kind of darkness we faced. But Elena had seen it all, hadn't she? She'd know what to do.

"Hey, Elena? You're freaking me out a little. You don't look like yourself right now."

I had the urge to hug her, to protect her. She was tough and could look after herself. So why did she look so scared?

"This Moloch demon," I said. "You're really afraid of him, aren't you?"

"That's a fucking understatement. He's a demon from hell. One of the most powerful, evil entities to exist. He's been around for thousands of years . . . thriving off of people's pain and misery. He feeds off of fear. Especially children's fear . . . "

Then a thought struck me. Judging by the way she was acting, maybe her fear wasn't random or abstract. Maybe it came from a very real place. A place at the back of her head filled with memories.

"This might sound crazy, but have you dealt with him before?"

Slowly, she nodded.

"Once," she said, picking at her nails. "Two years ago. I was investigating a child abuse ring in Manhattan. At first, the police thought the dickheads at the center of it were regular criminals. You know, human trafficking, that sort of thing. But after a little investigating, multiple witnesses started coming forward to say something darker was at play."

She paused for a breath and sat back in her seat as the weight of what she was about to say fell against her.

"The kids they interviewed," she continued, "the ones that survived, they described things that could only be called human sacrifice."

"You're telling me this abuse ring sacrificed *kids*?"

"It wasn't the abuse that people think of when they think of the usual news headlines, and soon the police were realizing that too. That's when I was called in."

She bit her lip, staring into the distance again as though lost in her memories of it.

"Moloch was ultimately the one behind it," she explained. "He operated through these criminals. They were all-powerful men. They thought that he could give them more power, more fame, more money, pretty much whatever they wanted. All they had to do was give him what he wanted."

"Children."

She stopped fussing with her nails and rubbed the heel of her hand against her eye. For a second, I was worried she was going to cry, but instead, she sat up straight, took a deep breath, and carried on.

"Yeah. This demon feeds off children," she said. "It's not exactly common knowledge. There's only a handful of religious scholars who've heard of him, but his history in this world is almost as old as the world itself. People wanting more power or luck or money have sacrificed children to him for centuries. For thousands of years, actually. It's done all over the world. Since he's a demon, he can appear differently to different people to get what he wants. So whether it's a witch doctor in Uganda or a cult in Tennessee, Moloch is ultimately the one behind it."

Goosebumps rose up the backs of my arms. I wanted her to stop talking, didn't want to hear another word she had to say about child abuse and demons.

"So . . . you think that's what's happening here?" I asked. Elena frowned as she thought about it.

"The thing is, he doesn't normally take so many kids at once. It's usually one here, one there. But if they're being taken underground, like what Haley told us, and the numbers being what they are, there's gotta be something bigger at play."

She bit her lip in thought, obviously not hearing a word I said.

"Logan . . . the case in Manhattan was the worst I've ever worked on. I don't want to . . . I don't think I can . . . "

Her voice broke and she swallowed hard.

"I don't know if I can do it again. To deal with that darkness. That demon."

Rising from her seat, she walked over to the window that looked down the hall. Mild chaos was still erupting throughout the building as young officers and seasoned detectives tried to battle with their ever-increasing workload.

"What are you thinking?" I asked her. "You look like you're hatching a plan."

"I just have a hunch."

"Tell me."

"Well, I'm thinking we should—"

"Sheriff, I was wonderin' if you—oh!" A young officer burst into McKinney's office who looked like he'd slept as much as I had. Dark circles lay beneath his eyes and his hair was sticking up on end. "Sorry. Thought the sheriff was in here."

"Last I saw, he was out there with you guys," I replied. "Everything okay?"

"It's pure insanity."

He drained the last of his coffee and tossed the paper cup into the trash before dragging his hands down his exhausted face and yawning.

"When was the last time you had a day off?" I asked.

"A day off?" he scoffed. "I don't remember."

He yawned again and leaned against the wall.

"You're FBI, right?"

"Right."

"And what do you make of all this?"

I thought about everything Elena had just told me and all the things I had experienced over the last few days. No one would believe it. I wouldn't haven't believed it myself a week ago.

"I think we've got a very complex case on our hands," I said.

He stared at me, waiting for me to elaborate, but I didn't. What more could I tell him? Tensions were running high through the station, and I didn't want it to reach full-blown hysteria by rambling about demons. The news would travel like wildfire to the reporters roaming around the parking lot. I did not want to be known as the FBI agent who confirmed that our top suspect was a demon named Moloch, who liked long walks on the beach and dabbled in child sacrifice.

"I just wish I knew what else I could do," the young officer sighed, rubbing the back of his neck. "I've done the interviews with the family members. Hundreds of them. I've lived here all my life and I know these people."

"Are you related to any of the missing kids?"

"No," he said, shaking his head. "I've searched the area, miles and miles of it looking for these kids but . . . " He grimaced as though he was physically in pain. "There's no sight of them. Nothing."

He lowered his head and gazed at his shoes.

"Is it true what they're all saying? That there's some sort of paranormal force behind it all?"

"That's just a rumor," I said, glancing at Elena. "What we need is some hard evidence."

"Like I said, I grew up here. I've heard the stories. Heard some of the noises in the woods myself. I'm not saying there's gremlins out there, but I wouldn't be surprised if there was something."

He rubbed his eyes and yawned.

"Just wish there was something more I could do," he said, walking back towards the door. "Something that can actually help instead of doing interview after interview."

Elena's eyes brightened and she whipped out her phone.

"Actually, there *is* something you could do," she said, waving him over to her side. She brought up the photo of the sigil inscribed onto the boulder we'd found at Sylvia's. "See this symbol? Have you ever seen that around town or out in the woods?"

"No, never."

"Are you sure?"

"Pretty damn sure. Think I'd remember it. It's a weird looking scribble, ain't it?"

"It's more than a scribble. I think it's a clue about whoever took all these kids. I want you to look around town and see if you can find it somewhere."

"Should I look anywhere in particular?"

"It could be carved into rocks or trees. Probably away from populated areas though."

She texted him the photo. Meanwhile, a look of confusion crept over his tired face.

"All of Yarbrough is surrounded by woods. I'm happy to help y'all, but it'll be like finding a needle in a haystack."

He zoomed in on the picture, taking note of every curve and line of the sigil.

I scratched my chin in thought, wondering what the best plan of action would be.

"Here's an idea," I said. "You've got a map of the places where the kids went missing, don't you?"

"That I do."

"Focus on those places. Start at the one nearest to the station and work your way clockwise."

"Sounds like a plan." Enthusiasm entered his voice as he straightened himself up. "I'll get started on that right now."

Taking an FBI business card out of my wallet, I handed it to him and tapped my cellphone number.

"Call or text me if you find something. Doesn't matter what time of day or night it is. If you find anything, take pictures and send them to Agent Rivera and me."

"I will," he said, looking at my name. "Senior Special Agent Hawthorne."

"And your name is . . . "

"Officer McKinney."

"McKinney? Any relation to the sheriff?"

"He's my uncle," he said, looking a little embarrassed. "But that ain't why I work here. Became a cop on my own."

"Oh trust me, I understand." I gave him a knowing smile. "My dad was in the FBI, and so was my grandpa."

"Ain't that something."

"Right then, let's get back to business. I'm ready to roll," Elena said, clapping her little hands together. The color had come back to her cheeks and she looked hell-bent on getting out of there. Officer McKinney gave her a polite smile and stepped out of the room.

"Nice meeting you, Agent Hawthorne. I'll be in touch."

With a mock salute to Elena and me, he darted out the door with a spring in his step.

"Awww, you made a new friend," she teased. "You think he's secretly an expert in demons?"

"No, but he's young and hungry and has something to prove because of his name. He'll be perfect."

I turned to her and saw she was trying her best to look normal, but I could still see the uneasiness in her eyes. She gave me a lackluster smile and reached for her previously forgotten Skittles. Chewing thoughtfully, she stared out the window. Another news truck was parked halfway down the road as though they were waiting for the right time to pounce. Soon, there would be more, and we had to have something of substance to tell them.

"What do you think our next step should be?" I asked, watching the truck.

"Sylvia," said Elena without missing a beat. "She saw something last night. Something that scared the ever-living shit out of her. She said it was like hell."

The thought of heading back to her house exhausted me. More dust, more cats, and infinite manic weirdness.

"She needs to tell us exactly what she saw."

"Agreed."

We both stared out the window, the two of us lost inside our heads as we watched the wind blowing through the trees.

"Do you trust Sylvia?"

The side-eye Elena gave me was in a league all of its own.

"Of course I trust her. Why would you ask something so dumb?"

"It's just that the rock with the sigil was on her property."

"Buried," Elena reminded me. "And you felt how heavy it was. You think she's capable of carving it and burying it? She's got arms like chicken wings. She could barely lift a bag of cat food. Don't tell me you think she's in on all of this."

"No, but it's hard to trust her when I know she's

keeping information from us. And don't forget she drugged me."

"That was an accident," Elena said, waving it off like it was nothing. "You got a mild dose of mushrooms. I've seen crazier shit in college. But I do agree with you that she needs to tell us *everything* she saw last night. I'm going to keep after her until I get answers."

"Fine," I sighed, and slipped my phone into my pocket. "Let's head over. But if she offers us anything to drink, I'm not taking it."

23

ELENA

"Coffee?" asked Sylvia as she poured herself a cup.

"No thanks."

"That'd be great."

I rolled my eyes at Logan and he gave me an unapologetic shrug.

"She just brewed it," he said. "I don't turn down a fresh cup of coffee."

Around him, a swarm of cats was slithering their way around his legs and trying to use them as a scratching post. I held back a smug snort of laughter, wondering how much he'd spent on that fancy suit. A chubby ginger cat with crinkly whiskers pawed at his shoelaces.

"Here you are, Agent Hawthorne," said Sylvia, handing over the cup of coffee with a smile.

"So, what can I do for y'all?" she asked. "It must have been a whole two hours since I saw you last. Have there been developments since then?"

"Of sorts," said Logan as he took out his cell.

"My my," said Sylvia. "Phones just keep getting smaller."

"I found an article about the sigil on that rock we found in your yard." Logan unlocked his phone with his thumb and pushed it across the table to her.

For a second, her face was blank. Then she looked closer, squinting as she scrutinized the symbol.

"No . . . " she whispered so softly we hardly heard her. "This can't be. That's the sigil of Moloch."

"You know who he is?" asked Logan. She looked up from the phone with obvious fear in her eyes. Then she slid it across the table to its owner.

"I've only heard of him. Bad people do bad things to appease him. He's a demon. He dwells in the underworld. What I saw last night . . . "

"You said it was like Hell," I interrupted.

"Yes . . . " Her face turned a sickly shade of gray as she held her hands to her face. "I'll never forget it. The fear. The screaming. The tears."

"Sylvia," I said, leaning towards her. "I know what you saw was awful, but you need to tell us what it was."

"No. I can't!

"You have to."

"I can't. It's too much."

She stood up and backed away from us until she was pressing herself up against the kitchen sink.

"I won't!" she screamed, the force of her voice taking me aback.

I rose from my seat and walked towards her, my hands outstretched towards her gingerly.

"It's okay, Sylvia. It's okay. We're here."

"It's *not* okay!"

Tears were in her eyes. She held her shaking, arthritic fingers to her face and sobbed.

"Please," she said. "Don't make me tell you what I saw. Don't make me say it out loud."

I glanced back to Logan, his eyes darting between me and Sylvia.

"I'm so sorry," I said to Sylvia, laying my hand on her shoulder. "I wouldn't ask you if we didn't really need you to."

She sniffed and wiped the tears from her face.

"But we have to know. If we're going to find the children, we need to know everything. I know it scared you, but can you please tell us what you saw? For the children . . . "

She sniffed and nodded again, holding out a hand to pet Lafayette, who had jumped up onto the sink.

"I suppose if it helps you find the children," she said, stroking his uneven black fur. "But I don't see how it can."

"Even the smallest bit of information could help us in a big way," Logan chimed in from the table. She looked back towards him before settling her eyes back on his phone.

"Moloch," she said. "Is he what this is all about?"

"Maybe. There's still a lot to find out."

A chill crept over her and she pulled her sleeves down over her goosebump-covered arms. I too felt the temperature drop in the room and looked around to see if any of the windows were open. When I saw they weren't, I shuddered. The energy in the room was changing fast, but was it because we were talking about Moloch? Or was I imagining it?

"Do you mind if we go to the living room?" asked Sylvia. "It's a bit chilly in here."

When Logan stood up, I noticed all the cats had disappeared. They were long gone, having left without making a sound. Even Lafayette was nowhere to be seen.

Weird, I thought. *I hope this doesn't mean they know something we don't.*

"Sure, Sylvia," I said, taking her trembling hand. "We'll go wherever you're most comfortable."

As soon as we stepped into the living room, I understood why all the cats had left the kitchen. It was late enough in the morning that the sunlight had become bright and hot, filling the living room with intense patches of sunshine that were ideal for napping in. Cats were draped on sunbleached furniture, spread across the threadbare rugs, and curled up on every cushion available.

Beside me, Logan looked at his watch and bounced his knee impatiently. That's what he got for not going on a run earlier. But I understood his frustration. I wanted to ask Sylvia more questions, but was afraid that if I pushed too hard she'd close herself off to me. I couldn't bear the thought of seeing her cry again. There was something so gut-wrenching about seeing an old woman sobbing.

"Right . . . " she eventually said, taking a seat on the couch across from us.

Between us on the floor was the spot of the previous night's remote viewing session. For a split-second, I imagined her body on the floor as she screamed in horror. Then I pushed the thought out of my mind and looked up into her face. She was forcing herself to smile, but I could see her eyes were glossy.

"Are you ready?" Logan gently asked.

"As ready as I'll ever be."

Her hands shook again as she clenched her fingers

around the hem of her skirt, fiddling with loose pieces of thread.

"I don't know where to start," she said, her eyes burning holes in the carpet.

"Hell," I prompted her. "You said you hadn't seen anything like it since you saw Hell."

"That's right . . . "

Her eyes remained fixed on the carpet, her fingers gripping her skirt tighter. I watched as she tugged on a piece of thread so hard it dug into her skin before snapping.

"It's okay," I tried to reassure her. "We're here with you. You're safe."

"I don't feel safe. Sometimes digging into your memory makes you feel like you've traveled back to a place . . . like it could suck you down a rabbit hole of feelings that you tried to forget."

Logan nudged me gently and nodded towards Sylvia. I took the hint and moved across the room to sit beside her.

"Memories can't hurt you," I told her, resting my hand on her back. But I knew that was a lie. Memories could hurt you more than a bullet wound. Or at least it felt that way sometimes.

"I mean they can't hurt you *physically*," I said. Taking her hand away from the hem of her skirt, I squeezed it tight. "The sooner you tell us, the sooner you can forget about it for good. And the sooner we can help find the children."

"Yes . . . Of course. The children."

She sucked in a deep breath and quivered as she exhaled.

"I saw them down there," she began, clenching her eyes shut.

"Down where?" Logan immediately asked. He leaned

forward in his seat, making a steeple with his hands. "Are they okay? Are they alive?"

Raising a hand towards him, I shot him a steely look to shut him up. It worked like a charm.

"Sorry," he said, leaning back and quieting his voice. "In your own time, Sylvia."

Her eyes were still focused on the floor as she continued.

"I said it was *like* Hell," she said. "I saw it once before. When I was younger and I didn't know how to control my psychic power. If you could call it that. Sometimes it feels like such a burden."

She paused, lifted her gaze from the carpet, and looked up to a photograph of her husband as though she was seeking strength from his face.

"It wasn't long after I lost him," she said. "I couldn't handle the grief. I missed him so terribly. All I thought of was seeing him again, just one last time. Of hearing his voice telling me he was alright. That *I* was going to be alright."

Her hand slipped out of mine and began scratching at the upholstery of the couch.

"So I did something I knew was wrong. I tried to contact him. Tried to reach the other side."

"But you said you had a psychic power," I replied. "Hadn't you ever done that before?"

"Not like this. This wasn't as simple as looking for information from the other side. This was reaching far, far into the underworld to seek out death itself. To envision that very essence of death, to understand it. It was wrong, of course. I had this warped idea that somehow I could not only speak to my husband but that I might be able to bring him back."

She looked back up at his photograph with a sorrowful expression.

"But that's not what happened," she said. "I didn't know what I was doing back then. Not really. Not like now. I wasn't experienced enough, and I was arrogant. Thought I could control my power enough to reach into the other side and be safe."

The look in her eyes darkened as she shook her head regretfully.

"Did you reach your husband?" I asked her softly.

"No. No, I never reached him at all. Instead, I made contact with an entity who masqueraded as him, who pretended to be him. The thing I met, I suppose you could call it a demon. It was evil anyway. So evil."

Her hands shook as she raised them to her face and wept.

"I remember reaching out to it, thinking it was my husband, but as soon as I made contact, he changed. He moved like he was melting. Then the damn thing was laughing at me. It shrieked and then it wasn't my husband's face I was looking at anymore. It was this black thing with hollow eyes and a tongue that lashed out like a fiery flame. The next thing I knew I was so hot . . . "

I looked down at Logan and saw the disbelief on his face. Or was it fear? Either way, I could tell he didn't want to hear what she was saying. For some people, knowing another side exists is too much to handle. But learning of other dimensions, especially ones most people have heard about, like Heaven and Hell? To know these places really exist? It's another step into the abyss of the unknown. It's the kind of thing that can turn a person crazy.

"I was so hot," she continued. "Everything around me was humid, dark, damp and decaying. I could barely see anything, but I could tell there were figures moving around in the dark. Creatures that climbed over each other, grabbing at the last bits of light that leaked down from Earth. There was screaming all around me. So much screaming that came from the kind of pain no one could ever feel up here in this world. It was the kind of pain that could only come from Satan himself."

Tears sprung from her eyes as she held a hand to her mouth and silently jerked forward as though she was about to vomit.

"And then there was the smell," she said. "It was the stench of death and sulfur, of rotten bodies and burning flesh. It was the smell of the worst of humanity."

She began rocking back and forth as she spoke, all the while fighting the urge to be sick.

"It was Hell I saw. I know it," she said. "I saw it with my own eyes. I felt the pain, the despair, the sheer desperation. There was a pit. Like a hole in existence that was filled with the screaming dead. It looked like the naked bodies of every single person sent to Hell had been thrown down in there. They stayed there for eternity. There was never a way out. I don't know how I knew that—it was just made clear. I remember looking at all the people, and I couldn't wrap my head around how big this pit was. It wasn't just miles deep. It went on forever and ever."

At last, she stopped rocking and lowered her hand. The tears fell freely from her cheeks, but she paid them no attention.

"The thing that took me down there just kept laughing. And all I could do was pray that I could be brought back to my life up on Earth. I prayed to know what goodness and light felt like."

Across the room, Logan stopped bouncing his knee. He

just sat there, wide-eyed and silent. It might've been the description Sylvia was giving us, or it might've been the fact that Lafayette was in his lap, kneading his thigh with his paws. One quick movement of a startled cat could be disastrous for his balls.

"So how did you make it back?" I asked her.

"I was released eventually. The demon let me go. Brought me back to Earth. I'd never been so grateful for anything in my whole life."

"Why do you think it took you down there? Why did it pretend to be your husband?"

"It was a trickster demon," she said with an air of authority. "That's the only explanation I can give. All of my terror gave him quite a show. He got what he wanted. It's as simple as that. I took my experience in Hell as a warning. That I had somehow trespassed into the other side without permission."

She wiped the tears from her face with the hem of her skirt and leaned over to the coffee table for her mug. She took a long gulp of the hot drink and sighed with relief. It was all out now. All those memories she'd kept locked up in her mind were now out in the open for a sympathetic ear to listen.

"So after that," said Logan, his voice barely audible above Lafayette's purring. "After that, did you give up on psychic work?"

"Agent Hawthorne, you know fine well that's not the case."

At last, she gave a smile. It was weak, but it was still a smile.

"I'll admit that I pushed the idea of using my psychic power to the back of my mind. I was simply too scared to use it. So I tried to forget I even had it. It took a long time, almost a decade to raise the courage to enter that realm again. And that was only because of the sightings."

"The sightings on your property?" I asked.

"Exactly. It felt like things were happening all around me outside of my control. Things that were tied to the land. I wanted to learn more, felt as though it was my duty as a citizen of Yarbrough to follow this path of knowledge to learn all I could about what was happening. That was when I set out to become a student of remote viewing. I liked how other strict psychic techniques had rules that you have to follow for your own safety. I couldn't make the same mistake again of summoning up any old demon that was just passing by. I had to be protected psychically and have full control of my consciousness. It took years of practice. The more I learned how to protect myself and learned the rules, the less afraid I was. At least, that was the case until . . ."

She set her coffee cup down and looked straight at me.

"That was until *you* came along."

Her shaky hand moved across to a plate of cookies on the table. She took one, the edges crumbling between her fingers leaving dusty pieces of chocolate on her tear-stained skirt.

"When you came I thought I could handle it," she said "After all, I'm not a novice anymore, but then . . ."

The tension returned to her voice. She tried to distract herself by biting into her cookie, but it made no difference.

"What I saw down there with those missing children . . . I could spend a lifetime learning to protect myself psychically but it wouldn't do nothing to stop the terrible misery I felt when I saw them."

"Was it really Hell you saw?" asked Logan.

"It certainly felt that way. It filled me with terror in

exactly the same way."

"So was it Hell or was it something *like* Hell?"

"It wasn't Hell itself. But the resemblance was too much. Where those children are is a perfect replica of Hell. You know how those casinos in Las Vegas try to recreate Italian canals or the Eiffel Tower? It's like that. It's close, but you know it ain't the real thing."

The energy in the room once again grew thick. The bright sunlight cast rays of heat across the room. All around the room, dozens of cats lay semi-comatose.

"They were all being held there," she said, looking down at her lap. "All the children."

"They're alive?" asked Logan.

"Most of them are."

It was a sentence that gave both grief and hope.

"Most of them?" I asked.

"There's dozens of them held in a pit underground within the faerie realm. They're screaming, crying, begging for their parents. They're terrified. Some are too young to understand what they're seeing, while the ones old enough to see what surrounds them are paralyzed with fear."

She swallowed hard and pressed on, eager to finish what she had started.

"They're all desperate to get out. All crying. All trying to get back to the surface world."

"Who are they down there with?"

"Creatures. Goblins. Guardians of the underworld. Like the ones you saw last night, Agent Hawthorne."

Logan said nothing, just maintained his poker face and nodded while petting Lafayette.

"Then there's the queen," she said. "An evil woman who has ordered they all be brought to her. I could see her leaning over the pit of children, tossing rotten food at them."

"Does she look like this?" Careful not to disturb the black cat in his lap, Logan took out his phone and showed Sylvia the picture Rylee had drawn of Solana. Sylvia's eyes widened and she nodded her head.

"That's her. Queen Solana."

"Do you know why she took the kids?" I begged to know. "Why would she kidnap so many in such a short period of time?"

But at the back of my mind, the pieces of the puzzle were falling into place. I could have guessed what she wanted them for.

"Power," said Sylvia. "She's going to sacrifice them so she can be the most powerful queen in The Hollows."

"Let me guess," said Logan from across the room. "She's going to sacrifice them to Moloch so she can gain power through him."

Sylvia raised her head to Logan and frowned.

"That's exactly what she's going to do!" she gasped. "She's made a deal with that demon."

"You said most of the kids are alive," continued Logan. "How do you know?"

"I can see them all in that pit. Most of them are alive, but there are so many and they're all piled one on top of the other. It's like an endless fight to get out of the pit, and it's impossible to escape. They'll never get out."

Silence hung heavy in the room. The sun was higher in the sky now that it was noon. Sylvia stood up, stepped over her cats and opened a window to let in some of the warm summer air.

"I never want to see anything like that as long as I live," she said. "The sound of them all crying, the fear of impending death . . . And then the queen's face. She thrives off their pain and misery just like that damned demon does. She loves every second of seeing them suffer."

She walked back to the couch but didn't sit down. Instead, she stood, unable to keep still as she fiddled with the sleeve of her blouse.

"If the children are being sacrificed," said Logan. "Then why are they all down there together? Why not kill them one by one?"

"I can't say for sure," replied Sylvia. "But my guess is that the sacrifice that's awaiting them is part of a bigger ceremony. And if it's to Moloch . . . Then it won't be just any ceremony. Think of the way the Aztecs sacrificed people. They didn't just beat them in the head with a rock. It was a big to-do."

"It sounds like Solana is waiting for the right day," Logan said while running his hand along Lafayette's rumpled, uneven fur.

"I believe so."

Sylvia walked over to the window and looked out towards the forest where the rock was found.

"I could hear her voice," she said, pressing a hand to the glass. "She said the most unspeakable things. She has no soul, no morality. All she desires is power."

I knew that more than anyone. What Sylvia had said churned my stomach, but at the same time, it motivated me. At least now we knew what was happening. Even if what was happening was awful, we knew what we were dealing with.

"What is her objective besides power?" asked Logan.

"Her objective?" laughed Sylvia, still staring out the window. "For her, there is only power."

She lowered her hand from the window and turned back around, leaning against the window ledge. Her face was pale and drawn, her whole body slumping with exhaustion. I could see the toll it had all taken on both her body and mind.

"I'm sorry," she said. "But I can't tell you anymore. I told you everything I saw."

"We appreciate it," I told her. "What you saw was awful. Evil."

"I'll never forget it."

She looked ready to collapse on the spot, her whole body weighing heavily against the window ledge.

"I'm sorry," she said, "But that knocked the bejesus outta me. I need to lie down for a bit."

"Of course. We'll be back soon."

"I'd like that," she said, trying her best to smile at us both. "I don't often get the pleasure of company. I've enjoyed having y'all around, even if it ain't all been good."

I reached out a hand for her to shake and she pushed it away.

"A handshake, Agent Rivera? I think we're a little beyond that."

Leaning in for a hug, she squeezed me tight.

"Come back soon," she said, kissing my cheek. "And make sure you bring that hunk with you. Lafayette's taken a liking to him."

"Well that was fucking awful," Logan groaned as we climbed back in the car. "I'd say that was probably the worst thing I've ever heard."

He let out a long breath and sagged his body against the seat while I rolled down the windows. Sylvia was a crazy, sweet woman, but her house left me gasping for fresh air. I took a deep lungful of air, then turned to see how my partner was doing. He was staring out the window until he felt my eyes on him. Then he turned and gave me the most pitiful look.

"Have you ever heard anything as bad as what Sylvia just told us?"

"Yeah."

"Of course you have." He narrowed his eyes and went back to looking out the windshield. "I don't even know why I asked you."

He folded his arms over his broad chest and sat there, sulking in silence. I glanced towards the rear of the Navigator so I wouldn't start laughing at him.

That's when I saw it.

Orange, sweet, bubbly nectar of the gods. The fucking motherload. And it was sitting on the floor of the back seat behind my fucking chair.

Four cases of Fanta. Four!

"Where did *this* come from?" I squealed, ripping a hole in the cardboard container. I pulled out a can and popped it open.

"Huh? Oh . . . " He was still sulking, but now he looked a little sheepish too. "I found that at the Piggly Wiggly when we were in Scruggsville. It was after you fainted."

"Oh honey, you remembered!" I gushed, then took a huge chug. I hadn't realized how thirsty I was until I drank half the can in one shot. I didn't give two shits that it wasn't cold. Sitting in Sylvia's dusty house without a drop to drink had left me parched.

"Yeah, well . . . surprise." He frowned until his bottom lip puckered just the tiniest bit. The little furrow in his brow had returned full force.

"What's wrong?"

"Oh, you know. Just losing my goddamn mind. *That's* what's wrong. I joined the bureau to go after terrorists and criminal masterminds. I didn't sign up for some megalomaniac faerie queen recruiting a demon from hell to kidnap kids for a mass child sacrifice. What the actual fuck? Don't you think it's all a bit far-fetched? I mean, yeah, I want to believe Sylvia. Really I do. She's a sweet lady, but come on."

"I'm sorry, Logan, but this is what we're dealing with."

We sat in silence, still parked in the driveway with the windows rolled down. I polished off the Fanta and reached in the case for another one.

"And how can you just sit there and chug your soda like this is just another job?" he demanded.

"Because it's just another job to me." I stifled a burp and slid my Fanta in the nearest cupholder. "Look. This is just one job. Next week or next month there'll be another one and it'll be just as fucked up. You can't let it get to you or you *will* lose your goddamn mind. I'm sorry your first case in the OCD had to be kids. It's not like I don't care. Not when I saw my mom get murdered and grew up in foster care. Anyone who hurts animals or children deserves total annihilation."

Leaning back against the headrest, Logan stared up the long driveway through the trees towards the road. I watched as his shoulders began to relax.

"So . . . this is just another day at the office for us?"

"Yep. You better get used to it." I pulled my seatbelt across my body and clicked it into place, careful to not touch the metal. "Maybe for our next assignment we'll get some nice terrorists who just happen to be poltergeists. Those cases are actually kind of fun."

"I need a fucking beer," he grumbled, twisting the key in the ignition. "Or ten."

24

LOGAN

"Power," I muttered as I started down Sylvia's driveway. "That's the whole point of all of this. Queen Solana wants power."

I heard a sarcastic snort from the passenger seat.

"Isn't that the point of everything? Fame and fortune and sex is just another name for power."

Elena was right, but it still felt hard to grasp. Killing all those innocent children and sacrificing them to a demon? How could anyone do such a thing? And for power? It wasn't something I could wrap my head around.

"You okay?" asked Elena from the passenger seat.

She was staring at her phone, looking at the picture of Moloch's sigil again.

"Honestly? No. I can't get that image out of my mind, of all the missing kids thrown into a pit like a bunch of rats. Fuck. We don't even do that to rats."

My stomach clenched tight. The whole situation sickened me.

Elena lowered her phone and rested a gentle hand on my arm.

"You'll be okay. The fact that you care so much means you'll do everything you can to save them. I'm finally starting to see why Chief Harris made us partners."

"You really mean that?"

"Yeah. And maybe I'm being a bit optimistic, but deep down I think we can save the kids. If Solana's waiting for the right moment to carry out her ceremony, that means we still have time."

"I suppose," I said, gripping the steering wheel tight. "But the whole thing just leaves a bad taste in my mouth."

"You want a Fanta? Nothing washes away the taste of human sacrifice like high fructose corn syrup and yellow number six."

I let out a bitter laugh, finding a strange comfort in her brand of dark humor.

"Sure, if you open it for me." I had my hands full navigating as the car bumped along the rocky dirt road. "How long is this driveway? Feels never ending."

"Sylvia definitely lives off the beaten path."

"In more ways than one."

We crawled along, our bodies rocking from side to side each time a wheel hit a rock or crevice in the road. Every few yards, a cat would dart out from the bushes or worse, decide to take a nap right in front of the car. Honking at them didn't work. The only effective way of moving them was for Elena to get out and shoo them away. One of them refused, holding his ground until she dragged it to its feet and plopped it down on the side of the road.

"Fucking cats!"

"And here I thought you were starting to like them," Elena laughed.

"*Like* them? They fucking ruined my suit!"

"You let Lafayette sit in your lap. I saw you petting him!"

"No, what you saw was me being nice to him so he wouldn't shred my nuts with his murder mittens."

Elena laughed so hard she snorted.

"That's basically the definition of cat ownership."

"I never want to see their evil little faces again. Look at these assholes over here."

I pointed at a gang of three tabbies traipsing down the side of the road.

"I bet they have a full day planned of terrorizing wild birds and shitting in people's yards. They act like they own the whole town."

"Well, they own part of it," said Elena.

"Hmmm . . . " I grumbled, edging the car around the little gang of whiskered hellions who barely glanced up in acknowledgment as we passed.

"Would you look at that?" I moaned at them. "Didn't even budge an inch. What a bunch of dicks!"

Elena raised her eyebrows at me and pursed her lips.

"Wow, you really do need a beer."

At last, the end of the driveway was visible and the main road came into view. As soon as the car rolled onto the smooth asphalt of the two-lane county highway, I breathed a sigh of relief.

"Thank fuck for that. Are you okay with having lunch at the Drunk Chicken?"

"As long as you don't give me shit about putting honey on my French fries, sure."

The drive back into the main strip of Yarbrough was short, but with the area being so hilly and sparsely popu-lated, it felt like we were driving through the wilderness. It was rare to see another vehicle on the road, unless it was one of Sheriff McKinney's officers or frantic people driving to the latest search site.

That was why it was even more noticeable when a large pickup truck pulled out of an almost invisible side road and crept up behind us.

"Would you look at that piece of shit?" I laughed as I adjusted the rear view mirror. "You ever seen a rust bucket like that?"

Elena turned round in her seat and stared out the back window at it.

"Looks like it came right out of a demolition derby. Especially with the lift kit. Do you hear it? Sounds like the muffler fell off about ten years ago."

I tried to ignore it and focus on the winding road, but it was impossible to not hear the growling of its engine. I kept flicking my eyes up to the mirror, and I noticed there was barely a panel on the truck that wasn't dented or rusted. What was left of the red paint had chipped and rusted to a miserable brown, and the windows were so filthy they looked like they'd been smeared with mud. At least that's what I thought at first. It wasn't until I took a closer look that I realized the windows weren't just dirty, they were blacked out with tint.

"Elena? What do you make of those windows?"

"They're . . . " she squinted and leaned further out of her seat. "They're tinted."

"That's weird, right?"

"Yeah. Windows like that don't belong on piece of shit mudding trucks like that, do they? They'd cost more than the damn thing's even worth."

"That's what I thought."

I picked up speed, eager to put a little distance between us and the driver. Not being able to see the driver's face put me on edge, and the way it was driving wasn't suspicious as such, just . . . peculiar. It kept trying to tailgate us, then backed off, only to do it again. I could detect some kind of road rage from the driver. Whatever had pissed them off, they had an intent to do something.

"What you thinking?" asked Elena.

"I dunno. Just . . . seems weird."

"I'm going to get a picture of the license plate."

"Good idea."

Reaching her phone out behind her, she snapped a picture through the back window of the Navigator.

"Got it?"

"Ugh. Yeah, but the thing's so dirty I can't make out the numbers."

She zoomed in on her screen to see better, but couldn't make out anything more than a brown blur.

"Should we ignore it?" she asked.

"Suppose so. It's not as if they're doing anything. I just had a hunch, that's all."

"Always trust your gut," she said. "That feeling is more powerful than you could ever believe."

I drove on, focusing ahead where I could see the first few houses of the town come into view.

"Do I turn right or left to get to the Drunk Chicken?" I asked.

"Left, I think."

Elena pointed to a road that looked like nothing more than a bicycle path snaking into the middle of nowhere.

"Are you sure?"

"Yeah. McKinney said it was the first right before town, and since we're coming from the opposite direction, we should take a left."

It didn't feel right, but trusting Elena's judgment, I

swung left and once again felt the asphalt give way to rocky terrain full of potholes and bumps.

Goodbye coccyx, I thought as the wheels hit the first hole in the road. The suspension on the Navigator was pretty impressive, given the state of the road. There was no way that rusty piece of shit truck would be headed in the same direction as us.

Or so I thought.

To my surprise, it swung in close behind us, driving way too fast for my liking.

"What the hell?" asked Elena, turning back round to look at it. "They're right on our ass!"

"This doesn't feel right."

"Speed up."

"I'm going as fast as I can around here! It's like driving on the fucking surface of the moon—with speed bumps and switchbacks!"

I hit the gas and we zoomed down the road a little further, but the truck behind us was only a couple of feet away from plowing into us.

"Are they speeding up?" I asked, looking in the mirror. "They are! Shit, what's their problem?"

I hit the gas again, moving perilously fast around the bend. If we'd been somewhere with wide open plains, I would've pulled onto the shoulder or driven into a cornfield. But we were in the heart of the Smoky Mountains, where unpredictable fog and steep slopes kept that option off the table. Hoping that nobody was coming in the opposite direction, I pulled over to the other side of the dirt road to let the dickhead behind us pass.

It didn't work.

"What the fuck are they doing?" I yelled. "We're federal fucking agents!"

"What are you gonna do, Logan? Stop the car and show them your badge? The driver's probably tweaked out on meth! They'll run you over!"

"Fuck, they're speeding up again. They're gonna hit us!"

"Hit the gas!"

"I *am*!"

"Go faster!" cried Elena.

"I'm trying not to drive us off a goddamn cliff!"

"I swear if they come any closer, I'm firing!"

Her hand moved down to the golden gun neatly holstered at her side. Since I'd met her I hadn't seen her give it much thought, let alone draw it. I wondered if she thought she was too good for crude, human weapons, but now she was gripping it tightly with an incredulous glare pulling at her face.

"I'm calling McKinney," she said, but as she reached for her phone, a crunch sounded as the car behind us plowed into our bumper.

"What the fuck!"

Elena's phone hit the floor on impact, dropping down to the floor mat. She reached down, fumbling for it, but before she could curl her fingers around it we were hit again. This time so hard that the Navigator jolted forward, the back wheels floating off the ground for a few seconds.

"That motherfucker's trying to run us off the road!"

"No shit, Sherlock!"

Part of me wanted to speed up and escape, but the bigger half of me wanted to screech to a halt and beat the living shit out of the driver. But this wasn't la-di-da Dupont Circle or Georgetown. This was the backwoods of Tennessee. People around here loved their guns. The last thing I wanted was to confront a meth head with an AR-15.

Behind us, the monster truck's engine growled even louder. I heard another crunch as we shot forward. The steering wheel slipped between my fingers as I briefly lost control. My stomach was twisting as I grabbed the wheel and coaxed our car away from the edge of the road.

"Call McKinney!" I shouted as I desperately tried to maintain control.

I felt the shock of being smacked extra hard from behind. There was a millisecond of quiet, and then we were hit with a wall of sound as the Navigator made impact.

Metal twisted and bent. Glass shattered. I could smell gasoline fumes and burnt rubber. Air was gushing around the side of my face, but I couldn't figure out why.

That's weird. I don't remember opening a window. What the fuck is happening?

I was breathless, frantic, and confused. I tried to see where my partner was, but all I could see was the blurry whiteness of the deployed airbag.

Is that blood? Why is it soaking through my shirt and pants?

A sharp, searing pain entered my head and there was a weird, gritty, metallic taste in my mouth.

Then everything went black.

25

ELENA

A shock wave tore through the entire car, shooting up through my body. Despite all the twisting in my seat, the safety belt had kept me from flying through the windshield. All I could feel was the stifling sensation of the airbag against the side of my face. It felt like I was being attacked by a giant marshmallow. Wrestling with it, I pushed it away from me and fumbled for the door handle.

My fingers clenched themselves around it with a crunch as a dozen shooting pains stabbed my fingers.

"Ow! Fuck!"

I looked down at my hand and saw blood where tiny shards of glass had punctured my skin. I brushed my hand on my jeans, getting the bigger pieces out.

"Logan?"

Looking across at his seat, I expected to see him sitting beside me, but instead, I saw branches from a tree that had thrust itself through the windshield as we hit it. On the other side of it, I could just about make out his head cushioned by his inflated, bloody airbag.

"Logan!"

I pulled the door handle and fell about three feet onto the ground, landing on my face in a patch of wildflowers. Crawling on my hands and knees, I staggered into the middle of the road and saw the full impact of the damage to the car. There was a v-shaped dent in the trunk, but that wasn't what made my stomach lurch. The Navigator had done a swan dive into a huge oak tree, which was the only thing that kept us from flying down the steep mountain slope. If we'd gone six inches to the left, we'd have rolled right down the mountain. If we'd gone six inches to the right, Logan would've been decapitated by the tree branch sticking through the windshield. It was sheer dumb luck that one or both of us wasn't dead.

I jogged over to the driver's side, my feet stepping on broken glass. Fortunately, that side of the car was tilted close enough to the ground so I could reach it. When I pried open the door I found Logan's face pushed deep into the airbag.

"Logan? Can you hear me?"

I reached in and shook his arm. Nothing.

"Logan?"

I knew it was risky to move a person after a crash, but I wasn't thinking straight. Panic had set in and adrenaline was coursing through me. Grabbing him by the shoulder, I shook him again.

"Logan!"

"Ugh . . ."

Inch by inch, he began to move as he grumbled and groaned.

"You're awake!"

"Yeah, yeah, I'm awake," he coughed, pushing himself away from the bloody airbag. "Why am I facing down?"

"We were in an accident. The car's stuck on a tree, but I

don't think it's going anywhere. Are you okay? Does anything hurt?"

"My head hurts a little," he said, still disoriented from the unnatural position he was sitting in.

Gradually, he came to grips with his surroundings, looking around like he'd passed out and woke up in a space-ship. He squinted as he stared at the smashed windshield, then the tree branch right next to his head. I watched as he started adding things up and let out a panicked garbled noise.

"What the . . . What the fuuuuck?"

"Logan, do you remember what happened?"

"The last thing I remember was . . . That fucking truck!"

"Yeah. It ran us off the road."

"Fucking asshole!"

He craned his neck up at the road as though he hoped to somehow still see them.

"They're long gone," I told him. "Nothing but birds and chipmunks out here. Are you sure nothing's hurt?"

He lifted his hand to his head, and when he pulled it away, it was covered in blood.

"Shit, you're bleeding pretty bad."

He looked down at me, slightly bewildered and a little afraid.

"Elena, I'm bleeding *everywhere*. I can feel blood all over my shirt and my legs. Is it bad? Am I going to die?"

Studying his clothing, I frowned, avoiding his eyes. The liquid was definitely centered around the crotch area . . . more on his right side than his left.

"Well . . . your clothes are wet, but . . . it's not blood."

Logan closed his eyes and groaned, although it wasn't in pain. Not physical pain, anyway.

"Fucking great. I fucking pissed myself, didn't I?"

I took a deep breath.

"Let's not worry about that right now. Can you move your arms and legs? Is anything broken? Ribs? Collar bone? Are you having any trouble breathing?"

"I'm fine," he insisted. I watched him unfasten his seatbelt and carefully climb out of the driver's seat.

"Sit down," I ordered, taking off my jacket. Then I peeled off my tank top.

"I'm so confused right now," he said, trying to avoid looking at the turquoise and lime green embroidered flowers that adorned my black bra. "I piss myself, and you start stripping. Don't tell me you're into watersports."

"You didn't piss yourself, dumbass," I said, folding my tank top into a neat little square. I fished a piece of tree bark out of his head and pressed my shirt against the wound. "It's Fanta. You had an open can sitting next to you when we crashed."

I watched his entire body relax as he sighed in relief.

"You don't know how happy I am to hear that."

"Yeah, well, you might change your mind once it dries and your balls get stuck to your leg." I tugged my jacket back up my arms and crawled inside the vehicle.

"What are you doing? It's not safe in there. You better not be grabbing a motherfucking Fanta."

I grinned to myself as I peeked under the passenger seat. It wasn't the worst idea he'd come up with since we'd started working together.

"I'm looking for my gun. It's custom made just for me. I can't exactly walk into the nearest Walmart and buy another gold-plated Glock." It took a few moments of digging through broken glass, leaves, twigs, and bits of tree bark. I heard a metallic groan as the car shifted a little.

"Elena? Get out of there!"

"Just a sec. I think I see it!" A little glint of gold flashed from beneath one of the cases of Fanta. "Yep! Found it!" I stretched my body, carefully lifting the twelve-pack off my gun. I'd switched off the safety before the crash, and I really didn't feel like accidentally shooting myself in the face. Another metallic groan sounded, followed by a high-pitched squeal and some cracking.

"*Elena!*"

Ignoring my partner, I grasped the handle and put the safety back in place while the groaning squeal got louder.

A powerful pair of arms grabbed my waist and yanked me backwards right as the tree branch holding the car in place snapped. Together, Logan and I watched as the Navigator tumbled down the mountain slope, flipping over and over until it skidded to a halt and burst into flames. My jaw fell as the fireball rose high above us, blanketing us with unnatural heat.

"That was too close," I heard him breathe into my ear. His arms were still wrapped around me, holding me tight against his body. I sank into them as I realized what he'd just done. If it hadn't been for him, I'd be melting into the upholstery right about now.

"You sure you're okay?" he panted while pulling me closer. He held me so tight it almost hurt, but I didn't complain. Instead, I rested the back of my head against his shoulder and felt the rapid beat of his heart through our clothes. Finally, he lowered me to my feet, but he didn't let go. For a long time, we just stood there together, watching in shock as the Navigator burned. Time withered away to nothing. Right then, all I wanted was to stay there feeling safe, but as I breathed in his smell and relished the feel of his warm, muscular arms, I kept remembering the image of the rusty truck and the sound of its revving engine.

"We should probably give McKinney a call and report this. The sheriff, not the nephew," I said, turning around to face my partner. His suit was ruined, his hair was a mess, and blood was running down the side of his face, but his blue eyes only reflected concern for me.

"Elena? Are you sure you're okay?"

"Yeah. Just a few bumps and bruises. Nothing to worry about." I backed out of his grasp and holstered my gun.

"Really?"

"I swear I'm fine. Just shaken up, obviously." I motioned toward the burning wreckage below us. "Can you call this in though? I left my phone in the car. Pretty sure the police radio's in there, too."

"I'm on it." He dialed the sheriff's office and I watched as he paced alongside the road, keeping things as brief as possible.

"Sheriff's out on a call but they're sending over a firetruck and a deputy to pick us up. Should be about fifteen minutes."

"Thanks." I stooped down to grab my folded up tank top and pressed it against his head. "You're bleeding like a stuck pig. Make sure to keep applying pressure until it stops, okay?"

"Yes, ma'am," he said, grinning at me.

"How can you be smiling when you just got bitch-slapped by an oak tree?"

Logan grinned even wider, then nodded at the burning vehicle.

"I was just thinking . . . now we don't have to fight over the radio station anymore."

"Good point," I said, snickering at his comment. "We should ask for a sunroof on the next car we get."

"I'll keep that in mind."

I went back to picking glass out of my hand. Now that the adrenaline was wearing off, shit was getting real. I was quickly going from nonchalant near-death breeziness to fucking irate that someone had almost killed us.

"You know, the more I think about what just happened, the more it seems to me that this was no accident."

Logan nodded, still holding my tank top against his head.

"Agreed. There's only one reason I can think of. We're too close to the truth. And someone around here doesn't like that."

I looked up into his face and pondered the weight of what he'd just said. Someone had attacked us because we knew too much? But who?

"It could be Davis," I suggested. "He seems like the type of guy who'd have a mudding truck like that. Plus I'm gonna go out on a limb and say he's not a fan ever since I kneed him in the crotch."

"He's definitely at the top of my list," Logan said with a nod of agreement. "Regardless, it's someone local. You don't drive like that unless you know every curve and bend in the road. I'd say they live nearby."

"What if someone's pissed that there's FBI here trying to solve the case and steal their thunder?" I suggested. "Whoever ran us off the road might not know what we've learned from Sylvia about those kids."

"Or they know we're closing in on them and they're getting desperate," he replied, staring into the flames of the burning wreckage. "There's a lot of possibilities. Whoever they are, and whatever their reason, they wanted us dead."

26

LOGAN

"Excuse me, ma'am, but about how much longer?"

"Almost done," said the nurse who was tending to the cut on my head. She'd been saying that for almost ten minutes. She also happened to be the same nurse who'd looked after Elena when she'd fainted. "I've seen a lot worse. Especially in the summer. This is nothing compared to a good old-fashioned lawnmower accident. Compared to that, this is just a little scratch. Anything above the neck bleeds more because you have so many blood vessels there."

I tried to stay still for her, but I kept glancing at my watch or my phone, checking the time and hoping to hear from Elena. We'd gone opposite directions after the wreck. I came here to Scruggsville urgent care clinic to have my head sewn up. She'd hitched a ride with a state trooper out of Knoxville to take care of rental car arrangements and get another phone. I wasn't worried about the trooper. Yarbrough wasn't her jurisdiction, so she had no skin in the game. She was simply there to help the sheriff's department look for the missing kids. She was doing us a huge favor by driving Elena to Knoxville.

It was a little over two hours from there to Yarbrough. Add in a half hour to pick up the rental and another hour to get a new phone, and Elena wouldn't be back until seven at the earliest.

After being run off the road, and after pulling her out of the car about five seconds before it blew up, I worried about her driving alone. I worried about her errands in Knoxville taking too long, forcing her to drive back in the dark. I probably didn't need to worry at all—the girl had more grit and determination than just about anyone else I knew, but still.

A text would be nice.

"There you go," the nurse said in a chipper voice as she tied off the last of my stitches. She took a step back to admire her handiwork before putting on a bandage. "You're lucky I do quilting in my free time. I bet you won't have much of a scar at all, if I do say so myself."

"Thank you, ma'am. I appreciate the extra effort."

With a warm smile, she headed towards the door before pausing as though she'd recalled something.

"Oh, I've just remembered. Sheriff McKinney is waiting to see you. Should I send him in?"

"Sure. Thanks again."

She sauntered out with a grin and a few seconds later was replaced by Sheriff McKinney's lumbering body.

"Agent Hawthorne!" he declared, blustering into the small exam room. He took one look at my orange soda stained, bloody, cat-scratched suit and nearly fell over. The bandage on my head must've been what put him over the top. "Good god, son! Are you alright?"

"Just a little scratch," I said, pointing to the bandage on my head. "Apart from that, I'm as good as new."

He lurched towards me, and for a second, I was worried

he was going to wrap me up in a big sweaty bear hug. Instead, he gently ruffled my hair like a concerned grandpa.

"I was so worried about y'all when I heard what happened!"

"No need to worry," I assured him. "Me and Agent Rivera are both fine."

"And I assume you've had the whole rigamarole of tests. You know, x-rays and whatnot?"

"No. That's not necessary."

"Of course it's necessary!"

"Really, we're okay. If we hadn't been buckled in it would be a completely different story, but we're fine. The car took the brunt of the impact."

McKinney shook his head and began wandering up and down the cramped room, taking two steps one way, then spinning on his heel and taking two steps back the other.

"It's disgraceful," he mumbled through his mustache. "Absolutely disgraceful. You're a federal agent for cryin' out loud! Not only that, but you're guests of this town. I'm so sorry, Agent Hawthorne. Really, I am. We'll find whoever did it. I promise we'll find them."

"They shouldn't be hard to find," I said, getting up from the exam table and collecting my jacket. "The truck was loud as shit. And it looked like shit too. Rivera got a picture—"

"She did?"

"Yeah." I ran my fingers along the edge of the bandage on the side of my head. "But her phone blew up in the car. I'd be surprised if it went to the cloud. I'll know more once she gets her new phone."

McKinney's eyes narrowed.

"You kids and your clouds." He wagged a finger furiously into the air. "We'll find out who's responsible. You have my word, Agent Hawthorne. We'll find those sons of bitches and we'll bring them to justice."

I felt relieved seeing him so eager to track down our attackers, but I also wanted him to shut up for five seconds so I could describe them.

"The truck was brown," I said. "I'm assuming it was red at some point, and . . . "

"Ah, so you didn't see it too clearly?"

"No, I could see it fine. It's just that it was all rusted and beat up and—"

"Sounds like it could be one of those Malones who lives out way, way past Sylvia's place. Weird family out there. Off the grid prepper types. Don't like outsiders much. Did you see a face?"

He finally stopped pacing and wagging his finger and looked dead into my eyes.

"No . . . I didn't see a face. Just the truck."

"Well now, that's . . . that's a damn shame. I'd be able to find them easier if got a description of his face. Anyway, I'm on it."

He urgently made for the door as though his ass had caught fire and he tore at the handle.

"Sheriff, don't you want some kind of statement or . . . "

He was gone, storming down the hall with the squeak of his boots disappearing into the distance.

"Knock knock," came a nervous voice. The deputy who'd been kind enough to bring me to Scruggsville urgent care appeared in the doorway holding two cups of coffee.

"What happened to Sheriff McKinney?" she asked. "He had a face like thunder."

"Yeah, he seems pretty stressed out right now. Is that normal for him?" I said, taking a coffee from the woman.

"He's probably embarrassed," the deputy said. "He

asked you here to help solve these kidnapping cases, and now the locals are going after you."

I took a drink of the coffee. It was terrible but at least it was hot.

"Hmm . . . He didn't seem embarrassed. He seemed . . . I don't know how to put it. Just . . . odd, I suppose."

It felt like all my FBI training had failed me right then. I was trained to monitor behaviors and speech patterns and derive intention from them, but McKinney just seemed like a jumbled mass of contradictions to me. I had no idea what he was thinking.

"Well, he's always been a little different," the deputy said with a faint grin. "Like how he has all those books about ghost stories in his office, or how he's going to retire and live off of that treehouse he built as an Airbnb. Maybe that's normal in places like New York and San Francisco, but around here, that's a little weird."

"Fair enough." I slung my jacket over my shoulder and the two of us headed out the door.

I looked down the hall in the direction McKinney had gone, mulling over what he'd told me about the Malones . . . preppers who didn't like outsiders.

There were dangerous locals who didn't like people like me and Elena. This town was small, and if Sheriff McKinney was related to other officers, chances were likely that he was related to other people in the area. Roots ran deep in little places like this. Alliances were forged through generations and seldom broken. Was this potentially dangerous Malone family related to the McKinneys?

It was a possibility. Sometimes these small towns felt like a law unto themselves. All I could hope for was that the town wouldn't close ranks against us.

ELENA

I pulled into the McKinney's empty driveway and parked our new rental car, then headed for the backyard after chatting with Martha for a few minutes. It was around eight-thirty, and the sunset had been so gorgeous that I'd taken the most roundabout way to get back to Yarbrough. It was hard to believe something so beautiful could exist in this world when there was so much ugly to contend with. Most of all, I thought about how lucky I was to be alive to see it. I'd be a smoldering pile of ash right now if it weren't for the football star up in that treehouse. Some people called it fate or destiny.

I called it Thursday.

I'd cried a little in the car on the way back to town and gotten it out of my system. Given my line of work, I'd almost been killed at least half a dozen times—maybe more. I'd just never had someone else save me. I felt stuck between being grateful and feeling like I owed my partner big time. Given our line of work, it wouldn't be the last time one of us saved each other's life. That was the whole point of having a partner—you didn't have to do everything yourself. You had help.

The wooden shutters of the treehouse windows were propped open when I climbed up the stairs. Logan was sitting on the bed, staring at his laptop in an old Quantico t-shirt and what looked like swimming trunks. He looked up at me from under the brim of a worn-out Washington Nationals baseball hat, and I just about died.

I could see it all over his earnest, adorable face. He was worried about me. He set aside his laptop and scooted to the edge of the mattress.

"You're back later than I expected. Everything okay?"

"Yeah," I said, tossing aside my purse and keys. "I took the long way back. Thought I'd watch the sunset."

"Damn. I missed the whole thing. I've been researching stuff online all night," he said, reaching for a bottle of water. He took a gulp and then gave me an expectant look. "So? What did you get us? Please tell me it's something with decent legroom."

"Chevy Tahoe," I gloated while jutting out my jaw in satisfaction. "With satellite radio and a sunroof."

"Nice. I'd say that deserves an award." Logan motioned towards a shallow cardboard box sitting on the bench next to his rolled-up sleeping bag. "Open it."

I took the three steps required to cross the little room and pulled the cardboard flaps apart. My eyes widened when I saw the haphazard mess of lumpy rainbow swirls and uneven clusters of glitter sprinkles.

"Unicorn cupcakes with homemade buttercream frosting," he announced. "The deputy who drove me to urgent care said her kids are raising money for a puppy. They've been running a lemonade stand every weekend since summer vacation started. When she told me they're expanding into bake sales, I couldn't resist."

"You mean, these are *edible*?" I asked, not looking away from the box of sparkling rainbow cupcakes. I felt like a tiger shark, and he'd chummed the waters a little too well. If he wasn't sitting right there, I'd already have shoved half of these in my mouth. Gathering all the restraint I could muster, I brought the box over and sat down on the bed next to him.

"You want one?"

Logan shook his head.

"Nah. I don't really like frosting."

He might as well have told me he didn't like puppies or kittens.

"How is that even possible? The frosting's the best part of a cupcake!"

"No, the *cake* is the best part of a cupcake," he argued with a grin. "The frosting's just there to cover up a sub-par baking job."

"No, the frosting is meant to *complement* the flavors of the cake."

Logan peered into the box, then raised a skeptical brow.

"How do you figure, when there's more frosting than there is cake? By your definition, that's like adding a stick of butter to a cup of popcorn."

"And?"

Logan rolled his eyes, but he was still grinning.

"Whatever. All I'm saying is that you can have a cupcake without the frosting, but you can't have a cupcake without the cake. And I like cake more than I like frosting."

I looked at him, then looked down at the box. Then I picked up a cupcake and used my finger to guillotine the massive heap of colorful, glittery frosting perched on top of it. More for me.

"Here," I said, presenting the bald vanilla cupcake to him with a bit of a flourish. "This is me sharing."

"Thank you," he said, and started to carefully peel away the paper wrapper. "Were you able to get a new phone?"

"Shrrrr . . . mmm hmmm . . . " I mumbled with my mouth full of frosting. With my free hand, I reached into my jeans pocket and waved the new phone at him. He snatched it out of my hand and studied the case briefly before giving me shit about it.

"You couldn't find anything with a little less bling?" He looked down his nose at the sparkly holographic turquoise and purple case, then set it down beside me.

"They had one with rhinestones, but those always pop off and look like shit after a few weeks. This one should hold up a lot better."

"Any chance you were able to recover that photo of the truck that ran us off the road today?"

"No," I said, finishing my cupcake. "My phone backs up every night so there wasn't enough time for it to upload to the cloud."

Logan frowned a little. He was still peeling the paper off his cupcake, while I was licking frosting off my second one.

"Did McKinney at least get a statement from you?"

"No. I haven't seen him since this morning in his office."

"He didn't call you while you were driving?"

"No, although Chief Harris called to say the judge approved of our wiretap request. He's already got a crew monitoring every line going in and out of the station."

"That's good news. Nothing from Sheriff McKinney, though?"

"Nope. Didn't even get so much as a text asking if I was okay," I said, raising a single eyebrow as I swallowed more rainbow frosting. "But he's been slammed lately. You saw what the station was like, between all the volunteers from neighboring towns and the media trucks. That's probably why he's not home yet."

More curious frowning from Logan.

"McKinney isn't home yet?"

"Nope. I talked to Martha when I got back and she said it wasn't like him to be out so late. She made him supper and it's still sitting on the table. Apparently, he always comes back for supper no matter what."

"Interesting . . ."

"Not really," I said. "He's a small-town sheriff with a serial kidnapper on his hands and a PR fiasco to manage. It's not like Yarbrough has a comms person to deal with it. The man's got his hands full. I'm sure collecting statements from us is on his to-do list. It's kind of hard to forget about a car exploding."

"Fair enough," Logan said, and finally took a bite of the cupcake. "I just thought he'd want an official report or something."

"Maybe the fire department took care of it?" I shrugged. "I don't know what their protocol is out here for that kind of thing."

I polished off my cupcake and put the box back on the bench, then kicked off my boots and flopped face down onto the bed.

"You don't have to get up," I said from where my face was mushed into the pillows. "I've just needed to do this all day. It feels so good, but it feels so wrong."

"What feels wrong?"

"Lying down for five damn minutes. We should be out

there finding those kids. Not binging on cupcakes and lying around in a treehouse."

"Elena, this isn't summer camp. We were in a major car crash today," Logan pointed out. "I can't believe neither of us broke a single bone."

"I've never broken a bone," I admitted. "Just other people's bones."

"Me either," Logan said with a chuckle. "I mean, minus that last bit. You'd think after playing football throughout high school and college that I would've had at least a few significant injuries, but I was always really lucky that way. It's nice to see that luck carried over to the OCD. We're lucky we only walked away with a few scratches."

"I know." I adjusted my pillow and stared out the window at the twilight sky beyond the trees. "But I can't help feeling like I should be out there. I know you said I can't pour from an empty cup, but I feel so useless lying here."

"Maybe you could answer some questions I have," he suggested and picked up his laptop. "I've been researching ever since I got back from Scruggsville."

"Researching what?"

"Paranormal stuff like remote viewing and demons and faeries."

Aww, Logan was doing his homework! And I hadn't even asked him to! I felt warm and fuzzy at the thought of him finally accepting more of what the Occult Crimes Division was all about.

"Impressive. What questions do you have?"

"First thing I need to clarify is what's the difference between faeries and fae? Or are they the same thing?"

"Fae is a general term for any magical creature that originates in the realm directly below this one."

"You mean the Hollows?"

"Right. So demons have magic, but they come from Hell, so they're not fae. They're demons. And ghosts and poltergeists can have some magic abilities too, like moving through walls, but they're human souls that are stuck on earth. So, not fae."

"Okay, then what's the difference between a faerie and a fae?"

"You know how bobcats and leopards and lions and tigers are all felines?"

"Sure."

"It's the same concept. Some fae are faeries like me, and some are goblins or nymphs or kitsune or elves."

"Elves?" Logan took off his hat, ran his fingers through his clean hair, then put it back on. He was clearly trying his best to stay open-minded. "Are they like Santa's elves or like Lord of the Rings elves?"

"Santa's elves are actually brownies," I explained. "It used to be common for them to help humans with their work as long as they were taken care of. The elves I'm talking about are more like Lord of the Rings. I've met a few. Most of them are dicks."

"Huh. Okay. What about wings?"

"What about them?"

"For example, do all faeries have them? Can you actually fly?"

"Ha! I wish! I'd love to be able to fly." I stretched and rolled onto my side, still snuggled into my pillow. "Not all faeries have wings, and some have wings but can't fly very far. Some of my ancient ancestors had them, but that trait died out a long time ago. We still have the bone spurs on our shoulder blades from where we would've had wings. It's kind of like how people used to have tails, but they've evolved to the point where they don't need them anymore. Now they only have teeny tiny tailbones."

Logan blinked as if he'd misunderstood me. He narrowed his eyes in confusion and sat up slightly to see me better.

"Wait—you mean you've got little baby wings? Is that why you're always wearing a jacket? I know you're not wearing it because of any dress code."

"I don't have actual wings . . . " I clarified, feeling a little uncomfortable. "I . . . I have bone spurs where they would've been. Wing spurs. They make my back look all bumpy. But you're right. That's why I always keep my back covered up."

Logan sat up even straighter, his eyes moving down my side, searching for some sign of them through my jacket. There was still a hint of suspicion in his eyes. It wasn't intense enough to call it skepticism, but it was definitely there. His lips were parted, hinting that he had a thousand questions dancing on his tongue but was afraid to ask.

"You wanna see them, don't you?"

He gave a little laugh.

"I mean, yeah. But don't feel obligated."

"That's just it—I *do* feel obligated." I sat up and wound my loose hair into a bun on top of my head. "You're in the OCD and you're not even sure if it's completely real or not. You're my partner and I want you to be able to trust me. I wouldn't show you my back if I didn't trust you. Maybe it has something to do with you saving my life today."

His face grew serious as he thought about what his next words would be.

"I couldn't have saved you if you hadn't woken me up and gotten me out of the car. Look—you're my partner. You might drive me crazy sometimes, but I swore an oath to always have your back. And speaking of backs, you don't have to show me yours if you don't want to. It's not your responsibility to make me believe in things I don't understand. That's on me. You don't owe me anything, Elena. I'm not into keeping score."

With that, he pushed the rest of his cupcake into his mouth and went back to scrolling on his laptop. I watched as he chewed, as he swallowed, as he licked his lips and then brought his thumb to his mouth, sucking the last sweet remnants of crumbs until his finger was clean.

I've never wanted to be a cupcake so bad in my life.

"So . . . do you want to see my back?" I asked.

"Yeah. The curiosity's driving me nuts."

He gave a modest smile and closed the laptop, then set it on the floor next to the bed. I turned my back to him and unzipped my jacket, pulling my arms out of the sleeves until they were free. I hadn't bothered finding another shirt to wear after my tank top had become an emergency bandage after the crash. The only thing left on my skin was my bra.

One hand at a time, I reached up and slipped each bra strap off my shoulders.

And then I waited.

I'd never shown anyone my wing spurs before. Not ever. Not people I'd slept with. Not even the nurses and doctors who did the FBI physical exams. I always wore a t-shirt or a full-coverage tank top. If Logan had asked me a few days ago to see them, I would have been offended at the idea of showing a human, but he wasn't *just* a human. He was someone I had grown to trust, someone I felt safe with.

A soft breath moved across my bare shoulder blades, and the strands of hair that hadn't made it into my loose bun tickled my neck. It was a warm summer night, but Logan's warm cupcake breath sent goosebumps down my arms and legs. I could practically feel his attentive, thoughtful gaze on my skin.

"I've never seen anything like that before," he said in a wistful tone. "Is it okay to touch them? You can say no."

I fought the urge to twist away from him, to hide my wing spurs away from his analytical eyes. He'd seen enough of my freakish bumps.

But even as those critical inner thoughts filled my mind, my head nodded and my mouth said, "Sure."

The mattress sank as he crawled closer behind me. Again, that warm breath tickled my neck as loose hairs danced across my skin. Again, that clean, verdant, woodsy scent filled my nose as his body crept closer to mine. I closed my eyes, my breath hitching and my back arching as his warm fingertips touched me where no other living being ever had.

"Does it hurt?" he asked, and lifted his hand away. "You flinched a little."

"No, it doesn't hurt." I looked over my shoulder at him and caught his gaze. His eyes were hidden by the brim of his ball cap, although I could see that his lips were slightly pursed. "I guess I'm a little sensitive, that's all. I'm not used to anyone touching me there."

"Hmmm . . . don't worry. I promise I'll be gentle."

I suddenly felt both of his warm hands on my back. His fingers spread out, grazing the skin, exploring each rise and fall of the protrusions on my shoulder blades.

"They feel like knuckles," he murmured behind my ear. Another soft shiver tingled across my body, culminating below my navel before melting away. I leaned back against him, reveling in the warmth that came not just from his touch, but his very being. I closed my eyes again, letting his fingers run up and down the length of each row of spurs.

"They kind of look like two tiny little mountain ranges going down your back."

Looking over my shoulder, I saw the deep fascination in his face as he caressed each bump with his careful fingers. Then his eyes flicked onto mine, so dark blue under the brim of his hat that they almost appeared navy. He had something on his mind. There was no mistaking that intense look in his eyes.

I kept waiting for him to say something . . . to *do* something. For the love of all that was holy—he had me right there in the bed, wearing nothing but jeans and a bra that was two unfastened hooks away from lying on the floor. I felt a dull ache between my thighs, no doubt coaxed there from the warm breath that kept hitting me, not to mention the firm hands exploring me. If stupid Logan would just make a fucking move, I'd let him slide my jeans down my hips and do anything he wanted.

Another ache spread through me. I could feel the liquid heat pooling in the crotch of my thong. I could smell how ready I was for him.

Please . . . just make a fucking move!

"Elena?"

Oh fuck oh fuck oh fuck—he's gonna do it!

I bit my lip to keep from squealing. "Yeah?"

"This might be a totally inappropriate thing to ask, but . . . "

Nope! No such thing as inappropriate! Whatever insane thing you're gonna suggest, I am down!

"Are you embarrassed by this part of your body?" He trailed a finger over my bumpy left shoulder blade, then crawled off the bed and grabbed his laptop. "Because you shouldn't be. I think your wing spurs are kind of awesome."

Nooooooo! screamed my pussy. The elusive man meat

317

had escaped our clutches yet again. So much for sexy times.

I yanked my bra straps back into place and slipped my jacket back on, zipping it halfway. I started digging around my bag for some pajamas while Logan plugged in his laptop and phone in our one stupid outlet.

"Yeah, well, I hate people seeing my wing spurs. I got made fun of constantly," I told him as I found the baggy t-shirt I slept in. "I've been called Lizard Chick, Frog Princess, Boney Bitch, Lumperina, you name it."

"Damn! Kids can be such assholes!" Logan said from the sleeping bag he'd unrolled.

"And every time I changed foster homes, I changed schools, which is probably why I hated gym class so much. I still hate the fucking gym."

"That sucks so much. Well, if you ever wanna go for a run or go to the gym with me, let me know. I promise I won't make fun of how you look."

I found my toiletry bag and started for the tiny bathroom, desperate for a shower. I stopped and turned to him.

"What if I showed up in a mankini? Would you make fun of me then?"

He took off his hat, tossed it aside, and ran his fingers through his hair, all while wearing a smug, boyish grin.

"There's only one way to find out."

At first, I thought I was awake. It wasn't until I looked around and realized I wasn't lying in the bed I'd fallen asleep in, but the one I used to lay my head down on as a child.

"What the fuck?"

I sat up, looked down at the green silk bed covers of my

childhood and buried my fingers into the cotton depths of my pillows. The smell of vibrant, living earth filled the room along with flowers, grasses, and mushrooms growing on the forest floor. It was the scent of the Hollows . . . of the Kingdom of Elphame. A scent I hadn't smelled since I'd been there last. It was so strong it threatened to overwhelm my other senses.

"Am I dreaming?" I said out loud, looking around my former bedroom.

It looked the same way it did on the day I left it, with books and trinkets strewn across the floor.

"Yes, you are dreaming, dearest."

I jumped at the sound of a voice from the corner of the room. A voice I never thought I'd hear again.

"Mom?"

Looking behind me into the back corner of the room, I saw a figure in the shadows sunk deep into the armchair I used to throw my dolls onto.

"Mom? Is that you?"

Slowly, the figure rose, and through the shadows emerged the patient, kind face I'd loved so much. I saw her rosy lips parted in a smile and her green eyes soothe my nerves.

"Mom!"

"Stay there," she said, holding a hand out.

"But I want to hug you."

"You will hug me again someday, but not today."

She shifted over to the end of the bed, her long gown falling gracefully around her slender frame. It felt as though not a moment had passed since the last time I saw her . . . as though it hadn't been two decades since the last time she held me, but two seconds. She looked just like she did on the day she died, only more beautiful.

"My goodness, Elena. You've turned into such a beauty."

"Aww, thanks, Mom. I look just like you."

She smiled and looked out towards the window. It was dark when I fell asleep in the treehouse, but here it was light outside, the misty air was a silvery shade of gray that gave the feeling of lingering between two worlds.

"We don't have much time," said my mom. "You have to listen carefully."

She pulled her attention away from the window and looked deep into my eyes.

"Elena, you're involved in something very big, very evil."

"Solana. I know."

"Not just her. She is summoning something truly evil, truly demonic, but you can stop it, Elena. I believe you really can."

"I'll stop Solana with my dying breath if I have to."

Mom smiled, but there was a bittersweet look in her eyes. Like she wanted to be happy but somehow wasn't allowed to be.

"How I wish I could have been with you when you were growing up," she said, sadly. "How I wish I could be with you now and see all the things you've accomplished. You're so strong. So, so strong. The Rivera family would be so proud of you if they only knew."

"I get my strength from you."

"I don't doubt that. Now you must use your strength to stop unspeakable evil. You must stop Solana before she hurts more children. If you don't stop her, she will summon Moloch . . . and blood will run deep when she does."

"Oh, believe me, I'm working on it."

She looked back towards the window, but her eyes saw

nothing beyond the glass. Instead, her gaze turned inward to her own thoughts.

"I have to go soon," she said, growing restless.

"No, wait!"

"Before I go I must tell you two things . . . and you must listen."

"I always listen to you, Mom."

She leaned further down the bed towards me, reaching out her hand to me, but her fingers couldn't quite bridge the gap between us. It was as though she was somehow forbidden from touching me, like if she inched closer something terrible would happen.

"That man you sleep with," she began. "Logan Hawthorne . . ."

"My partner?" I asked, completely baffled that she knew anything about him. "Technically, we're not sleeping together, we're just sharing a room. And even if we *were* sleeping together, I know he's not a faerie like us, but—"

"Regardless of his birth, he is a good man. Pure of heart. Keep him close."

"Um . . . could you be more specific?" I asked. A laugh escaped my lips before I could stop it. It was *my* dream, after all. I had questions.

She shrank back away from me and glanced over her shoulder as if she was being watched.

"The second thing will save you all," she said. "It will stop Solana from unleashing chaos and forcing her evil up into the surface world. It will save the children of Yarbrough. It will bring them back."

Hanging on her every word, I leaned towards her, my heart hammering hard in my chest.

"Do you remember your way around the castle?" she asked, holding out her hand towards the door.

"Of course. It's our home! I mean, it used to be our home."

"Then you'll remember the library."

"Yeah!"

When I was a child I spent tons of time in the library, although there was a section that I was forbidden from entering. I remembered its green door down in the lower level of the castle. No one could enter that area except the high council and my mom and dad. There were rumors around the castle that ancient secrets were kept in there, magical ones that were too powerful for ordinary subjects to know about. Even as a young princess, and the heir apparent, I was never allowed to see them.

"Now is your time to learn what lies inside that part of the library," my mom explained. "Now is your time to learn the secrets it holds."

"How exactly do I do that?" I asked, bewildered.

"You will know how."

She stood up and walked back to the armchair in the shadows, sinking herself deep down into it.

"Mom, wait!"

I still had a thousand things to ask her, and a thousand more to tell her. I wanted to tell her I loved her. Wanted to hold her and smell her comforting, familiar scent. I wanted to feel like I was a kid again, safe in her arms.

"I must go," she said, dissolving into the darkness.

"But Mom! What about the library!"

"You will find what you need within its walls," she breathed, her figure shrinking into the shadows.

"Wait, don't go! How can I get into the library? Solana lives in our castle now!"

I leaped off the bed and ran to the chair, but as I reached it, I saw it was empty.

"Mom? Mom! *Mom!*"

A short, sharp gasp stung my chest as I struggled to breathe, and the next thing I knew I was sitting upright in bed, crying. My hair was still wet from my shower, and my heart was thundering so fast it felt like it was about to explode.

"Elena?" called a voice nearby. "You okay?"

"I had the craziest dream!" I cried.

"So I gathered," Logan said, reaching over and turning on the little light above the bed. He looked down at me and stepped into the bathroom, coming back with something in his hand. "What was it about? Your mom?"

"Yeah . . . "

Looking out the window, I saw it was still dark. Beneath me, there were no green silk sheets and no earthen smell of the fae realm. The summer night air was fresh, but it wasn't the same as it had been in my dream.

"Here," said Logan, handing me a wad of toilet paper as he sat down next to me. I wiped my eyes and blew my nose as I tried to gather my bearings.

"It didn't feel like a dream," I told him, throwing the used toilet paper at the little trash can in the corner. I missed. "My mom came to see me. It felt so real. She was sitting where you are now and it felt so real."

Logan gave a sleepy, sympathetic smile and wrapped one of his long arms around my shoulders. I kept waiting for him to offer words of wisdom or try to bring up how he dealt with things when his own mom died, but he just sat with me, rubbing my shoulder, giving silent comfort.

I recalled what Mom had said about him . . . that he was pure of heart, that I should keep him close. As I looked into his eyes, I wondered how to interpret her message. Given that he'd pulled me out of a car seconds before it blew up, he was definitely a good person to have nearby.

"My mom told me how to solve this case," I told him.

"Oh yeah? What did she say?"

"That I had to go into the library," I said.

"Yarbrough doesn't have a library."

"No, I mean the library in the castle I grew up in. She said there was something in there that would help lead us to the missing children. But I don't know how I could get in there."

"Can't you go in the same way you came out?"

"Technically, yes, but there's a bounty on my head, remember? If I set foot in the Hollows, let alone Elphame, Solana would have me killed on sight."

"Then it's a good thing you don't have to be there in person," Logan said with a wink.

"Huh? What do you mean?"

"What I mean is, I think there might be a way to get you in that library without entering the fae realm. A way Sylvia knows about."

"Ohhh . . . right . . . " I said, nodding slowly. One last shudder rippled though me, leaving behind relief and a desperate need for sleep.

"My mom also said to keep you close."

"Oh yeah?" he smiled softly. "How close?"

"I'm not really sure," I shrugged.

"Do you want me to stay here until you fall asleep?"

I felt my face flush ever so slightly. "If you don't mind."

"I don't mind." He scooted down until he was lying down next to me. "If your mom came back from the grave and said she wanted me to stay close, then I'll stay close." He reached up and turned off the light, laughing softly in the dark. "You know I'm a momma's boy."

28

LOGAN

"Agent Rivera! And Agent Hawthorne! How nice to see you again!"

"I feel like this place is my second home now," I laughed, stepping into Sylvia's hallway, nearly tripping over three cats in the process. Thankfully, I'd decided against wrecking my other suit. I'd gone with hiking boots, a dark blue polo shirt, and my favorite tactical pants, made specifically for walking through briars and thorns. The cats would be no match for me.

"I had a feeling you'd both be back here," said Sylvia, leading us both down to the kitchen. "I just baked cookies."

The smell of cinnamon and sugar permeated the house, giving a much-needed break from the fragrance of rotting wood and cat piss.

"That's so kind of you," said Elena, taking a seat at the kitchen table. After sleeping in late, I'd gone for a run. Then we'd gone to the diner for lunch, where she'd eaten a full order of chocolate chip pancakes topped with whipped cream, a strawberry milkshake topped with more whipped cream, and a doughnut. But that didn't stop Elena from grabbing a cookie off the metal baking sheet. I swear that girl had a hollow leg.

It was still hot, and she winced as it burned her finger-tips, but that didn't stop her from sinking her teeth into its sweetness.

"Mmm . . . These are great!" she said with her mouth full and reached for another one. "I've got the biggest sweet tooth."

"I'm surprised you have any teeth at all," I said, taking a seat beside her and removing my Nationals hat. But there were a lot of things that surprised me about Elena. Her sugar consumption was by far the weirdest.

"As nice as it is to have company, I assume you came here for a reason," said Sylvia, taking a seat. "What's brought you back again so soon?"

As she sat down across from me, her eyes landed on the bandage on my temple.

"Goodness, Agent Hawthorne. What happened to you?"

"Someone tried to kill us," explained Elena with her mouth still full. "But we're fine."

"Someone tried to kill you?"

"It's just a scratch," I said as Elena dipped her hand into the tray for cookie number three. "We came to ask you more about remote viewing."

Sylvia tensed in her seat. I could tell she wasn't in the mood to be sent on another psychic adventure.

"Not for you," I quickly added. "For Elena. We need you to show her how to do it."

"Really?" Sylvia asked, grinning widely at the prospect of someone seeking out her expertise.

"Really," Elena said, gulping down the mouthful of

cookie. "I need you to guide me somewhere. A place from my childhood."

"You do? Oh, Agent Rivera! I'd be delighted to help you on your journey! But I won't do it unless you promise me one thing." She leaned closer to us, giving Elena a stern look. "This place you're going. Is it dangerous?"

"No. I don't think so."

Elena was smiling as she spoke, the corners of her delicate mouth curling up as she chewed. I could see the excitement in her, the light in her eyes. I could almost see her want to bounce up and down in her chair like a kid stepping into Disneyland.

Sylvia slid her hand across the table and grasped Elena's fingers.

"Are you are sure it's not dangerous? I could never forgive myself if . . . if you got hurt."

"It's my childhood home," Elena said with a dismissive wave of the hand. "It's only dangerous if someone sees me there. That won't happen, will it? No one will be able to sense I'm there, will they?"

"No. You'll be looking at things just like you were watching them on TV. But things will be more vivid. You'll be able to feel the temperature and smell your surroundings. You'll even be able to taste things. You'll feel the pain or happiness of whoever you see."

"It sounds like the most immersive virtual reality experience," I grinned.

"That's exactly it," said Sylvia. "It's like being there in real life. It's not for everyone."

We all fell silent for a moment, looking at each other as we contemplated what we were about to do.

"You won't be alone," Sylvia eventually said to Elena. "I'll guide you. I'll be with you every step of the way."

"Me too," I chimed in. "On this side, anyway."

Elena smiled and polished off her last cookie.

"I'm ready," she said, wiping her hands on her jeans. "Let's do this."

We were back in the living room once again, the three of us sitting cross-legged on the floor as the early afternoon sunshine poured through the windows. The light and the warmth was so strong it was almost oppressive, and I found it impossible not to yawn. All around us, cats congregated and draped themselves on every available cushion and piece of furniture.

A gentle meow sounded nearby, and a moment later I felt a soft nuzzle against the back of my elbow. I looked down and saw Lafayette's dark face looking up at me with wide green eyes.

"Hey, little dude."

He meowed back in greeting and I scratched under his chin, then ran my hand down his patchy, unevenly shaved black fur. It was meant to appease him and send him on his way. Instead, he took it as an invitation to climb into my lap. I scrubbed my hand down my face as he morphed himself into a furry loaf shape across my inner thighs. The only thing separating his murder mittens from my balls was a pair of boxers and these fancy tactical pants. I guess it was time to see if they were a good investment or not.

"Alright then, Lafayette . . . go on and make yourself right at home, I guess."

Lafayette looked up at me with a serene expression and began to purr in response. I swear he was grinning at me. It wasn't a sweet, friendly grin, either. It was the kind of grin you give when you're secretly telling someone to go fuck themselves.

"He likes you," said Sylvia, smiling sweetly at us. "He's always been aloof, but he likes you quite a bit. He told me so."

Sure he did, Sylvia. Sure he did.

She was sitting near the coffee table, lighting what felt like the hundredth white candle. Beside her, Elena fidgeted impatiently. Every so often, her eyes would flick over to mine, but when I returned her gaze, she would glance away. I'm sure she was nervous. The last time we'd done this, Sylvia's face had caved in and been replaced with a black hole of chaos. I thought about that happening to Elena and tried to put the image out of my mind.

"Okay, are we ready?" Sylvia asked.

"As ready as I'll ever be," replied Elena.

"Okay, I want you to hold this."

She placed a pen in Elena's hand and poised it over a sheet of paper.

"Did you bring a blindfold? It might be hard to keep your eyes closed the entire time."

I fished one of my neckties out of my pants pocket and handed it to Sylvia, who tied it around Elena's head.

"Now, you're a beginner, but you're fae. You should have enough natural psychic ability to do this," she said. "But you haven't done this before. You'll have to follow all of my instructions to the letter. Do you understand?"

"I do," promised Elena, gripping the pen tighter.

"Okay, I want you to think of where you want to go. Name the place."

"The library," said Elena.

"Be as specific as you can, honey. There's a lot of libraries out there."

"I want to go to the library in my parents' castle."

"Good. Hold the image of it in your mind."

Elena clenched her jaw tight and pressed the tip of her pen to the page.

"You got it?"

"Yep."

"Okay . . . Now I want you to be there. Not just dream you're there, but really be there."

"How do I do that?"

"You switch off your conscious mind," explained Sylvia.

"How could I ever do that!"

"Stop talking. Stop thinking. Stop doing anything. Just be . . . Just be in your subconscious."

Elena clenched her jaw even tighter, but I could see she was struggling to complete the impossible task.

"Just be in my subconscious?" she repeated. "I don't know how to do that."

"Okay," said Sylvia, moving so she was sitting behind Elena. "Where do you feel that you live?"

"Huh? I live outside of Washington, DC."

"No, I mean your feelings. Where do they live?"

"In my head, obviously," said Elena, becoming annoyed.

"No, no! I mean your true feelings. When you're angry, where do you feel it? When you're sad, where does that darkness lie? When you're feeling lovey-dovey about someone, where in your body sparks to life?"

Elena thought for a second, then placed her free hand onto her stomach.

"In here."

"That's right," said Sylvia, reaching around to cradle Elena from behind. "In your gut. That's why it's called a gut feeling, right? You're an FBI agent. You go after the bad guys. You must've had a gut feeling before about a case. A hunch maybe?"

"Yeah," said Elena. "All the time."

"We're going to draw on that feeling now," said Sylvia, placing her hand over Elena's.

The two of them sat there, holding onto Elena's stomach as though it held the key to everything. Given how much she was capable of eating in a day, I wouldn't have been surprised to learn it had magical abilities.

"Draw on this gut feeling," said Sylvia. "This is where the subconscious lies."

Elena fell silent for a moment, but I could see her whole body relax.

"I'm there!" she suddenly blurted out. "I'm in the castle! I don't mean I'm just imagining it—it's like I'm really there! I can smell it. Oooh, I can feel how cold the stone walls are. I can . . . feel the breeze coming through the open windows."

Although her eyes were still shut, her face was filled with wonder.

"Where are you?" asked Sylvia.

"I'm on the staircase that goes down to the lower level of the castle. It's dark. Pretty damp. It's nothing like what it was when I was a child."

"What do you hear?"

"Distant murmuring," said Elena. "Like there are dozens of people above me. I can hear their voices traveling through the ceiling."

Suddenly, she shuddered like she'd come across something hostile.

"What is it?" asked Sylvia.

"This was my home when I was a kid," she said.

"Except it's nothing like I remember it. It used to be happy. But now it's . . . dark."

"Explain the darkness," urged Sylvia.

"It's seeping out the walls. It's evil. It followed someone here. It followed Solana . . . "

"Solana lives in your family's castle?"

"Yeah. She takes a lot of pride in living there after killing my parents," seethed Elena, her throat pulled tight with anger. "She's been breaking down all the positive energy my parents left and replacing it with evil."

"And where is Solana now?" asked Sylvia.

With a mind of it's own, Elena's arm jumped into action and began dragging the pen all over the page. With Lafayette still planted in my lap, I scooted over to see what she was drawing. The image of a large throne was being scratched angrily into the paper.

"She's in the great hall," said Elena through clenched teeth. "That bitch is sitting on my mom's throne!" Her cheeks grew red with anger, and she gripped the pen so tight her knuckles turned white. "But she can't see me," Elena went on. "She can't see that I'm here in her home. *My* home . . . "

"Good," replied Sylvia. "You make sure to keep your distance. You're just a ghost passing through space and time."

Elena nodded, but her anger failed to dissipate.

"Okay, go down to the library," instructed Sylvia. "Can you go back down?"

"Yeah, I'm back in the stairwell."

"What do you see?"

"Mold. Slime. Decay. The walls are crumbling down here. There's dirt and grime everywhere. It doesn't look like anyone's been down here in years. Maybe decades. Maybe since my parents died."

"Can you see the library?"

"I can see the door. It . . . It used to be green, but the color's faded. Now it's just muddy looking. It's falling off its hinges, and the handle is rusted."

Raising a hand off her stomach, she pushed through the air as though she was opening a door.

"Oh, you guys . . . it's so sad down here," she said, her face crumpling around the blindfold. "No one's been here in ages. It's like they forgot all about it." She moved her face down as though she was staring at the floor. "It's all falling apart. The books . . . There's thousands of them but they're all rotting away to nothing."

She hung her head sadly.

"For someone who's so obsessed with power, Solana sure doesn't give two shits about reading and learning."

Raising her head as though she could see through the layers of the castle to the room in which Solana sat, she said, "She thinks books are for the weak."

Then she lowered her head, her closed eyes focusing on something in the distance.

"Do you know where in the library you need to look?" asked Sylvia.

"No."

"That's okay. Let your gut instinct guide you."

Returning her hand to her stomach, she felt for a hunch, that gut feeling that was to tell her where to go.

"I think I have to move closer to the back of the room," she said. "To a hidden compartment. It's . . . I think it's beneath the floor."

"What do you see?" asked Sylvia. "You need to tell us

everything as you move through that space. It'll help you stay in the moment. Describe everything around you."

"There are pages of dusty books scattered on the floor. There's a small window. No, not quite a window, but a hole in the wall that used to have a thick piece of glass across it. It's smashed now, broken in a storm and never fixed. Wind and rain flow in here. It's destroying everything."

She went silent again, her eyes flickering beneath her lids.

"Now what do you see?" asked Sylvia.

"A wet floor covered in leaves. A table that's been knocked over."

"What do you smell?"

"Mold."

"What else?"

"Sadness."

"You smell sadness?"

"I mean I smell all these rotten pages and it's making me sad."

"What do you feel in your stomach?"

"I feel like I have to keep walking to the very back of the room. Ugh, I can taste the air. It's nasty down here. Everything's all covered in rot and dirt and years of damp air and dead leaves. My mom would've cried if she'd seen it like this."

"Try to focus," urged Sylvia. "Walk to the back of the room like your gut keeps telling you."

"Okay."

"Now what do you see?"

"Nothing."

"Nothing at all?"

"Just a wall. There's nothing on it. There used to be paint on the bricks, but it's peeled away. I can see little shreds of paint chips on the floor. They're green and look just like the leaves beside them."

"Are there no books?" asked Sylvia.

"Nope. Nothing."

"What about this compartment you spoke of?"

"I can't see anything. Just a wall."

"Think. Feel your instinct. There must be something."

"But there's really not!" cried Elena. "I don't see anything. I don't think this is working. Clearly, my gut feeling is wrong."

"It's never wrong!" snapped Sylvia. "It's never ever wrong. You must listen to it closer. Do whatever it tells you."

"But . . . "

"Do what it tells you!"

"It's telling me to . . . "

Elena frowned as though she was confused by her own feelings.

"It's telling me to dig."

"Dig where?"

"At the bottom of the wall."

"Alright. Then dig!"

Elena pushed her hands out in front of her as though she was scrambling through the ether, her tiny fingers pushing and pulling at the wall in front of her.

"I feel something," she gasped. "A loose brick!"

"Can you move it?" I asked, being drawn into her excitement.

"Yeah! Holy shit—it's coming out of the wall!"

I watched as her fingers pulled out the imaginary brick and set it down at her feet.

"Now what's happening?" I asked her, forgetting all about the cat purring in my lap. "Elena, what do you see?"

"There's a hole in the wall. A compartment."

"What's in there?"

Without hesitation, she thrust her hand into the hole, her fingers clenching around something large and heavy.

"It's a book!"

"What book?" Sylvia and I called out in unison.

She lowered her blindfolded gaze to what lay in her hands.

"It's a book of spells. It's my mom's old book of spells."

29

ELENA

It didn't matter how long ago my parents were killed—I could never forget my mother's handwriting. I grew familiar with it from the moment I was old enough to read, although I never thought I'd see it again.

Looking down, I felt the thick crumbling pages of the book in my hands and brushed my cautious fingertips down over the paper. My fingers came away with dust and debris, but the ink remained steadfast on the page.

"Elena?" came Logan's voice. It was deep, warm, powerful, yet so distant. It sounded like it was coming from somewhere inside my head while simultaneously coming from some place far, far away.

"Elena, the book of spells. What does it say?"

"It says too many things to explain," I said, gingerly flipping through the pages.

Undoubtedly, the book was the one thing I was meant to find. Quickly, my eyes devoured the pages as I tried to find whatever I was destined to find.

Use your gut, I thought to myself. *Use your subconscious, your instinct.*

My fingers were working independently from my body as they made their way through the book. Page after page after page . . . until they rested on one page in particular.

"Can you still hear us?" asked Logan.

"I can hear you fine," I replied.

"What are you seeing right now?"

I looked down at the page. Is this the one that my subconscious chose for me? Was it the one my mom wanted me to find? A feeling in my gut was telling me it was. There was an unwavering sense within me that this wasn't just the section I was supposed to find. This was *the* page I was meant to find.

My eyes fell upon the words at the top of the page and my heart beat a little fast, but not from fear, but from elation.

"I'm looking directly at the solution to our problems," I said, trembling with excitement. "A spell that will stop Solana for good."

"What is it?" Logan begged to know.

"Please, Agent Rivera—tell us!" urged Sylvia

I held the book close to me, feeling my mom's spirit through each and every word she'd written on that page.

Thanks, Mom, I thought as I squeezed its old pages in my hands. *You may have finally put an end to all of this.*

"Elena! What does it say?" asked Logan again.

"This is the spell," I began, a smile forming on my lips. "My mom named it The Greater Ceremony to Mute all Evil. Looks like we can use this to—"

Before I could get the words out, a thump and a thud sounded from overhead. A second later came the rush of footsteps down the ancient staircase.

"Who treads there?" came a booming male voice.

Spinning around, I looked through the doorway out to

the staircase at the sight of four of Solana's guards running towards me. There was no mistake that I was as real to them as the swords in their hands.

"Sylvia! Get me out!" I screamed. "They can see me!"

"Wake up, Elena!" she shouted. "You're not there! It's only in your mind. You're safe in my home. You're sitting on the floor with me and Agent Hawthorne. Lafayette is purring in his lap and there's a plate of cookies sitting beside you. You're not really there!"

I could hear her voice, but it appeared to do nothing. I was still trapped in the vision in my head, the guards getting nearer and nearer.

"It's not working!" I screamed again.

"Elena, wake up!"

I felt solid arms around my shoulders and suddenly I could sense Logan by my side. I could smell his woodsy skin and hear his powerful voice piercing through my thoughts.

"Snap out of it, Rivera!" he shouted.

I felt a hard jolt, like I'd fallen from a great height and landed hard back into reality. When I opened my eyes, I saw Sylvia's and Logan's shocked faces.

"Elena, are you alright?" Logan asked from above. I realized he was still holding onto me, although I was too shaken to move.

"Welcome back," smiled Sylvia. "My goodness, that was quite an adventure, wasn't it?"

"I thought I was supposed to be like a ghost, but they could see me! They looked right at me!"

"Your spirit is more stubborn than most," said Sylvia. "And you possess a natural talent that's stronger than I realized. They could see you on the other side because you were really there."

I frowned in confusion. That didn't make sense.

"How could I be there when I was here?"

"Simple. You were in both worlds."

Feeling dizzy and overwhelmed, I sank deep against Logan's arms. He was a wall of muscle—he could take it. It was only then that I felt the cramp in my right hand. I was still gripping onto the pen. To my surprise, I'd been putting it to use.

"What the hell?"

We all looked down at the notebook to see a long line of writing and symbols identical to the ones I'd seen in my mom's book. It was even written in her handwriting; my eyes and my brain had essentially photocopied it right down my arm and onto the page.

"Holy fuck," Logan gasped when he recognized what I'd done. "You wrote the whole spell out?"

Relief flooded through my aching hand as I forced it open and let the pen fall to the floor.

"The Greater Ceremony to Mute all Evil," I sighed. "From the looks of it, you have to read this rhyme. This magical rhyme about banishing evil with . . . "

"With what?" asked Sylvia.

"Yeah, with what?" Logan asked, taking the notebook out of my lap. He scrutinized the page, but he couldn't read a single syllable. It was written in Old Fae. I'm pretty sure they didn't teach that at any known universities.

"Apparently all we need are pure hearts and noble intentions," I said, struggling to sit up on my own. Logan let go of my shoulders and gave me a quizzical look.

"We're going to fight this evil queen with noble intentions?"

"Hey, I didn't write the spell! I'm just telling you that's what it says."

I scanned my eyes quickly over every word. There were

verses to say, peculiar phrases that had to be spoken in a certain order, and all in the presence of moonlight. According to my mom's instructions, this would banish and mute all evil, but only if the words were spoken by someone with a pure heart and noble intentions.

Logan shook his head, chewing on his bottom lip as he gave it another minute to register.

"We're supposed to defeat Solana by reading her a poem?"

"Yep. That's the plan, unless you come up with a better idea."

30

LOGAN

I didn't notice my phone buzzing in my pocket until Elena gently elbowed me in the ribs.

"You gonna get that, or what?"

"Oh! Right." I grabbed my phone and held it to my ear. "This is Special Agent Hawthorne."

"Uh, hey there. It's Officer McKinney."

It took me a minute to put together the old name with the young voice. It was the sheriff's nephew.

"Right, right. I'm kind of in the middle of something. Is it important?"

"Yes, sir. I wouldn't have bothered you if it wasn't."

"Of course. Give me a second."

Giving both Sylvia and Elena an apologetic look, I stepped out of the room and hurried down the hall and onto the front porch. A gust of fresh air greeted me, and I drew in a deep breath, staring into the trees around the property. I couldn't explain why, but got the feeling something was watching me from behind the bushes and wildflowers.

"Okay, I'm here now. So, do you have something for me?" I asked Officer McKinney.

"Heck yeah! You were really onto something with that weird rock."

"Did you find more?"

"Ten of them."

"Ten? No shit?"

"Yeah, well, that's how many I've found so far. I think there'll be more."

I looked over my shoulder down the hall to Sylvia's living room. Elena was still kneeling over the spell she had just scribbled out. The day was already weird, but I knew it was about to get a whole lot weirder.

"Where did you find them?" I asked. "And are you sure they're the same as the one I showed you?"

"I'm positive, Agent Hawthorne. I've taken photos of all of them. They're identical. I emailed you pictures, but I can text them to you if you want."

"That would be great. Can you send me coordinates while you're at it? A link to a pin on a map would be ideal."

McKinney took a breath as though he was trying to calm down.

"Yeah! Definitely! But you'll never guess where I found them."

"Tell me."

"The rocks were all buried around the places with the most disappearances. Except some weren't even buried at all! Just a little covered up with leaves and branches."

Now it was my turn to steady my breath.

"What do you think this means?" he asked.

I knew exactly what it meant, but it wasn't his job to know just yet.

"I'm not sure," I lied, not wanting to panic him. The rumor mill in town was churning nonstop, and I didn't need any more gossip compromising this case. If any of the officers knew what Elena and I were dealing with, that news would spread like wildfire through the entire county.

"It's weird, though, right?" he continued. "Someone must've had pretty in-depth knowledge of the area to put them in those places. And it ain't like those rocks are small. They're heavy as all get-out! Why would anybody drag a bunch of boulders out into the woods like that?"

"Beats the hell outta me why someone would go to all that effort. Could be some kind of ninja artist like Banksy. You should look him up and you'll see what I mean," I said to McKinney, bringing the conversation to a close. "Good job, officer. You did well."

"Anything more I can do?"

"Just keep doing what you're doing, and send me all the pictures you have, along with that location. I'm sure I'll talk to you later."

As I hung up, light footsteps approached from down the hall. I turned to see Elena standing on the other side of the screen door, clutching the notebook in her hands. She looked exhausted, although she managed to give me a judgy little side-eye.

I knew that look. It meant we had work to do.

31

ELENA

"Who was that on the phone?" I asked Logan. "Was it Harris? Does the wiretap team have any information yet?"

"It was Officer McKinney," he said, putting his phone away. "Sheriff's nephew found more of those boulders with Moloch's sigil."

"How many did he find?"

"Ten of them so far, and he thinks there's a few more in the area. He found them where the highest concentration of abductions occurred."

I shuffled over to the old porch swing and sank into the seat, half expecting it to come crashing down, and giving zero fucks if it did.

"That's not good," I groaned, leaning against one of the dirty chains holding the porch swing in place. The lumpy, cold metal felt good on my face. "That many stones in one area sounds like someone's building a doorway to Hell. If I wanted a direct line to Moloch, that's how I'd go about it."

"We can't afford to lose another kid," Logan huffed. "I think we should do the spell now."

"We have to wait until the moon rises," I yawned. "That's when magic's at its most powerful."

Logan put his hands on his hips, ambling down the length of the porch until he'd come full circle back to me.

"You alright, Elena? You look like you haven't slept in days."

My eyes fluttered open. I didn't even realize they'd been shut until I opened them.

"That remote viewing session turned my brain into mush," I confessed. "I'm so tired I could fall asleep right here."

Logan turned and peered through the screen door, then lowered his voice.

"If that crazy cat lady put something in those cookies and drugged you, I'm arresting her ass."

"Dude, she made them before she knew we were coming over," I reminded him. "Calm the fuck down. I think I'm tired because even though my body didn't go anywhere, my brain just traveled thousands of miles to get to my family's castle."

Right then his phone buzzed again and again. When he looked at it, he frowned.

"That's weird. Officer McKinney just sent me the location where all those stones are. Looks like they're not that far from here. Actually . . . Elena . . . "

"Yeah?" I snapped my head up and tried to focus on the satellite image he was shoving in my face. He zoomed out of the screen a little.

"Look how close Sylvia's house is to that Pinkie Pie hiking trail. That's the trail where Rylee and a bunch of other kids disappeared, remember?"

"Yeah, I remember. There was an ash tree off the trail."

"Right. But we were new to town when we went out

there. We didn't meet Sylvia until later, so we didn't know how close her house was to that trail."

"We should go check it out." This time I yawned so wide that it almost split my skull in half. Then I hoisted myself up, only to sink back down onto the bench. "Gimme five minutes."

"Jesus, Elena. You sure you're just tired?" Logan knelt down in front of me, looking at me with that deep-rooted, ever-present concern.

"I promise. I just need to lie down for a little bit. Maybe a half-hour?"

"Do you want me to drive you back to the treehouse, or do you want to stay here while I go check on those stones?"

"The living room couch will be fine," I said, taking his hand as he helped me up and onto my feet. "Hopefully the cats won't mind."

Logan snickered as we walked into the house.

"If they have a problem with it, they can take it up with me."

I woke up rested and refreshed, with the sound of purring in my ear. Lafayette was curled in a ball under my chin. I rubbed my eyes and reached over to pet him, confused by how dark the room had become. It was bright and sunny when I'd fallen asleep. Maybe a storm had rolled in.

I sat up and looked out the windows. The sky had melted into a wash of orange and pink and blue, and I caught a whiff of pizza coming from Sylvia's kitchen. Above the cheery notes of an old Dolly Parton song, it sounded like she and Logan were playing cards.

I frowned and reached for my phone, double-checking the time.

Quarter to nine.

Damn.

Why hadn't my partner woken me up sooner? Didn't he want to tell me what he'd found out about the boulders on Sylvia's property?

Lafayette meowed and stretched, then hopped off the couch and slinked towards the front door. I followed him and stepped onto the porch, watching as he made a beeline for the trees beyond the yard. Nightfall was coming hard and fast, and the crickets and frogs were singing up a storm. I was about to head inside when I heard a mechanical rumble in the near distance.

I knew that sound.

It sounded an awful lot like the monster truck that had run us off the road. The growling, choking exhaust quickly silenced itself into the night, and then a car door banged shut.

There was no way that Logan or Sylvia could hear what I was hearing. Even without Dolly Parton serenading them, they were human. Their senses weren't half as sharp as mine. Right as I thought about grabbing Logan to help investigate, I heard him let out a big belly laugh.

That idiot probably found the apple pie moonshine, I thought as I peered down the dark hall. I needed to get a license plate number off that truck, but I didn't need all six feet and seven inches of Logan's drunk ass tripping on logs and ruining the element of surprise. His carefree laughter was grating on my nerves.

If I wanted something done right, I was going to have to do it myself.

Propelled by anger, I headed for the trees, determined

to put eyeballs on whatever vehicle was out there. Maybe it wasn't even that rusty, muddy truck after all, but a couple of teenagers making out in the back seat of a station wagon. I needed to know.

My legs struggled to climb over countless fallen logs as my pants caught themselves on brambles. Ahead of me, the thick foliage grew dense and dark. I started to think this was a dumb idea. I wasn't even sure I was headed in the right direction. I took out my phone to send Logan a text and let him know where I was going.

No signal.

Well, I'd already come this far. Sylvia's house was out of sight, on the other side of a small hill I'd climbed. I started to get the feeling that I wasn't the only one out here. Maybe there was someone on the other side of the dense thicket in front of me. But every time I stopped to listen, all I heard was the sound of frogs, crickets, and mosquitoes.

So many mosquitoes. They were flying all around me, filling my ears with their faint, high-pitched hum. What the hell was I thinking, crawling through the Tennessee woods in the middle of summer without bug spray? I debated whether or not I should go back for it.

Just then I heard something lower in pitch than the mosquitoes. I took another step, swatting at the bugs around me as I strained to listen. Hmmm. Nothing. Maybe I was imagining things.

I was just about to turn around when I heard it again. I froze in place and held my breath. It was a voice . . . a male voice cutting through the darkness.

And as I honed in on what he was saying, my stomach turned.

"Accept this offering, almighty Moloch!" came the voice through the tree. "Rise, and let fire bring you near!"

For a second, I was frozen in total shock. Then my pulse exploded as my curiosity took hold. Against my better judgment, I moved closer to the voice.

Who is that?

"Hail Moloch, demon-bearing king. Accept this gift as a symbol of my devotion!"

I edged deeper through the darkness until I could just about make out the faint glow of firelight. Crouching at the edge of the brambles, I watched as the small flickering flames illuminated a large, lumbering figure. It was definitely a man. And judging by the scent mixed in with the burning sticks and logs, he was human. I squinted, trying to see his face, but he was turned away from me. All I could see was a dark silhouette of his huge body against a backdrop of fire.

"Hear me Moloch!" boomed his voice. "I am your servant on Earth!"

Fear and anger gnawed at my gut. This bastard had to be part of Solana's plan, but how?

Forgetting all about the mosquitoes, I edged closer to the fire, trying my damnedest to stay quiet, but of course, my foot found its way to a dried-up twig. It snapped beneath my boot.

Fuck.

The chanting came to an immediate halt. I froze in place, wishing I could somehow make myself invisible. Through the leaves, I could see him glance left, then right. By some act of divine intervention, he turned back towards the fire and resumed his ritual.

"My Lord Moloch! I am your son, your devotee, your disciple! Take this gift, this symbol of my devotion!"

I tried to get a better look through the thorny stems and thick leaves, but I still couldn't make out the man's face.

Growing more and more impatient, I edged my way further to the right, hoping to circle around them. Maybe then I could see this asshole's face.

Instead of seeing his face, the first thing I saw was the distinct shape of a rusted out pickup with a lift kit. The windows were tinted and the doors were covered in dents. I could even see the way the mud was splattered across the license plate.

No. Fucking. Way.

Whoever had tried to kill me and Logan was now standing just a few feet away from me. Not only that, but he was in league with Moloch . . . and probably Solana. Now if only I could find out who he was. My heart told me to reach for my gun and yell 'freeze!' I'd jump on the son of a bitch and arrest him myself.

But the rational part of my brain was telling me to play it cool and be sensible. If things went wrong I could die out here, and Logan and Sylvia would be none the wiser. I cursed myself for not telling them where I was going.

Why the hell did I leave them in there playing cards and listening to Dolly fucking Parton? Logan should be with me right now!

I looked over at the truck, then back to the chanting figure, trying to come up with a plan that didn't completely suck. He was still yelling into the night, his voice so loud the leaves trembled. With the way he was carrying on, there was no way that Logan and Sylvia wouldn't have heard him.

Then I remembered how they were laughing and talking shit over their card game, and how loud the music was playing. I looked over my shoulder towards the run-down house, but I couldn't see any sign of it. It may as well have never existed.

I decided my best plan of action would be to get closer

to the truck. Maybe there was something inside that could point me in the direction of who drove it. I was hoping for some registration papers in the glove box, a paystub, a cigarette pack—*anything* that could tell me more about the driver. Stepping sideways with my hand on my gun, I held my breath and drew closer. All the while I kept my eyes firmly on the figure of the man. The closer I got to the truck, the more the trees gave way to the small clearing where it was parked.

I still couldn't see a face.

Creeping to the edge of the truck, I saw a sizable dent in the hood from where it rear-ended us. It was such a piece of shit that it didn't make much of a difference to the overall appeal. It looked like it was owned for the sole purpose of crashing into other vehicles.

I glanced up at the figure as I stepped around to the driver's side. He was occupied with his ritual in front of his little bonfire, utterly clueless to my presence. Not being able to see through the tinted window, I curled my fingers around the door handle and pulled ever so slightly, expecting the door to just fall open.

Welp. That was a mistake.

For some god-awful reason that I'll never know, that piece of shit truck was fitted with a car alarm. The quiet night was immediately filled with the ear-blistering shrieks of the horn and sirens going off. The man spun around, fully lit by the firelight, revealing a face that I never imagined capable of hurting more than a box of jelly donuts.

"Sheriff McKinney?"

His jaw fell when he realized who was out there with him.

"Agent Rivera?"

He stepped towards me and I pulled out my gun.

"Don't come another step closer! What the fuck are you doing, huh?"

"Rivera . . . You were never . . . " He looked at my gun and laughed, his expression exaggerated by the flickering firelight. "Don't be a silly girl now," he said, chuckling to himself. "What are you going to do, shoot me with that shiny toy gun of yours?"

I wanted to be angry, wanted to scream some hard-ass threat at him, but I couldn't. It wasn't because I was afraid. I was just so hopelessly disappointed. Seeing him standing there, trying to invoke Moloch made me want to weep for humanity.

"You were supposed to be on our side!" I yelled over the car alarm, keeping my Glock pointed at his chest. "You were supposed to be *finding* the missing kids, not . . . not being part of whatever the fuck this is!"

I stepped closer to him, my gun still raised. His expression changed as I neared, changing from amusement to something darker . . . something akin to hatred. There was no trace of the man I'd met when I first arrived in Yarbrough. I was looking at a stranger.

As I got closer, I saw what he was doing. Down at his feet was a large, gray rock that had been carved with Moloch's distinctive sigil.

"It was you . . . " I sneered. "You put this rock out here. You're the one who's been creating those symbols to Moloch!"

"I was trying to but you arrogant assholes had to go dig it up. Had to go around digging *all* of them up! And getting my nephew involved too?"

He shook his head and looked down at the rock, which I realized was meant to replace the one we'd uncovered. It wasn't until now that I fully grasped just how good an actor the sheriff was. I'd shown him my photo of the sigil and asked to look through his collection of paranormal books, and he hadn't shown *any* sign of concern. If anything, he was as confused and dumbstruck as I was.

"Don't look at me like that," he drawled, his voice forcing itself out over the sound of the car alarm. "You're supposed to be the best federal agent there is at this kinda shit. Supposed to be expert in all this stuff and you had *no idea* what was going on beneath your nose the whole time!"

He laughed with a calmness that surprised me, running his hand over the top of the rock before stepping away from it. He looked at it for a second as though he was regarding it with great reverence, then he turned to face me.

"I had fun with you while you were here," he said, putting a hand on his hip as he shot me a curious look. "I always wanted to meet you, you know. You've got a reputation that precedes you."

He glanced back down at the rock, then pinned his eyes back to mine.

"People in occult circles, they talk about you. Talk about the little pink-haired girl with the big green eyes that can take out monsters. But you ain't so special, are you? Maybe if you weren't so busy thinking about the dick on that partner of yours you would've been able to do your job right. You might've been able to catch me sooner."

He laughed to himself.

"You're the one who called us in," I reminded him. "You wanted me on the case! Why? To amuse yourself? To see if I was worth my reputation?"

"I needed to know what you knew," was his abrupt reply. He laughed again, his voice grating on my nerves. I was half tempted to shoot him just to make him shut up.

"Ever heard the phrase keep your friends close and your enemies closer?"

He smiled into the faint firelight, impressed with himself and his questionable intellect. He was grinning like he'd just won this huge, morbid, deadly game. Of *course* nobody in this tiny little town would suspect their own sheriff . . . a man whom they'd known for decades. And, lo and behold, he was as evil as Solana.

I wanted to shoot him dead right then and there. I wanted to see his blood splatter across the small boulder that lay near his feet.

The car alarm still blared. Coupled with the adrenaline and anger in my bloodstream, it was giving me a splitting headache. In front of me, McKinney just kept smiling. It was a nasty smile . . . one that said I needed to get this fucker in handcuffs before he did something stupid.

"Now, come on, little girly. If you know what's good for you, you'll put down that weapon."

Little girly . . . Who the fuck does he think he's talking to?

I gripped my gun tighter and stepped towards him, but it only made him laugh.

"What do you think you're doing with that tough girl act?" he chuckled. "You think you could ever arrest me? Think you could . . . what? Bring me to justice? No one would believe a word you said. Not around these parts."

I blocked out his words. He was trying to undermine me and make me doubt myself. It was a cheap tactic and I wasn't falling for it. He folded his arms in front of his chest and continued to laugh, but as I grew nearer, I started to think his bravado was just an act. He knew I'd caught him red-handed, and as I neared him, I could see a flash of fear in his eyes.

"Turn around," I ordered. He did as he was told albeit with a smirk on his lips. "Hands in the air."

He wavered for a moment, keeping his arms crossed.

"I said, hands in the fucking *air*!"

Slowly, he raised his hands up over his head. I stepped closer, my gun trained on his head, but as I faced his back, I was aware of his gargantuan size. Before, I'd seen him as nothing more than an overstuffed, weathered old teddy bear. But that softness was no longer in him. I was now acutely aware of his strength and size.

"Lower your hands behind your back."

Slowly, he began moving his wrists behind his spine as I reached for my handcuffs. But before my hand could connect with them, a flash of movement in the dark took me by surprise. That motherfucker had reached out, grabbed my right wrist, and twisted with such force that I dropped my gun.

McKinney spun around, the smirk still on his face.

"You dumb bitch," he snarled. "You think you can arrest *me*? I'm the fucking sheriff!"

Pain shot up my arm as he twisted it with his great big meaty hand. I looked down for my gun and tried to reach for it, but he had a vice-like bone-crushing grip on my arm. The pain was so strong I couldn't stop myself from screaming, but my anger was stronger.

I lashed out, kicking him hard right below his kneecap. He yelped as my steel toe cap cracked the bone, but all I'd really managed to do was make him even angrier.

"You fucking *bitch*!" he yelled while tightening his grip on me before slamming me face-first into the ground. His knees were on my back, pinning me into the sticks and leaves and dirt with all of his weight. His enormous hands reached up for my throat, and although I tried to kick and scream, it made no difference. My legs were growing limp as consciousness began to fade. And as much as I would've liked to close my eyes and surrender my life to see my mom and dad again, I was stubborn as hell. I refused to go into the afterlife willingly.

My vision was getting blurry, although I saw a black shadow leap out from the edge of the clearing. Over the sound of the car alarm, I heard a cat screaming and yowling somewhere above my head. McKinney took one hand off my neck long enough to let me gulp as much air as I could. There was a soft crushing sound and a thump in the leaves, and then I saw Lafayette lying in a heap in front of me.

With the last ounce of energy in my body, I tried to fight against the monster on my back. Right as everything started to turn black, I heard a shot ring out through the trees. Then a second one. Then a third.

They pierced the forest air even louder than the car alarm. Not a split second later, the air was sucked back into my lungs as the hands around my neck fell away. The world came back into my eyes in vivid technicolor as I coughed and spluttered, crawling onto my hands and knees.

"Elena!"

Logan's voice traveled through the darkness and I searched for him through the trees. I wanted to get up on my feet and run to him, but my body refused. Instead, I stayed firmly in place, paralyzed by the pain in my throat as I sucked in one lungful after another of the sweet night air.

"Elena!"

I saw him kneel down beside me, crouching low to take a close look at me. The smell of him soothed me immediately as he ran a hand along my back.

"Logan," I managed to croak out. "The Sheriff . . . Lafayette . . . he killed him . . . "

"Looks like that scrappy little cat did a hell of a number on that shithead's face," Logan said, noticing the little heap of raggedy black fur lying nearby.

"It's going to be okay," he said. "You're okay. I got you."

With curiosity getting the better of me, I turned my head ever so slightly and saw a heap on the ground beside the rock. McKinney's body lay motionless. The only movement came from the flickering fire near his lifeless body. With his face covered in deep cat scratches, blood trickled out his right temple from a perfectly circular bullet wound, and there were two more holes in his chest. He was dead. There was no denying it. But his eyes were wide open and staring at the sky, glossed over and empty.

"Oh, shit . . . " Logan groaned in a way I'd never heard before. "Lafayette's still alive. Fuck . . . the little guy's suffering."

He reached for his gun and aimed it at the cat's head.

"Stop!" I cried, and crawled over to his little body. He was lying on his side, twisted in a way that wasn't cute at all. His bright green eyes were wide with fear and pain. "If he's still alive, I can heal him!"

Logan holstered his gun and moved out of the way, and I placed my hands as gently as I could on the cat's chest and stomach. I took a deep breath and willed my energy and vitality into his body, imagining an invisible needle and thread stitching up his internal bleeding and broken bones. The insanely long nap in Sylvia's living room and the sheer amount of adrenaline running through me lent itself well to the act of being funneled into a half-dead cat. Within a matter of ninety seconds, Lafayette went from a twisted mess of broken bones to getting up on his feet and arching his back.

He barely had time to blink before Logan scooped him

up and held him close against his chest. There were tears in his eyes, and he blinked furiously to keep them from falling. Seeing the way he was snuggling against Lafayette's chest, I gave him a soft smile.

"Shut up. So what if I like this cat?"

"I like him too," I grinned, reaching out to pet him. "He helped save my life by clawing the shit out of Sheriff McKinney. I think he deserves a can of tuna all to himself."

Lafayette turned to look up at me, not as grateful as I was expecting, but then again, he was a cat. And then, still looking at me, Lafayette tilted his head.

"Really?" he said. "I helped save your life, and the best you can offer me is a tin can of fish? Try again."

3 2

LOGAN

Elena stared at Lafayette, then me, and I'm sure I had the biggest, stupidest grin on my face.

"I fucking *told* you he could talk!"

"I . . . I don't even know how to respond to this," Elena said, looking at Lafayette with less curiosity than I was expecting. I suppose if she dealt with ghosts and demons on a regular basis, a talking cat wasn't quite as difficult for her to wrap her head around.

"How about you don't say anything?" Lafayette suggested. "But I do expect more than a can of tuna."

"I brought you back to *life!*" Elena countered. The black cat squeezed his eyes shut briefly, then looked at her with a smug little grin.

"I wasn't dead."

I looked down at the cat in my arms. So many emotions were flooding through me all at once. I was way more excited about Elena saving Lafayette's life than I thought I'd be. And holding him close and petting him helped distract me from the fact that my partner had almost been murdered, and that I'd shot and killed another person.

"Please tell me you shot the sheriff," Lafayette said from my arms. "That guy is the worst."

"He's dead," I replied. "You said so yourself."

"Fine, whatever," Elena said, standing up. "I can't stand this noise anymore."

I watched her make her way over to McKinney's body to dig in his pockets until she found his keys. Aiming the fob at the truck, she squeezed it and to our relief, the alarm stopped. I had no idea the silence would be so deafening. For a moment, the three of us stared at McKinney, trying to process what we were looking at. I'd never drawn my firearm in the line of duty, and now I'd killed someone. I'd have to call my superiors and let the authorities know what happened. There would be an investigation and forensic tests would be conducted. It would have to be decided whether I was truly culpable for what I did or if it was a clean shot.

But the second I saw McKinney with his hands around Elena, my hand reached for my gun like a reflex action. I knew what to do immediately and there was no hesitation. He was killing my partner, so I took him out.

It wasn't until his body hit the ground that the realization of what I'd done came over me. Even now, I could barely believe what I'd seen or done.

"You did the right thing," Elena said before I could get too deep into my own head. Her feet crunched through the foliage as she walked towards me. "He's as much a part of these kidnappings as Solana."

"I had no idea he was involved in . . . "

I didn't need to finish my sentence. She knew what I was thinking because she was thinking the same thing too. We didn't know he was one of the bad guys. How had the wool been pulled over our eyes so easily? Was it the slightly incompetent small-town sheriff act that he put on so well? Had we not even bothered to consider him a suspect because we didn't think he was smart enough to get away with it?

"We need to do the ceremony," said Elena, still looking at Lafayette in my arms. "That's all that matters right now. We can worry about that dickhead sheriff later. And if he somehow gets eaten by a few dozen hungry cats . . . " she paused and lifted an expectant eyebrow at Lafayette. "If he gets eaten by cats, I guess I can't help it."

"I'll see what I can do," Lafayette said in between deep purrs.

Elena raised her hand to her neck as she spoke, her voice still raw from being nearly strangled to death. Holding the cat in one arm, I leaned in and brushed the hair from her throat. It was dark, but in the light from the fire nearby, I could make out the start of bruises forming across her skin. They looked like the fingerprints of a ghost.

"You're right about focusing on the ceremony," I agreed. "All that matters right now are those missing children. We can report McKinney as soon as we're done."

Elena nodded in agreement.

"Let's get a move on," she said, and kicked dirt onto the fire to smother it out. Pale moonlight filtered through the trees, with glints of bright white peeking out from beyond the leaves. "It's a full moon tonight. If we're going to get the spell right, we don't have any time to waste."

33

ELENA

"Okay," I said, taking a deep breath. "I'm ready."

We were standing outside the door to the kitchen, gathered on the back patio where Sylvia's pots of herbs were growing. The moonlight was bright enough that we didn't need the light from the kitchen, although it was nice to have options in case a cloud passed by.

The instructions I'd written that explained the ceremony were gripped tight in my hands. As I looked at the words I'd written on the page during my remote viewing session, I silently thanked my mom. They were her words communicated to me and through me—the way I saw it, she was the one saving those missing children. I was just the vessel through which her words could be spoken.

In front of me, Sylvia and Logan waited. Sylvia was excited. Logan was clutching onto Lafayette, petting him to alleviate the uncertainty of what was to come. There was a great sense that we were awaiting something of cosmic proportions to happen, but weren't sure what. I knew the words on the page were magic, but what exactly would they do? Would they crack open the ground to reveal the

Hollows hidden beneath it? I didn't know, but I was about to find out.

"Let's begin," said Sylvia. Logan set Lafayette down on the concrete and watched as he led a significant number of cats into the woods towards Sheriff McKinney's body. Logan and I shared a glance but said nothing.

Instinctively, we drew closer until the three of us stood in a circle. I placed the page down between us, securing the corners with small stones to keep it in place. I looked into the eyes of both Sylvia and Logan and was given an affirmative nod from each of them. Alright. We were actually doing this. Time to stop fucking around.

With a big, deep breath and my hands clenching onto them both, I began reciting the first line from the page.

"From goodness born, a seed of gold . . . "

I paused for a second, feeling embarrassed as shit by the sound of my own voice. It felt like I was reciting a poem at school.

"Go on," urged Sylvia. She gave me a warm, encouraging smile and squeezed my hand as I started again.

"From goodness born, a seed of gold shall pierce the veil and strike out bold."

As I spoke, something behind us stirred among the trees. We all turned round to see nothing but darkness, but it definitely felt like something was out there. We were being watched. I just knew it. The hairs along my neck began to prickle with excitement. Spurred on by the fact that my words were having an effect, I continued.

"From heaven high, it shines through dark, and burns a light in a glimmering arc."

"What was that?" gasped Sylvia as she looked around the patio. "I heard a rumble."

"I heard it too," said Logan. "It sounded like it was coming from beneath us."

I had also heard it. I just didn't want to be the first one to say so. It was a subterranean tearing sound that grumbled deep beneath our feet. I could feel the sensation travel up my legs and shake my bones. My words were obviously being heard from the Hollows below.

"Keep going," Logan urged. "Something's happening."

I held his hand so tight it hurt and he squeezed back. Right then, I felt connected to him more than I'd ever felt connected to anyone in my whole life. Sure, we were partners, but it was so much more than that. We'd saved each other from death . . . more than once. I felt like we were inseparable, two parts of the same whole.

In that moment, I never wanted to let go of him.

There was energy flowing between us like electricity traveling up our arms and I knew he felt it too. As I held his hand and felt his energy merge with mine, I felt that all of time was one, that all humans and fae and all other living beings were one . . . that all worlds were one . . . that me and Logan were one.

That powerful sensation spread through me like an explosion of blissful white heat. It unfurled itself from deep within my body and spread out far beyond my physical form. I could feel it rise all around me like an aura of energy, and as I looked up, I thought I could even see it. A glimmering arc of gold. A seed of goodness to extinguish all evil. It shone through the night brighter than the moon and the stars. The essence of a pure heart and noble intentions. It was the greatest light of all.

"Purity of heart shines bright to mute all blackness," I continued. "It leads the light to burn through darkness!"

The light around me grew brighter and bolder as it

started to swirl around us. First, it was slow like honey . . . then it was like a missile of light seeking out its target.

Sylvia and Logan stared up in awe as it glittered through the air, but our wonder at the spectacle wouldn't last long. Below our feet, the rumbling grew louder. At first, I thought I was just imagining the ground rocking back and forth. Then I realized I was actually losing my balance as the earth trembled. I looked down and saw cracks begin to form where my feet stood. The cracks began to branch out like spiders' legs through the concrete and dirt. Sylvia screamed and tumbled backward as the ground shattered under our feet.

"Sylvia!"

She fell away into the shadows behind the potted herbs, and I couldn't see where she landed. It all became a blur as the light mixed with the dark and the ground quivered and shook.

"Logan!"

"I'm right here!"

Somehow, his hand managed to remain tight around mine.

"I'm not letting go!" he shouted. "You have to finish the spell!"

"But Sylvia!"

Trying desperately to see her, I searched the ground, but all I could make out was a heap on the ground.

"Finish the spell!" Logan yelled. "You have to!"

I tried to see the words on the page, but the paper was fluttering wildly on the shaking ground with most of the stones fallen loose from its corners. Just one remained, but as I tried to focus on the words, that too fell away.

"No!"

I fell to my knees and caught the page just as it blew up from the ground. Logan landed beside me, gripping hold of my sleeve.

"I'm not letting go!" he yelled. "Keep reading!"

Struggling to keep my balance, I held the page tight and leaned into Logan for strength. Then I looked up at the sky and saw the arc of glimmering light still hovering above us.

"Banish thee evil to bowels below! Where captivity holds thee for eternity! Those pure of heart will cleanse us all with blessed divinity!"

The rumbling beneath us grew louder. The cracks in the ground snaked out deeper and longer until giant fissures ran through the mud. I saw the horror in Logan's eyes as he focused on something from below us. As I followed his gaze I felt his horror.

An acid green light was coming out from the fissures, creeping like fog as if it was attempting to escape to the surface of the earth.

"Elena . . . " came a growl so deep from within the earth. It didn't sound like a voice, but like the wind . . . like something that could only be uttered from the deepest elements. It sounded like evil. It sounded like Solana.

"Elena . . . "

The wind picked up around us, whipping at our faces as it whistled in our ears. I could hear all the boards within Sylvia's house creak as it struggled to remain upright, and hear the hissing of all her cats as they scattered deep into the woods like rats off a sinking ship. The trees, previously shrouded in darkness, soon became illuminated in the unnatural, toxic green glow.

"Solana!" I screamed. A ferocious hatred came bubbling out of me that I couldn't control. "Solana, I know you're here!"

Her response echoed through the trees as her sickly green aura filled the air.

"I knew we'd meet again," she laughed. "I always knew you would fall into my hands."

Logan's grip on me was still tight. It was the only thing keeping me grounded. The wind lashed my hair as my feet struggled to stay planted on the shuddering ground. Through the turmoil, I started to catch glimpses of a silver dress billowing in the wind, of large black eyes, and a cruel, merciless smile. I could feel her glowering at me, her hatred burning into my body.

Leaves and branches were ripped from the trees as hatred flew out of her like a hurricane. It rocked the earth to its core, shaking tree roots and rocks and banishing woodland animals from their homes. Birds fled from their nests, screeching into the night, while rabbits and mice scurried through the grass in search of safety.

Through it all, I gripped the ground and the page in my hand, determined to continue. With the elements whipping at my face, I looked up through the strands of my fluttering hair and saw feet walking towards me. They were bare, the skin blackened and shriveled around the toes.

Logan held me tighter as she approached. I could feel the piercing cold emanate from her as she neared. The goosebumps up my back intensified until a deep chill had permeated my spine.

Gradually, the rest of her legs appeared, long, spindly twigs no thicker than the bones beneath her flesh. Each step she took released more of her green aura into the ground. I could smell the sickening despair oozing from her as she came closer. It was the stench of decay and rot and misery. It was the stench of evil.

"Do you really think you can cast me out with a spell?" she roared.

I looked at Logan and his eyes implored me to continue with our work.

"Finish it, Elena!" he insisted.

Holding up the page towards Solana I thrust it at her.

"From goodness born, a seed of gold shall pierce the veil and strike out bold!"

A roar escaped Solana's mouth that came from somewhere so deep within her it sounded as though it had risen from the deepest pit of Hell.

"From Heaven high, it shines through dark, and burns a light in a glimmering arc!"

"Stop!"

She screamed and fell to her knees, her hands outstretched towards me, trying to push me away. But each time I saw her get close, I'd look to Logan and felt that burst of energy within me. I could do anything with him beside me. And as I took his hand, I felt the blistering white light of our pure hearts and our noble intentions shoot out from both of us.

"Purity of heart shines bright to mute all blackness," we both shouted. "It leads the light to burn through darkness!"

A wretched, anguished scream leaked out of Solana's lungs as she fell onto her front, clutching her chest.

"You'll die!" she cried. "You'll *die* for this! No one is immune to corruption! No one's heart is truly pure! You will *never* banish me!"

She crept away from us on her hands and knees, her blackened fingers clawing at the dirt. She was no longer the powerful, beautiful being I'd once known her to be. She was nothing but a grub wriggling on the ground, trying to hide from the light.

"It's working!" said Logan.

Around us, the elements soothed themselves as the wind died down and the ground knitted itself back together and became still. At last, we could find our footing and regain our balance. And the eerie green light that was once flowing from Solana was now nothing more than a soft glow that trickled from her weakening limbs.

"You will never banish me," she whimpered. She looked so pathetic now that she'd been stripped of her power. She could make all the empty threats she wanted to—there was no coming back, and she knew it.

It was time to finish what we started. Hand in hand, Logan and I stood over her failing body and recited the words that would end her reign of terror.

"Banish thee evil to bowels below. Where captivity holds thee for eternity."

"No . . . !"

"Those pure of heart will cleanse us all with blessed divinity!"

"No. No! NO!" She raised her hands to her ears. "Stop!"

I could see the pain as she twisted up her body and writhed on the ground.

"Those pure of heart will cleanse us all with blessed divinity!"

"Please, I'm begging you!"

She squirmed in agony, rolling onto her back as she reached out her claw-like hands towards us. Was she actually begging us for help? Or was she trying to fight back and take us down with her last dying breath? I didn't care.

"Those pure of heart will cleanse us all with blessed divinity!" we yelled for the last time.

As though drawn together by an invisible force, our

bodies fell together in an explosion of fire and light. For that brief moment in time, we stopped being FBI agents in some human-run department. We were sacred knights sworn to protect those on Earth against the darkness that existed in the great beyond.

Beside us, Solana jerked and spasmed one last time, then fell limp onto the ground, her body dissolving into blackened ashes that melted into the mud. Then she was gone, leaving nothing but a dark space on the ground like a scorch mark. The night became sweet and balmy again, and the summer air filled with crickets chirping and frogs singing.

"She's . . . I think she's gone," Logan said in a daze as he finally let go of me.

For a long while, neither of us could speak. We could only look down at the spot where Solana had melted into nothingness. The only thing left of her was a stain.

I was still clutching the page of my mom's spell, although the corners of it had been torn and shredded from the wind. I listened as the sounds of the forest returned to normal. An owl hooted as it flew back to its hollowed-out tree trunk. And somewhere deep within the foliage, a family of rabbits hopped into their warren.

Then, among the sounds of the animals, a woman moaned in the shadows. It was followed by a confused grumbling.

"Sylvia!"

We rushed to her side and found her pulling herself to her feet. The elderly woman was tough as nails.

"Sylvia, are you okay?" I asked, wrapping my arms around her.

"Sure, baby, I'm fine. Just got a little ding on my head." I stepped back to see her rubbing at her scalp where a bump was forming. "I must've been knocked out in the ruckus." She stopped rubbing her head and looked at me and Logan. "Did we do it? Did your mamma's spell work?"

"Yeah! It worked better than we could have imagined!"

A teary smile flickered on her face and I hugged her again. Logan joined in, wrapping his arms around the both of us.

"Oh, my dears," said Sylvia, holding us close to her like we were her favorite grandchildren. "You must know how proud I am of you. So very proud. Do you know what I think we all need?"

"A shot of your apple pie moon—"

Before I could finish my sentence, a sound pierced the night that made us all freeze. Then we heard it again.

A child's unmistakable cry.

"Over there!" I gasped while pointing towards the noise. I started to run, straining to look and listen with my heightened fae senses. Logan was right behind me, then in front of me, pushing through the brambles like a human shield. Thorns tore at his arms and my hair as we zeroed in on the voice.

"Hello?" I called out, pulling away branches.

The crying grew louder. Then, through the deep thicket, a small figure appeared. Curled up in the fetal position wearing a pink unicorn t-shirt, purple leggings, and little red tennis shoes, a young girl sobbed and stared up at us with enormous hopeful eyes.

"Rylee?" Logan cried, scooping her out from beneath the brambles and into his big, strong arms. "Where did you come from?"

"I don't know!" Rylee wailed. "I was down under the ground and now I'm here. Where's my mommy and daddy?"

"Don't worry, hon. We'll get your mommy and daddy," he assured her, pulling her up onto his hip. "We'll get your mommy right away."

As we soothed the young girl and tried to calm her down, we heard another cry coming from deep within the bushes and brambles. Then another . . . and another. We looked around in disbelief.

"They're coming back . . . " said Logan, shocked but elated. "Elena! They're actually coming *back*!"

34

LOGAN

"Promise you won't forget about me."

"How could I, Sylvia? We'll never forget you."

"You'll come back and visit?"

"I hope so."

The sun had risen over Sylvia's house, bringing a new day filled with hope and promise.

Sheriff McKinney's body had been collected hours ago, driven to the morgue where an autopsy would be conducted. The officers and forensic analysts didn't know what had truly happened. They never could. But the one thing they did know was that I had killed their beloved sheriff. I was an FBI agent, an outsider, some prick in a suit who firmly believed in the paranormal.

It was safe to say I wasn't too welcome on the scene.

Around the house, a forensic team bustled around, busy collecting soil samples and whatever else they could gather to get some kind of clue as to how the children had all returned at once. And of course, what happened to the ground. Although they had mostly joined back together, a web of fissures ran out like stretch marks from Sylvia's house, making it look like an isolated earthquake had destroyed the earth. Between the geologist, the surveyor, and a building inspector, they were able to convince Sylvia that her home wasn't structurally safe to keep living in. She took it a lot better than I expected.

"I'll just move in with my niece Bernice. She's been begging me to come live with her." She turned to look at her crumbling plantation home. "This place has a lot of memories, but a lot of them are sad. It's time to move on. I'm thinking about donating the property for public use since it's right by all the hiking trails. Maybe they can tear down the house and put up a picnic shelter or something? That would be nice."

I couldn't help but be skeptical of Sylvia's upbeat attitude.

"What about all your cats?" I asked. "Does your niece have enough room?"

Sylvia started to laugh.

"Enough room? Agent Hawthorne, she's got a mansion on thirty acres! That's plenty of room for me and the kitties. And her wife's a vet, so they can help me spay and neuter all the ones I haven't been able to take in myself. I could stay on top of it when I was younger, but people kept dumping batches of kittens at my house. It got to be a bit much for my arthritis, you know? I just hope the cats leave Bernie's Bees alone."

Elena scrunched up her nose and gave Sylvia a closer look.

"Wait a minute . . . are you saying that your niece Bernice is the owner of Bernie's Bees?"

Sylvia nodded and gave a modest smile.

"I don't like talking about it. People get all kinds of weird when they find out you're a multi-millionaire. I invested in Bernie's business when it was just a few hives in her backyard. She started out selling honey and beeswax candles at the farmer's market. Now her little hobby is worth over a billion dollars. So yes . . . me and the kitties will be just fine."

I felt a lump in my throat as I realized how badly I'd misjudged this poor woman just for being an eccentric cat lady in a run-down house.

"I'm going to talk to you every day and see how you're doing," said Elena to Sylvia, giving her another hug.

"You are?"

"In here," she explained, tapping the side of her head. "You taught me a really useful power. I can see the world from inside my head. That means I can keep an eye on you."

"You use that power wisely," Sylvia said, wagging a finger at her. "It's more powerful than you could ever know. If you just want to catch up, use a telephone."

"Okay, I promise."

As we stood on Sylvia's porch, a gathering of cats spilled out the porch and rubbed themselves against their owner's legs. I looked down and saw my old buddy with the messed up haircut.

"Lafayette!"

I bent down and scratched the top of his head. He responded by raising himself on his back legs and rubbing his head vigorously against my hand. His green eyes were looking directly into mine. I could just imagine him saying he deserved more than a can of tuna for helping save my partner's life.

"Aw, he really likes you, Agent Hawthorne," Sylvia said with a smile.

"Think I've got a soft spot for the little guy myself."

"You know . . . I wouldn't be offended if you were to offer him a home. He's a very special guy, but cats have a way of choosing their people. And I think Lafayette's chosen you. He told me. He talks, you know."

I gave her a surprised look and she shot me a wry smile.

"Oh, there's no way I could have a cat," I told her. "I work too much. Have too many commitments. I'll never be home now that I've been promoted."

Sylvia opened her mouth to protest, but was interrupted by the sound of footsteps battering across the cracked ground.

"Agent Hawthorne!"

I turned to see young Officer McKinney jogging towards me. He was wearing a poker face, but I knew by the look in his eyes what he was thinking. I mentally prepared myself to get reamed by the nephew of the man I'd killed.

"I'm so sorry about your uncle," I said to him, raising my hands. "I did what I had to do. I . . . "

"I get it, Agent Hawthorne. I know you were just doing your job." He looked sadly down at his boots and sighed. "Can't believe he's gone. He's the center of this town."

"I mean it. I really am sorry."

"Is it true that he tried to kill Agent Rivera?"

Elena answered his question by pulling her long pink hair away from her neck, revealing the large purple bruises around her throat that couldn't be anything but fingerprints. McKinney's eyes widened in shock.

"Jesus! I didn't know the old man had it in him! I guess you can't ever truly know someone. I think my uncle kept a lot of secrets."

"It would seem that way."

"The rumors are circulating already," the officer continued. "They're saying all these crazy things about him . . . that he was partly responsible for the children disappearing. That he helped them get captured."

Neither of us said a thing. Elena and I just let him speak his thoughts.

"They're saying he did it for some messed-up power grab that involved demon-worship! They're saying he's Satanic. Can you believe any of that?"

Again, neither of us said a word.

"His body was found next to one of those rocks," he said. "It had a big symbol on it like the one you made me look for."

Lifting the cap off his head, he ran a hand through his hair and blew out a long exhale through pursed lips.

"I just can't believe any of it," he said. "This will kill his family. Poor Aunt Martha . . . "

"But think of the children," interrupted Sylvia, turning the conversation to more pleasant things. "I hear they've all come back safe and sound."

"That's another thing I can't believe," said McKinney. "They just reappeared. Just arrived in the night. Some were found wandering along the side of the road and others just appeared where they had first vanished. It's like they all just fucking materialized out of thin air! Some even walked through the night and got themselves back home."

"That's . . . remarkable," was all I could say. What else could I possibly tell him?

"Remarkable's an understatement," said McKinney. "It's a damn miracle! Whoever heard of such a thing?"

We all fell silent as we contemplated his question. Not even Sylvia had anything to say. She was content to let the matter be dealt with by the authorities. Like Elena and I, she understood that nobody would ever believe the truth . . . not unless they'd been there to see it firsthand.

Beside me, Elena patted me on the arm, tapping her finger near my watch. I knew what that meant.

"We have to get going," I told him and Sylvia. "Gotta get back to DC now that we've given all our statements."

"Oh, right. Of course," said McKinney. He reached out to shake Elena's hand and then mine, but it felt wrong. I'd killed his uncle. No matter how evil he was and what he had done, it still felt wrong.

"I take it you won't be swinging back around Yarbrough anytime soon," he said, taking a step back towards the porch steps.

"You never know. Maybe when we come back you'll be the new sheriff."

He smiled weakly and dropped his hat back on his head.

"Maybe," he said as he started to walk away. "Well, take care."

"Do you really have to leave so soon?" Sylvia asked as she looked up at me.

"I'm afraid so."

"I'll admit I'm sad to see you go. It's been wonderful knowing you."

We gave her one last hug and said our goodbyes before heading in the direction of where Officer McKinney had gone.

"Wait!" she said, as we reached the steps. "Agent Hawthorne, are you sure you won't take that cat?"

We all looked towards the front door where Lafayette sat staring right at me expectantly. His tail swished violently from side to side.

"I honestly can't," I said, trying to tamper down the guilt welling up inside of me. "I mean, sure, me and Lafayette have history, and yeah, he seems to like me, but I'm just not a cat person."

"Hogwash," Sylvia said, raising an eyebrow at me. "I can tell by the look on your face that you'll change your mind."

35

ELENA

I relaxed into the back of my middle seat on the plane, enjoying the G-forces of takeoff. It was my favorite part about flying. Well, and also the view. And being among the clouds. And landing.

Okay, so I just loved flying.

I blame it on being descended from faeries with wings.

I turned to my partner, who was grinning like a lovesick teenager.

"When Sylvia said she thought you'd change your mind, I didn't think it would literally be twenty seconds later."

"What can I say?" Logan gazed down at something sitting by his feet. Tucked safely under the seat in front of him was a soft-sided cat carrier that we'd picked up on the way to the airport. A pair of bright green eyes were peering through the mesh side panel. "I guess I really *am* a cat person. At least when it comes to this little guy."

"You'll make a great cat dad," I told him.

"Thanks," he laughed, and pulled the carrier into his lap. "You hear that, little dude? I'm your Paw-Paw."

Flattening his ears, Lafayette glared at Logan from inside his mesh carrier.

"I am *not* calling you that."

"Fine. How about I give you a chin scratch instead?" He reached his hand into the carrier and Lafayette rolled onto his back to expose his tummy. I watched the two of them cuddling, rolling my eyes at the saccharine sweet spectacle. Eventually, Lafayette curled into a ball and promptly fell asleep.

"So, it's over," said Logan, leaning his head back against his seat. "It feels like the whole thing was a dream."

"More like a nightmare."

He looked towards me and gave a faint but warm smile.

"Thank you," he said.

"For what?"

"Just . . . for everything. I know we got off to a rocky start, but now I can't imagine working with anyone else."

I stifled a yawn. The energy I'd used to heal Lafayette's injuries and perform my mom's spell had taken a toll on me.

"Nothing like a few near-death experiences to bring us closer together, huh?"

"I suppose so," Logan agreed. "Speaking of . . . if you wanna use my shoulder for a pillow, go for it."

"Thanks," I said, turning to look out the window. I watched the misty Smoky Mountains fade away as we ascended through the clouds. Beside me, Logan's eyes flickered shut and Lafayette purred in his carrier. The weight of the last few days landed on me and I felt exhaustion tug at my eyelids. The last thing I saw as I drifted off were puffy white clouds caressing the plane's wing.

"You did it," came a gentle voice through my dreams.

"Mom?"

I looked around and saw I was no longer on the plane, but back in my childhood bedroom once again. My mom was sitting in the armchair in the corner of the room, smiling.

"You did it, Elena," she said, standing up to hug me.

"No, Mom. We *both* did. I couldn't haven't done it without you."

Pulling me into an embrace, I sank into her arms and felt her love and warmth. It felt so good I almost cried.

"He's a good partner for you," she said, giving me a squeeze. "I love you, Elena."

"I love you too, Mom."

I looked up at her face and reached up to touch her cheek, but before my hand could reach her, she dissolved into nothingness.

A hard thump jolted me awake and I was instantly thrown out of my dream. Looking out the window, I saw the plane gliding along the runway at Dulles International.

"That was a bumpy landing," said Logan. I yawned and rubbed my eyes.

"Was I asleep the whole time?"

"You were out cold. You were mumbling in your sleep, too, like you were talking to someone."

"Yeah, I had the nicest dream," I said with a wistful grin as the plane came to a halt.

"Was it about cupcakes and Fanta?" he asked, grinning wide, then pointed to his light blue shirt. There was a dark blue wet spot on the shoulder. "You drooled on me again."

I felt my cheeks start to burn, but it went away as he stood up and put on his jacket. It covered the spot just fine.

"Don't worry. Your secret's safe with me. I got your back, Elena."

"I suppose the least I could do is buy you a beer," I said with a nonchalant toss of my hair.

"I think we both deserve one," he said with a wink. "Maybe something stronger."

Standing up and grabbing my things, I exited the plane and stepped into the terminal. The late afternoon sun was shining brightly on the asphalt runway and I was eager to spend the rest of the day relaxing in a bar somewhere with nothing to worry about but what song to pick next on the jukebox.

Unfortunately, fate had other plans. Before we could even sit down at the nearest terminal bar, my phone rang.

"It's Harris," I grumbled groggily as I looked at my screen. "Guess he wants to know if we've landed."

Answering with a yawn, I waited to hear a big congratulations from him. What I got instead was a rapid-fire of words that instantly woke me up more than Mountain Dew ever could.

"Agent Rivera, I need you and Hawthorne back in the office immediately. You're both needed on a case. There've been reports of bodies piling up in Boca Raton, and they're all missing their blood. Sounds like another goddamn vampire. I'll brief you both when you get here."

He hung up abruptly, leaving me to stare at my phone.

"What was that about?" asked Logan, puzzled.

"We've got a new case," I told him. "A vampire in Florida. Looks like we're gonna have to take a raincheck on that beer."

🐈

Will Logan turn into a crazy cat dad?

Can Elena say no to a cupcake?

Could things finally heat up between these two???

All questions will be answered in the second book of my Faerie Files trilogy, Catnip & Curses.

VIP SECTION

Dying to for more? Love going behind the scenes?

Join Emigh's reader group!

As a VIP at Club Cannaday, you'll get exclusive content nobody else gets to see, author updates, new release alerts, free audiobooks, and **"The List,"** crammed full of Fantasy & Paranormal Romance bestsellers & new releases.

**Get VIP status at
emighcannaday.com/newsletter**

I can't wait to see you there!

Emigh Cannaday

ALSO BY EMIGH CANNADAY

The Faerie Files

Urban Fantasy Romance

Wiretaps & Whiskers

Catnip & Curses

Hexes & Hairballs

The Annika Brisby Series

Urban Fantasy/Paranormal Romance

The Flame and the Arrow

The Silver Thread

The Scarlet Tanager

The Darkest of Dreams

Song of the Samodiva

The Novi Navarro Chronicles

Fantasy/Paranormal Romance

Prince of Persuasion

Crown of Contempt

The Sloane Spadowski Series

Dirty Rom-Com/Contemporary Romance

ABOUT THE AUTHOR

Fun Fact: Emigh sounds just like "Amy"

Emigh Cannaday lives in Wisconsin with her rock star/winemaker husband and a rambunctious pack of Welsh Corgis. She grew up drawing and painting but now uses words to illustrate her offbeat & elaborate daydreams.

When she's not hoarding houseplants or cuddling corgis, she spends her free time testing out new recipes on her friends & family.

Printed in Great Britain
by Amazon

23217726R00229